Praise for Gr...

The Take

'Quite simply, *The Take* is the best police procedural I've read this year'   Harlan Coben

'A great British police procedural. Faraday is a fine creation'   Michael Connelly

'Another Detective Inspector, another superb series. In *The Take* Hurley marries an intensely strong sense of place with believable and flawed characters. An exemplar of classic crime fiction'

Waterstone's Books Quarterly

'The story goes at a fair pace and won't disappoint'
Time Out

'Second instalments in police series are often disappointing, but this one is even better than the first'

Mat Howard, *Morning Star*

Blood and Honey

'Hurley's decent, persistent cop is cementing his reputation as one of Britain's most credible official sleuths, crisscrossing the mean streets of a city that is a brilliantly depicted microcosm of contemporary Britain . . . The unfolding panorama of Blair's England is both edifying and shameful, and a sterling demonstration of the way crime writing can target society's woes'   *Guardian*

This is Graham Hurley's second novel to feature DI Joe Faraday and DC Paul Winter. An award-winning TV documentary maker, Graham now writes full time. He lives with his wife, Lin, in the West Country. Visit his website at www.grahamhurley.co.uk

By Graham Hurley

THE TAKE
A DI Joe Faraday Investigation

Graham Hurley

An Orion paperback

First published in Great Britain in 2001
by Orion
This paperback edition published in 2002
by Orion Books Ltd,
Orion House, 5 Upper St Martin's Lane,
London WC2H 9EA

An Hachette Livre UK company

Printed and bound in Great Britain by
Clays Ltd, St Ives plc

The Orion Publishing Group's policy is to use papers that
are natural, renewable and recyclable products and
made from wood grown in sustainable forests. The logging
and manufacturing processes are expected to conform to
the environmental regulations of the country of origin.

www.orionbooks.co.uk

In memory of Norman Shaw
1940–2000

Acknowledgements

My thanks to the following for their time and patience: John Ashworth, Katie Brown, Deborah Owen-Ellis Clark, Roly Dumont, Tony Johnson, Bob Lamburne, Colin Michie, Phil Parkinson, John Roberts, Pam and Ian Rose, Pete Shand, Matthew Smith, Steve Watts, Sandra White and Dave Young. Thanks, as well, to my agent Antony Harwood and my editor Simon Spanton for their encouragement and advice. My wife, Lin, supplied the coffees, the warmth and the laughter – all of them beyond price.

TAKE (*vb. tr.*)
Of a hawk or falcon, to catch (quarry or lure)
Encyclopaedia of Falconry, Adrian Walker

A policeman should be the most forgiving person
in the world if he gets the facts right.
Graham Greene, *The Heart of the Matter*

Prelude

Another grey summer's day, spitting with rain.

Faraday was one of the last into the crematorium car park, abandoning his Mondeo, buttoning his coat and ducking along the path towards the front of the building. The larger of the two chapels was already full. It smelled of furniture polish and the kind of flowery scent you squirt from an aerosol. Faraday slipped into a pew at the back, acknowledging a nod here and there, aware of the bareness of the place, burying himself in a random page of the English Hymnal.

> There is a blessed home, beyond this land of woe
> Where trials never come, nor tears of sorrow flow.

Fat chance, Faraday thought, closing the hymn book with a soft but perceptible thud.

The cortège appeared ten minutes later, delayed by a tanker spill on the motorway. The coffin was bigger than he'd expected and he wondered about its weight. Vanessa had been the slightest of women but, in a darkening world, the brightest of candles. She'd brought energy and commitment and an infectious good humour to a job that was never less than daunting. She applied to herself and to others the highest of standards. On bad days, and there were many of those, she'd made going to work a pleasure.

I

Faraday was still gazing at the coffin, still wondering about the burden these men had shouldered. Could you measure loss in pounds or kilos? Had the undertaker's men with the bowed heads and the clasped hands seen her wrecked body before screwing down the lid?

Vanessa's mum was supported on both sides by relatives, her small white face shadowed by an enormous hat. She peered around her, plainly bewildered. Lately, Vanessa had been talking of early Alzheimer's, trying her best to minimise the harm her mother might do to herself. Hence the weekly supply of pre-cooked meals. And hence, perhaps, the state of the Fiesta's brakes.

The service lasted no more than twenty minutes. Friends, relatives and, it seemed, half of Southsea police station did their best with the hymns. A vicar who seemed never to have laid eyes on Vanessa talked of her passion for hill-walking. Then came the moment when the canned music swelled and the vicar ducked his head in silent prayer.

Watching the curtains close on Vanessa's coffin, Faraday thought of the last time they'd shared a proper conversation. It would have been a couple of days ago. She'd had a problem with next month's duty roster and she wanted to know whether there was a likelihood of any more abstractions. After seven brief months as a management assistant, she knew as well as Faraday that the question was impossible to answer. A stranger rape in Fordingbridge or a drive-by killing in Southampton could rob them of yet more pairs of hands, sending another little administrative tremor through the rapidly emptying divisional CID room.

He and Vanessa had discussed the roster for the best part of half an hour. She was as tireless and quietly efficient as ever, but short of prophecy there was no real

2

way he could help her. In the end, with the sweetest of smiles, she'd nicked the last of his jammie dodgers and scrawled NBC across a yellow sticky, fixing it to the top right-hand corner of the paperwork. NBC was her own contribution to the ever crazier world of performance indicators and management acronyms. In Vanessa-speak, it stood for No Bloody Chance.

The curtains were fully closed now and feet were beginning to shuffle in anticipation of the end of the service. Across the aisle, Willard was exchanging a word or two with his DCI and Faraday caught the lift of an arm as the DS checked his watch. Willard, he knew, was due at headquarters for a conference which started at eleven. If the M27 was open again, he might just make it to Winchester in time.

Faraday returned his prayer book to the back of the pew and closed his eyes for a moment, trying to rid himself of the images that had haunted him ever since he'd asked to see the traffic file. The guys in Photographic spiral-bound the colour prints between blue covers. The shots that really hurt showed the interior of the Fiesta. The shell of the car had deformed beyond all recognition. The engine had come back through the dashboard and the driver's seat had slipped forward, crushing Vanessa against the steering wheel. The contents of her handbag – money, make-up, two ticket stubs from a recent visit to the UCI – were strewn across the remains of the passenger seat and there were three library books among the wreckage in the footwell. One of them, a Catherine Cookson novel, was webbed with something glistening and scarlet and it had taken Faraday several seconds to realise that he was looking at blood. Vanessa had bled to death. In the dry prose of the post-mortem report, her left femoral artery had ruptured, shock and blood loss killing her before help was at hand.

Faraday opened his eyes again. Heads were bowed. The vicar was intoning a final prayer. Then, from nowhere, a butterfly appeared. It fluttered up the aisle, darting left and right, before coming to a halt, as if making some kind of decision. Faraday stared at it, transfixed, and as he did so it came back down the aisle at head height, zig-zagging towards the door.

Butterflies, like birds, were one of Faraday's passions, a solace, an escape. He knew about them, knew where to look for their newly hatched eggs, knew the colour of their larvae after the first and second moults. He could map their migration routes, and their habitats, and their distribution. Above all he knew their names, not simply in English but in Latin as well.

The butterfly gone, he gazed numbly towards the curtained altar, letting the dull colours slowly blur. The Red Admiral butterfly, he thought. *Vanessa atalanta.*

Outside, the promise of rain had given way to a thin drizzle. Ignoring an invitation to inspect the floral tributes, Faraday made his way back to the car park. The overwhelming temptation was to look for the butterfly. Was it down by the road, feasting on buddleia and lavender? Or had it flown north, bound for the row of evergreen shrubs that edged the long curve of the drive? He didn't know, and he realised that he didn't care. It had come and gone like a ghost. Simply to have glimpsed it was enough. Vanessa Parry would never see her thirty-fourth birthday. End of story.

The car park was beginning to fill with mourners for the next funeral. Unlocking his Mondeo, Faraday suddenly became aware of a white Vectra Estate. It was parked three spaces along from his own car. The driver was wearing a green anorak and his head was turned

4

away. Faraday withdrew his key and walked across. The lettering along the side of the Vectra read WESSEX CONFECTIONERY – TRADE AND RETAIL. Must be a replacement motor, he thought. No question about it.

Faraday bent to the window and tapped on the glass. The driver ignored him. He tapped again, looking at the huge bouquet with its cellophane wrap laid so carefully on the big cardboard boxes of crisps in the back. The handwriting on the card might have belonged to a child. 'Sorry', it said. There was no name.

At last the driver looked round. He had a chubby young face, with a couple of days' growth of beard. His hair looked freshly gelled and he wore a tiny diamond stud in his right ear. He gazed up at Faraday, vacant, stupid. Faraday hesitated a moment, then wrenched open the door. He knew the traffic file by heart. Matthew Prentice. DOB 21.10.74. Four previous convictions, all for speeding. Just about right, Faraday thought. You were on the mobile that morning. Or making notes on your little clipboard. Or doing any bloody thing except driving properly. Bastard.

The driver was trying to get out of the car. Faraday blocked him with his body.

'You killed her,' he said softly. 'You know that, don't you?'

Two days later, Sunday night, a woman set out to take her boxer puppy for a walk. She lived in Milton, an area of narrow-fronted terraced houses which lapped the edges of Southsea and Fratton. She had the dog on a lead and she carried a torch.

The woman's route took her out onto the path which skirted the edge of Langstone Harbour. Five minutes' walk and she'd be among the ponds and bushes that covered Milton Common, the featureless scrubland between the busy Eastern Road and the water's edge. It wasn't countryside, not real countryside, but in one of the most densely packed cities in the country, it offered a rare chance to get away from the hassle and the traffic. The dog loved the place almost as much as she did.

Tonight, for the first time, she was going to let the puppy off the leash. She'd discussed it with her kids and they'd both agreed it wouldn't be a problem. Tyson was as good as gold. No way would he dream of straying.

She bent to slip the chain around his neck. The dog looked up at her for a moment, as if she'd made some kind of mistake, then bounded off towards the nearest of the ponds. Within seconds, she could hear the rustle of wildlife among the reeds at the water's edge. Just like Tyson to look for new friends.

Lighting a cigarette, she began to wander towards the pond, taking her time, enjoying the breeze off the harbour. Weatherwise, it had been a crap day – more bloody rain – but the sun had come out late afternoon and the bloke on the telly was promising something half-decent for the next couple of days. If it lasted through to the weekend, she'd maybe take Jordan and Kelly for a treat. Get over to the Isle of Wight for a day on a real beach. The thought of the kids chasing Tyson through the shallows brought a smile to her face.

The cigarette gone, she called the dog's name. She thought she heard an answering yelp and the usual pell-mell tumble, but she wasn't sure. She called his name again. This time, for definite, nothing. By now, it was nearly dark. Out across the water, she could see the lights of Hayling Island. Half a mile behind her, the orange glow of the Eastern Road.

Switching on the torch, she followed the path towards the pond. The more noise she made, the better.

6

'Tyson!' she yelled. 'Tyson!'

Still nothing. For the first time, she felt a prickle of apprehension. What if the bloody animal had got lost? What if it had gone after some duck or other and didn't know how to swim? She reached the edge of the pond. Her eyes followed the beam of the torch as it swept across the water. A splash as something small and black swam quickly away. But no Tyson.

Then, suddenly, there came a stir in the bushes directly behind her. Flooded with relief, she swung round. She had the torch in one hand, the lead ready in the other. Daft bugger.

'Tyson . . .' she began.

A man was standing in front of her, no more than a metre or two away. He was wearing a tracksuit of some kind and she could see gloves on his hands. She brought the torch up, then screamed. A Donald Duck mask covered his face, and the moment she took an involuntary step back he began to make quacking noises, really loud, like he was laughing. The gloves fumbled at the waistband of the tracksuit bottoms, pulling them down, exposing his erection. She stared at it, then up at the mask again, feeling the chill of the water around her ankles, not knowing what to do. This isn't happening to me. No way.

The man took a step towards her, the quackings turning into a deep, throaty laugh. Instinct told her to run. The moment she moved, he blocked her path. She could smell him now, the sour reek of cheap tobacco. More quacks. And another step towards her.

For a moment, she just stared at him. Then, from her right, came the sound of splashing and a familiar bark. Distracted, the man in the mask looked away. Seeing the puppy, he began to turn, and as soon as he moved she took her chance. Lashing out wildly with the lead, she caught him around the head. She did it again as he lunged towards her, the tracksuit bottoms still around his knees. Tyson, by now, was yelping fit to bust. Play time.

Later, giving her statement, she couldn't remember how long they'd struggled. It might have been seconds. It felt like for ever. She'd tried to knee him in the groin, tried to fight him off, but what had brought the nightmare to an end was the moment he'd caught her hand, forcing back her fingers until she was screaming with pain. It was the screams that drove him off. One minute he was all over her. The next, he'd gone. Making her way back towards the lights of the Eastern Road, she'd wept like a baby. That bad, it was. That fucking horrible.

One

Monday, 19 June, early morning

Unable to sleep, Faraday was up by half-past five, nursing his second cup of tea. It had been light for over an hour, a pale grey wash spilling over the mud flats of Langstone Harbour. At half-tide, from the upstairs study, he could see turnstones strutting across the pebbled flats, pausing from time to time to poke around in the pools of standing water. Several of them seemed to follow the mooring lines that snaked out to dinghies and larger craft marooned by the sluicing tide, and he watched a group of three as they squabbled over a yellow smudge of mussel. Aggressive behaviour was rare among turnstones, but over the last few months he'd noticed a number of episodes like these. Must go with the territory, he thought. Inner-city turnstones. Bred to be stroppy.

He turned back from the view, eyeing the mountain of paperwork on his desk. All the years he'd been living with J-J, he'd made it a rule never to bring work home. That, of course, was impossible. It was a rare evening when the phone didn't ring at least a couple of times. But paper was different. That belonged in his other world, and with the challenge of bringing up a deaf child to meet, he'd made bloody sure it stayed there.

But Joe-Junior had been gone for the best part of a year now, a gangly, loose-limbed twenty-two-year-old who'd blissfully surrendered himself to a sharp-faced

French social worker from Caen, and the months of living alone had nagged away at Faraday's resolve until it was rare not to return with his battered briefcase bulging with stuff he never seemed to have time to sort out at the office. Minutes of meetings he could barely remember. Agendas for meetings he'd do his best not to attend. Amendments to Force Standing Orders. Thick briefs on upcoming European legislation. Incomprehensible strategy papers from the Social Services policy group on child abuse and the At Risk register. Home Office updates on service performance indicators. Risk assessments on more or less everything. Hundreds of thousands of words that were somehow expected to make him a better detective.

Faraday emptied his mug and picked up the yellow pad he normally kept by the telephone. The duty DC had answered the call from the control room about last night's Donald Duck incident. By the time he'd got to the woman, she was up in Accident and Emergency at the Queen Alexandra hospital getting her injuries sorted out. She'd evidently gone straight home after the incident because she'd left her kids by themselves, and by the time a uniformed patrol had made it to her house, she'd changed into a dressing gown, dumping all her clothes in the washing machine. She'd felt dirty, she'd said. This pervert had touched her. Pawed her. Pressed himself up against her. All of which, in the DC's dry phrase, was a bit of a shame. Because, even with the washing machine's filter for examination, nothing makes forensic evidence more difficult to recover than a cupful of BioSurf and the hot-spin cycle.

At the hospital, X-rays had confirmed two broken fingers and a fractured wrist and the DC had piled insult on injury by arranging for a police surgeon to take scrapings from under her fingernails, plus a couple of hairs from her head, for later matching if they were lucky enough to pull in a worthwhile suspect. After discharge from the hospital, he'd driven the woman back to the ponds by the harbour where three uniforms were waiting to identify the scene of crime. The woman had done her best to try and work out exactly where she'd been jumped, but in the dark she'd got hopelessly confused and in the end they'd taped off the whole area, waiting for daylight before beginning a proper search.

This was the third time this year that someone in a Donald Duck mask had exposed himself to local women, but so far there'd never been any suggestion of rape. The DC, on the phone, was still unclear in his own mind whether the guy had simply been trying to defend himself from the flailing dog lead or had had something more substantial in mind, but either way, it didn't really matter. The woman's injuries turned a potential nuisance into grievous bodily harm. Crown Court, for sure.

Faraday made his way downstairs, musing on the irony of the case. The incident had taken place barely a hundred yards from his house, here beside Langstone Harbour. Had he been in on Sunday night, he'd probably have heard the woman yelling. A piece of luck like that could have saved him the chore of organising a proper inquiry, getting bodies out there, knocking on doors, asking questions, taking statements, raising actions, looking for leads. They'd have the bloke locked up by now, tidied away, not too much paperwork, minimal fuss. Luck like that might even have stirred a modest herogram from headquarters. Exemplary vigilance. In the best traditions of the force.

As it was, though, Faraday had driven out to the New Forest, beyond Southampton, and spent a couple of priceless hours wading through the still-wet heather, waiting for the first churring of a pair of breeding nightjars. He'd visited them last year and the year before. They arrived in May from Africa, shy, dun-coloured birds, almost impossible to spot in their daytime scrapes among the gorse. Only at night would they emerge, fleeting silhouettes against the last of the sunset as they hunted for insects and moths. They flew in spurts, twisting and gliding, the churring noise issuing from the syrinx in their throats. Stand absolutely still, as Faraday had done, and a couple of handclaps might bring on the birds in big swoopy circles, curious to check out this stranger in their midst. He'd played the game for the best part of an hour, the birds softening his rage about Vanessa, and with the light finally drained from the night sky, he'd driven back down the road to a favourite pub and offered a private toast to her memory with three pints of Romsey bitter. Allies like Vanessa were hard to find. Dead, he knew that the ongoing war would be that much more pitiless.

He put a couple of slices of bread under the grill and looked half-heartedly for bacon. The fridge, like so much else in the house, was beginning to fall apart. The place needed a thorough going-over. Sills and window frames on the weather side of the property were showing signs of rot and he'd known for months that it was time to get out the ladder and the sandpaper, but the one thing he was never short of was excuses. Another ruck about overtime allocations. Another outbreak of vehicle thefts. Another crisis with a dodgy informer.

The thought of bacon finally abandoned, he buttered the toast, wandered through to the living room and stood in front of the big glass doors that opened on to the harbour, disappointed to find a thick grey ledge of cloud where the sun ought to be. The light was flat and lustreless. The water was the colour of lead. Even the oyster-catchers, normally so pert, seemed to have difficulty stirring themselves. Sometimes, just sometimes, Faraday felt his whole life could do with a stiff scrub-down and a coat or two of Weathershield. Something to keep the rain away, for Christ's sake. Something *bright* for a change.

Paul Winter, against his better judgement, finally agreed to accompany his wife to the hospital. It wasn't about taking the time off (though that was the excuse he'd offered her) and it wasn't that he didn't think she meant it when she woke him up early and asked him to be there. It was just this thing about the Queen Alexandra. He hated the big hospital on the hill. He hated the kind of people who went there: overweight, ugly, greyfaced. He hated the bossy, in-yer-face posters on the corridor walls: don't smoke, don't drink, don't shag. He hated the heads-down weariness you encountered in the lift. And he hated, most of all, the feeling of resignation, of *defeat*, that overwhelmed you the moment you stepped inside the place. Life was about seizing opportunities, about playing the game to maximum advantage, about staying ahead of the pack. Hospitals, especially big anonymous ones like the QA, were for the also-rans.

Joannie's appointment card directed them to the gastro-intestinal clinic. She'd been to the GP twice since Christmas, complaining of pains beneath her rib cage. The first time, she'd come away with tablets for dyspepsia. The tablets had made no difference at all, and the second time the GP had referred her to the QA for tests and a scan.

By now, she wasn't eating properly or sleeping well. Winter, cheerfully dispassionate, put it down to her ongoing failure to get on *Who Wants To Be a*

Millionaire? As an ex-teacher, she was certain she could get at least as far as £64,000, a conviction which made Winter a willing accomplice when it came to making the calls to the contestants' line after the show. Sixty-four grand would make all the difference. Sixty-four grand might even put daylight between himself and the likes of Faraday.

The fact that he'd been paper-sifted out of contention for the DC vacancy on the Drugs Squad – the fact that he hadn't even made it to the fucking interview board – still rankled, and the knowledge that it was Faraday who had shafted him made the insult even worse. 'Fails occasionally to see the big picture', Faraday had written, a form of management-speak that suggested Winter was a law unto himself. This was a judgement Winter himself wouldn't necessarily dispute, but that wasn't the point. The point was that Winter had got Faraday a result on the Oomes case, and Faraday *still* didn't understand that one good turn deserved another. '*Fails occasionally to see the big picture*'. A killer phrase like that, and Winter was lucky not to be back in uniform, posted to traffic cones and the challenge of the lost-property store.

Winter had read last January's copy of *OK!* twice before Joannie's name was called. She took his arm and followed the nurse into the office at the end. The consultant got up the moment they appeared at the door, extending a hand to Joannie, and as soon as Winter saw the expression on his face he knew something terrible had happened. Bad news was like a smell. There was no disguising it.

The consultant was tall, with a long, bony face and the hint of a northern accent. While Joannie made herself comfortable, he ducked his head to check a file.

'What is it?' Winter heard himself say. 'What's wrong?'

Despite everything, he hadn't once given the possibility of anything serious a moment's thought. Joannie was as strong as an ox. Twenty-four years of marriage – countless fallings-out, countless makings-up – told him that she was immortal. However badly he treated her, whatever he got up to, she'd been there for him. Her capacity for punishment, for forgiveness, was infinite. Now this.

The consultant took a tissue from a box on his desk and went through the motions of blowing his nose.

'Mrs Winter,' he began at last, 'you'll forgive me, but I'm afraid there's no point in beating around the bush. Conversations like this can be difficult. If you feel you need . . .' He left the sentence unfinished, nodding at the box of tissues.

Fucking Kleenex? Winter was on his feet now.

'Just tell us,' he said. 'What is it?'

For the first time, the consultant spared him a glance.

'Mr Winter?'

'That's right.'

'Please sit down. There's no reason to make this more—'

'I asked you a question.'

'And I'm about to answer it.' He turned his head. 'Mrs Winter, I'm afraid . . .'

Joannie reached up for her husband, tugging him back. With some reluctance, Winter sat down. The consultant's tone had changed. His eyes were on the file again and he sounded like he was reading a death sentence. Winter had heard judges more sympathetic than this.

'Pancreatic what?' he said.

'Carcinoma, Mr Winter.'

'What's that?'

'Cancer.'

'*Cancer?*' Winter stared at him, suddenly chilled. 'You're joking. Joannie? *Cancer?*'

There was a long silence. From the waiting room came the rattle of a tea trolley. Then Joannie's voice, smaller than Winter had ever heard it.

'You're sure?'

'Positive, Mrs Winter.'

'Can you' – she hesitated – 'do anything?'

'Alas, no. We can try and make life easier for you, maybe a small operation, just to tidy things up . . . but no, long-term, I'm afraid no. This is a particularly aggressive cancer. You have secondaries in the stomach and liver. There are drugs, of course. Palliative treatment. The hospice. But I wouldn't want to mislead you about the outcome.'

'So . . .?'

'About three months, Mrs Winter.' The consultant inched the box of Kleenex towards her. 'Though even in a case like this it's hard to be precise.'

Faraday had been at his desk at Southsea police station for several hours by the time Cathy Lamb arrived for their regular Monday conference. She'd driven down from Fratton nick where she had an office of her own. The old divisions of Portsmouth North and South were in the process of amalgamation into a single super-division, and in the consequent administrative uncertainties, Cathy had seized her chance. CID was short of Detective Inspectors to fight the rising tide of so-called volume crime, and with Faraday's support Cathy had made it to acting DI. Responsibility suited her. She'd been in the job a couple of months now, and she plainly loved it. A big woman, crop-haired with an open, outdoors face, her gaze was steadier than ever.

'How's your little treasure, then?' She nodded back towards the big open-plan CID office along the corridor where Vanessa's replacement was punishing the photocopier.

Faraday pulled a face.

'She's got some kind of agency for Beanie Babies,' he said. 'She brings the bloody things in every day, trying to flog them. Drives the blokes mad.'

'Why don't you tell her not to?'

'I did. She doesn't listen.'

Faraday got to his feet and shut the door. The new management assistant was called Joyce. She was an overweight American in her early forties, the kind of woman who from day one had presumed an intimacy which didn't exist. With Vanessa, Faraday had been only too happy to offload endless administrative baggage, including material which was extremely sensitive, freeing up precious time he could devote to something worthwhile. With this woman, that kind of trust was out of the question.

Cathy seemed amused.

'I hear her husband's in the job.'

'That's right. He's an Inspector at Southampton. As useless as she is.'

'Nice to keep it in the family, though.'

'Yeah, kind of two-for-one offer. Makes life twice as bloody difficult.'

'Is she here for ever?'

'No idea.' Faraday nodded at the file on Cathy's lap. 'What's the score, then? Anything interesting?'

Faraday's own CID boss was Willard, and the Detective Superintendent had made it clear that he expected Faraday to keep a watching brief over Cathy's stewardship of Portsmouth North. Acting DI at twenty-eight was going some. The girl would need supervision.

Cathy ran quickly through the usual tally of minor crimes: thefts from vehicles, vandalism, shoplifting, house burglary, warehouse break-ins, and, from the weekend, four serious assaults. In theory, she had six detectives and a couple of Sergeants to do the legwork, but as an ex-Sergeant herself she knew that the staffing figures were largely fiction. It was a rare week when at least a third of her guys weren't either abstracted for major inquiries elsewhere, sorting out the backlog of training courses they'd missed, or filling in for other divisions stripped even barer than hers.

'Then there's Winter,' she added. 'Called in sick this morning.'

'Nothing minor, I hope.'

'Actually, it's his wife. He had to take her to the hospital.'

'Winter? Looking after his missus? You're sure it was him?'

'Had to be. Said it might take all day.'

Faraday made a note on his jotter. It took real determination to resist change, but in his early forties Paul Winter was still an old-style DC, wholly unreconstructed, a man for whom the difference between criminality and innocence was never less than subjective. As such, he was the perfect specimen of the old Portsmouth Mafia, a brotherhood of like-minded detectives who'd thrived on alcohol, patronage and favouritism in more or less equal measure. Unlike his ex-colleagues, though, Winter had survived the CID culture changes of the eighties and some of the newer intake still viewed him with awe. Winter, they said, had a rare talent for getting inside the heads of the bad guys, for winning their trust and opening their mouths, for tying them into schemes so complex, so byzantine, they defied description. This interpretation of Winter's MO was both colourful and compelling, but to Faraday, the truth was altogether simpler. On a good day, just, Winter stayed legit. The rest of the time he was as bent as the low-life he gloried in putting away.

'Give him a call,' he said briskly. 'No hospital appointment lasts all day.'

A frown ghosted across Cathy's face. She was about to dig in, but Faraday didn't give her the chance.

'How's Pete?' he said. 'Climbing the walls yet?'

Pete Lamb was Cathy's estranged husband, a uniformed Sergeant from Fareham nick. As leader of one of the force's tactical firearms units, he'd been suspended pending the outcome of an internal inquiry after shooting a suspected drug dealer on an early-morning bust. That was bad enough, but what had turned poor threat perception into a potential jail sentence was the result of a subsequent blood test. Breaking every regulation in the book, Pete had been drinking. Thanks to some inspired work by Pete's lawyer, the inquiry would probably take a couple of years to resolve certain issues about the admissibility of evidence from voluntary blood tests, but in the meantime, still on full salary, he was forbidden to take other paid work.

'He's fine,' Cathy said.

'Not bored out of his skull?'

'Never. It's June. He's still got shares in the boat, and Cowes is coming up.'

'Is he still living with his mum? Over in Gosport?'

'Not any more. He's just got a flat in Southsea. Whitwell Road.'

'Nice?'

Cathy gave him a look, then softened it with a smile.

'Oldest trick in the book,' she murmured. 'How would I know?'

For the third time in as many weeks, Pete Lamb made his way through the second-hand book shop, pushed past the boxes of *Reader's Digest*s at the back, and clumped up the bare wooden stairs to the office on top. He'd known Malcolm Garrett from Mal's days as a DS at Fareham, and now that Mal had turned early retirement into a new career, Pete saw every reason to develop the relationship. A tatty room overlooking Southsea's Albert Road wasn't the greatest commercial address in the world, but, as Mal kept pointing out, this was just the start. After decades of neglect, the city was beginning to boom. And big money always brought with it the need for special kinds of investigative expertise.

'Bird called Liz Tooley.' Mal gestured towards the kettle on the shelf by the door. 'Water's still hot. Help yourself.'

Liz Tooley headed the residential sales operation at Gunwharf Quays, an enormous harbourside redevelopment scheme that was fast turning thirty-three acres of ex-Navy land into an aspirational lifestyle fantasy. Already it had sucked in a hundred million pounds' worth of investment. Retail names like Ted Baker, Tommy Hilfiger and Gap had finally secured a unique retail niche in the city, and plans for three hundred luxury harbourside apartments would no doubt do wonders for Portsmouth's social mix.

'They're flogging the penthouses for half a million quid,' Mal grunted. 'You put down a grand for starters, then ten per cent, then the balance on completion. They've got people queuing round the block. Half a million quid. For some poxy flat. Can you believe that?'

Pete could. Living in Gosport, on the other side of the harbour, he'd regularly been taking the ferry across, and the view on a sunny morning from the upper deck was more than enough to explain the rush to buy. Gunwharf Quays lay between the cobbled streets of Old Portsmouth, huddled around the harbourmouth, and the national treasure trove that was the Navy's Historic Dockyard. The site was still chaotic, a busy muddle of diggers and piling-crews beneath the soaring construction cranes, but even without a look at the glitzy brochures the potential was obvious. A couple of minutes' walk, and you'd be sitting on a train at the harbour station. Ninety minutes later, you'd be at Waterloo. For someone with a London job and a yearning for premium maritime views, Gunwharf Quays would be the dream address.

Pete was trying to get the lid off the Kenco jar.

'So what's the problem?'

'She's lost a buyer. Not lost him, exactly. It's more complex than that.'

The guy had taken an option on three flats, two of them penthouse apartments, all of them with waterside views. One had been for himself. Another for his mother. The third for a South African chum. Once the apartments were ready, the guy would be parting with nearly a million and a half pounds.

'That makes him worth finding,' Mal pointed out. 'Because his time is up.'

He'd signed and paid for the thousand-pound options on 23 May, making an appointment to hand over the ten per cent deposits two weeks later. The appointment had been for late afternoon on Tuesday, 6 June, and he'd made a little joke about D-Day, inviting the sales girl to mark the occasion by accepting his invitation for dinner. The sales girl had pleaded pressure of time so he'd settled for a meet on site instead.

'He didn't show?'

'No. And when they tried the numbers he left, they got nothing. His option expires tomorrow, but they're naturally bolloxed about pissing him off if there's some genuine reason he never made it on the sixth. So, sunshine, I just thought . . .'

Pete had abandoned the coffee jar for a packet of Jaffa cakes, fumbling in his leather jacket for a notepad.

'Name?'

'Pieter Hennessey. Spelled P–I–E–T—'

'He's South African too?'

'Yeah. I've got the numbers and stuff on a sheet from Liz. Guy's a surgeon of some kind. Been in the UK for years now. Here.'

Pete looked briefly at the sheet. With the phone numbers were three addresses, one in Beaconsfield, one in the New Forest and the third in Harley Street.

'Private practice?'

'So I gather. Apparently the guy earns a fortune, though at their prices he'd bloody have to.' He paused, impatient as ever. 'What d'you think, then?'

Pete glanced up, wiping a smear of chocolate from the corner of his mouth. Had they tried the other two buyers? His mother? His mate?

'Yeah. They've got phone and fax numbers in Cape Town but no reply so far. It could be they don't exist, of course. Hennessey says he's acting as proxy but there's no real proof.'

'So he could be buying these places as a spec?'

'He could be. They don't like that, but he could be.'

'OK.' Pete scribbled himself a note. 'How long have I got?'

'Couple of days.' Garrett relieved Pete of the Jaffa cakes. 'That's all the Gunwharf lot are prepared to pay.'

Paul Winter was contemplating yet another pot of tea when his mobile rang. It was Cathy Lamb at Fratton nick, wanting to know where he was.

'At the QA.' The lie was automatic. 'Why?'

'How's it going?'

'Crap, love. You know what these places are like. Wait, wait, wait.' He paused. Next door, in the lounge, he could hear Joannie crying again – tiny, choking sobs. He closed his eyes and put the phone to his ear. 'They want us now, boss. Call you back?'

Without waiting for an answer, Winter ended the conversation.

Joannie was curled into her favourite recliner. Already, in less than an hour, she seemed to have physically diminished. She looked pale and thin and beaten. The spark had gone, the energy, the life. She was a stranger in their little bungalow, not Joannie at all.

'Love,' he began, 'it'll be—'

'Don't.'

'Don't what?'

'Don't say it. Don't say anything. It's just the shock. I'll get over it in a minute. Just give me a bit of time.'

She looked up at him, doing her best to summon a weak smile, then buried her face in her hands, her whole body rocking back and forth. Winter was on his knees beside her, carefully moving the empty cup to a safer place, feeling hopelessly inadequate. On the shelf above his head their single goldfish flapped slowly around the bowl. He put his arms round his wife and watched it for a moment or two, trying to work out what to say, realising that he didn't know. He thought he'd got the world sussed, and he'd been wrong. He thought life owed him no surprises, and here he suddenly was, completely helpless. Not an operation. Not a week or two in hospital. But a death sentence. Delivered, in Winter's view, without a shred of compassion.

'Wanker,' he said softly. 'Complete tosspot.'

'Who?'

'That bloke. Your specialist.'

Joannie, who'd rarely seen anything but the brighter side of life, shook her head. It wasn't the consultant's fault. He was only doing his job.

'His *job*? His job is to make you better. Not sit you down like that and tell you there's no point even bloody trying. What are these people *for*, for God's sake? We pay their wages. We build them all these bloody hospitals. There are drugs. Machines. All kinds of stuff. All he's got is a white flag. Fuck him. Just fuck him.'

He shut his eyes, close to tears himself. Rage and self-pity. Then he felt Joannie's hand on his, stroking and stroking.

'It'll be all right,' she was saying softly. 'I'm still here.'

A minute or two later, standing in the kitchen, Winter realised he'd just washed the same cup three times. Can't cope with this, he told himself. No bloody way.

Opening a drawer, he pulled out a drying-up cloth. Beautifully ironed, it smelled of fresh air. Shutting his eyes again, he visualised a line of washing in the garden, the way Joannie pegged the big stuff in the middle, the way she planted the pole so the sheets never snagged on the rose bushes. Twenty-four years she'd been doing that. Twenty-four years he'd taken it all for granted, every single time. And now she was next door. Dying.

He'd left the mobile on the side. Cathy was in her office.

'We're through at the hospital, boss.' He tried hard to sound normal. 'What have you got for me?'

Faraday was reading the front page of the *News* for the second time when the duty DS from Fratton phoned. Joyce, ever gleeful, had left the midday edition on his desk. DONALD DUCK RAPIST STRIKES AGAIN ran the headline. MOTHER FLEES IN TERROR.

'We've had a bloke at the front desk, sir,' the DS was saying. 'Not sure about the strength but we thought you might be interested.'

'What's it about?'

'His daughter. He thinks she's been molested.'

Faraday was leafing through the paper. A search of the area around the ponds was still going on, but the *News* editorial left it in no doubt that the city's women deserved a better deal from the police. Three incidents in a row. Three chances to nail the guy. And absolutely nothing to show for it. This was the kind of nonsense that sent the suits at headquarters racing to their PCs. Any minute now Joyce would be bending over his shoulder, reading the first of the e-mails.

'Molested by who?'

'Her lecturer.'

The DS named a college in the city. The girl was on some kind of media course. The lecturer taught drama and film studies. According to the father, she'd been pressured into sleeping with him. She was a good girl, weak-minded but a good girl. Bloke needed sorting out.

Faraday at last closed the paper. The college was up in the north of the city, part of Cathy Lamb's patch.

'So why me?' he enquired drily. 'Can't you lot cope?'

'It's not that, sir.'

'What is it, then?'

'His address, for a start, and hers. They both live

down your way. She's in some kind of bedsit in Southsea. He's got a place in Milton.'

Faraday reached for a pen. The Donald Duck incidents had all occurred around the edges of Langstone Harbour. Milton was half a mile away.

'And?' he said.

The DS paused a moment, then laughed.

'This is the father talking,' he said, 'but apparently he's got a thing about dressing up.'

Two

Monday, 19 June, noon

Winter stood in a room at the Marriott hotel, staring down at the view. The sun had come out at last, and from the seventh floor the city was laid out at his feet: rows and rows of gleaming yachts in the nearby Port Solent marina, the motorway threading across the wide spaces of the harbour, the big black silhouettes of the cranes in the naval dockyard and a cluster of sentinel tower blocks far away in the haze. Half-close your eyes and it might be somewhere foreign and exotic, an island city ringed with blue. For a view to start your morning, you could certainly do worse.

'Will you be wanting to bring other guys up here? Seal the room off?'

The manager was a softly spoken Scot and his recent dealings with the Drugs Squad had fuelled many a laugh at the social club bar down at Fratton nick. Only last month, the drugs guys had used the hotel to set up surveillance in expectation of a big cocaine delivery. The wholesalers were coming down from Manchester and trans-shipping in the hotel car park. Teams of three from the Drugs Squad had organised a twenty-four-hour watch – still cameras, video, the lot – but the bad guys hadn't shown and on the third day, under their noses, some local scrote had turned up with a rusty old Transit and nicked the hotel lawnmower. They'd all watched him do it – back the van up, open the rear doors, wrestle the bloody thing in – yet none of them had even made a note of the Transit's registration number. Too busy sizing up the big picture, Winter thought bitterly. Too fucking grand to bother with a £1700 slice of volume crime.

The hotel manager was still waiting for an answer. Winter finally dragged himself away from the view, back to the room. On the manager's instructions, nothing had been touched.

'Tell me again,' Winter grunted. 'The guy booked in and paid?'

'Yesterday afternoon. Cash. No problem there.'

'But you're worried about this?'

'Aye, and the bathroom, too.'

Winter looked round. There'd certainly been some kind of disturbance. An armchair had been upended and there were shards of china from a smashed tea service on the carpet by the telly. Next door, in the bathroom, blood had dried on the splashback tiles around the handbasin. Not a vast amount of blood, but more than enough to warrant the maid putting a call through to the manager.

Winter inspected the bloodstains more closely, in search of the splatter patterns that might indicate use of a weapon. Stab somebody with a knife, or use a cosh or a hammer on their skulls, and the moment you withdrew the weapon was the moment you sent little drops of blood over your shoulder, flecking the surfaces behind. On this occasion, though, Winter could find no such evidence. The blood was restricted to the tiles around the basin. The guy might have cut himself shaving.

Winter nodded to himself and then bent to an empty glass on the shelf beside the bath and sniffed it. He was going through the motions, his brain on automatic, and he sensed that the manager knew it. Not that Winter really cared.

'What's the guy's name?'

'French. Angus French.'

'And you say he's checked out?'

'He's left, certainly. His clothes have gone, as you can see, and we can't find his car. He wouldn't need to check out.'

'Nothing from the minibar?'

'No.'

'No phone calls?'

'Not on our system.'

'Nothing downstairs? The restaurant? Breakfast on his tab?'

'Nothing.'

Winter was inspecting the contents of the little wicker basket of goodies by the sink. Bath gel. A shower hat. A complimentary bar of herb-scented soap. The latter was one of Joannie's favourites. He weighed it in his hand and then slipped it into his pocket, trying hard not to picture her huddled in the recliner at home.

'You're not bothered?' the manager said at last, looking pointedly at the bloodstains.

'I've seen worse.'

'But you'll understand our concern? Calling you guys in?'

'Yeah, but I don't think you've got a problem here. Bloke's on his own, gets pissed, staggers around a bit, cuts himself somehow, drowns his sorrows.' He picked up the glass and offered it to the manager. 'I'd say Scotch, but you'd be the expert.'

The manager was looking at the glass.

'You'll not be bringing in forensic, then? Or a photographer?'

'No point. It's not even a damages claim, is it?'

'No, but—' He shrugged. 'I guess it's up to you.'

'I'd leave it. Anything else comes up, give me a call.'

Winter gave him a card before stepping back into the bedroom. The manager glanced at the card, took a final look at the blood crusting beside the basin, then shrugged again. Next door, Winter had returned to the window.

'That bloody lawnmower of yours,' he mused. 'Ever get it back, did you?'

It was lunchtime before Faraday had the chance to pursue the message from Fratton CID. Rick Stapleton and Dawn Ellis had been part of the team mounting the search after last night's Donald Duck incident and they had little to report. They'd come away with a boxful of used condoms and enough empty lager cans to fill a couple of supermarket bags, but the guy they were now referring to as 'DD' hadn't obliged them by dropping anything really helpful, like a pair of keys, or a nice little slip of paper with his name and address on it. They'd managed to match the woman's trainers against a footprint on the edge of one of the ponds, but the surrounding mud was a mess of overprints and they'd found nothing worth even a photograph.

Faraday let them finish before mentioning the call from the DS over at Fratton. Dawn was a slight, fine-boned twenty-five-year-old with a sharp intelligence and a chaotic love life. Stapleton, seven years older, was fiercely gay and lived with his partner, a Southsea restaurateur, in an exquisite Victorian terrace near the seafront. To Faraday's surprise, they made a good team. Stapleton, who happened to own a Suzuki 1100cc superbike, was one of those guys who tackled most of life's corners at a thousand miles an hour, and Dawn was one of the few individuals who could slow him down. The fact that she very obviously fancied him had fuelled months of office gossip, but it was Vanessa, typically, who'd put her finger on the essence of this strangely effective partnership. Dawn, she'd concluded, had a passion for lost causes, and in Rick Stapleton she'd found herself the perfect specimen. The guy was superglued to his partner. Even Dawn, with her wardrobe of trophy rugby shirts, didn't have a prayer.

'I've got an address on the Donald Duck job,' Faraday said at last. 'Definitely worth a visit.'

Stapleton was studying the slip of paper Faraday had handed over.

'Who's Beavis?'

'He's the guy who made the complaint. Thinks his daughter's at it with her teacher.'

'How old is she?'

'Eighteen.'

'That makes it legal, doesn't it?'

'Not if he's wandering around at night in a mask.'

Dawn looked briefly troubled. Faraday, for once, was sounding like Rick Stapleton. Assumptions first, evidence a distant second.

'Why would we put him in the frame?' she enquired.

'We might not. It's a punt, that's all. He lives close by. The father thinks he's over-sexed. He might be into dressing up. Run last night past him, and the other dates, too. Joyce is sitting on the file.'

Joyce was perched on a corner of her desk, demolishing a doughnut. Tuned in to the conversation, she licked the sugar from her fingers and reached back to open a drawer. Dawn Ellis got there first, grabbing Joyce's arm moments before she toppled onto the floor. A second or two later, the contents of the open drawer caught Dawn's attention.

'What's this?' She began to giggle. 'And this?'

She pulled out a handful of magazines, full colour. Well-muscled young men in a variety of come-on poses. All of them naked, and most of them in a state of some excitement. Faraday joined her. The magazines were German. *Der Fleisch*.

'Are these yours?' Faraday was gazing at Joyce, amazed.

'Of course they're mine. Three pounds a month including postage. A little man in Hamburg sends them over.'

Stapleton reached for one of the magazines, flicking through it with growing interest. He kept himself in trim with near-nightly runs along the seafront, bounding along in wraparound sunglasses and a pair of scarlet shorts. Dawn was watching him carefully.

'Speak German do you, Rick?'

'No chance.' He was looking at Joyce. 'How about you?'

'Me neither.' Joyce beamed at him. 'Be my guest.'

Cathy Lamb found Winter beside the coffee machine at Fratton police station. Just back from the Marriott hotel, he was trying to work out why his thirty pence had failed to produce a shot of Gold Blend, creamer, two sugars.

'How's your wife?'

Winter didn't take his eyes off the cash read-out.

'Fine,' he said stonily. 'Why doesn't this bloody thing work?'

'You need another ten.' She pointed at the price tag alongside the Gold Blend logo. 'Here. Have one on me.' She put a coin in the slot and watched the plastic cup drop into place. 'There's a stack of stuff come in. We need to talk.'

'No can do, boss.' Winter shook his head. 'I'm buggered for the rest of the day.'

'How come?'

Winter, waiting for the cup to fill, wouldn't look at her. He had paperwork going back the best part of a week, he said. He had two CPS files to sort and neither would wait. On top of that, she'd sent him to the Marriott.

'And?'

'Very dodgy. There's evidence of a fight and the bloke's disappeared.'

'What evidence?'

'Blood all over the bathroom.'

'You want to get a SOCO in?'

Winter ducked his head towards the cup. SOCO was CID-speak for Scenes-Of-Crime Officer. Putting a SOCO into the Marriott was the equivalent of pressing the alarm button, and though Cathy wouldn't think twice about giving him the go-ahead if circumstances justified it, there were serious financial implications. A full forensic search of the hotel suite would carry a hefty price tag.

'The manager's sealed the room off,' he lied, 'but I thought I'd make a few calls first.'

Kevin Beavis lived in Fratton, barely half a mile from the police station. The history of Portsmouth was writ large across the city's face – street after street of tightly packed terraced houses pushing outwards from the naval dockyard – and the fields of Fratton had disappeared under a wild frenzy of nineteenth-century speculative building. Piped water and the tram had brought a measure of comfort and civic pride to the area, but nowadays much of that spirit had long gone. There were curls of dog shit beside Kevin Beavis's front door and one of the windows beside it had been boarded up with plywood. Across the plywood, in red aerosol, someone had scrawled 'Becks Sucks'. Waiting for an answer to her second knock, Dawn Ellis obliged Rick Stapleton with a translation.

'Football talk,' she explained. 'In case you were wondering.'

Beavis was a tall, bulky man in his early forties who filled the narrow entry. His sagging jeans were stained with engine oil and the lumberjack shirt hadn't seen the inside of a washing machine for weeks. His big jowly face was buttoned with tiny eyes, jet-black, and a savage side-parting gave his whole body a curiously lop-sided look. If you were launching an inquiry into inbreeding, then Kevin Beavis was definitely where you'd start.

The moment he saw Stapleton's proffered ID, he extended an enormous hand. Stapleton ignored it.

'Just a word or two, Mr Beavis,' he said. 'Inside, if you don't mind.'

The house was a tip: bare boards in the hall, and a glimpse of a motorcycle frame propped up on a raft of breeze blocks in the front room. The kitchen lay at the back of the house, the sink full of motorcycle parts, the single window misted from a recently boiled kettle. Both Stapleton and Dawn Ellis refused Beavis's offer of tea.

'We understand you made a complaint,' Dawn began. 'Regarding your daughter.'

Beavis nodded. His daughter's name was Shelley. She was a bright girl, clever, not like her mum or dad, and she'd done well. At school they'd said she was college material, definitely. She liked films and plays. She wanted to be an actress. She read a lot. In fact, she read all the time. Which was why she'd ended up with a pervert like Addison.

'Who's Addison?' Stapleton was making notes.

'Her teacher. Lecturer-bloke. Up at the college. You can smell it on these people. You don't have to read books to know.'

'Know what, Mr Beavis?'

'Know what he's after. Teacher? Bollocks. He's after Shel. Stands out a mile, know what I mean?'

Shelley had been at the college nearly a year, enrolled on some kind of drama course. At first, she'd been happy to do her studying at home, where she'd always lived, but after Christmas she'd moved out.

'Where to?'

'Friend's place, so she says. Down Southsea.'

'Address?'

'Rawlinson Road. Dunno what number, but that doesn't really matter, does it, because I don't suppose she lives there, does she? No, mate, she lives with him, lover boy, Mr Paul fucking Addison, and I'm telling you something I hate to say in front of a lady, but that bastard is a disgrace. Ought to keep his dick to himself. Know what I mean? And something else, too. All that fancy talk, all that Hollywood shit about making her famous. He knows my Shel. He knows how easy it is with her. Bloke needs sorting. He's lucky I came to you lot first.'

Stapleton had abandoned his notebook and was gazing into the sink. Among the entrails of a rusting cylinder head, he'd recognised the remains of a bacon sandwich, the bread crusts black with engine grease.

'You mentioned something about dressing up,' Dawn was saying, 'when you went to the nick at Fratton.'

'Exactly.' Beavis poked a grimy finger at her. 'Ponce that he is.'

'What kind of dressing up?'

'He makes Shel wear all kinds of gear. Says it helps

her get in touch with her feelings. Says it'll put her on the road to Hollywood.'

'How do you know all this?'

'She tells me. She comes dancing in here and her head's full of it. How they play these games together. How he makes her dress up. How he's going to put her in the movies. How she needs to get in touch with her fucking feelings. You know about all this feelie-feelie shit? Feelie-feelie, my arse. I can tell you where he feelie-feelies her, and you don't need no A levels to fucking work *that* out.'

Stapleton blinked. The sight of Beavis at maximum revs was far from pretty. A film of spittle had pooled in the corners of his mouth and the wreckage of the man's teeth, broken and yellowing, disgusted him.

'Dressing up's not a crime,' he said carefully.

'No, but that's just the start of it.'

'Start of what?'

'What they gets up to. What *he* gets up to. With my Shel.'

'Are you saying he's been harassing her? Do you have dates? Instances? Specific allegations?'

'Not exactly, but it's obvious, isn't it? Girls like Shel, they think he's God. He tells them he'll sort out their grades and stuff, give them good marks, and they believe him. He tells them they'll be in the shit unless they come across, so what else are they expected to do? It's a tough old world, mate. My Shel, protected all her life, she don't stand a chance. Bloke should be put down. He's an animal, I'm telling you straight.' He paused, then seized the kettle. 'You sure about that tea?'

He plunged the kettle into the wreckage in the sink and turned on the tap.

'Another thing,' he muttered. 'He makes her wear masks.'

*

36

Cathy Lamb was still wondering about Winter when her phone began to ring. In any other circumstances, she'd have sat him down and given him a bit of a shake about the log-jam of jobs piling up, but there was something in his manner that she'd never seen before. In four years as his DS, she'd got used to his deviousness and sleight of hand, but not once had she seen him so subdued. Even knock-backs like the Drug Squad job failed to dent his self-belief. So what had happened?

She reached for her phone. It was Pete, her estranged husband.

'Big favour,' he said at once.

'Not again.'

'Fraid so.'

He gave her a name. She scribbled it down, then read it back to him..

'Pieter Hennessey,' she said. 'Pieter spelled the South African way.'

'Yeah. Apparently the guy's some kind of surgeon. I don't think he's got form but it would be useful to find out. Any chance?'

Cathy was still looking at the name. Over the last couple of months, she'd helped Pete out with a vehicle registration check and a peek at an ex-DC's service record. She'd never enquired why he wanted them, and when he'd offered to split whatever fee he was getting, she'd hit the roof. If he was really moonlighting, then he was digging himself a bloody great hole and the last thing she intended to do was join him. Occasional evenings at the Wine Vaults and a curry afterwards was one thing. This was quite another.

'What do you think?'

'I think you're crazy.'

'About Hennessey, though.'

'It's difficult. And unfair.'

'OK. Forget I asked.'

Cathy blinked at the phone. His voice was warm. He was apologising. And he seemed to mean it.

'I'm sorry, Pete,' she began, 'but—'

He was laughing now. He owed her a meal and a drink, he said. Her choice of wallpaper for the new flat had been inspired. The refurb had come to less than he'd thought and he had enough for a new futon.

'What's buying a futon got to do with me?'

'Nothing. Except you're good at that kind of thing.'

'Testing them out?'

'Choosing them.'

'For someone else to christen?'

'That's a difficult question.' Pete was laughing again. 'And bloody unfair.'

Winter retraced his steps through the QA hospital. Left at the big fountain. On past the shop. Down to the second set of lifts. Up to the first floor. He had the measured tread and sightless gaze of a man possessed. Nothing would deflect him. Not reason. Not prudence. And certainly not the possibility that the next ten minutes might solve absolutely nothing. All his life, he'd seized the initiative. Now was the worst possible moment to stop.

When he got to the gastro-intestinal clinic, he found himself looking at a row of empty chairs. Up at the far end, where he and Joannie had meekly accepted their fate, the consulting-room door was shut. He rapped on it twice and walked in.

The consultant was writing notes in a file. Winter loomed over him, his hands flat on the desk, his breath coming faster than he'd have liked. For a moment or two, the consultant ignored him. Then he put down the fountain pen and looked up. He had the air of a man who'd spent all day waiting for this small moment of peace, only to find it snatched from his grasp.

'Can I help you?' he enquired icily.

'We need to talk. Now.'

'I'm afraid that's impossible. Make an appointment. Ring my secretary. She's back in the morning.' He nodded towards the door. 'On second thoughts, leave her a note. It might be quicker.'

Winter reached across and capped the fountain pen, then laid it carefully beside the file. This time, the consultant was even more direct.

'I'm asking you to get out of my office,' he said. 'You have no right to be here.'

Winter ignored him. Six hours ago, this man had ruled a heavy black line across Joannie's life. There'd been no apologies, no explanations, no possibility of treatment, just the starkest of warnings that her time on earth had come to an end, that her train was about to leave. To Winter, to any half-decent husband, that was unacceptable. She'd been to the GP in good faith. In good faith, he'd given her tablets. When they hadn't worked, she'd come for tests and a scan. At no point had anyone suggested cancer. At no point had there been the remotest possibility that his wife was beyond the reach of modern medicine. She was forty-three, for God's sake. She had plans, dreams, a future. They both did. Now this.

'So you see why we have to have a little talk,' Winter concluded, 'before I do something really silly.'

'Like what?'

Winter didn't respond. The only threats that mattered left everything to the imagination. Twenty-five years in the job had taught him that.

'I want to know what steps you intend to take,' he said at last, 'when it comes to treating my wife.'

'There are no steps, Mr Winter. I know it's a hard thing to accept but I'm afraid that's the situation.'

'Really?'

'Yes. I can't tell you how sorry I am but I thought we'd been through all this already.'

'No.' Winter shook his head. 'We've been through something else. We've been through a little game you guys play when you're up against the clock, or something looks just a touch difficult, or the bean counters who run this place have run out of cash for the really expensive drugs, the ones that sort these bloody diseases out.' He was leaning over the desk again. He could feel the consultant's minty breath on his face. 'I'm here to tell you that we'll pay. I don't care how much it costs. We'll sell the bungalow. I'll raise a loan. I'll cash in all my insurances. I'll score a ton of heroin. Any bloody thing. But I want you to make her better. That's Joannie, by the way, my wife. Not the case number you disposed of this morning.' He held the consultant's eyes for a second or two extra, then smiled. 'Deal?'

The consultant was reaching for the phone, doing his best to contain his temper.

'Whether you mean to insult me doesn't really matter,' he said quietly. 'We've done what we can, and all I can say once again is that I'm sorry we've run out of options.'

'Sorry isn't enough.'

'So I gather. If you want a miracle, I suggest you talk to a priest. Your wife has my sympathies. And so, strangely enough, do you.'

Winter stared at him a moment. The consultant was waiting for the phone to answer.

'Who are you ringing?'

'Security.'

Winter took a tiny step backwards and began to laugh.

'Try nine-nine-nine,' he said, 'and have me arrested.'

'I'm sure that won't be necessary, Mr Winter.'

'Too bloody right.'

Winter kept his visiting cards in his inside pocket. Beneath the Hampshire Constabulary crest was his name and a CID contact number. He laid the card beside the telephone, turned on his heel and left.

Three

With fifteen minutes to spare between meetings, Faraday dug out the photocopy he'd taken of Vanessa Parry's RTA file and reached for his phone. Fatal road traffic accidents attracted a great deal of paperwork: an on-the-spot report form, witness statements, photographs, the findings of the motor engineers who took the crashed vehicles apart, and finally the painstakingly detailed analysis from the Accident Investigation boys over at Winchester. The latter, the work of a hard-pressed two-man unit with far too many accidents to attend, normally took at least a couple of weeks to come through, and so far Faraday, despite several phone calls, hadn't seen it.

'Traffic.'

Faraday recognised the gruff tones of one of the duty Sergeants.

'DI Faraday. Is Mark Barrington there?'

Barrington was the motorcycle patrolman who'd attended Vanessa's accident, a newish recruit three years into the job. Faraday had tracked him down via the traffic HQ at Fratton police station and Barrington had obliged with a look at the file and a detailed personal account of what appeared to have happened at the site of the accident. The Sergeant was infinitely less helpful.

'Barrington's not here,' he said briskly.

'Is he back later?'

'I doubt it. He was early turn. He's gone already.' He paused. 'Something I can help you with?'

Faraday was looking at the rough sketch plan that Barrington had made once the ambulances had been and gone. Larkrise Avenue was up in Drayton, a long, straight suburban road with parked cars on both sides narrowing the through-way to a tight squeeze. The two cars, Vanessa's Fiesta and the Vectra Estate, had met head on about a third of the way down. There had been no evidence on the road of skid marks from either car, though the tarmac had been gouged as the Fiesta was spun backwards by the impact. The sketch was necessarily rough and begged all kinds of questions that only the Accident Investigation report could answer.

'It's the Larkrise Avenue fatal,' Faraday began. 'I'm after the AI report.'

'It hasn't arrived.' The Sergeant was blunt to the point of rudeness. 'But when it does, we'll sort it.'

'I'm sure you will. Vanessa Parry was on our support staff.'

'So I gather. Excuse me saying so, sir, I know it's family, and I know you're all upset, but we're giving it our best shot, OK?'

Faraday listened to the Sergeant staking out his bit of territory. Twenty years in the job had taught him a great deal about turf wars, and the no-man's land between traffic and CID was never for the faint-hearted. The traffic guys had more than enough to do. Mark Barrington was a promising young copper. The Sergeant had no reason to question his handling of this particular episode. The preliminary query about the Fiesta's brakes was unfortunate but it might be best to wait for the full AI report. If developments called for

43

some kind of CID involvement, Faraday would be the first to know.

'No offence, sir. But I'm sure you see what I mean.'

'Of course I do. When do you expect the AI report?'

'To be frank, I've no idea.'

'What about the mobile?'

'What mobile?'

'The lad Matthew Prentice had a mobile with him. Barrington found it in the Vectra, along with all kinds of paperwork. I suggested he raise a C63 on it. I was just wondering whether he'd had any joy.'

'You suggested *what*?'

A C63 was the form you filled in to bid for access to data from one of the mobile phone companies. A printout on a particular number could pinpoint the time and duration of a call, plus a name and address for the voice at the other end.

Faraday permitted himself a grim smile. The sergeant was wound up tighter than a spring.

'Just a thought I had,' Faraday said lightly. 'Your lad found the mobile switched off. That isn't necessarily conclusive.'

'So what are you suggesting . . . sir?'

'I'm suggesting that Prentice had at least a minute to sort himself out after the impact. He wasn't hurt. He wasn't unconscious. Had he been on the phone, he'd have switched it off.' He paused. 'As I understand it, there were no witnesses.'

'Did Barrington tell you that?'

'He didn't have to. There are no witness statements in the file.'

'You've seen the file?'

'I'm looking at it now.'

The Sergeant was speechless. Faraday pressed on.

'Prentice was lucky,' he said. 'No witnesses except for

44

the other driver, and Vanessa is dead. That gives him every incentive to claim amnesia, and as I understand it, that's exactly what he's doing. Got up in the morning. Drove to his first call. Then it all goes fuzzy. Can't remember driving into Larkrise Avenue. Can't remember any Fiesta. Can't remember killing my management assistant. The AI report might help him fill in the blanks. And if it doesn't, then maybe we ought to be thinking about his mobile. No?'

There was a long silence, then the Sergeant came back. He'd given up arguing the toss about Mark Barrington. He'd talk to his Inspector. Not about the ins and outs of the Larkrise Avenue RTA but about bloody CID muscling in on Traffic. You do your job, I'll do mine. OK?

Faraday let the storm pass, then bent to the phone again.

'Death by dangerous driving. Am I right?'

'It's on the cards, certainly.'

'Crown Court? Hefty fine plus a ban? This guy's a commercial rep. He'll get himself a decent brief. He'll plead tools of the trade. Take my licence away, I'm out on the street.' He paused. 'Number one, we need to get this guy off the road. Number two, it might be nice if he had his tiny mind concentrated.'

'Like how?'

'Like a couple of years inside.'

'On a death by dangerous driving?'

Faraday let the laughter subside.

'No,' he said quietly, 'perverting the course of justice. Courts just love that. In case you'd forgotten.'

Rawlinson Road lay at the heart of Southsea, a once fashionable address attracting generations of naval officers and their families to the imposing bay-fronted houses. A century and a half later, disfigured by landlords squeezing rents from multi-occupation, it had become a neighbourhood you'd do your best to avoid. Awash with litter, choked by cars and vans half-parked on the pavement, it was now a regular port of call for drug dealers, noise abatement officers and harassed officials from the Social Services acute response teams. Even the trees looked unloved.

Shelley Beavis, according to the accommodation secretary at the college, shared the basement at number 21. Access to the flat was round the side, a length of slimy paving under permanent bombardment from a dripping overflow.

She answered Dawn's knock with some reluctance, a sleepy-eyed, barefoot eighteen-year-old in jeans and a thin cardigan, peering out from a mop of tousled blond hair. Dawn's first reaction was to wonder whether she was Beavis's daughter at all. Genetics plainly owed nothing to her willowy body and flawless complexion.

'Police?' she said blankly, when Stapleton showed his ID.

The flat was subterranean, pools of semi-darkness smelling of day-old joss and a serious damp problem. Thick, crudely suspended blankets hung at the barred window in the front, and it took Dawn several seconds to map the room where Shelley appeared to live. An unmade single bed in one corner. A baize card table supporting a battered-looking hi-fi stack. Posters of Ralph Fiennes and Brad Pitt. Bits and pieces of food, chiefly biscuits and crisps. Piles of paperbacks and magazines lapping at a dinner plate on the floor. The dinner plate obviously doubled as an ashtray, and Stapleton studied it with interest while Dawn explained the reason for their visit.

At the mention of her father's worries about Paul

Addison, Shelley shook her head. Her father had no right to go on like that about Paul. Her life was her own. She didn't want to talk about it.

'Is he right, though? Is there some kind of relationship between you?'

'I don't know what you're talking about.'

'I'm talking about you, Shelley. You and Paul Addison.'

She shook her head again, turning away. Her father was off the planet. He'd always hated her going to college. Woolies or B&Q would have been more his mark. Somewhere he could keep an eye on her. As for Paul, it was all a fantasy.

'That's what he says.' It was Stapleton's turn to take up the running. 'He says he dresses you up.'

'That's right, he does. We both do. It's called role play. It's part of the course. Is that illegal?'

'Not at all. Unless . . .' He shrugged. 'Unless you're not up for it.'

'Not up for what?'

'Shagging.'

'Is that what he's saying? My dad? We dress up and then shag?'

'Something like that. Only you're not keen. That's what's bothering him.'

Shelley said nothing, and then crossed towards the window to let in some air. As the light caught her face, Dawn thought she saw the faint remains of a bruise beneath the girl's left eye.

'We're really here to help,' she said softly. 'You'd be wise to trust us.'

The faintest smile crossed Shelley's face, but she didn't reply. As far as she was concerned, their little chat was over. Stapleton bent to the carpet and retrieved the dinner plate, counting at least three roaches among

47

the litter of stubbed-out butts. Then he looked Shelley in the eye and nodded at the plate. Shame to taint a nice relationship like this with anything as silly as a visit from the Drugs Squad.

At length, Shelley shrugged.

'OK,' she muttered, 'he might have . . . you know . . . tried it on.'

'Might have?' Stapleton was frowning. 'You'd know, surely.'

'Yeah, but . . . these things . . . it's me as well, you know.'

'What does that mean?'

'I dunno. I dunno what you want.'

There was a long silence. Dawn could hear the steady drip of water from the overflow outside.

'Rape isn't trying it on,' she pointed out.

'No, I know, but—'

'Are you telling us he raped you?' Stapleton this time, the smile gone. 'Just yes or no, love.'

'No, but . . . I dunno.'

'Have you had intercourse with him?'

Shelley was biting her lip. Stapleton asked the question again. She didn't reply. Dawn had circled behind her.

'So whose idea was it?' she enquired softly. 'His or yours?'

'What idea?'

'Shagging.'

'I didn't say that.'

'You don't have to. We've been there. No games, Shelley. Just tell us.'

'But it's not like that. It's nothing like that. Honest.'

Dawn turned away, leaving her to Stapleton.

'Then why's your dad so uptight?' he enquired.

'You tell me.'

'That's not an answer, love.'

'But I'm telling you. I don't know.'

'Yes, you do.' Stapleton was in her face now. 'Addison tried to get his leg over and you were bloody upset and you told him what happened and he came to us and now you just want us to go away. Isn't that it?'

'The last bit' – she stepped away from him – 'definitely.'

She was frightened, Dawn could tell. In terms of anything useful, anything evidential, they were light years away from a result, but they'd stumbled on something here, and she could tell that Rick felt it too. The girl was confused. She couldn't quite make up her mind what role to play. There were knots inside her that deserved untangling, secrets she might be persuaded to share.

Dawn caught Stapleton's eye again and nodded at the door. Shelley watched him every step of the way as he left the room.

'It's first on the left,' she called. 'Keep pulling to flush.'

The two women looked at each other. Dawn tried to narrow the gulf between them with a smile.

'Tell me about the masks,' she said softly.

The girl stared at her.

'He told you about that? My dad?'

'I'm afraid so.' Dawn felt for a pen. 'An address would be good, Shelley. Just for starters.'

Paul Winter was in a traffic jam at the city end of the motorway, waiting for the queue of vehicles to drain down on to the big roundabout that would take him back to Fratton nick. His boiling anger with the consultant had gone now, replaced by a feeling of numbness. He'd been blanked by the world of medicine.

Short of crank diets or a sudden attack of religious faith, there seemed to be absolutely nothing he could do. Maybe Joannie was right after all when she told him they had to accept it. Maybe she really was going to die. He shook his head, gazing sightlessly at the auto parts van on his left. Even a half-smile from the girl at the wheel failed to rouse him.

His mobile began to chirp on the seat beside him. He looked at it a moment, totally disinterested, then picked it up. It was the manager from the Marriott hotel, the Scots guy.

'It's about our friend Mr French,' he began.

'Go on,' Winter grunted.

'I did some asking around. Just out of curiosity.'

'Yeah?'

'He had a meal in the hotel last night. Paid for it with his credit card. I checked out the slip and his name's not French at all.'

'Maybe he was using someone else's card.'

'Not if he signed, surely.'

The traffic was beginning to move at last. Winter waved the auto-parts girl into the gap in front.

'Faked the signature,' he said. 'Happens all the time.'

'And that's not illegal?'

'Of course it is. If you've got the time to chase it and get a positive ID on the fella.'

'Would that include video?'

'Video?' Winter was forcing himself to concentrate at last. Of course they had video. Even B&Bs had video these days. Shit. 'How many cameras have you got?' He tried to make the enquiry sound casual but knew he hadn't a prayer. First the lawnmower. Now some doze of a DC who hadn't had the wit to enquire about video.

'More than a dozen,' the manager was saying. 'Including reception.'

'And you're telling me you've got a decent mug shot?'

'Several.'

'OK.' Winter reached for a pen. 'Give me the name he used. I'll check it out.'

'Pieter Hennessey,' the manager said. 'Pieter spelled the Dutch way.'

Faraday brooded all afternoon about the accident in Larkrise Avenue. He brooded through a meeting on the implications of the European Convention of Human Rights. He brooded through a departmental run-in on the monthly overtime figures. And by the time Joyce appeared at the door of his office with a pile of internal correspondence, he was more or less certain that his raid on Traffic's turf deserved some decent camouflage.

The Sergeant would have gone bleating to one of the uniformed Inspectors by now. From there, it was only a phone call to someone way up the ladder, probably the uniformed Superintendent. He'd doubtless have his own views on Faraday's lack of manners, and by the time the inevitable phone call came, he ought to be prepared. He hadn't the slightest doubt that Vanessa Parry's death was akin to murder. And murder deserved more than the attentions of a promising young patrolman.

Joyce was wanting to know whether he wanted tea or coffee.

'Neither, thank you. How urgent is this lot?'

'Most of it's bubblegum. The stuff you need to worry about is on top.'

'You've been through it?'

'Yep. Just ask for triage next time you call.'

The wryness of the comment brought a smile to Faraday's face. The contents of Joyce's bottom drawer had come as something of a surprise, not least because her husband had always been banging on about his fitness routines. Listen to him over the course of one of the interminable Mess dinners at Netley and you'd think she'd married Super Dick. Evidently not.

'Traffic have been on,' she continued. 'The Chief Inspector wants a word.'

'I bet he does.'

'You want me to get him for you?'

'No, thanks.'

She looked down at him a moment. She had huge bosoms, fifties gloss lipstick and a head that seemed too small for her body, yet the legs beneath her pleated skirt, as more than one DC had commented, were amazing. Did she work out alongside her husband? Was that another of her little secrets?

'This is about the guy who mashed Vanessa,' she said, 'isn't it?'

Faraday blinked. A mind reader, as well as a connoisseur of German gay porn.

'What makes you think that?'

'I'm guessing, but something tells me I'm guessing right.' She paused. 'We never did get to talk about Vanessa, did we?'

'No, we didn't.'

'Well, I guess some day we should.' She reached for his empty cup. 'Before it gets to be a problem.'

Four

When Cathy Lamb finally ran Winter to earth, he was sitting by himself in the canteen, nursing a cup of coffee. She joined him, not making the running, not even attempting to begin the conversation. He'd know what was on her mind. He was a detective, for God's sake.

At length, he looked up. He seemed surprised to see her.

'Nice,' he said, 'outside.'

She leaned towards him. This wasn't an exchange she was keen to share.

'I'm really sorry about your wife but there are things in this life you just shouldn't even think about doing.'

'Is that right?'

'Yeah. And one of them's badmouthing the guy who has to break the news. You're lucky he's not taking it further. He could see you in court for what you did.'

'Allegedly.'

'OK. So what's your version?'

'My version?' Winter looked contemplative, the expression of a man for whom consequences were no longer of any interest. 'Simple. Guy tells Joannie she's history. Guy explains she hasn't a prayer. Joannie has a problem with this. Hubbie returns to sort one or two details out.'

'He's saying you threatened him.'

'He's right. My mistake was leaving it there.'

53

'You could lose your job over this, Paul.'

'Yeah? And what's second prize?'

Cathy sat back in the chair for a moment, exasperated. Nothing in Force Regulations had prepared her for this.

'How did Joan take it?' she asked at last.

'Badly. Like we all would.'

'Where is she now?'

'At home.'

'By herself?'

'Yes.'

'Then why aren't you with her?'

Winter began to toy with the empty cup of coffee, running his finger round and round the rim, and Cathy was reminded of a child in class, caught out, robbed of an alibi or an explanation.

'You going to bollock me, then?' Winter was staring at the window.

'I just did.'

'And is that for the record?'

'No. It's just you and me. I managed to talk him out of taking it any higher. Just.' She reached out for his hand and felt him flinch at her touch. 'Go home, Paul. Be with her.'

For the first time, he looked her in the eye.

'You've got a pile of stuff. You told me this morning.'

'It's all crap. It can wait.'

'The Marriott thing needs sorting. I can't just walk away.'

'You can, Paul. I'm telling you to.'

He leaned forward across the table, pushing the coffee cup to one side, and explained again about the trashed room. The bloke had been using a false name and now he'd disappeared. Didn't that lot deserve a bit

54

more investigation? Or was it shoplifting and car thefts from here on in?

Despite herself, Cathy felt a stirring of interest.

'Have you got a name for this guy?'

'I've got two, like I said. He signed in as French and paid for a meal as Hennessey. Must be exhausting, keeping track.'

'Paid for a meal as what?'

'Hennessey.'

'You've got a Christian name?'

'Pieter. Spelled funny.'

Cathy was frowning. She got up and went to the cooler for a cup of water. When she got back, the frown was still there.

'I'm serious about taking time off. It's not just you, Paul, it's Joan.'

Winter nodded, saying nothing. Cathy swallowed a mouthful of water. She seemed to be having trouble trying to frame the next question.

'You remember Pete? My ex?' she said at last.

'Ex?'

Winter was looking at the thin platinum ring on her finger. The shooting incident involving Pete Lamb had also flushed out an affair he'd been having with a young probationer on division. Cathy had thrown him out of the marital semi and for months afterwards the CID office had been running a book on when she'd bin the wedding ring. The fact that no one had ever collected had surprised most of them, but not Winter. As he knew only too well, there were worse things in a marriage than screwing around.

'We keep in touch,' she said defensively, 'and it might be an idea if you gave him a call.'

'Why's that?'

'This guy you mentioned. Hennessey.' She emptied the cup. 'I think Pete might have something to say.'

Dawn Ellis and Rick Stapleton had been parked up for less than ten minutes when Addison returned to his small, neat terraced house a couple of streets back from Milton's busy parade of shops. Stapleton checked his watch. Half-past four.

'College hours,' he said in disgust. 'What a doss.'

They got out of the car, feeling the heat bubbling up from the road, and intercepted Addison while he was still fumbling for his house keys.

'DC Ellis. DC Stapleton.' Rick pocketed his warrant card. 'You are . . .?'

'Paul Addison.' He looked from one to the other. 'What's this about?'

'A word, sir, if you don't mind. Inside might be more private.'

Addison shrugged, then led the way into the house. Stapleton judged him to be mid-thirties. He wore Wrangler jeans with a nicely weathered leather belt, and a stone-grey Ben Sherman shirt. He carried a buckled leather bag on a strap over one shoulder and a folded copy of the *Guardian* in his other hand. His hair, cropped fashionably short, was beginning to grey and lent the tanned, evenly featured face a certain maturity. Paul Addison wouldn't have been out of place in the classier weekend colour supplements, the kind of aspirational figure you'd associate with after-shave or trekking boots. The contrast with Kevin Beavis couldn't be more complete.

'You want coffee or anything?'

Stapleton said no, but Dawn settled for a glass of water. They both heard the fridge door opening in the kitchen and the clink of ice cubes dropped in a glass.

Dawn looked round. Two rooms had been knocked into one, and through the arch in the middle, towards the back, she could see some kind of video set-up, two TV monitors on a desk with a control panel in between. Lines of video cassettes were racked on the walls, each one carefully labelled, and there were more videos in cardboard boxes on the floor.

'Nice.'

Stapleton was admiring a series of black and white photos mounted on clip frames on the chimney breast. The use of light was distinctive to each, the low slant of winter sunshine casting hard-edged shadows across bleak expanses of upland moor. Wooden bookshelves filled the alcove beside the chimney breast. The lines of paperbacks seemed to be arranged alphabetically, lots of French poetry and American new-wave crime fiction, but Stapleton was back with the photos when Addison returned.

'Pennine Way?'

'Dartmoor.'

'You take them yourself?'

'If only.' He handed Dawn the glass of water. 'I go down there a lot. There's a gallery in Bovey. A local guy's produced a whole book of them.' He waved them towards a low, chrome-framed sofa and hooked a canvas-backed director's chair towards him with his foot. 'How can I help you?'

Dawn was looking at a framed poster on the other wall, a swirl of greens and misty yellows with sails poking through. EXPOSITION DES BEAUX ARTS, it read, MUSÉE D'ORSAY.

'What were you doing last Friday night?' she enquired.

Addison took the question in his stride.

'Working,' he said.

'Where?'

'Here' – he nodded towards the back of the room – 'editing video tape.'

'Alone?'

'Yes. Why?'

Dawn ignored the question. Stapleton was consulting his notebook.

'Two other dates,' he began, 'February nineteenth and April twelfth. Do you keep a diary?'

'Yes.'

'Do you want to check it?'

'Listen . . .' Addison had a tiny frown on his face. 'Wouldn't it be easier if you just explained what this is about?'

Stapleton offered a helpful smile, then described the series of incidents featuring a man in a Donald Duck mask. The ongoing investigation had thrown up his name and they were simply keen to eliminate him from their inquiries.

'Thrown up how?'

'I'm afraid I can't tell you, sir.'

'But someone told you it was me? Is that what you're saying?'

Disbelief was giving way to derision. Crazy people. Crazy thought. Dawn suggested that the diary might help them clear all this up. Then they'd be out of his hair.

'OK, why not?' Addison shrugged and left the room. He was back within seconds, unfolding a Psion organiser. 'Those dates again?'

Stapleton gave him the dates. On 19 February he'd been in London most of the day on a conference; 12 April was a blank.

'So what does that tell us?'

'The nineteenth I can remember coming back here. I'd have been at home.'

'Could anyone corroborate that?'

'I doubt it.'

'No social life?'

'I didn't say that.'

'What about April?'

'The same. I'd be teaching during the day. Back here for the evening.'

'Witnesses?'

'Probably not. Most nights I'm either editing or marking. Stuff I prefer to do alone.'

'So we've only got your word for it? All three dates? Is that what you're saying?'

Addison was beginning to tire of these questions. Dawn could sense it.

'There's a problem with one of your students,' she began.

'Who?'

'Shelley Beavis.'

'What about her?'

Dawn outlined the father's complaint. Addison held her gaze, unblinking.

'*Raped* her?'

'That's what he's saying. Or at least that's what he thinks it amounts to.'

'And what does she say?'

'She's a bit confused.'

'What does that mean?'

'It means that she wouldn't tell us.'

'Wouldn't tell you whether I'd raped her or not?' He began to laugh. 'Are you guys serious?'

Dawn glanced at Stapleton. He had a pen out now and he was making notes.

'Shelley mentioned dressing up,' he said. 'Costumes and masks and stuff. Is that right?'

'Yes.' Addison nodded. 'She's doing a drama module. She wants to be an actress. Did she tell you that too?'

Stapleton ignored the question.

'Do these sessions happen here?' His gesture took in the whole house.

'Yes. Though "sessions" would be the wrong word. Some parts of the curriculum you can only reach through interactive role-play. It's highly structured, believe me.'

'And she's alone when this happens?'

'Yes. And she's alone because she's very good. In fact, she's outstanding. In this city, talent like hers deserves a little attention. Most of the students I teach have difficulty getting up in the morning. Shelley's in a class of her own.'

Stapleton was bent over his pad again, smiling.

'Attention,' he said quietly. 'I like that.'

There was a long silence. Addison looked pointedly at his watch.

'Are you through? Only I've a life to get on with.'

'We need to be clear, Mr Addison.' It was Dawn this time. 'Do you have any kind of relationship with Shelley Beavis?'

'Of course I do. She's a student of mine. I teach her. I watch her learn, watch her develop. From where I'm sitting, that's a privilege as well as a pleasure, but if you're asking whether it ever goes further than that then the answer's no. We don't hold hands. We don't go to the pub together. We don't screw. I talk. She listens. I teach. She learns. It might sound simple, and in many ways it is.'

'Nice speech.' Stapleton was smiling again. 'Why so passionate, Mr Addison?'

'Because I'm frankly pissed off with the line you're taking. You barge in here. You've obviously made up your minds. And now all you want is for me to make some crass admission about a relationship that doesn't exist. Don't invent mischief where there isn't any. Life's complex enough as it is.'

'Is it?'

Dawn let the question hang in the air. She thought she detected a hint of colour beneath Addison's tan, but she wasn't sure. Stapleton began to ask about the masks again.

'They're upstairs. Along with the other stuff, the costumes and so on.'

'Mind if we have a look round up there?'

'Of course not.'

Stapleton glanced across at Dawn. The premises search forms were outside in the car. Dawn was back within a minute, showing Addison where to sign. This sudden formality sparked another shake of the head from Addison, but he scribbled his signature readily enough, carefully folding the carbon copy and leaving it on the mantelpiece. Shelley's been on to him already, Stapleton thought. She's phoned him on his mobile and told him about our little chat in the basement flat.

Dawn told Addison she preferred to look round with him in attendance. Just in case.

'Just in case what?'

'Just in case there's any problem later.'

'With what?'

She smiled at him, not saying anything, then gestured towards the door. They both left the room and Stapleton listened to their footsteps on the stairs before he wandered through to the back room. Overhead, he could hear drawers opening and closing, then the bang of a wardrobe door. He paused beside the edit suite.

The master power switch was mounted on the left of the controller. He flicked it on, watching the monitors come to life. The play and record machines were on the floor and there were cassettes in both. Curious to know what preoccupied Addison evening after evening, he peered at the control panel, then pressed one of the two play buttons.

The screen on the left-hand machine fizzed for a second or two, then the picture stabilised. A man was making love to a naked woman on her hands and knees. Light from an open hearth fire in the background flickered over their bodies, and in the gloom beyond there was a hint of roughcast stone walls. As Stapleton watched, a voice stopped the action. The camera began to move, circling the bodies on the floor. The woman was young, no more than twenty. She had olive skin and a long fall of thick black hair. The shot closed on the woman's buttocks. The man's genitals swam in and out of focus and then the camera steadied and he began to make love again, long deep strokes, taking his time.

Stapleton heard footsteps coming back down the stairs. His finger found the pause button and he turned in time to catch Dawn coming in from the narrow hall. She was shaking her head, obviously disappointed.

'*Spitting Image* masks,' she said. 'Reagan, Thatcher, the Queen, Madonna, but no Donald Duck.'

Her eyes left Stapleton and he stepped aside to give her a better view. She stared at the screen for a long moment before Stapleton hit the pause button again and the action recommenced. Addison was coming downstairs.

'Shit.' Dawn glanced towards the door. 'No wonder he stays in most nights.'

Winter met Pete Lamb for a drink in Old Portsmouth –

Pete's suggestion. He was down there already sorting out some charts at the Sailing Club and he'd be happy to talk about Hennessey. Booze was cheap at the club but the bar didn't open until eight, so they walked across to the Still and West, a pub at the very tip of Point, a finger of land curling in from the harbour-mouth.

'He's gone missing,' Pete said at once, 'which is where I come in.'

They were sitting at a table outside, the sun still hot. Ferries churned in and out through the harbour narrows, and across the mouth of the Camber Dock, a couple of hundred metres away, there was a perfect view of the construction site that would soon become Gunwharf Quays.

Pete was talking about the new apartments.

'*How* much?'

'Half a million. That's top whack, of course, for the penthouse suites on top.'

Winter turned to peer at the forest of cranes. Hard to imagine anyone paying half a million quid for a stake in that chaos.

'Have you seen the plans?'

'You're joking. I live in a bungalow. In Bedhampton.'

'Then you should. I'll get you a brochure. Suit you down to the ground.'

He explained briefly about his deal with Mal Garrett, picking up the odd day here and there, background inquiries, relieved that Winter didn't bother with the usual health warning. Of course it was dodgy taking work while suspended, but in a way it wasn't the money at all. More the chance to keep his hand in.

'And Cath?'

'Won't touch me with a bargepole. Thinks I'm potty.'

'Potty, bollocks. She wouldn't have suggested this if that's what she thought.'

Pete hid a smile, not pursuing the point. They were here to talk about Hennessey. Where did Winter want him to start?

Winter told him what had happened at the Marriott. What was Pete's interest?

'He's skipped the deadline on three of those flats. We're talking way over a million and the management want Mal to find him before they foreclose on the option. That's not the half of it, of course.' He paused, looking at Winter. 'You're telling me you don't know about this guy?'

Winter shook his head. 'Should I?' he grunted.

Pete held his gaze a moment longer, checking for the wind-up, then disappeared into the pub for refills. Back with another couple of pints, he settled down again.

Hennessey was a gynaecological surgeon. His speciality was hysterectomies and he had a reputation for whipping out middle-aged wombs quicker than anyone else in the business. He had a private practice in Harley Street and also did work for the National Health Service. In the eighties and nineties, he'd done very nicely for himself. Hence his interest in the real estate.

'So what's the story?'

'You're really telling me you haven't heard of this guy?'

Winter shook his head again. Just the mention of the word 'surgeon' brought the blood pulsing to his head again and he took a deep pull at his glass to steady himself. He should have given the consultant a seeing-to while he still had the chance. There were some kinds of hurt that only violence could sort out.

'So what happened? What did this guy do?'

Pete was warming up now. Hennessey had been in

the papers only recently. Dozens and dozens of operations had gone disastrously wrong. According to the experts, hysterectomy wasn't rocket science, yet Hennessey seemed to have been crap at it, cutting the wrong tubes, leaving damaged tissues unstitched, causing all kinds of post-operative mayhem in his race to get through the patient list. Perfectly healthy wombs had been chopped out after misdiagnoses. Women had been left incontinent for life. One or two had nearly died. And all because this butcher kidded them he knew what he was doing.

Winter nodded grimly. Bastard medics.

'He's up before the GMC for clinical malpractice and the victims are suing. Loads of them. Lots of individual actions.'

'He'll carry insurance,' Winter said at once. 'They won't hurt him personally.'

'You're right, but he won't work again, not after that kind of publicity. The guy's history as far as cash flow is concerned. Which may explain why he's trying to lay hands on three of these flats.'

Pete explained about the other two proxy names. Like Mal Garrett, he'd tried to raise both Cape Town numbers and failed. Inquiries lodged with the South African telephone authorities had not yet been answered, but Pete had already concluded that all three would, in reality, belong to Hennessey. On a rising market, he could put down a ten per cent deposit on each apartment and sell on before they were even completed. Alternatively, if he could raise the capital, he could complete on all three and earn himself a hefty capital gain once Gunwharf Quays was a truly prestigious address. Either way, he'd be looking at a five-figure profit – easy money if you could afford to be in at the start.

'So you don't think he's done a runner?'

'Can't see why he would. The publicity's over until he has to appear before the GMC. He knows he won't be working as a surgeon again, not in this country anyway. But he'd stick around for long enough to make a killing, wouldn't he?'

Winter's gaze returned to the Gunwharf site. Pete was right. Make a killing. Dead right. Of course he'd stay. Anyone would.

'Do you have any pics?'

'I've got cuttings. *Guardian*, *Independent*, *Telegraph*. There are mug shots in all of them. Take photocopies if you want.'

'Anything else?'

'A couple of addresses. Apparently he lives in some huge pile in Beaconsfield, but he's baled out for the time being and taken a rented place in the New Forest.'

'How do you know?'

'He fancied the bird at the sales office. Tried to get her over for dinner. Here.' He took an envelope from inside his leather jacket. 'Address and phone number. I've been trying all day, but no joy.'

Winter was thinking fast. Finding Hennessey would be a pleasure, one small act of vengeance. He'd do it for Joannie's sake. For her.

Pete was examining the bottom of his empty glass.

'So how will you get all this past the management?' he enquired.

'Management?'

'Cathy. How will you justify the time and effort? Given that the guy hasn't actually done anything.'

It was a good question. Winter sat back, watching one of the big cross-Channel ferries nosing out through the harbourmouth. In his experience, the best investigations started off like this, with coppers like him chasing

66

shadows. You had to feel it in your bones. You had to sense opportunities, temptations, and know with absolute conviction that some bastard would be trying to square them away. That's how the world worked. That's what kept the country moving. People like Hennessey, backs against the wall, reaching for a big fat apple on someone else's tree.

'I think he's probably dead,' he said slowly, 'though don't ask me why.'

Winter was back home by half-eight, his footsteps lightened by another couple of pints after Pete Lamb had left. His wife was in the lounge, curled up on the sofa in her dressing gown watching *Peak Practice*. There was a bowl of tomato soup, half-finished, in her lap and a small circle of crumbs on the carpet beneath her feet.

Winter stood by the door. It was still sunny outside, a thin strip of light between the drawn curtains, but already the room felt like a tomb. On the TV, two GPs were arguing the toss about an X-ray of someone's knee.

'Leave it out, Joannie,' he said softly. 'Not more bloody medics.'

She looked up at him, the unvoiced question all too obvious. *Where have you been?*

'Work,' he explained simply. 'Never stops.'

After the third glass of Rioja, Faraday felt better about screwing up the chilli con carne. For once he hadn't followed the recipe. He'd chopped up onions and garlic extra fine and sweated them in oil. He'd stirred in a spoonful of tomato purée and a daub or two of Marmite. He'd added the mincemeat, with plenty of pepper and salt. And only at the end, with Ruth at the table in the kitchen, had he realised that he'd forgotten to buy fresh chilli. Shielding the stove with his body, he'd made do with cayenne pepper, but that wasn't the point. Chilli con carne without chilli? What kind of cook was he turning into?

It was the third time this month Ruth had come over for dinner. After the loss of her husband and son, way back last year, he'd let a decent interval pass before trying to convert a strictly professional relationship into something slightly cosier, but to his surprise the transition had been painless.

She'd slipped into his bed as easily as she'd slipped into his life. Sleeping together hadn't been altogether successful – far from it – but they seemed to have settled on a relationship flexible and forgiving enough to make room for a sexual disappointment that had been obvious from the start. Faraday hadn't been with a woman since the death of his wife, and nearly twenty-two years of bringing up his deaf son had done nothing to rid him of memories of the relationship which had shaped his life. As Ruth herself had put it, sleeping with Faraday was like a *ménage à quatre*: Joe, herself, J-J and the ghost of the long-dead Janna. Was it any kind of surprise that she no longer stayed over?

Oddly enough, from where Faraday sat, it didn't really matter. Ruth was as centred and fathomless as the day he'd first met her, doggedly pursuing his own conviction that an admirer of hers had been murdered, and nothing that had happened since had stripped her of any of the fascination she held for him. Mystery came as naturally to her as the clothes she wore – Indian cotton prints, baggy pantaloons – and she brought to his life a deep sense of challenge that he was quite unable to define.

That's maybe why it didn't work in bed. The truly

68

inner Ruth lay beyond the simple physical questions. Whichever key opened her lock, he was never quite able to find it, and as a consequence they'd slipped into a comfortable companionship, freed from either obligation or routine. Sometimes, like now, they'd see quite a lot of each other. Other months, when Faraday was even more preoccupied than usual, they might have time for no more than a phone call. When people asked him whether there was anyone special in his life, Faraday would answer yes. When they asked him if he was involved with anyone, he would, with some regret, shake his head.

They were clearing away the plates when Faraday heard a squeal of brakes outside. He glanced at his watch. Nearly half-past ten. Ruth raised an eyebrow but he shrugged, making his way to the front door. A bulky figure in a grey suit was standing outside in the half light. Faraday thought he recognised him, but he couldn't be sure.

'Boss?'

He was right. It was Paul Winter. Faraday stepped aside, inviting him in. It was obvious at once that Winter had been drinking.

'D'you mind?'

'Not at all. Something that can't wait?'

Winter laughed, a thin, mirthless chuckle.

'Yeah. Sort of.'

Ruth was still in the kitchen. Faraday did the introductions, but it was obvious that Winter wanted a private word. Faraday frowned. Years of history between the two men offered not the slightest clue for Winter's visit. Was it work-related? Or had Winter something else in mind?

Ruth was already hunting for her house keys. When

Faraday offered to open another bottle, she shook her head.

'I ought to be off,' she said, 'leave you two to it.'

With Ruth gone, Faraday took Winter into the big sitting room. The last time Winter had been here was the night they'd been trying to crack Charlie Oomes. Winter had gone at him hammer and tongs in the interview room at the Bridewell, going over his story time and time again, bringing a fresh brain to the tissue of lies the man had woven around himself. Yet when the clock finally stopped, and Oomes was still running rings round them all, it was Winter who'd found an alternative resolution for the age-old tension between crime and punishment. It might not have been orthodox, and it certainly wasn't legal, but the knowledge that Charlie Oomes had taken a beating in the showers on the remand wing at Winchester nick brought Faraday a small warm feeling of satisfaction. Winter's way wasn't Faraday's way. But, with every other option exhausted, it had worked.

Langstone Harbour lay in the darkness outside. The big sliding doors to the lounge were still open and the night wind spiked the room with the scent of seaweed and newly cut grass. Ruth had promised to keep an eye out for a decent mower. Something motorised. Something Faraday wouldn't have to push.

Winter was sitting on the sofa with a big glass of Scotch, talking about the incident at the Marriott hotel. How the guy had checked in under a false name. The mess he'd made of the room. The blood around the hand basin next door. Faraday knew him in these moods. He was setting the scene, baiting a trap.

'So what's it worth?' he said at last.

'You tell me, boss. On the face of it, fuck all. But you get an instinct, don't you?'

'And what does that tell you?'

'It tells me the guy was attacked.'

'Do you have a name?'

'Hennessey. He was a surgeon.'

'Was?'

'Yeah, and I can think of several thousand women who'd gladly see him dead.'

Faraday reached for the bottle and splashed more Scotch into Winter's empty glass. The name Hennessey rang bells.

'Gynae surgeon? Cocked up lots of operations?'

'That's right. You'd have seen him in the papers.'

'So what's the evidence? At the Marriott?'

Winter was staring at the photos on the wall. The photos were Janna's work, Faraday's dead wife. She'd had a talent as mysterious as Ruth's, only in her case it revealed rather than hid itself. He'd kept the photos ever since she'd died, in exactly the same place on exactly the same walls, part of the geography of his life, and he must have mentioned them to Winter the last time he'd been here because he seemed to recognise them. He was pointing to a shot of Puget Sound during a snowstorm. Seattle had been Janna's home town.

'That's where I am,' Winter said quietly, 'that's exactly where I am. Snowed in. Totally fucked.'

Faraday blinked. This wasn't about the Marriott at all.

'What's happened?'

Winter glanced round at him.

'Cath not told you?'

'No.'

'Joannie's got cancer. Three months, give or take. How do you cope with something like that? Eh?'

The question was genuine. And, more importantly, Faraday knew that Winter wanted him to answer it. His own wife had been taken by cancer. Same brutal news. Same brutal outcome.

'I'm sorry,' Faraday said quietly. 'Truly sorry.'

'I don't want sorry. I want advice. How do you cope? What do you do? I'm telling you, I'm fucked, snowed under. I need clues, boss. Know what I mean?'

Faraday nodded. He'd been a younger man when Janna died, much younger, but at the time youth hadn't helped at all. Whenever it happened, you looked death in the face and refused to believe it.

'It must seem unreal.'

'It does.'

'And bloody unfair.'

'Yeah. And it gets worse.' Winter gestured down at his ample belly. 'It gets you like you don't know what to do, how to react. I just want to. . .' He stared at the empty tumbler, leaving the sentence unfinished.

Faraday reached for the bottle of Bell's. A moment or two with the memories of Janna's final weeks and he could do with a refill himself. Day after day in the tiny bungalow over at Freshwater Bay, doing his best to nurse his infant son. Endless nights, watching his wife asleep, wondering whether she wasn't already dead. People had it wrong about death. It was never pretty, never comforting.

'You'll need time off,' he said. 'Serious time off.'

'But it could take from here to Christmas. Probably will.'

'Exactly. But that's why you need the time. I'll sort something out tomorrow. Give you a ring, eh?'

The question seemed to rouse Winter. He got up on one elbow, the Scotch still in his hand.

'It's not that,' he said at last. 'It's not the time off. That's not why I came here. It's something else. A thing like this, it kills you, kills you stone dead. A woman.

Your wife. You live with her for all those years, and then bang, this happens, and you're really on the spot. I can't look her in the eye any more. I just can't.' He looked up at Faraday. 'You know what I mean, boss? About women? The kind of bloke they think you are? And the kind of bloke you know you really are?'

Faraday nodded, turning away. He had another bottle of Bell's in the kitchen.

'That's well put,' he said softly.

Five

A double-dose of ibuprofen and three cups of tea had failed to do anything for Faraday's splitting head. At best, the regular Tuesday morning senior management team sessions with Hartigan were a test for his patience, a reluctant genuflexion towards organisational flow charts which seemed to change almost monthly. Normally, Faraday survived these meetings by seeming to go along with all the bullshit about information cascades and service performance indicators, and then sounding the usual weary note about conditions down on the street. This morning, though, he doubted whether he could even manage that.

Hartigan was his divisional boss, a uniformed Superintendent with barely a year in the rank. Unlike Bevan, his predecessor, whose down-to-earth coppering had won Faraday's deep respect, Hartigan had come newly minted from the headquarters assembly line. Scoring top grades on the Bramshill Senior Command Course, and winning high praise from the Winchester apparatchiks for a lengthy paper on the methodology of SWOT analysis (Strengths! Weaknesses!! Opportunities!!! Threats!!!!), he'd descended on Portsmouth with a mission to transform the city's policing.

Like most of his colleagues, Faraday had at first assumed that Hartigan's zeal was a gesture, no more significant than an introductory handshake, but it had slowly dawned on him that this small, intense little man with the buffed nails and carefully trimmed moustache really meant it. Pompey was a tough case, but he was going to turn the place around. And afterwards, once the dust had settled, he'd find himself behind an even bigger desk.

'Now then' – Hartigan had one perfect fingernail anchored halfway down the agenda – 'the Good Neighbours Initiative.'

There was a murmur of anticipation around the conference table. Of the six officers present, five were uniformed. Only Faraday spoke for CID. He sat back, eyeing the coffee pot as Hartigan launched into one of his mantras about the importance of putting a smile on the city's face. Listen to Hartigan in this mood, and you'd think he was running a travel agency.

'We can only cope with so much negative publicity,' he was saying. 'We have to get Paulsgrove behind us.'

Paulsgrove was a sprawling council estate on the lower slopes of Portsdown Hill, in the north of the city, a carefully planned post-war refuge for bombed-out families. Since then, socialist good intentions had slowly fallen apart under the weight of poverty, broken families and an epidemic of petty crime, and the estate had recently become a national byword for anarchy and mob violence after a series of paedophile riots. Faraday, who knew the area well, had some sympathy for most of the folk who lived there. Getting by on a pension or dole money was hard enough. Living alongside the estate's hardcore of loonies, inbreds and psychopaths would stretch anyone to the limit.

Hartigan, more self-important than ever, had decided the city needed a bit of a boost. Put Pompey pride before Paulsgrove paedophilia and the crime rate would sink overnight. Salvation, he announced, was staring us in the face. A hundred million pounds' worth of investment. Architecture to be proud of. Unrivalled views. Decent people in decent housing and all kinds of retail goodies to raise the tone. Faraday, like everyone else around the table, waited for Hartigan's call to arms, the magic phrase that would transform this battered old punchbag of a city.

'Gunwharf Quays, gentlemen.' Hartigan looked around him. 'That's what should be concentrating our minds. How we help them make it work. Why we need to think even harder about good neighbourliness.'

Neighbourliness, Faraday knew, was code for Portsea, a couple of square miles of towering council blocks and rusting Transit vans that surrounded the new jewel in Portsmouth's crown. Portsea, like other inner-city areas, was disfigured by poverty and petty crime. Some of the neediest people in the country lived in Portsea, and the sight of well-heeled buyers queuing for half-a-million-pound harbourside apartments would do nothing for their self-esteem.

Hartigan was cross-examining his Chief Inspector about the latest crime figures for Portsea. Vandalism and street violence were on the increase. So were thefts from motor vehicles. Hartigan looked pained.

'We need to tackle this.' His hand chopped down on the table. 'It's an undertaking we need to make. We have to be pro-active. Community meetings and poster campaigns simply aren't good enough. Joe?'

Faraday knew the summons was bound to come. Although he also reported directly to Willard, his

Detective Superintendent, the divisional structure meant that Hartigan claimed ownership of his services. The DI belonged to him, not Willard. Faraday and his team of detectives was a divisional asset to be deployed as he, Hartigan, felt fit. Look for a way of nipping trouble in the bud – targeting known troublemakers, setting up surveillance, feeling a few collars – and Faraday would be tasked with delivering, in the fashionable phrase, the appropriate outcomes. He wasn't a detective, not as far as Hartigan was concerned. He was a crime manager.

Faraday gazed numbly at his copy of the agenda. After the Good Neighbours Initiative came Crime and Citizenship. The morning could only get worse.

'This undertaking you mentioned, sir . . . to whom, exactly?'

'The Gunwharf Quays people. I've had a couple of meetings, and I have to say I'm impressed. They're born troubleshooters. And they want to know we're on their side.'

'Is that in doubt?'

'Not at all, Joe, not at all. But these people speak the language of results. We can flannel them all we like, but they're not stupid. Words are cheap. They want to see that we mean it.'

Faraday suppressed a smile. He'd seen the glossy brochures for Gunwharf Quays, with its promises of 'world-class shopping' and 'lifestyle malls'. If anyone understood the power of language, it was surely the developers.

'We can try and up our game,' he said carefully, 'but in the end it's about resources.'

'Of course, Joe, of course. So what are you proposing?'

'I don't know, sir. Give me a couple of days. I'll get something down on paper.'

Hartigan glanced at his watch.

'Thursday? Close of play? Something I can table at our next meeting? Something you might like to come along and present?'

Faraday had a sudden vision of Hartigan taking him along on some kind of lead and introducing him with the appropriate flourish. Meet Joe Faraday. My tame DI. He reached for his pen and scribbled something on his copy of the agenda, hoping to God that Hartigan would move on. Maybe he could task one of his DSs with drawing up some half-arsed plan. Maybe, if it looked good enough on paper, he might even blag some of that precious overtime reserve he knew Hartigan kept in his bottom drawer.

Hartigan was still eyeballing him, his head lowered, his pen in his hand, eager to tick yet another box.

'Last thing Thursday, Joe? Is that a yes?'

Winter was wondering about the possibility of a free breakfast when the manager finally emerged from his office. He'd been on a conference call with the Marriott high command up in London. He had the promised video tapes ready and waiting.

Winter followed him back into his office. An image of a man in a light zip-up jacket quivered on the TV monitor in the corner. He was standing at the reception desk, his wallet in his hand. Judging by the angle, the camera must have been mounted on the back wall, slightly above head height.

'That's him. Hennessey.' The manager was glancing through a sheaf of notes on his desk.

Winter stood over the monitor, staring at the figure on the screen. A long, fleshy face. Jowliness verging on plump. Receding hair, combed sideways over a balding skull. Thick lips. Square, rimless glasses. And, most revealing of all, a big, self-confident smile, the smile of a man used to being in charge. Winter had yet to pick up the cuttings from Pete Lamb but he had no doubt that this face fitted the bill. Pieter Hennessey. Butcher of the Year.

'You've got hard copy of this?'

'Of course.'

'One for me?'

'No problem. You want to see the rest?'

The night manager had already dubbed footage from the other cameras onto this single tape. The next image showed two men in the big revolving door which led out to the car park. Hennessey was on the left – same jacket – and the bulk of his body partially obscured his companion. The other guy was slightly taller and a good deal less fat. He was wearing jeans and a suede jacket and his face was turned away from camera.

'Is this the best you can do?'

'I'm afraid so. The system records single frames every three seconds. Otherwise we'd be forever changing tapes.'

Winter nodded. Hennessey's mystery companion seemed to be offering the surgeon support, his arm locked around Hennessey's ample waist. Either that, or Hennessey was being marched out against his will.

The manager pointed his remote at the screen, and the image changed again. This time the two men were out in the car park, and as the sequence jumped from image to image, it became apparent that Hennessey was indeed damaged goods. In some of the shots, he was plainly nursing his left arm, his whole body sagging to one side, and when they got to a black-looking Mercedes in the far bay, it was Hennessey's companion who first folded the surgeon into the passenger seat, and then got in behind the wheel. The last shot showed the back of the car as it turned towards the main road. Winter made a note of the registration.

'Copies of those, too. If you don't mind.'

'I'll get them done this morning. Have them sent over.'

'I'll need the tapes as well. For evidence.'

'OK.' The manager permitted himself a small, private smile. 'No problem.'

Winter was thinking ahead, planning the wall he'd build around Hennessey.

'You've still got the credit-card slip?'

'Aye.'

'I'll need that too, please.' He glanced at his watch. 'The room you showed me. We ought to give it a proper going-over.'

The manager glanced up, sorting through the paperwork on his desk, still looking for the credit-card slip.

'Too late, my friend. I had the maid clean it.' The smile had returned. 'After you said you weren't interested.'

Back in his office, Faraday called for Rick Stapleton and Dawn Ellis. On the phone, first thing, Stapleton had already briefed him about the lecturer, Addison. They'd arrested him on suspicion of producing material liable to deprave and corrupt, and gone through his house again, more thoroughly this time. This second search had failed to produce any evidence of a Donald Duck mask, but they'd seized seven boxes of video tapes and, at Dawn's suggestion, a pair of walking boots with mud and grass on the soles. Of the black tracksuit reported by all three victims, there'd been no trace.

Booked in by the Custody Sergeant down at the Bridewell, Addison had spent the night in the cells. They'd interviewed him for a couple of hours in the early evening with his solicitor present, and he was due a second session this morning, once the brief could make it back to the Bridewell.

'So where are we?' Faraday waved his two detectives into chairs the other side of the desk.

'He's got an explanation for more or less everything.' Stapleton was flicking through his notes. He sounded disappointed.

'What about the tapes?'

'He says they're legit. No kids. No animals. No violence. No anal. Just straight sex. He's running some kind of business. Says lecturing's crap money.'

'Business?' Faraday had seen the videos next door in the CID office, the cardboard boxes stacked to desk height.

'It's all through a student of his from last year, Albanian girl, comes from somewhere in Kosovo. Apparently she was a bit of an artist with the camera. She did her three years on the course and graduated with a first.'

'In porn?'

'Yeah.' Stapleton nodded. 'Good as.'

The girl, according to Addison, had returned to Kosovo and begun to make skin flicks. Her trademark was moody lighting and quality performers. On both counts she was only interested in the best, and the deal with Addison was simplicity itself. She admired his editing skills. He had his own gear. She liked him, trusted him, as a guy. So how about sending back the rushes for him to view and edit? Addison, naturally, had said yes, and now spent most of his evenings churning out premium-quality porn videos. The masters went to duplicating houses in London, mainly for transfer to DVD.

'Where does he sell them?'

'He doesn't. She does. Apparently she's got some kind of agent, German guy. He sorts out the European end of it. The rest go back to Kosovo for the squaddies. They buy them by the lorryload. Neat, eh?'

'Do we believe him?'

'We may have to. He's got all the paperwork: invoices from the duplicating house, faxes from the Albanian girl, even copies of cheques she's sent him. It all stacks up.'

Faraday glanced across at Dawn.

'Nearly eleven hundred quid in a good month.' She rolled her eyes. 'Imagine getting paid for a job like that.'

'What about the videos? Have you looked through them all?'

'You're joking, boss. There are hundreds of them. In fact, we were wondering . . .'

'What?'

'Whether you might lend a hand. It's easy on the eye, most of it. And you can always fast forward.'

Faraday sat back, not saying anything. Dawn smothered a yawn. She looked exhausted.

'What about the Donald Duck dates?' Faraday said at last. 'Where was he?'

'At home, editing,' Dawn said. 'Wouldn't you be? Money like that?'

'Corroboration?'

'None. Works alone, he says.'

'What about the boots you mentioned? You want to send them to forensic?'

'No point, really. He says he takes regular walks out by the harbour, says it's the only place to go, apart from the beach.'

'And he walks round by the ponds there?'

'Yep.'

'He volunteered that?'

'Absolutely.'

Faraday nodded. The more he prodded, the worse it got.

'What about the girl? Shelley?'

'Denies ever touching her. Admits she comes round regularly, always alone, but says it's strictly teacher–pupil. Even if he's lying we can't have him. The girl's eighteen. Who she screws is her own affair.'

'And what does she say?'

There was a silence. Dawn and Stapleton exchanged glances. Then Dawn frowned.

'She's the bit that doesn't add up,' she said. 'At least, not to me. She's not telling us something. And I think she's frightened, too.'

'Of him?'

'I don't know. She might be. He's pretty sorted, you know, pretty cold. I don't think we've shaken him once.'

Faraday scowled, then reached for a pen. It was hard not to share their sense of disappointment, but from where he sat there were still, in Hartigan's favourite phrase, pathways forward. Time to sort this man out. Time for a battle plan.

'He'll have a perv bag stashed somewhere,' he said. 'He'll keep everything in it: the mask, gloves, tracksuit, trainers, the full kit. It'll be in a lock-up. A friend's place. Boot of his car, maybe.'

'We checked the car. Nothing.'

'Find keys at all when you searched?'

'Nothing he can't explain.'

'Address book?'

'We're going through it now.'

'OK,' he said, 'then here's what else we do. Number one, get on to the Paedophile Squad at Netley. Some of the Vice boys are still there. Check out the position on the tapes. They'll know what we can do him for. He might have history, too. It'll be on their database.' He paused. 'Have you talked to the college?'

'Not yet. Normally they don't want to know.'

'Granted, but there may have been complaints about him earlier. That gives us leverage. Use it.' Faraday was thinking about the cassettes. 'Our Albanian friend. You've got an address?'

Stapleton consulted his notebook.

'Pristina.'

'Excellent. Talk to the Foreign Office. Those blokes from Major Crimes over in Kosovo. The least they can do is check her out.'

Stapleton scribbled a note to himself, smiling. A couple of CID from the Major Crimes Suite at Fratton had been abstracted to help out with the big forensic operation over in Kosovo. He'd been tapped up himself, but the prospect of disinterring all those dead bodies had turned him off. A year underground did terrible things to human flesh and a night or two chatting up a porn queen might be just what the Major Crimes blokes needed.

'OK.' Faraday was gazing out of the window. 'How thorough was the search you did? This guy's premises?'

'Not bad. There's a bit of garden at the back, and a little shed thing. We had a nose round that, too.'

'Do it again. Properly. And make sure he knows.'

'We're seeing him at eleven with his solicitor. We'll take them with us.'

Dawn and Stapleton made their way towards the door. Faraday called them back.

'Another thing,' he said. 'Those tapes.'

'Yeah?'

'Tell Joyce to sort me out a player. I'll make a start on a couple of boxes.'

Winter was looking at an e-mail from one of the PNC operators when Cathy Lamb appeared in the CID room. He'd been right about Hennessey. According to the entry on the Police National Computer, the Mercedes in the hotel car park was registered in the surgeon's name.

Cathy, he knew at once, was having a bad day.

'So what happened?' she grunted. 'At the Marriott.'

Winter told her about the video. There'd been a fight in the room. The other guy had marched Hennessey away.

'Abduction,' he said, 'at the very least.'

'You're serious?'

'Absolutely.'

'Where's the evidence?'

Winter began to describe the trail of surgical mistakes Hennessey had left in his wake. There were people who were angry about the man. Very angry. Angry enough to make a physical point or two. Cathy wasn't having it.

'That's hypothesis,' she said. 'I asked you about evidence.'

'Blood. All over the bathroom.'

'Get a SOCO in. Close it down.'

'I can't.'

'Why not? I thought you told me the manager had sealed the room.'

'He had. Then he unsealed it.'

'Why?'

'Pressure on bookings. They needed the room. You know how it is, Cath. Big business, bottom line. These guys have to meet performance targets like you wouldn't believe.'

Winter was at his most plausible when he was lying, and Cathy knew it. Short of phoning the manager herself, though, there was little she could do.

'You're telling me the room's been cleaned?'

'Yeah.'

'So there's no forensic at all?'

'Unlikely. He's saying he'll talk to housekeeping about cleaning rags, just in case, but' – he shrugged – 'I wouldn't put money on it.'

'So what have we got, then? Evidentially?'

Winter stared up at her, recognising the challenge. He'd seen Pete Lamb's press cuttings by now and he was word-perfect on Hennessey's body count.

'Let's start with motive,' he said. 'This guy's been mutilating women for longer than you can imagine. People trust doctors. They assume they know what they're doing. They assume they care. They assume they're honest. This guy wasn't any of those things and it took years for anyone to twig. By that time, dozens and dozens of women had got themselves screwed because of him. Screwed's exactly right. They might just as well have laid on their backs with their legs open, and you know what? Most of them did precisely that. They let him in and he fucked them up.'

'What's this got to do with the Marriott?'

'Everything. In my book you're looking at a revenge killing. You're married to one of these women. Or you're her brother, or her lover, and you've gone through all the right channels, written all the letters, gone to your MP, done every fucking thing to try and get this bastard banged up. But nothing happens, nothing that gives you any satisfaction. OK, the guy might go in front of some committee or other, might get his wrist slapped, might even get struck off. But what kind of justice is that? Your missus is incontinent. She'll smell like a fish for the rest of her life. Because of him. So what do you do?' Winter spread his hands wide, his case made.

Cathy let him calm down a moment.

'You need time off, Paul,' she said quietly. 'You need to be at home with Joan. Not here, cooking up some fantasy about a hotel guest.'

Winter was staring at her. It was all there. Right in front of her nose. And she still didn't get it.

'You don't believe me?'

'I believe you're in a state. Anyone would be. You should be at home. Looking after your wife.'

Winter shook his head.

'I don't want to be at home. I'm a detective, Cath. This is what blokes like me do.'

'Listen, Paul.' She paused, picking her words carefully. 'I've got a stack of jobs up to here.' She raised her hand to her head. 'And it would be really really helpful if you could see your way to helping shift them. I know you've seen Pete. I know he's wound you up. But we're not here to run errands for estate agents.' She stared at him, pale with anger. 'Do I make myself clear?'

'Perfectly.'

'And you'll stoop to doing something half-useful?'

'Of course I will.'

'Good. We'll have a meet this afternoon, try and sort everything out.'

Winter waited until she'd left the office before he

phoned Faraday. They'd left on good terms last night, sharing a great deal more than a bottle of Bell's. At three in the morning, Winter had been perfectly happy to take his chances at the wheel, but it was Faraday who'd insisted on calling a cab. Nothing bonded guys quicker, Winter concluded, than talking about the bad times.

'It's me, boss. I've been having a think about that offer of yours.'

'About what?'

'Compassionate leave.' Winter was still looking at the door. 'I just want to say you're right. I ought to be at home. For Joannie's sake.'

Six

Addison and his solicitor watched while Dawn Ellis and Rick Stapleton searched the house again. The morning's attempt to re-interview him had come to nothing. Addison had simply repeated last night's story, blank-faced, cold-eyed, refusing to rise to any of Stapleton's carefully phrased suggestions. No, he'd never had a relationship with *any* of his female students. No, hours of watching porno rushes had done nothing for his libido. And no, he'd never had the urge to extend role-play to a Donald Duck mask and an audience of total strangers.

Afterwards, snatching a cup of coffee with Dawn before they both drove Addison back to his house, Stapleton blamed the solicitor for the lack of progress, but Dawn wasn't so sure. While it was true that his brief, an ambitious young Oxford graduate, had a reputation for making the going as tough as possible, Dawn had been watching Addison carefully and had drawn a very different impression. Here was a guy who was used to making up his own mind. The brief, able as she might be, was there as a legal backstop.

They started at the top of the house, working their way methodically from room to room, pulling out drawers, opening cupboards, sifting through shelf after shelf of carefully labelled box files. Addison was almost obsessively organised – separate drawers for underwear and socks – and Dawn tidied up after Stapleton, aware of Addison monitoring their every move. Once again, this wasn't the behaviour of a guilty man. On the contrary, his interest seemed to be purely domestic. He'd made a habit of filing his life away, and he wanted everything back exactly where it belonged.

The house wasn't big, and an hour was enough to have drawn a comprehensive blank. Their knowledge of Addison now extended to trekking holidays in Nepal and a passion for certain kinds of modern jazz, but they'd found absolutely nothing that could conceivably link him to the Donald Duck incidents.

With the kitchen back in one piece, it was Addison himself who suggested they take another look at the garden. Stapleton looked at him in some irritation.

'Why so keen?'

'I just want this thing cleared up. Once and for all. Is that a problem?'

They went out into the little yard at the back. The sun blazed down on the tiny patch of grass and Dawn could see where the depth of Addison's tan had come from. The garden was walled on three sides, trelliswork woven with honeysuckle and wild roses, and the borders at the foot of the brickwork were a mass of carefully chosen shrubs. There wasn't a corner of Addison's life that hadn't been thought out, and this sun trap must have offered the perfect escape between the frustrations of teaching and the prospect of yet another evening in front of the edit machines, splicing one heaving body against another.

There was access to an alley at the rear of the property through a newly painted wooden door. Beside the door, tucked into a corner of the garden, was the shed Dawn and Stapleton had searched the previous day. They did it again, this time hauling out the sunlounger and electric mower to search behind shelves neatly stacked with weedkiller, plant nutrients and tins of gloss paint. Again, nothing.

Emerging into the sunshine, Dawn and Stapleton exchanged glances. Then Dawn's eye caught one of the larger shrubs on the other side of the door to the alley at the back. There was something tucked behind it, something shiny. She beckoned to the solicitor, pointing it out, then bent to retrieve it. Her fingers brushed through the thick-bladed leaves. She could feel the shape of a face, some kind of nose, and then, at the back, a twangy length of elastic. She pulled it clear, stepping back. Addison was staring at her. Stapleton had raised an eyebrow.

A Donald Duck mask. In mint condition.

Joannie was in the kitchen, buttering a slice of toast, by the time Winter finally made it home. She looked up at him in some surprise. She'd slept well last night, asleep long before Winter had returned from Faraday's place, and she'd still been dozing when he'd left for work. According to the note he'd left beside the kettle, he'd be busy all day. Yet here he was, reaching for a couple of slices of wholemeal and feeding them into the toaster.

'Where's the car?' She hadn't heard him drive in.

'Outside. In the street.' Winter was trying to find the raspberry jam. 'How's tricks?'

'Fine. I feel fine.'

'Great.' He unscrewed the jam jar, waiting for the toast to pop up. 'Lovely day.'

'I know. I've been out in the garden. Shall I get the other chair out?'

'No.' Winter shook his head. 'I thought we might take a little drive.'

'*Drive?*' Joannie looked startled. 'Together, you mean?'

'Yeah. Just you and me.' He glanced up at her, as if struck by a sudden thought. 'How about the New Forest?'

Faraday had just put the phone down on Rick Stapleton when Joyce finally appeared with a video machine. He looked up, smiling, as she wheeled the trolley into the office.

'Result,' he muttered. 'On the Donald Duck job.'

Joyce, unbidden, was sorting out the venetian blinds. A hot morning had developed into a flawless afternoon, and the office was flooded with sunshine.

'Young lad came up from Traffic this morning,' she murmured. 'I left you a note.'

'Did you?'

Faraday was looking at the chaos of his desk, paperwork stacked everywhere. Instinctively, he began to sift through the biggest pile.

'It's on top,' Joyce said drily, 'where I left it.'

Faraday found the note. Mark Barrington, the motor-cycle patrolman who'd been first on the scene at Larkrise Avenue, had paid a visit.

'What did he want?'

'You, poppet.'

Faraday stared up at her. *Poppet?* Joyce ignored him.

'It's to do with that pile of junk Vanessa was driving. The Fiesta.'

'It was her mother's, not hers.'

'Sure. Point is, Accident Investigation and the mechanic who went over it got their heads together and they figure no way was she to blame. The Fiesta had all but stopped. The brakes weren't brilliant, but they did what they were supposed to do.'

'And Prentice?'

'Prentice was a no-no.'

'A what?'

'A no-no. He wasn't about to tell me *anything* about Prentice. Guy says he needs to talk to you. Hence my little note.'

She did a little curtsy, and left the office. Moments later she was back with two boxes full of video tapes, her chin resting uncertainly on the top.

'This may take a while,' she said. 'We ought to be thinking comfort here.'

Out she went again, this time returning with a portable air fan. Plugging it in, she cleared a corner of Faraday's desk and switched it on.

'Health and safety,' she explained, bending to insert the first of the cassettes. 'Remote's in the out-tray. Second button down starts the action. Enjoy.'

She left the office for the last time, closing the door behind her, and Faraday was left wondering whether she'd meant the fan as a joke, realising that he simply didn't know.

Winter and his wife drove west, towards the New Forest. The traffic was light for midsummer, but in a rare concession Winter kept his speed below eighty, modest enough for Joannie to be able to enjoy her favourite cassette. Winter had never really fathomed the appeal of Celine Dion, but the last thing he wanted was a squabble about their choice of music. If she wanted to listen to *The Reason* three times on the trot, so be it.

North of Southampton, Winter stopped for fuel, returning to the car with a bagful of sweets. The sight of the Werther's Originals brought a smile to Joannie's face.

'Must be Christmas,' she murmured, tucking them into the glove box. 'I should be ill more often.'

Heading west again, she began to talk about what lay ahead, practical steps they might have to take, decisions about diet and sleeping arrangements, and maybe a good look at their respective wills.

'Sleeping arrangements?' Winter wouldn't take his eyes off the road.

'It'll get difficult, Paul. I was reading this article. You don't want to be awake all night, running round after me. You know what you're like if you don't get your full ration.'

'We're talking sleep here?'

Winter risked a grin, slowing down even more as a huge truck thundered past, not sure that the joke was altogether appropriate. The grin turned into a smile as her hand found his thigh. He glanced across at her.

'You look all right to me,' he said. 'In fact, you look bloody fit, losing a bit of weight like that.'

'Thanks.'

'I mean it. Doctors can be wrong, you know. They're not always the bloody experts they claim to be. Maybe we should get a second opinion.'

'He is a second opinion. The GP was the first. The consultant's the end of the line. It's pointless going any further. I'm there now. And it's not as hard as you think it is.'

'Dying?'

'Accepting it.'

Winter shook his head, lost for words, and moved into the outside lane again. A second opinion was a good idea. He'd do something about it. Except a second medic might be as fallible and useless as the first.

Joannie was musing again, this time about a move to a hospice. Winter was appalled.

'*Hospice?* What's wrong with home?'

'Nothing. I'm not talking about this week, or next. It's nothing desperate. But there'll come a time, love, there really will.'

Her hand still lay on his thigh. He wanted to reach down for it, to cover it with his own, but he didn't.

'I'll look after you,' he said automatically.

'No you won't. You say you will and I'm sure you mean it, but we both know you won't. Not when the time comes. Not when I need you.'

Winter heard the rustle of sweet papers as she retrieved the Werther's from the glove box. When she'd unwrapped a couple he opened his mouth to let her pop one in.

'You're pissed off with me, aren't you?'

'Not at all. You only get fed up with people who let you down.'

'I let you down. All the time I let you down.'

'No you don't.'

'You mean that?'

'Yes. To know a man, you stick with him.' Her hand was back again. 'I stuck with you.' She squeezed his thigh.

'But you needn't have.'

'You're right. But I did, surprise, surprise.'

'And you don't regret it? Now? When this happens? All the other stuff you could have done with your life, and you stayed with me? You don't regret that?'

'Not at all.'

'Why not?'

'Because I love you.' She glanced across at him. 'And I have no expectations.'

Winter drove on in silence, poleaxed by this simplest of confessions. No flannelling around. No dressing it up. No fancy-fancy. Just the way she felt. Close to tears, he swallowed hard and wiped his nose with the back of his hand.

A big blue sign swam into view. The Lyndhurst exit. He signalled left. Slowing for the roundabout, he glanced across at Joannie. She seemed lost in her thoughts.

'Where are we going?' she asked.

'Little place I need to look at.'

'Why?'

'Just a job I'm on.'

Joannie nodded, permitting herself the ghost of a smile.

'See what I mean?' she said at last.

Faraday watched the videos for the best part of an hour, an endless sequence of couplings, nothing bestial, nothing harrowing, every variation of a twosome or a threesome or, just once, a fivesome covered from every conceivable angle. In time, slowly, he got to recognise the shape that Addison had imposed on the videos, the way he'd used his editing skills to tease and taunt, to delay or speed up the action, just the way that women, in real life, took subtle charge of a relationship.

There were echoes here of Ruth. Nothing obvious. Nothing to do with technique, or endurance, or the very vocal delight a woman might take in being pleasured by a particularly dextrous lover. But something buried much deeper in the rhythm of each individual piece, in the way that a sudden, unexpected change of angle would confound every expectation. Ruth was like that. Not in bed, necessarily, but in her everyday life. He'd think he'd got close to her. He'd think he'd touched her in small but important ways. And on the basis of these shared moments he'd make certain assumptions: that she cared about him, that they were embarked on roughly the same journey. But then something else would happen and his little file of scrupulously gathered evidence would be suddenly worthless, thanks to a chance remark, or the ghost of a smile so secret, so opaque, that he knew they could never be truly close. Ruth didn't do close. Not the kind of sturdy, ongoing, day-by-day close he really needed. No, she did something else, and one of the reasons the relationship survived at all was the challenge of trying to define what that something was.

Once, in an unguarded moment, he'd described her as every detective's wet dream. Far from taking offence, she'd asked him to explain, and as he fumbled his way towards some kind of rationale he'd realised exactly what it was that fuelled this strange compulsion of his to keep chasing her. Everyone, he said, was a series of dots. Connect the dots in the right order and the person was revealed. It happened time and again in his professional life – with colleagues, with witnesses, with suspects. It had happened, over the course of a single wet afternoon in Seattle, with Janna. It had happened, over twenty-two long years, with his son, J-J. But never with Ruth. She was every detective's wet dream because her case was so obviously worth cracking. Yet the harder he tried, the more he became aware of his own inadequacies. She was, in her own phrase, beyond reach.

Faraday shook his head, slotting yet another video into the machine, forcing himself to concentrate on the job in hand. Whatever parallels he might concoct between all this naked flesh and his feelings for the elusive Ruth were irrelevant. What mattered – what always mattered – were the links you began to detect as the trawl for evidence produced more and more material. That's what these videos were – more dots to be connected – and the longer he watched, the more obvious the emerging pattern became.

The love-making, after protracted foreplay, would gather speed. The woman, often straddling the man, would be seconds away from her climax. And then, quite suddenly, she'd ease herself away, busy hands stroking and fondling, tongue dipping, mouth opening, while all the time her eyes never left the man's face, and instead of a climax, instead of the graphic 'money shots' they peddled in the sex shops down Fratton Road, there'd come a long moment of stillness before the love-making dissolved to something totally unrelated: a shadowed dawn in the mountains, the fall of water over moss-green rocks, a flight of swan-like birds with the misty outlines of a marsh beneath.

Quite what the squaddies in Kosovo would make of material like this was anyone's guess, but Faraday found himself getting more and more intrigued. What point were teacher and pupil trying to make? Was this some kind of artistic collusion, videos made to an agreed plan, or was Addison sending some message of his own?

The signature camerawork offered a clue. The stuff was beautifully shot, beautifully lit, but what was especially revealing were the series of murmured off-camera directions, just audible, to which the lovers always responded. This, presumably, was Addison's star pupil, the Albanian camerawoman who'd so quickly parlayed a three-year degree course and turned it into a profitable career. She was the one in control. She was the one who plotted the moves. She was the one who stilled the action while she busied around with her camera, hunting for yet another angle. So what was she after, apart from money?

Faraday didn't know, couldn't possibly guess, but the

longer he looked at the videos, the more he bought the collusion theory. Addison and his star pupil were as one. They must have been close. They must have had a relationship. They must have rehearsed a lot of this stuff, belly to belly, over the three years of her course. No other explanation fitted. The partnership, the mirrored understanding, was simply too close.

So where did that leave the current investigation? As far as the girl, Shelley, was concerned, Faraday assumed they must be at it. As Rick Stapleton had pointed out, screwing an eighteen-year-old wasn't a crime, but that wasn't really the point. If Addison was having a relationship with Shelley, and denying it, then he was a liar. And if he'd lied about Shelley, then it was perfectly possible that he'd lie about everything else. Hence the mud and grass on the bottom of his hiking boots. Hence, more importantly, the mask in the garden.

Faraday pulled the second box of videos towards him and extracted one at random. It was a different make to the others, different box, and there was a scrawled name on the label that had since been smudged. He inserted it into the player and reached for the remote. Seconds later, he found himself looking at a girl of about eighteen, fully clothed. She had a mass of blonde curls and a striking face. She was sitting at some kind of table and there was a dark-blue curtain filling most of the space behind her.

A voice from nowhere, a male voice, said, 'All right?' Local accent. Gruff, flat-vowelled Pompey. The girl nodded, composed herself, then began to talk to the camera. She wanted to say thank you for this chance to explain why the course was so right for her. She wanted to be as honest as she possibly could. She wanted to explain about her total determination to make it as an actress. The voice, by no means strong, began to falter.

She hesitated, swallowing hard, and then a hand went up to her mouth and she began to redden with embarrassment. Moments later, the hand came down again, and her face broke into a wide grin. Different girl. Different message.

'I don't know how to say this,' she began, 'but I really, really fancy you. I'm not just saying it. I do. I've been watching you. It's the way you walk, the way you hold yourself, the way you use your hands all the time. You're so, I don't know, *cool*. And it's not just me, either. Except I'm the only one to' – she suddenly held up a square of card – 'admit it.' She paused. 'Wipe the last bit, OK?'

Faraday reached for the remote and fingered the pause button. There was a name on the card, big black lettering, and it took him a second or two to decipher it.

'Shelley Beavis', it read. 'Course 99/M1A'.

Seven

Tuesday, 20 June, mid-afternoon

The village of Newbridge straggled along a winding country road on the north-easterly edges of the New Forest. Acorn Cottage was a pebbledash bungalow with flaking yellow paint, drawn curtains and ankle-high grass lapping the crazy-paving path that led to the front door. Paul Winter rang twice, waiting for at least a minute before setting off on a circuit of the property. Joannie was still in the car, debating whether to risk a Werther's Original on a depressed-looking pony that was nuzzling the trim on the passenger door.

There was a garage to one side of the house with locked wooden doors at the front. Winter peered in, shading his eyes against the glare of the sun. The garage was empty apart from a bicycle, a rusting lawn mower and the usual collection of garden tools. There were oil marks on the concrete run-in that led out to the road, but they appeared to be old. Round the back of the bungalow, Winter prowled from window to window, trying to see through the cracks in the curtains, testing catches, wondering about access. Returning to the front, he gazed up at the alarm over the front door. It looked new, but there were scratch marks visible around the metal where it was seated against the pebbledash and he thought he detected a slight dent. Directly beneath the alarm, the flower bed was over-grown with weeds, recently disturbed, and when he parted them, he found himself looking at twin dents in the dry soil. Someone had been here with a ladder.

At length, he returned to the car. Joannie was standing in the road. The pony had been joined by a friend and they were both studying her with half-hearted interest. She turned away from them at Winter's approach and did her best with a smile. It was nicer out in the fresh air, she said, though she wasn't sure she could stand the heat for too long. Winter remembered an old flat cap he kept in the boot for winter visits to Fratton Park for the football. He retrieved it, gave it a slap or two against the rear wing, and handed it over.

'Wear it backwards,' he told her, 'keep the sun off your neck.'

The red-brick bungalow next door to Acorn Cottage definitely looked lived-in. Both windows were open at the front and Winter could see a line of washing in the garden at the rear A woman in her mid-fifties came bustling down the hall to answer his knock. She was wearing an apron and a pair of rubber gloves. Winter showed her his ID card and asked her about the property next door. He was on a missing-person inquiry. Did she know a Mr Pieter Hennessey?

The woman pushed a wisp of greying hair out of her eyes. It was Dr Hennessey, not Mr. And he'd been back only yesterday.

'You saw him?'

'Yes.' She had a soft country accent. 'Well, the car actually.'

'What kind?'

'Black one. Big one. His for sure. I've seen him driving it.'

'And you definitely saw him?'

She frowned, then shook her head.

'Well, no,' she said. 'It was only here two ticks, the

car. One minute I looked. The next it had gone. Must have been him, though.'

Winter asked her about the alarm system. Had it gone off recently?

'It's always going off. Blasted thing.'

'And what happens?'

'We called the police first. Then afterwards there was no point. It's the wind or something. No one seems to know. My husband got so mad with it he went up there and gave it what for. That's why he's lent me a key.'

'Who?'

'Dr Hennessey. Every time it goes off, I just go in and reset it. I've got the code written down. Scares you to death, them things.'

The woman led the way back to Acorn Cottage and opened the front door, disappearing inside to disable the alarm before inviting Winter in.

'I'll be back at home,' she said. 'Help yourself.'

Despite the weather, the house smelled damp. Winter slipped on a pair of disposable gloves and moved from room to room, trying to build himself a picture of the life Hennessey had made for himself here. It was a way-station, a pit stop, no question about it. Cheap furniture, bare walls and tatty, unlined curtains that must have come from some other property because barely any of them fitted properly. In the kitchen, there was margarine, bacon, milk, three cans of lager and an open tin of corned beef in the fridge. The milk was still fresh, just.

A room at the back, small and dark, had been used as a bedroom. The bed was unmade and the sagging double mattress was slightly too big for the frame. A pair of sandals lay on the fraying rush mat beneath the window, and there were clothes hanging in the ward-robe by the door. Winter hauled out a light summer suit and held it up beside himself, remembering the ample figure from the hotel video stills. Hennessey was an inch or two under six feet. A thirty-eight-inch waistband sounded about right.

Next door to the bedroom was a poky lounge that Hennessey seemed to have converted into a study. A single cardboard box on the floor served as a dump for old receipts and there was a brand-new Dell computer on a small square table, pushed against the curtains that blocked the flooding sunlight. Winter switched the computer on. While he waited for it to boot up, he reached for the telephone and dialled 1471. The last unanswered incoming call had an 0207 prefix. Winter made a note of the number and then pressed the re-dial facility, curious to know to whom Hennessey had last placed a call. The phone began to ring at the other end. After a while, a woman's voice.

'Marina. How can I help you?'

Winter was looking at the prefix on the print-out on the phone – 01534?

'I think I've got the wrong number,' he mumbled. 'Where exactly are you?'

'St Helier.'

'St where?'

'St Helier. Jersey. This is the marina.'

Winter apologised and rang off. Another note. Might Hennessey have an interest in boats?

The computer was ready now, and among the files in the directory were two tagged *Patients/A* and *Patients/B*. Winter opened them both, quickly realising that *Patients/B* contained the names of women angry and mutilated enough to have initiated legal action. In all, he counted fifty-two case histories, complete with names, addresses, phone numbers and brief medical details. On the mantelpiece at the back of the room, he'd noticed a box of new floppy disks. He fed one into the computer and downloaded the contents of the *Patients/B* file. Returning to the file directory, he hunted in vain for details of Hennessey's personal finances, then gave up, browsing instead through a selection of correspondence, trying to imagine the disgraced surgeon banged up in this threadbare bungalow, committing a lifetime's medical butchery to his hard disk.

One particular letter caught his attention. Judging by the address, a legal-sounding partnership in High Wycombe, it must have gone to his solicitor.

Dear Iain,
    Thanks for lunch. It's a relief to know we're on the same wavelength. Some women want it all. Why they didn't take the trouble to listen to me in the first place is a complete and enduring mystery. Every operation carries an element of risk – as any consultant will confirm. Explain that as patiently as you can, and they still don't take any of it on board. Is it something about me, d'you think? Or are they as brainless as they seem? I'll let you have an e-mail address as soon as I'm hooked up.
    Yours, aye, Pieter.

Winter added the letter to the patient files on the floppy, stung by the depth of the contempt Hennessey showed for his patients. First injury, he thought, and then insult. Bastard.

Through the tiny vertical slit in the curtains, Winter could see his wife. She was still standing by the car, his old grey cap perched on the back of her head. She was looking round, very slowly, the way you do when you're trying to commit a view to memory. She'd always liked the country, which was one of the reasons they'd settled in Bedhampton, on the slopes of Ports-down Hill, rather than find somewhere in the city itself. They had a decent bit of garden at home and they could be out in rural Hampshire within minutes. Here, though, was different. Here really was the country, thousands of acres of forest, and what made this scene all the more gutting wasn't the fact that she so obviously loved it, but the knowledge that she might never see it again. Hence the expression on her face: pleasure salted with a kind of numbness. And hence Winter's renewed rage at finding a letter like this.

Abandoning the computer, Winter bent to the card-board box again. What he wanted, what he *needed*, was a lead on the state of Hennessey's personal finances. Read properly, a bank statement was as good as a map. You logged the credits and the debits, jigsawed patterns of expenditure, looked for sudden aberrations, followed the footsteps wherever they led. If Hennessey had indeed done a runner, it might well show in the account transactions. If he'd come to grief, that too might have led to a mystery withdrawal. Either way, access to his bank statements would give Winter a flying start.

He found them in a Waitrose shopping bag at the bottom of the cardboard box, wedged into a rusting bulldog clip. The most recent statement was on top, a list of the usual standing orders plus a page and a half of cheque withdrawals. One particular transaction on the second page caught Winter's eye. On 6 June, Hennessey had withdrawn £115,000 in cash. The sum had been covered by an earlier transfer of £133,000 from a deposit account, leaving Hennessey with an end-of-month balance of nearly £18,000 – a useful nest egg if you anticipated disappearing for a while. Winter made a note of the account number, and then the date of the

£115,000 withdrawal, before folding the June statement into his jacket pocket. Getting access to personal finance data was tricky these days and some banks went as far as demanding a court order, but there were still ways and means of smuggling out the odd detail without going through the hassle of applying to a judge.

Several minutes later, armed with the floppy disk, Winter was back with the woman next door. He'd finished at Dr Hennessey's. He was grateful for her help.

She peered up at him.

'OK for me to lock up again?'

'Absolutely.'

'You think anything's happened to him?'

'I doubt it.'

He gave her a pat on the arm, eager to bring the conversation to a close, then paused.

'Nice man, is he?'

The woman nodded at once.

'Real charming,' she said. 'Real old school. Trust him with your life, you would.'

Faraday sensed the disappointment in Dawn's face the moment she and Rick Stapleton returned to Southsea CID. He called them both into his office and sat them down. The two boxes of videos were still on the floor, though by now he'd switched off the fan.

'Well?' he said.

They'd brought Addison back to the interview room at the Bridewell. The mask, safely bagged, was ready for despatch to forensic for checks, but in Stapleton's view there was no point waiting for the result from the labs. Under the Police and Criminal Evidence Act, they had just twenty-four hours to hold Addison in custody. The time limit was due to expire in ninety minutes' time.

Unless Faraday managed to secure a twelve-hour extension from Hartigan, they'd have to let him go.

'Has to be him,' Stapleton said. 'Guy lives in the right area. Eats, sleeps, breathes sex. Admits he takes walks where they all happened. Can't alibi himself for any of the dates. And now turns out to be hiding a Donald Duck mask. What the fuck else do we need?'

Dawn was looking at her hands. Only when Rick got truly excited did he stoop to swearing. Faraday picked up a cassette he'd left on the desk.

'What about his brief?'

'She's advised him to say nothing. He's still denying it, still insists he's had nothing to do with any of them. I'll give him full marks for nerve, sad man.'

'And the mask?'

'Says he's never seen it before in his life. Surprise, surprise.'

Faraday glanced at Dawn. She anticipated his next question, throwing a sideways look at Stapleton.

'If we were right about the girl putting a phone call through after we saw her, why would he risk leaving it in the garden?'

'He was at work.' Stapleton couldn't hide his impatience. 'And we were sitting on his front door when he got back.'

'But we searched that garden after we nicked him,' she insisted, 'and the mask wasn't there then.'

'We had a quick look round. On the way to the shed.'

'Wrong. I had a proper look.'

'Behind the flowers and stuff? Funny, I could have sworn you were with me.'

Dawn shrugged. In certain moods, conversations with Rick were always like this. He'd made up his mind. The clock was ticking. Charge the guy. Bang him up. The small print would sort itself out.

Faraday stooped to the video player. Seconds later, Shelley Beavis appeared on the screen. She did her party piece about wanting to become an actress and then confessed her passion for Paul Addison. As the placard with her name came up, Dawn looked less than surprised.

'Funny kind of rape,' she murmured.

There was a long silence. From the harbour, miles away across the city, came the faint parp of a ship's siren.

'OK,' Faraday said at last, 'so where are we now?'

Stapleton leaned forward on the chair. Irritation heightened his normal glow.

'The guy's guilty as fuck, boss. The girl's irrelevant, I've always said so. What we're after is the wanker who goes poncing around with the mask. It has to be him. Has to be.'

Dawn shook her head, equally forceful.

'But why? Why would he want to do it? The guy's educated, good-looking. We've got nothing on him from Vice and the college report no complaints. What does he get out of exposing himself?'

'Pass.' Stapleton rolled his eyes. 'I thought we wanted a result, not an explanation.'

'But what if the result's wrong?'

'It's not wrong. It can't be. It all fits. Maybe the guy's tired of all that straight sex. Maybe he's jaded. Maybe it's a power thing. Maybe he hates Walt Disney. Maybe he needs to take a few steps back and pretend he's some inbred retard who only gets it up in disguise. Maybe it's role-play. Yeah' – he nodded – 'maybe it's that. Maybe he gets a bit pissed at night, and forgets himself and takes things too far.'

'We didn't find one bottle,' Dawn reminded him, 'not one.'

'You're right. So how much proof do you need? I'm telling you. The guy's seriously weird. Doesn't drink. Doesn't smoke. Just screws himself silly. With all those students.'

'What makes you think that?'

Stapleton stared at Dawn in disbelief.

'You don't think he helps himself?' He nodded towards the screen. 'Bird like Shelley turns up? Can't wait to come across? You don't think he takes a break from all that heavy porn and tries out a move or two for himself? This is social worker talk, love. We're just here to put him away.'

'Quite.'

'Meaning?'

'Meaning I'm not sure.'

Dawn stole a glance at Faraday, embarrassed by a conversation which had got out of control. In these moods, fuelled by a conviction dangerously close to hysteria, Rick could give enthusiasm a bad name.

Faraday was trying to compute the strength of the case against Addison. Stapleton was right. Circumstances would certainly argue for his face behind the mask, but the hard evidential truth was that circumstances weren't quite enough. A confession would be favourite. Confirmed by a positive match on the mask from forensic.

Faraday glanced at Stapleton.

'You've organised a swab?'

'Yeah.'

A mouth swab would be enough to establish Addison's DNA. The swab would accompany the mask to Lambeth for forensic checks. Only one of the three women had confirmed physical contact with Mr Duck, and she'd washed her clothes within the hour, but the Scenes of Crime boys had retrieved her jeans and T-shirt from her airing cupboard and thought there might just be a chance of rescuing something useful. A hair. A single fibre. Not that it mattered. Addison's DNA inside the mask – from snot or scalp dandruff or sputum – would be more than enough for Faraday.

He glanced at his watch.

'I'll go and see Hartigan about an extension. Twelve hours won't make any difference to the forensic, but we ought to have another go at him.' He frowned. 'Once he's had a bit of a think.'

Eight

Addison's solicitor returned for the evening interview. She'd argued the case against detaining her client for a further twelve hours, pointing out that indecent exposure didn't even warrant the power of arrest, but Hartigan had ignored her, contending that Sunday's assault was serious enough to justify a custody extension pending further inquiries.

The solicitor's name was Julia Swainson, and the jungle drums at the Magistrates' Court suggested she was cutting a swathe through some of the city's older legal fraternity too bored or desperate to care about their marriages. Not just an Oxford degree. Not just an implacable determination to succeed. But a lean, gym-honed figure and a slightly crooked smile that spoke, to Dawn, of mischief and curiosity.

Her presence in the interview room beside Addison stiffened Stapleton's determination to put the lecturer away. Not only was he screwing the tastier students but he was clearly making a major impression on his legal adviser as well. The coolness of the guy under fire. The fact that he never betrayed anything more than a faint irritation at this intrusion into his well-ordered life. Stapleton was beginning to hate him.

He started the three audio cassettes, announced names and times, and then asked Addison about the Shelley Beavis video.

'Souvenir, is it? Keepsake? Trophy?'

Addison and his solicitor exchanged glances the way good friends might at a party, an unspoken acknowledgement that they were in the company of lesser mortals. Dawn knew exactly what was coming next.

'This has nothing to do with the offence in question,' Julia said silkily. 'As far as I'm aware, Shelley Beavis has made no complaint.'

Stapleton gave her one of his fuck-you looks, but Addison interrupted. He had absolutely no problem talking about Shelley. What, exactly, did Stapleton want to know?

'I want to know about the video, the one where she says she fancies you. Why did she do it? Why did she put all that stuff on tape?'

'It's an exercise all my students go through. At the start of the first year I ask them all to give me a video statement. I want to know why they're on the course, what they expect, where they want to get to. It's a way of concentrating minds. It makes them think.'

'And are they all as frank as Shelley?'

'Of course not. She was exceptional.'

'Because she said she fancied you?'

'Because she did it so well.'

'So *well*?'

For a moment, Stapleton was lost. Dawn, sitting beside him, came to the rescue. In these situations, it paid to be frank.

'I don't understand you, Mr Addison,' she said. 'What exactly do you mean?'

'Shelley wants to be an actress,' he pointed out. 'It's rare to find someone so young prepared to think so laterally.'

'You're saying she made it all up?'

'I'm saying she was giving me a performance. She

realised the potential of the video. She realised what an opportunity it gave her. It was a stage. She took advantage of that.'

'How do you know?'

'She told me. When we talked about it.'

'She told you that she didn't fancy you?'

'She told me she was playing a role. I'd asked them all to come up with something original, to think hard about what they did with the tape. Most of them were pretty clueless. Shelley wasn't. She was clever. She seized her opportunity. I applauded her.'

'Did you believe her?'

'Yes, I did. She caught my attention. That's what a good actress does.'

Addison sat back, patient, articulate, waiting to see where the interview might go next. He might have been conducting a seminar on a particularly difficult subject. His air of self-possession, of command, was almost tangible.

'So when you realised she didn't fancy you . . .' It was Stapleton this time.

Addison looked him in the eye, then shrugged.

'No problem.'

'You didn't try and press it?'

'No.'

'Never tempted?'

'No.'

'So why is her father so convinced that you took advantage of her?'

'I have absolutely no idea. Perhaps you should ask him.'

'We did. He seemed pretty clear about it.'

'And Shelley?'

Stapleton didn't reply. Dawn was watching the solicitor. She had her fountain pen out and she was making notes on a big yellow pad. Dawn then turned to Addison.

'I want to ask you about the mask again, Mr Addison. You've told us you'd never seen it before.'

'That's correct.'

'So how did it get there?'

'I have no idea. There's access to the garden from the alley at the back.'

'But you say the door's locked most of the time.'

'It is. But it's not an enormous wall. It's not wired or anything.'

'You're suggesting someone climbed in? Planted it?'

'I'm saying it's possible.'

'But why would anyone want to do that?'

For the first time, Addison faltered. The easy, seamless pattern of question and answer, prompt and response, came to an end. Dawn repeated the question. Addison said he didn't know.

'Do you have enemies, Mr Addison? At the college, maybe? Colleagues with some kind of grudge?'

'Everyone has grudges, especially in my business, but I can't believe any of them would do that.'

'Who, then? Who'd go to all the trouble of climbing your wall and hiding the mask like that?'

'I've no idea.'

'It would be somebody who knew, wouldn't it?'

'Knew what?'

'Knew that you were in trouble already.'

The solicitor's pen came to a halt. She looked across at Dawn.

'My client wasn't in trouble. I thought we'd made that clear already. There's been no complaint from Shelley Beavis and there's nothing actionable as far as the video tapes are concerned. My client is here to defend himself against a possible charge of grievous bodily harm regarding last Sunday's incident by the pond. Until the mask appeared, there was no pertinent evidence to link him with that.'

Rick Stapleton jumped in.

'The hiking boots? The lack of an alibi? A preoccupation with sex?' He was talking to Addison now. 'I'm not sure you're taking this as seriously as you ought to, Mr Addison. You have a great deal at stake here.'

'That sounds like a threat.'

'Not at all. Three women have been frightened witless. One of them has been physically injured. She won't be taking that dog for a walk for a long time. Not just because of her hand, but because it'll take months before she gets her confidence back.'

'I agree.' Addison nodded. 'But you're talking to the wrong man. I wasn't there. It wasn't me.'

'Can you prove that? In a court of law?' Stapleton was staring at him. 'Because quite soon you might have to.'

Addison raised an eyebrow, then sat back in his chair, leaving his solicitor to interject once again. She might have been talking to a child.

'We have nothing to prove. The burden of proof is on you.' She glanced at Dawn. 'May I have ten minutes alone with my client?'

Faraday was still at his desk, wrestling with the overtime sheets, when he heard the tap at the half-open door.

'Mr Faraday, sir?'

It was the young lad from Traffic, Mark Barrington. He was wearing a full set of motorcycle leathers and cradled a bulky white helmet. Acutely uncomfortable on CID territory, he had the look of a burglar disturbed during a particularly dodgy break-in.

Faraday beckoned him into the office.

'Shut the door,' he said. 'Joyce tells me they had another go at the Fiesta.'

'That's right, sir. The engineers and Accident Investigation. Seems the Fiesta was well under the speed limit.'

'And Prentice?'

'Didn't see her until the last.'

'Does he say that? Admit it?'

'No, sir. He still says he can't remember anything.'

'How many times have you seen him?'

'Just the once, sir. For the full statement.' He unzipped his jacket, producing a thick wad of photocopied sheets. 'It's all in there, sir. I'd appreciate them back when you've finished.'

He was already edging towards the door. Faraday left the photocopies untouched on the desk.

'What about the phone? Prentice's mobile?'

Barrington paused by the door.

'That's proving a bit tricky, sir. I filled in a C63 and the Inspector endorsed it, but I think there's a bit of a hold-up with Vodafone. They're talking about a four-week waiting list.'

'Who says?'

'My Sergeant, sir. He took the call.'

Faraday at last reached for the photocopies. The question he couldn't answer was why the lad had taken the risk in coming over here to Southsea nick. Traffic belonged on the first floor at Fratton, a tightly managed fiefdom with absolutely no time for the scruffy layabouts in CID. Not only that, but he'd brought a copy of the AI report with him, a gesture that could turn good intentions into an extremely difficult interview with his Sergeant.

'You were the last to see her alive,' Faraday murmured. 'Vanessa Parry.'

Barrington's grip on the door handle slackened. He muttered something about trying to give her CPR – cardio-pulmonary resuscitation, the last-chance kerb-side bid to revive a bursting heart. Barrington was looking thoughtful. He nodded at the photocopies in Faraday's lap.

'I made a note of the phone number in red Pentel,' he said. 'It's Prentice's mobile.'

Rick Stapleton looked at his watch for the second time. Addison and his solicitor were still in a huddle outside in the corridor. He could hear the low murmur of voices and, once, a little burst of shared laughter.

'They're taking the piss,' he said in disgust. 'Why don't we just get it over with and charge him?'

Nearly a year of working with Rick had taught Dawn a great deal about patience. In these moods, he was like a kid denied his rightful due. Most suspects would have caved in by now, bowing to the sheer force of Stapleton's conviction, but not Addison. Addison was outside, cooking up another little surprise.

'Take it easy,' Dawn told him. 'Let him sleep on it. We've got half a day yet.'

'He's guilty.'

'So you keep saying.'

'This is a waste of bloody time. You know it and I know it. If I was the guvnor, this would all be over.'

Dawn thought of Faraday's natural caution.

'If you were the guvnor, you'd be carrying the can when the CPS slung it out for lack of evidence.'

'You're joking. The forensic'll be back by next week.'

'Yeah? And what happens if there's no match?'

Stapleton stared at her. The blank incomprehension in those big blue eyes made her laugh.

'I didn't hear that,' he told her. 'Whose bloody side are you on?'

Footsteps down the corridor announced the return of Addison. He stepped aside to let Julia into the interview room. Neither of them made any attempt to sit down.

'My client has a proposal to offer,' the solicitor began. 'He's prepared to take part in an ID parade.'

Stapleton began to laugh.

'It was dark,' he pointed out, 'and the bloke was wearing a mask. What kind of parade's that?'

'It's not the mask the witnesses might be interested in.'

'No?' Stapleton was looking lost again.

'No. As we understand it, the nature of the complaints has to do with . . . ah . . . exposure. Am I right?'

Dawn nodded. 'In all three cases.'

'Excellent. In which case, we would suggest' – she glanced at Addison – 'an ID parade with a difference.'

There was a long silence. Dawn was staring at the solicitor. She'd been right about the mischief, righter than she could possibly have known. Was this a legal first? Or just a wind-up? She began to ask for clarification, but Stapleton got there first. He sounded slightly awed by the practicalities.

'You mean a willy parade? Ten guys getting it up?' He made a loose gesture at belly level. 'For real?'

Back home by half-eight, Faraday began to read the accident report for a second time, realising at once that it was a mistake. There were some things he could – should – do here, steps he could take, but nothing would ever blunt the impact of those hideously perfect photographs. Even in black and white, after their passage through the photocopier, they were far too graphic for Faraday's peace of mind. Vanessa Parry was dead, and no post-impact investigation would ever change that.

Putting the photocopies back in their envelope, Faraday collected his binoculars from the study upstairs and set off along the towpath for the distant smudge of Farlington marshes, an RSPB bird reserve at the top of Langstone Harbour. It was still warm, and the afternoon sea breeze had eased to the faintest stir of air. Striding north at a faster pace than usual, Faraday could smell the scents of summer, the richness of the harbour-side grasses spiked with wild honeysuckle, grateful for the distractions of memory.

June, for father and son, had been a time for squabbling. As far as Faraday was concerned, high summer was a hiatus, a largely empty bridge between the vivid passage of spring migrants – wheatears, chiff-chaffs, willow warblers – and those golden days in early autumn when the first of the Brent geese returned from their breeding grounds in the far north. To wake up to their comical honking across the eel-grass was to know that summer was over. Time to struggle into an anorak and a pair of sturdy boots. Time for some serious birding.

J-J, on the other hand, loved June. A neighbour had a little dinghy on a harbourside mooring that dried out at low water. He taught J-J how to row, gave him a key to his garden shed, and told him to help himself to the oars and rowlocks. J-J, who'd swum like a fish since the age of seven, needed no encouragement. In all weathers, he'd be out there, an increasingly tiny dot through Faraday's living-room window.

It wasn't that J-J was blind to birdlife. On the contrary, birds – their plumage, the way they flew, their habitats, their tiny offspring – had been one of the shared secrets that had cemented the bond between father and son, an entire world they'd made their own. No, it was simply that J-J, in common with many deaf kids, lived through his nerve ends. He loved the kiss of sunshine on his near naked body. He loved the surge of the harbour beneath the dinghy. And he loved most of all the smell of crusted salt on his skin at the end of a hot, hot day. Faraday remembered him now, perched on a stool in the kitchen, offering his skinny little arm for his dad to sniff.

Up on the marshes, Faraday walked along the seawall until the other birders had shrunk to dots in the distance. The tide was low, and he found a comfortable perch before raising the binoculars and taking a precautionary sweep across the gleaming spaces of the harbour. A tiny scatter of little terns on an outing from their colony on a nearby island. A handful of lapwings windmilling around. The constant chatter of sedge warblers from somewhere behind him, heard but so rarely seen. Apart from that, nothing.

The binoculars came briefly to rest on the distant silhouette of his own house, still shimmering in the heat at the very edge of the harbour. A nudge to the right, and he was looking at the acres of scrub and bushes that fringed the ponds between the water and the Eastern Road. Against the setting sun, it looked remote and impenetrable, untouched by the bricks and mortar that covered the rest of the island, and he found himself musing about the tracksuited figure in the Donald Duck mask who'd managed to taint even this last relic of wilderness.

More and more, he realised what policing – detective work – really entailed. In the Home Office research papers and on the more fanciful courses it was all proactive, staying-ahead-of-the-game, intelligence-led stuff, but in practice he and his blokes were rarely more than sweepers-up. Society had hit the buffers during the eighties, he knew this now for certain, and all that remained was to poke around among the wreckage, connecting one torn wire to another in a wildly optimistic bid to put the lights back on.

Sometimes, absurdly gratified, they got a result. Other times, they eyed each other through the drifting smoke, trying hard not to gag. Vanessa Parry hadn't been killed by a pervert, or a psychopath, or some animal with a record as long as your arm. No, she'd had the life crushed out of her by a twenty-five-year-old with a diamond stud in his ear who'd been too busy on the phone to see where he was going. No one would care much about restitution or justice, and in any case there wasn't much point because the poor woman, through no fault of her own, was dead.

Faraday put the glasses down. If you were looking for a metaphor for a wider madness, it was all there. Fifty miles an hour down a suburban street. A car full of crisps and fizzy drinks. An appointment at some pub or other. The need to squeeze in just one more phone call. And the second it took you to look up and realise you were metres away from killing that frightened-looking lady in red. A very big bang. Lots of broken glass. And then silence. It was that bloody sad.

Faraday's mobile began to chirp ten minutes later. He was on his feet again, completing the long circuit of the seawall. It was Rick Stapleton with news about Addison's proposal for an ID parade. At first, Faraday thought he'd been drinking.

'He can't, boss,' Stapleton pointed out. 'He's banged up.'

'I meant you.' He could hear Stapleton laughing. Against the darkening sky, a pair of mute swans. 'Whose idea was it? Addison's or the brief?'

'Pass. The brief tabled it.'

'Then she's either off her head' – Faraday was still watching the swans – 'or she's playing games. What do you think?'

'She's sending us a message,' Stapleton said at once. 'She thinks we've got no chance. She's that confident. We should charge him. Get it over with.'

'And the Custody Sergeant?'

'He'll support a charge.'

Faraday strained to hear the last swish-swish of the swans' wings before they vanished, then bent to the phone again. The final decision on a formal charge lay with the Custody Sergeant. If he thought the evidence justified it then Faraday saw no reason to delay any further.

'Charge him,' he said. 'We're talking GBH here. What's the bail situation?'

'We're contending the guy's a public menace. The Sergeant's agreed to keep him in.'

'Charge him,' Faraday repeated. 'Go for it.'

By the time Winter returned from the kitchen with a fresh pot of tea, Joannie was asleep again. He poured her a cup, leaving it on the little table by her elbow before settling into the file again. He'd printed out Hennessey's patient notes on his PC upstairs, and now he was cross-checking them with the newspaper reports he'd lifted from Pete Lamb. Fifty-two case histories. Healthy wombs ripped out. Bladders punctured. Infection spread. Lives either risked or, on an all-too-permanent basis, wrecked. Was he imagining things here? Or were there fifty-two reasons why Hennessey himself might be history?

On a pad by his elbow, Winter had been keeping track of exactly where these women lived. Hennessey had been a consultant at a hospital in West Sussex, saving his private patients for appointments in Harley Street, and there were clusters of victims dotted around Arundel, Littlehampton and Bognor Regis. One in particular had caught Winter's eye.

Dierdre Walsh was a fifty-two-year-old widow from a village near Arundel. She'd gone to hospital with a diagnosis which suggested a urinary problem. Hennessey, in his wisdom, had persuaded her to consent to a hysterectomy as well, claiming she'd risk cancer if her womb stayed in place. In the event, though, the botched operation had left her in chronic pain, worse by far than anything she'd experienced earlier, and incontinence had added insult to injury. Embarrassed by social contact, and too ashamed to risk applying for a job, this poor bloody woman had been consigned to an eternity of days and nights alone. When she'd asked Hennessey what had gone wrong, he'd accused her of making it up, a dismissal confirmed by a terse comment in Hennessey's own notes. 'Largely psychosomatic', he'd written. 'NFA'. NFA meant No Further Action.

Joannie stirred in her armchair and rubbed her eyes. Winter put the paperwork carefully to one side and gave her the tea. She took a sip or two, then pulled a face.

'Cold,' she said.

She looked down at the slew of papers across the carpet, then up at her husband. She could feel the remains of her supper still lying heavy in her belly, but she didn't want to make a fuss. Winter was buried in his file again. At length, she struggled to her feet and stifled a yawn. She thought it might be nice to spend a couple of days with her mother in Brighton. They might pop over together. Make it a bit of a break.

Winter glanced up. He didn't seem to have been listening.

'I'll run you over there, love,' he grunted. 'First thing.'

Nine

Hartigan's secretary was still clearing away the cups from an earlier breakfast meeting when Faraday appeared at the door. There was a plate of Danish pastries on the sideboard where the Superintendent displayed his various trophies, and Faraday eyed them with some anticipation. The summons from Hartigan had meant skipping his usual bacon sandwich. He was starving.

'Sir?'

Hartigan waved him into a chair in front of his desk. The desk, as usual, was nearly empty.

'Gunwharf.' Hartigan nodded towards the conference table. 'A couple of their guys were up here this morning for a get-together on our strategic partnership strategy. We were chatting afterwards. Apparently we have a mutual interest in a man called Hennessey.'

Faraday struggled to recall the name, then remembered the night Paul Winter had turned up at his home. Hennessey was the disgraced surgeon who'd been involved in some fracas at the Marriott. Since then, Faraday hadn't heard a thing.

'The Gunwharf people are up to speed on the Marriott business. It seems the man represents a great deal of money to them. Can I assume we're looking for him? Vigorously? And can I assume you'll keep me in the loop?'

Faraday blinked, instinctively uncomfortable with this new interpretation of strategic partnership. He pointed out that any search for Hennessey would be governed by the circumstances of his disappearance. With all due respect, his detectives weren't in the business of running around for a bunch of London developers.

Hartigan ignored the remark.

'I'm here to keep the peace, Joe, and from where I sit that's a pretty elastic phrase. Our Gunwharf friends are important to this city. As far as Hennessey is concerned, they're naturally keen to be in the loop as well. It isn't a problem. I said we'd be delighted to keep them briefed.'

'We?'

'Me, Joe. I'll keep them briefed. That's why it's important you keep me abreast of developments.' He paused. 'So what's the status of the inquiry?'

The last thing Faraday was going to admit was his own ignorance. There was a point of principle at stake here, and if it took a bit of footwork to defend it then too bad.

'There isn't one, sir.'

'I beg your pardon?'

'There's nothing to investigate. The guy's not around. That's not a crime.'

'The state of the hotel room?'

'He had a row with someone.'

'False name on the check-in form?'

'He paid cash. The name he used was immaterial.'

'What about the video evidence? Hennessey staggering to a car at God knows what hour? Another man involved?'

Faraday hesitated for a moment longer than he'd

have liked. This was new to him. He had to tread carefully.

'To my knowledge, we have no direct evidence of a crime. The damage to the room was minimal. The man Hennessey chose to leave early. The fact that he hasn't been seen since is of absolutely no significance. There are millions of people out there. We can't chase them all. Not without good reason.'

'He represents more than a million quid to the Gunwharf people.' Hartigan paused. 'You didn't know that?'

Faraday shook his head. 'Should I?'

Hartigan explained about the options on the three flats. The ten per cent deposits were now owing, and beyond that the balance on completion. He sounded, Faraday thought, like an estate agent.

'But maybe he doesn't want to take up the option. Isn't that a possibility?'

'Of course it is. But there's another possibility, too. Maybe he can't take up the option. Because something's happened to him.'

'Like what?'

'I don't know, Joe. I thought that's what you people were for.' He was beginning to lose patience. 'Or are you too busy poking around in traffic files?'

Faraday phoned Cathy Lamb from his office. A certain kind of anger had emptied his mind of all the usual clutter. He wanted to know about Hennessey. And, even more importantly, he wanted to know about the Gunwharf management.

Cathy was as dismissive as he'd been.

'It's a non-runner,' she said. 'The bloke's disappeared, of course he has, but what am I supposed to do about it? He doesn't live in this patch. He doesn't work here. He was just visiting for the night. And now he's gone.'

'Is anyone on it?'

'No.'

'What about Winter?'

'Yeah. I've given him seven days' compassionate. Like you told me to.'

'But how far had he got? Before he bailed out?'

Cathy went through the case Winter had made to her and Faraday agreed that Winter was chasing ghosts. A long list of surgical mistakes didn't add up to a murder inquiry. Not without a great deal more evidence.

'That's what I told him.'

'How did he take it?'

'You know Paul. He just smiled. That meant he thought I was being a prat.'

Faraday nodded, letting some of the anger seep away. There were, after all, some reasonable people around, and Cathy Lamb was one of them. He described his meeting with Hartigan. The Gunwharf people knew all about the incident at the Marriott. They knew about the false name Hennessey had used, about the damage to the room, about the pictures on the video tapes, the lot. In fact, for at least a day, they'd known more than he did. How come?

'Haven't a clue.'

'But it must be your end, Cath.'

'Like who?'

Good question. Faraday thought long and hard, trying to resist the obvious conclusion, then gave up.

'Winter,' he grunted. 'Has to be.'

Paul Winter stayed for as long as he could bear at the tiny flat Joannie's mother called home. The flat was on the fourth floor of a walk-up conversion half a mile back from Hove seafront, and the eight flights of stairs left their mark on Joannie. She sank into a seat by the window, her face the colour of putty. Her mother, a small, slightly querulous woman called Marge, fussed around with a towel, mopping the sweat from her forehead, shooting Winter the odd look as if to blame him for the climb. Minutes later, refusing a second cup of tea, Winter checked his watch, mumbled an apology and said he had to leave. He'd be back the moment Joannie decided she'd had enough. In the meantime, no partying.

Joannie looked up at him, too exhausted even to pretend she got the joke, then offered her cheek for a brisk peck. Winter left his hand a moment longer on her shoulder. He could feel the bones beneath the dampness of the thin cotton.

'Bye, love.'

Outside, he stood for a moment in the street, feeling the warmth of the sun on his face. Brighton had never ceased to excite him – the piped icing of the Regency crescents on the seafront, the cheerful scruffiness of the terraces behind – and he watched a couple of young girls on the pavement across the road, striding beach-wards. They wore jeans and scoop-necked halters. A couple of towels and a bottle of wine poked out of the tall one's bag. They were sharing a joke about some bloke or other, agreeing the guy had definitely been worth it. Laughter went with this place, and good times, and easy sex, and Winter followed them down towards the sea, remembering the way it had been for him and Joannie in the early days.

They'd met at a party in Portsmouth, Winter the probationer PC with all of nine months' service, Joannie doing her time at the local teacher training college. They'd got it on almost at once, pissed as rats on a blanket in the back of Winter's borrowed van. Weeks afterwards, summer as always, Joannie's term had come to an end and she'd gone back to Brighton for a fine-weather job collecting money on the deckchairs. Her mum and dad had a property in Portslade, a bay-fronted terraced place with a caged budgie in the window, and both parents worked, which meant that she had the run of the house on her frequent days off. There was a bed in her room she'd inherited from an uncle, bigger than a single, and when Winter was on nights he'd take the train across and they'd spend the day screwing. Joannie had been a brilliant shag, quite brilliant, really up for it, really wild, and Winter remembered the night shifts afterwards, dead on his feet on beat patrol, just aching for somewhere to steal an hour's kip.

He was on the seafront now, looking down at the beach as the girls unpacked their little bag. He loved the smells of this place: seaweed, suntan oil and the tang of sizzling onions from the burger van across the green-sward. He and Joannie would wander along the prom late on summer afternoons, still an hour to go before the train went, just yacking. In those days Joannie used to talk at a hundred miles an hour, dreaming about the little house they'd one day buy, the colours she'd paint it in, the way she'd do the bathroom so that every morning started exactly right. She wanted bright colours, flowers and a big, big window with sunshine flooding in. Oddly enough, when the dream came true, that's exactly what happened. Except that the house was in Pompey and they could only afford the top half of it.

So where had he gone wrong? At first, Winter had blamed it on marriage, on the institution itself. It was nothing to do with Joannie, nothing personal, just the feeling that he'd somehow been trapped and needed to demonstrate a little independence – just to prove it still all worked, just to reassure himself he was still the irresistible screw Joannie had fallen in love with. This had been OK the first couple of times, but then his little excursions, his little adventures, had become a kind of habit, and in the end he'd been forced to the conclusion that he was just greedy. He fooled around with other women not because his marriage wasn't good, not because kids had never happened, but because he just couldn't resist another screw. It kept his hand in. It made him feel good about himself. And a man who felt good about himself probably had a marriage to match.

Odds on, Joannie had probably guessed anyway. There were too many late nights, too much crashing around in the bathroom in the early hours of the morning trying to scrub another woman's smell off his face and crotch before he fell into bed. She'd never made an issue of it, never sat him down and asked the harder questions, and when he thought about it now he realised that deep down she'd always treated him like the kid he really was. In the end, she'd known he would always come home. Because home was where it really mattered.

Winter abandoned the seafront and made his way back to the flat where he'd left the car. At the corner of the street, he gazed up at the net-curtained fourth-floor windows, still unable to grasp the real implications of the consultant's bombshell. If what the guy had said was true, then Joannie would never see another Christmas, another pantomime, another early daffodil. The world of calendars, of tax returns, of bargain winter breaks was suddenly meaningless. She'd die before her mother, her sister, even the bloody dog. It was that unfair.

But what could he do about it? The fact that he couldn't get beyond this big fat question mark had begun to obsess him. He knew where his duty lay. He knew that Cathy and Faraday and the rest of them were right, that he should be up there with Joannie, giving her support, warmth, company, reassurance, a crutch to lean on as the path steepened over the next few months. But somehow he couldn't do it. Not because he didn't love her. But because it was just so fucking *passive*.

Life had rarely laid a finger on Winter, but when it did – like the recent knock-back on the Drugs Squad application – he was up on his toes again within minutes because that's how blokes like him handled themselves. Someone takes a poke at you, you whack him back. Someone in a white coat tells your wife she's on Death Row, you get out there and do something about it. But what?

Fighting the temptation to cross the road and climb the stairs, Winter fumbled for his keys and returned to the car. The files he'd so carefully collated on Hennessey were still lying on the rear seat. Getting in, he reached back for the top one and pulled out the name and address.

Dierdre Walsh. 2 Buttercup Cottages, Amberley.

Addison appeared before the magistrates at the end of the morning session. Despite two nights in the cells at the Bridewell, he appeared as neat and self-possessed as ever. Look hard and you might have sensed a hint or two of exhaustion in the dark brown eyes, and maybe a suggestion of impatience in the way his fingers drummed on the wooden lip of the dock, but Dawn knew that the magistrates were impressed by appearances. This man was a fellow professional. He had a decent address, a degree, a full-time job. Were they really prepared to commit him to Winchester prison on remand?

The CPS solicitor thought they should. In his view, Addison represented a threat to the public at large and should be subject to custodial remand. Julia Swainson, Addison's brief, disagreed. Her client profoundly resented the implications of the charge laid against him. The damage already done to his private and professional lives was incalculable. He was wholly innocent, and when the time came to prove it, he most certainly would.

The magistrates retired. Back again, minutes later, they consulted with the clerk of the court on a legal point. Then they announced that Addison would be granted bail on condition that he didn't go within half a mile of certain designated areas within the city. The areas included the waterside ponds, Farlington Marshes, Hilsea Lines and the entire length of the footpath that skirted Langstone Harbour. The implications were obvious. If he was to dress up as Donald Duck again, he'd have hundreds of witnesses within spitting distance.

Dismissed by the magistrates, Addison turned to leave the dock. As he did so, he caught Dawn's eye. She thought he was smiling, but she couldn't be sure.

Faraday met his CID boss, Detective Superintendent Willard, for lunch in a pub in Eldon Street. Willard was involved with an ongoing Crown Court case and had half an hour between CPS conferences. The lunch was at Faraday's request.

Willard, in every sense, was a big man. A greying fringe of beard softened a face that wouldn't have been out of place on a poster for a boxing promotion, and he had a physical presence which dominated even social exchanges. His empire extended to the whole of the county's Eastern Area, a chunk of territory which included the sprawling conurbation of Portsmouth, Havant and Waterlooville, and he'd brought a certain bluntness to the job that had lifted heads and done wonders for morale. He was a detective's detective. He had no time for political correctness and civic grandstanding. His blokes were out there on the ground to nail the bad guys. Faraday liked him a great deal.

'What's the score, then?'

Willard shook the remains of a bottle of brown sauce over his steak and kidney pudding as Faraday explained about the incident at the Marriott. There was no point trying to snow Willard so he came clean about his conversation with Hartigan. His divisional boss wanted to keep a finger in Hennessey's pie. Faraday was more than happy to fight his departmental corner, but he wanted to be sure that he'd got this thing in perspective. Was there really enough evidence to throw serious effort at the surgeon's alleged 'disappearance'? Or was Faraday missing something here?

Willard had no interest in point-scoring as far as his colleagues were concerned. Whatever he felt about career-obsessives like Hartigan he kept strictly to himself. His sole purpose, in his own phrase, was to add quality to investigations, and that meant dishing out available resources with a strict eye on potential outcomes. It was like backing horses. Never waste your money on a rank outsider. Not unless you'd heard a whisper you could trust.

He made Faraday go through every particle of known evidence about Hennessey. Faraday told him everything he'd learned from Cathy Lamb. At length, Willard nodded, spearing another forkful of steak.

'Adds up to fuck all,' he grunted. 'But keep listening, eh?'

Ten

Wednesday, 21 June, early afternoon

Winter had phoned ahead, catching Dierdre Walsh on the point of setting off for a visit to Arundel library. He'd explained that he was making inquiries in connection with Pieter Hennessey and would appreciate a moment or two of her time. When she asked whether it was really important, he said yes.

Buttercup Cottages lay in the middle of the tiny village of Amberley, number two the smaller half of a picturesque timber-framed building that looked as if it might once have been a pub. A square of lawn at the side of the house had recently been mown and the nearby compost heap was topped with fresh grass cuttings. At two in the afternoon, rolled in an empty bottle inside the tiny porch, there was already a note out for the milkman.

Dierdre Walsh was an anxious, thin-faced woman who looked a good deal older than fifty-two. She wore a pair of baggy brown corduroy trousers and a pale blue cardigan over a red and white check shirt, and the moment Winter stepped inside the house he understood why. Despite the heat outside, the place had a definite chill. There was also a smell, sharp and acrid, that Winter at first mistook for cat's piss. Only later did he realise that the stench was only too human.

Dierdre had already prepared a tray of tea, and to Winter's relief, they sat outside on a tiny flagstoned patio at the back of the house, dispensing with small talk within seconds. This was a woman who'd lived with the consequences of Hennessey's work for the best part of a year and time had done nothing to soften the anger she felt at the treatment she'd received at his hands.

Meeting Hennessey, she said, had been a straightforward referral from her GP. He was a gynae consultant at the biggest of the local hospitals. He was the man you went to if you had a problem 'down there', and she felt lucky to have got to the top of his patient list within weeks.

'Lucky? Can you imagine that?'

She sat bolt upright in the sunshine, her bony fingers knotted in her lap, her face shadowed by an ancient straw hat. This was the first time Winter had had the chance to picture Hennessey in action, to get a flavour of the man.

'What was he like?'

'*Like?*' She was watching the plate of chocolate biscuits slowly melting in the sun. 'He was like you'd imagine any old-style consultant to be. He was loud. He barked a bit, especially when he laughed. If you were a nervous type like me he could be a little bit intimidating. People like Hennessey make you feel very small. It's a special little knack they have. Small and stupid.'

Winter nodded, thinking of Joannie's consultant. Not intimidating, exactly. Just superior.

'They think they know it all,' he agreed, 'and they don't.'

At the hospital, Hennessey had had access to the results of some smears she'd had taken. He'd also examined her himself, an experience that even now sent a shudder through her thin frame.

'Big fat fingers,' she said, 'fingers like sausages. And

absolutely no finesse. At the time, you think nothing of it. In fact, you tell yourself you're making a fuss. But later, when you realise just how hopeless the man really was, you kick yourself for putting up with it all.'

The scan and the examination had led Hennessey to the conclusion that Dierdre needed more than a bladder operation. Her womb should come out as well.

'There was no discussion,' she said. 'He just told me that was what he was going to do.'

'Did you ask why?'

'Of course I did.'

'And what did he say?'

'He just laughed. He thought it was amusing. Then, when I made a bit of a point of it, dug my heels in a bit, do you know what he said? He said I wouldn't be needing it any more so he'd be doing me a favour. He made it sound like some kind of house clearance, you know, getting rid of all the junk. He had absolutely no idea how hurtful that can be, a woman of my age, a woman of *any* age. It was horrible. Quite horrible.'

'But there had to be a medical reason, surely?'

'Oh, I think there was. Later, when I kicked up a fuss about what had happened, he said some of the cells they'd stained looked pre-cancerous. But why didn't he explain that at the time? Instead of playing God?'

Playing God. It was a good image, Winter thought. It fitted them all, every single one of them. The power to turn this woman's life into a constant misery. The power to hand Joannie a death sentence.

He jotted down a note to himself, listening to Dierdre describe the afternoon she'd surfaced after the operation. Then, and for days afterwards, she couldn't understand the constant dampness between her legs, and the smell. At first she'd put it down to some kind of post-operative reaction. It was the body sorting itself out, the nurses told her. The constant trickle of warm urine would soon dry up. But it didn't. Not in hospital, not during convalescence at a friend's house, and not for a single moment over the weeks and months to come. She leaked like an old tap with a dodgy washer. And the image, once again, was Hennessey's.

'He *said* that?'

'Those very words. I'm not making it up, Mr Winter. It was when I insisted on going back to see him. I was upset, naturally. I wanted him to do something about it.'

'And?'

'He just said I'd have to put up with it. He said it was wear and tear. An old tap' – she nodded – 'with a dodgy washer.'

'Nothing to do with him?'

'Absolutely not. When I asked, he said there was nothing more he could do for me.'

'No apology?'

'*Apology?* People like Hennessey don't apologise, Mr Winter. They're not in the apology business. And you know why? Because they're never wrong. Mistakes are something that other people make. Never them. As far as he was concerned, he'd done a thoroughly professional job and that was that. If I wanted anything else done about my' – she made a loose gesture towards her lap – 'waterworks, then I'd be better off going to see a plumber. Can you imagine a *doctor* telling you that?'

Hurt and outraged, she'd sought a second opinion. The consultant on this occasion was a good deal kinder but confirmed that her incontinence would remain chronic. Hennessey was right. There was nothing to be done.

'Did he explain why you'd got the problem? This second quack?'

'Of course not. They never do. They just cover up for each other. He probably knows. In fact, I'm sure he knows. But the last person he's going to tell is me. Isn't that amazing? It's my body he's wrecked, my life I have to cope with, yet none of them are man enough to come clean.'

'You're sure it was Hennessey's fault?'

She looked at him for a moment, despairing, then pulled herself together.

'All I know is this. When they put me under, everything worked the way it should. When I came round afterwards, I was leaking like a sieve. The person in charge of me in between was Hennessey. It's simple logic, Mr Winter. It had to be him.' She paused, then gestured at her lap again. 'Do you know what I'm wearing under this lot? Plastic pants, like a baby, and four nappies a day.'

Later, before Winter left, she fetched a box file from the house. Other Hennessey victims had got together and compared notes. They were all women, and in many cases the stories were the same. A bluff arrogance you'd ignore in the belief that this man knew what he was doing. A botched operation that went horribly wrong. Months and months of post-operative pain, the wounds salted by Hennessey's blunt refusal to accept any particle of blame. She quickly sorted through the inch-deep pile of letters, and as she did so Winter glimpsed names he recognised from his own research. Finally, with a little grunt of pleasure, she found what she was looking for.

'Here,' she said. 'Do you have a pen?'

The girl's name was Nikki McIntyre. Unlike most of

Hennessey's victims, she was young, still in her twenties. She was also extremely striking, beautiful even, and if Winter was really interested in seeing what kind of havoc a man like Hennessey could wreak, then he could do no better than pay her a visit. She lived in the Meon Valley, and her story deserved the widest possible audience.

Winter scribbled down the number and enquired whether Dierdre happened to know where Hennessey had gone. Were she or her lawyers still in touch? Had there been any contact recently?

Dierdre shook her head. She hadn't seen Hennessey for months – which was probably just as well.

'Why's that?' Winter was on his feet now, ready to leave, eager to progress the investigation.

Dierdre was shuffling the letters back into order. She closed the lid on the box file and finally looked up.

'Because on bad days,' she said, offering Winter a thin smile, 'I could cheerfully kill him.'

Mid-afternoon, Dawn Ellis made time to have a second crack at Shelley Beavis. With Addison formally charged with GBH the pressure had eased slightly on the Donald Duck job, but she didn't share Rick Stapleton's faith in the strength of the file they'd be preparing for the Crown Prosecution Service, and she anticipated all kinds of questions from the CPS lawyers. There were bits of the jigsaw that didn't fit properly. And one of them was Shelley Beavis.

Rawlinson Road was in its normal state of urban squalor, and the chaos wasn't helped by a newish BMW 7 series half-parked on the pavement across the entrance to Shelley's basement flat. Dawn glanced at the car as she edged past. There was a tangle of sports gear tossed into the passenger footwell – white shorts, hooded top, blue socks – and a pair of brand-new Reebok trainers in an open box on the back seat. A cut-out in the shape of a blue number nine football shirt hung from the driving mirror.

Dawn negotiated the steps to Shelley's front door. There was a yellow stick-it over the Yale lock and she peered at the message. 'Jimmy's', it read. Nothing else. Just 'Jimmy's'. Jimmy's was a café-bar a couple of minutes' walk away. The chrome-and-leather decor attracted a certain clientele – hard-drinking car dealers, guys running contraband tobacco, call-girls from the quality end of the trade – and often featured in the late-night disturbance reports.

Dawn knocked twice and waited to see whether anyone was in. When there was no response, she turned to go, then stopped. Something had happened to the wood around the door lock. She eased the stick-it away and took a good look. Where the door met the frame, there were gouge marks in the timber. Someone had been trying to get in, either with a jemmy or some kind of chisel. As far as the area was concerned, this would be par for the course. Student flats, in particular, were favourite targets for walk-in thieves and the crime stats were heavy with nicked PCs and audio gear. But successful or otherwise, what was especially interesting about this break-in was the fact that it was so recent. Two days ago, when Dawn had been here with Rick Stapleton, the wood around the lock had been undam-aged.

Making a mental note to check the burglary ring-ins, Dawn returned to the pavement. It was by no means certain that the note on the door had come from the owner of the BMW, but there was something about that single word, Jimmy's, that roused her curiosity. It was so peremptory. So blunt. It wasn't a message at all. It was a command. Jimmy's. *Be there.*

The moment she stepped into the café-bar from the street, Dawn knew that luck was with her. Shelley was sitting on a stool at the bar. She had a cigarette in one hand and a bottle of Becks in the other, and as soon as she recognised Dawn she turned at once to the man beside her, doing her best to use his body to shield her face.

The bar was tiny, no more than a couple of paces from end to end. Dawn ordered a cappuccino. Shelley had nowhere to hide.

'Hi.' Dawn grinned at her. 'How are you?'

Shelley shook her head, lost for words. Close to, she had a bruise on her right cheek bone, the swelling beginning to close her right eye. The damage, like the gouge-marks on the door, looked very recent.

The man beside her had turned round. He was tall and slim and wore an Armani T-shirt under a beautifully cut linen suit. His head was shaved and he had the kind of tan that spoke of long afternoons on the beach. There was something slightly Italian about him, a practised languor, and the way he flaunted an obvious fitness made Dawn wonder about the Beamer up the road, with its little blue number nine man dangling from the rear-view mirror. Was this the guy who'd chucked his sports gear in the footwell? The guy who'd left the note?

'Awright, then?'

Broad Pompey, not an Italian at all.

'Fine, thanks. You?'

He nodded, smiling down at her. Dawn had rarely been so frankly appraised. He ran his eyes up and down her body. She was wearing a T-shirt cut tighter than usual and he didn't bother to disguise his approval.

'Name's Lee.' He extended a hand. 'Mate of Shel's, are you?'

Dawn glanced across at Shelley. She wanted to be anywhere but here.

'Yeah.' Dawn nodded. 'Kind of.'

'College, is it?'

Lee was looking at Shelley. Shelley nodded at once, a quick jerk of the head.

'That's right.'

'Gonna introduce us then?'

Dawn stepped in, introducing herself. Nothing could disguise the panic in Shelley's eyes. Not that Lee was interested in Shelley any more.

'Good gig is it, college? Only I fancy that, one day. Girls like you and Shel, can't go wrong, can you?'

Dawn rode the patter with practised ease. Three years on the squad had given her a lifetime's insights into the male psyche, and it was child's play to deal with chat-up lines like these.

'Suit like that, you should be in a real city,' she said. 'Wear quality gear round here, you'll get arrested.'

'What for?'

'Nicking it.'

Lee thought that was really funny, and Dawn recognised a new light in his eyes. Cathy Lamb was right when she said that laughter was the best aphrodisiac.

'What are you studying, then? Media stuff? Same as Shel?'

'People.'

'What?'

'People. I study people.'

'You joking? Is this a wind-up?'

'Not at all. Anthropology. That's what I study.'

'Shel?'

Still unsure, Lee was looking to Shelley for confirmation. This guy hates being bested, Dawn thought. Especially by a woman.

'Yeah. Anthropology.'

Shelley could barely get the word out. There was something more than panic in her eyes. She looked terrified.

Lee turned back to Dawn.

'How come we've never met before, then? Friend of Shel's?'

'Different course,' Dawn said at once. 'Different part of town.'

'Where do you live, then?'

'Fareham.'

'*Fareham?*' He put his hand on her arm a moment. 'You could do with a real drink, not a bloody coffee. What's there to do in Fareham?'

'Plenty. If you know where to look.'

Lee raised an eyebrow, more interested than ever, then circled an arm around Shelley. Dawn saw the way the girl physically flinched at his touch, slipping off the barstool and wriggling free.

'Gotta go,' she muttered, draining the last of the Becks. 'Late already.'

Lee glanced at his watch and nodded. Then returned to Dawn.

'Get Shel to drop you an invite to one of our little parties.' He grinned down at her. 'You'll love it, you will.'

As soon as they'd gone, Dawn moved to a table in the window, watching them walk down the road, back towards Shelley's flat. Despite the suit and the sun tan, Lee couldn't quite eradicate the trademark Pompey swagger. He walked from the shoulders, his hands plunged deep in his trouser pockets, and when he came across an empty can, he couldn't resist sidefooting it through someone's open front gate.

Beside the BMW he stopped and unlocked the door. Shelley had disappeared. He shouted something at her, then ducked into the car. Rawlinson Road was one-way, the traffic flow heading south. As Lee stopped opposite Jimmy's, Dawn fumbled for a pen. T456GHB.

Eleven

Wednesday, 21 June, late afternoon

Winter had been home less than ten minutes when Faraday phoned. He hated the bungalow without Joannie. The spaces she'd made her own – the kitchen, her chair in the lounge, the spare room at the back where she stored her trophies from the car-boot sales – were suddenly empty without her physical presence. Winter knew only too well that this was a reality he was going to have to get used to, but the fact remained that it spooked him.

Faraday wanted to know how Joannie was getting on. He sounded warm and supportive, even mellow.

'Fine, boss,' Winter said at once. 'She's asleep at the moment, tucked up in bed.'

'And does it help?'

'What, boss?'

'Being at home?'

Winter said yes. Faraday had been absolutely right. The news had gutted them both, but a trouble shared was a trouble halved. If Joannie was awake and standing beside him now she'd be the first to agree. Having the old man around had done her the world of good.

Winter caught sight of a prescription on the mantelpiece. She'd forgotten to take it to Brighton. He'd have to send it on.

'Boss,' he began, 'this Hennessey thing. I've been

thinking. If I manage to make it back over the next couple of days, what's the strength?'

Faraday told him to forget it. He'd been talking to Cathy. As strapped for bodies as ever, he doubted whether she could spare him for even a couple of phone calls on the Hennessey business. Compassionate leave was different. Looking after your dying wife was a priority. Unlike the hunt for some half-arsed surgeon who may or may not have disappeared.

'By the way,' he added, 'the Gunwharf Quays people seem to have got themselves in the loop. You wouldn't have any ideas about that, would you?'

'Gunwharf Quays?' Winter was thinking about Pete Lamb. 'Haven't a clue, boss.'

'You're sure?'

'Absolutely. Prices like that, they're way out of my league.'

'I wasn't thinking of you buying in. I was asking you whether you'd been talking to the Gunwharf lot. A yes or no will do.'

Winter ignored the question. He was determined to make the Hennessey inquiry official.

'Remember Charlie Oomes, boss? That was no expense spared, wasn't it? Or is my memory playing tricks?'

Charlie Oomes was a London businessman whom Faraday had tried to put away for charges connected with a particularly intractable murder. At the time, everyone had said that Faraday was off his head even to think about going after Oomes, but Faraday had ignored them all.

'That was different,' Faraday muttered.

'You're right. You were the guv'nor.'

'That's not what I meant.'

'I know. But it's like you and your missus. I know how you must have felt now.'

'About my wife?'

'About Oomes. It's a gut thing, isn't it? An instinct? You know the guy's got himself in the shit and it's just a question of trying to work out how.'

Winter began to go through it all again – the mistakes Hennessey had made, the women he'd maimed, the retribution that doubtless awaited him – but he could tell that Faraday's heart wasn't in it. If Winter was really determined to return to work, then God knows there was plenty for him to do. By Cathy's calculations, the current caseload was unprecedented, a breaking wave of volume crime that threatened to swamp them all. Under these circumstances, an allegedly missing surgeon was the last thing on her mind.

Winter nodded, telling Faraday he was sorry to bend his ear. He was probably right about Hennessey, and in any case it was all academic because he had his hands full with Joannie. He'd been right about her, as well. They'd sort it out together. Just like Faraday said they should.

'Anything else I can do to help?'

'Nothing, thanks, boss. But cheers, anyway.'

'For what?'

'Understanding.'

It was early evening before Dawn Ellis returned to the basement flat in Rawlinson Road. She rapped on the door, hearing music inside. There was no sign of the BMW.

Shelley Beavis looked half-asleep. Her hair was more tousled than ever, and she was wearing a long green T-shirt that came down to her knees. Her legs were bare except for a tiny anklet strung with turquoise and red beads. The last thing she wanted was another conversation with Dawn Ellis.

Dawn pushed past her, into the flat. The smell of weed was overpowering.

'You can't do this,' Shelley was saying.

Dawn ignored her. She went quickly through the flat, making sure Shelley was alone. When she got back to the cavernous front room, Shelley was sitting cross-legged on the floor, staring at the remains of a Mars bar.

'He's coming back,' she said stonily. 'You've got to get out of here.'

'Why? He likes me, doesn't he? Wasn't that the vibe?'

'He likes anyone' – she looked up – 'with tits like yours.'

Dawn stared down at her for a moment. Girls like Shelley Beavis made her feel powerfully maternal. She needed something wholesome in her stomach and a bit of a cuddle. She also needed talking to. There were sandals and a pair of jeans on the floor beside the bed. Dawn tossed them across.

'Get dressed, love. I'll take you for a drink.'

'I don't want a drink. I want to stay here.'

'OK.' Dawn shrugged. 'We'll just wait, then.'

She sat on the bed. A copy of *Loaded* lay open at an article on women's favourite fantasies. Dawn began to read it, wondering what else you could do with a pre-warmed cucumber and a pot of Greek-style yoghurt, aware of Shelley struggling to her feet again. She had some difficulty with the jeans and abandoned the sandals for a pair of trainers. On the point of leaving, Dawn gestured at the magazine.

'Yours?' she enquired.

Shelley threw her a look.

'You have to be joking,' she muttered.

They went to a pub behind the seafront, Shelley's choice. This time in the evening, it was full of visitors off the beach, families with kids who'd come in for the cheap food and Happy Hour drinks. Dawn found a quiet alcove near the back, knowing that this was the last place for a man with a Beamer and a nice Italian suit to be seen.

Dawn returned with the drinks.

'Who is he?' she asked.

Shelley didn't want to say. She was mellowed out to the point of near silence and all that bothered her was all the crap that had gone down in Jimmy's.

'What crap?'

'You and me being friends. You being at college. Studying whatever it was.'

'You went along with it,' Dawn pointed out. 'Would you have preferred the truth?'

'Of course not.'

'Then what's the problem?'

'The problem? The problem is he fancies you.'

'So what? I'm a big girl.'

'Yeah, but . . .' Shelley shook her head, then buried her face in her hands. 'D'you know what that involves?'

'Give us a clue.'

'He's mental, that's what it involves. He's off his head. And now I've got myself in this situation, having to go along with all this garbage about you being a student. He wants a number. He wants to phone you. You don't need any of this. And neither do I.' She reached for her pint and swallowed a long mouthful. The cider seemed to clear her mind. 'So just . . .' She made a loose, slightly apologetic gesture at the space between them. 'Leave me alone, eh?'

Dawn didn't say anything. A couple of dads were taking on their respective kids on the pool table. A potted cue ball brought a squeal of dismay from a small boy in glasses.

'You still haven't told me his name,' Dawn reminded her.

'That's because I don't want to. Can't, more like it.'

'*Can't?*' Dawn reached across and tried to touch her face where it was bruised, but Shelley recoiled. 'Did he do that?'

'No.' She shook her head.

'You're lying.'

'I'm not.'

'Yes, you are. His name's Lee Kennedy. He's got a house up in North End. Salamanca Road, number forty-five. He's got previous for assault, three separate occasions, and a string of driving offences. The last guy he nutted spent a couple of days in hospital. This is just the official version. God knows what else he's done.'

The realisation that Dawn already knew about Lee Kennedy brought the conversation to a halt. Shelley stared at her drink, refusing to say a word. At length, Dawn leaned over the table. She wanted Shelley to listen very hard because she was only going to say this once.

'Have you read the local paper? We charged Paul Addison with grievous bodily harm this morning. He's got himself bail, so he's not banged up, but headlines like "Donald Duck Arrest – Lecturer Charged" aren't going to do his career any good. I don't know whether you've been in touch at all but in my book you haven't begun to play fair by him. There's stuff you haven't told us, Shelley, and if you care about the guy, now might be a good time to start.'

Dawn sat back, reaching for her drink, taking her time. She hadn't discussed her doubts about Shelley Beavis with Faraday, or even with Rick, because working practice made few allowances for hunches.

They'd blame a conversation like this on her time of the month. Or worse.

'Well?'

The colour had drained from Shelley's face. Unless she was an even better actress than Addison had suggested, Dawn swore she was hearing this for the first time. At last, she looked up. Her voice was barely audible.

'No bullshit?'

'Absolutely not. He'll end up in the Crown Court. On trial.'

'And after that?'

'Depends. If it's guilty, he'll go down.'

'Prison?'

'Of course.' She nodded. 'Not nice at all. And probably not fair, either.'

'You think he's innocent?'

'I didn't say that. Ask me whether we've got the whole story, the answer's no. So . . .' She offered Shelley a cold smile. 'Why don't you make a start? Here and now?'

Shelley thought about the proposition, running a perfect fingernail around the rim of her glass, and Dawn watched her turning it over in her mind. She'd been right about the girl, she knew it. There was much, much more to come.

Finally, with some reluctance, Shelley shook her head.

'I can't,' she said. 'I just can't.'

'He frightens you, doesn't he? This Lee?'

She nodded, totally candid at last.

'He'd frighten anyone,' she said. 'In some moods he's just off his head.'

'And he hit you.' Dawn nodded at her face. 'Did that.'

'Yes.'

'You have a relationship with him?'

'We shag, yes. I wouldn't call it a relationship.'

'So why not bin it?'

'I can't.' Her fingers briefly touched her swollen cheek. 'Not until he lets me.'

Dawn looked her in the eye. There were possibilities here, maybe even the beginnings of trust.

'We can do things,' she said slowly, 'take certain steps.'

'Like what?'

'Witness support. Find you somewhere else to live.'

'But you don't know what he's like.'

'You're right, we don't, but our gang's bigger than his, believe me.'

'He'll find me, I know he will, whatever you do he'll find me. He's that kind of bloke. He never gives up. Never. That's what's so scary about' – she frowned – 'this.'

'What's "this"?'

'You and me being friends. He's made up his mind about you. I know he has. That's the way he goes about it.'

'Goes about what?'

'You don't want to know.'

'But I do, Shelley, I do.'

Dawn relaxed, studying Shelley over the table, making a decision of her own. Then she leaned forward again.

'OK, then,' she said, 'we'll play it a different way. Here.' Dawn found a scrap of paper in her jeans pocket. She scribbled down a number and handed it across. 'That's my mobile. Tell him he's welcome to phone. And tell him the interest is mutual.'

Shelley stared at the number, her eyes blank. The

penny took longer to drop than Dawn had expected. Finally, she looked up.

'That means you're still supposed to be my friend,' she said. 'That means I've got to carry on pretending.'

Dawn nodded.

'GBH can carry fourteen years,' she said softly. 'You ought to think about that, too.'

Cathy Lamb met her estranged husband, Pete, in the Wine Vaults off Albert Road. Casks of real ale lined the wall behind the bar and Cathy took the risk of investing in a couple of pints of Summer Lightning, just like the last time, back in the early spring, when she'd amazed herself at how easy it had seemed, and how natural.

Pete had found a table in the room next door. Nearly a year apart had changed him, Cathy thought. No longer haunted, no longer edgy, he had the look of a man quietly pleased to have found himself in one piece. He'd put on a little bit of weight, which suited him, and he seemed to have suddenly developed a taste for nicely cut shirts.

'Cheers.' Cathy lifted her glass. 'Who does the shopping?'

Pete allowed himself a private smile.

'Sexist question,' he murmured. 'And one you wouldn't expect me to answer.'

'Nice, is she? In the job, by any chance?'

'I wouldn't know, love. Who ever bothers with conversation these days?'

'I'm a detective, Pete, remember? And detectives always think the worst.'

'The worst?' Pete offered her a quizzical smile. 'If only.'

'You mean there's no one?'

'I mean there's no one important.'

'And that's the best you can do?'

'Sadly, yes.'

Pete touched his glass to hers, an old gesture that brought this particular conversation to an end, and Cathy resigned herself to letting it go, surprised to realise just how badly she wanted to find out the shape this new life of his had taken. You can't live with a man for so many years and not get to know him. Where was he getting it from? And how much did she matter?

He wouldn't tell her. Instead, he wanted to know about this new job of hers. Who was working for her? Who was giving her hassle? And, most important of all, whether or not she'd be putting in for the next promotions board.

'DI for keeps? You have to be joking.'

'It's a pain?'

'It's not that. It's not even losing all the overtime. I expected that. I've watched Faraday long enough to know what goes with the turf. It's just so' – she frowned, hunting for the right word – 'relentless. You think you're getting on top of it. You scoop up a few villains, get a result or two, make a night of it in the bar, then next morning you wake up and start all over again. It never bloody stops. Not from either end.'

She described the pressures from headquarters, and from her own divisional Superintendent. The never-ending demands to beat performance target after performance target. The blizzards of paperwork. The fact that no one really knew what their political masters were after. They claimed to have priorities, lots of priorities, but in the end you got to realise there were so many that absolutely nothing got to the top of the heap. When it came to working out what politicians wanted, *really* wanted, she'd finally sussed the truth: that they were all equally clueless.

'None of that would matter,' she continued, feeling herself getting wound up again, 'if we were brave enough to ignore them. But no one ever does. Some twat in the Home Office has a bright idea on the seven thirty-three and within minutes we're chasing around again. Some councillor from Paulsgrove writes to the paper and you'd think it was World War Three. It's hard enough keeping up with the scrotes on the street, but I'm beginning to think the suits are even worse.'

Pete was down towards the bottom of his pint. In this mood he knew he'd only have to encourage Cathy with a nod or a frown and she'd bang on for ever. Instead, he changed the subject.

'I was out of order,' he said, 'the other day.'

'What?'

'About this bloke Hennessey. Asking you to check him out for form.'

'You're *apologising*? I don't believe it.'

Pete nodded. He'd pushed his luck as he always did, and now he wanted to say sorry. If she fancied another curry, it would be his pleasure. In the meantime, he was off to the bar for another couple of pints. As he began to get up, Cathy reached across, stopping him.

'Tell me something,' she said. 'Only, Faraday's been on at me.'

'About what?'

'This Hennessey. How come the Gunwharf lot know so much about what happened at the Marriott?'

'I told them. Paul told me and I passed it on.'

'Why?'

'Because that's the deal. They're paying me to try and find the bloke and I have to keep them briefed. It's called money, Cath.'

'And does Winter know that?'

'Of course he does. It's tit for tat. I feed him stuff, he feeds me. C'mon, Cath. This isn't rocket science.'

'Sure, but that doesn't make it right, my love. They'll crucify you if they find out.'

Pete smiled, amused by the concern in her voice, then departed to the bar, returning with another couple of pints. Cathy was still troubled by her ex-husband's casual reliance on police resources and was determined to make him understand the kind of risks he was running, but what puzzled her just now was Winter. In the canteen, he'd had a vehemence about Hennessey she'd never seen before. Normally he was so laid back, so *cool*. Not this time.

'So what do you think?' She was frowning. 'About this surgeon guy?'

Pete took the top off his pint and wiped his mouth with the back of his hand.

'To be honest, I haven't a clue. But I've read the cuttings, and incompetence would be a kind word.'

Twelve

Hating the silence of the bungalow, Winter went to the pub to read the file on Nikki McIntyre.

Her DOB, according to Hennessey's own notes, was 23 September 1972, which made her twenty-seven. Over a period of seven years, Hennessey appeared to have operated on fifteen separate occasions, though the dividing line between examinations and some formal surgical procedure wasn't altogether clear. Much of the medical jargon was impenetrable, offering no clue to the nature of Nikki's condition, but what was obvious was her status as a patient. From the start, she'd opted to go private, drawing on an insurance scheme to pay Hennessey's bills. The bulk of the work had been done at the Advent Hospital in South Kensington, and attached accounts had itemised the breakdown on each of the invoices Hennessey had sent to BUPA on her account over the course of their relationship.

Winter refuelled at the bar before returning to do the sums. Subtracting monies owed to the hospital for the hire of consulting rooms and an operating theatre, plus fees paid for anaesthetists, agency nursing staff and the hire of secretarial help, Winter was left looking at the figure which had accrued directly to Hennessey. Over the seven-year span, the surgeon had pocketed just under £40,000 for whatever damage he'd inflicted on Nikki McIntyre.

Winter sat back, gazing at the sum. It was enormous. It was the kind of money that would pay off his own mortgage with five grand to spare. It was a large enough figure maybe to have bought Joannie an extra year or two of time. There were wildly expensive drugs that could work that kind of miracle. Winter had read about them in Joannie's copies of *Hello!* magazine. That's how the super-rich kept their sleek figures and gleaming teeth. By buying a stake in immortality.

Returning to the notes, Winter did his best to tease a little sense from the entries in Nikki's file, but even when he managed to get a fix on a word or two, or even a complete sentence, he was none the wiser. The terms used were hopelessly technical. You'd need a couple of years at medical school to stand a prayer with this lot.

Emptying his second pint, Winter was suddenly struck by another thought. So far, he'd somehow imagined that Hennessey's career was well and truly over. Summoned before the GMC, and about to be pursued through the courts, the man had doubtless done the sensible thing and retired. Given earnings like these, he'd have stashed a pile in some offshore, tax-free account and – if he was still alive – would by now be planning a new life abroad.

His recent visit to the Marriott may have been a preparation for that. He'd have bits and pieces to tidy up. He'd have a house to sell, the New Forest cottage to vacate, other assets to turn into hard cash. Somewhere along the line, his past had caught up with him in the shape of the other figure in the video surveillance tapes, and in his heart Winter was sure that Hennessey was already dead. But say he wasn't? Say he'd somehow survived the attentions of the looming stranger in the suede jacket? Say he was still out there with his scalpel and his stethoscope, the freelance butcher of every woman's worst nightmare? Say, God help us, he was planning *more* operations?

Winter grunted to himself, then checked his watch. Motivation in the job had never been a problem with him. He went after criminals the way you'd do something about a bad smell. It was instinctive. It was necessary. But this was something special, an inquiry that personal catastrophe had turned into a near obsession. Whatever happened, dead or alive, he had to find Hennessey. Just to get his own back on life. He was still a copper, for fuck's sake. He could still bait traps, match motive to opportunity, back the bad guys into a corner and watch them destroy themselves. That's what two decades of CID work had taught him. They were the craft skills he took from job to job. There'd never been a situation he hadn't turned to his own advantage. Never.

Outside, in the car park, he phoned Nikki McIntyre's number on his mobile. At length, a male voice replied.

'Captain McIntyre. How can I help you?'

There was an edge of impatience in the question. It was getting late. There was an etiquette here, unspoken rules. Winter explained his interest. He was investigating the disappearance of a man called Hennessey. He had some questions to ask Nikki McIntyre. Where might he find her?

'You won't,' the voice said. 'Talk to me instead.'

'About Hennessey?'

'Indeed. You're a policeman, you say?'

'A detective. CID.'

'Excellent. Nothing will give me greater pleasure.'

Faraday sat in the restaurant, towards one end of the long table, slowly getting drunk. Conversation ebbed and flowed around him, little eddies of gossip and laughter, and he let himself float along, not really caring where the evening led. For once, he was well and truly off the leash.

He'd been attending the French language course all year, ten months of Wednesday evenings out at the city's sixth-form college, barely a mile from where he lived. He'd signed up for a good practical purpose: to improve what little French he possessed to the point where he could visit his son in Caen and risk a conversation with the woman he now showed every sign of wanting to marry. Communicating with J-J himself had never been a problem. Sign language, plus a private vocabulary of deeply personal gestures, had proved flexible enough to cope with anything they'd ever wanted to say. But talking to Valerie was an altogether trickier proposition. She'd learned enough sign to get through to J-J, but her English was far from perfect and she had a natural reluctance to risk much of her real self in a language she didn't really understand. Up to Faraday, then, to meet her at least halfway.

He seized a new bottle of red wine and began to replenish the glasses around him. He'd started the evening classes with some misgivings, not at all sure that he'd be able to cope, but to his surprise he'd felt immediately at home with the mixed bag of largely mature students who'd also turned up. The job rarely lent itself to excursions like these, uncontaminated by the demands of a particular inquiry or investigation, and he'd found himself relishing the chance to plunge into other people's worlds on the basis of nothing more than a shared adventure.

There was a guy who restored furniture for a living, over in Hayling Island, and made frequent trips to France to buy various bits and pieces in village auctions. Another bloke was a motor mechanic who wanted to jack it all in and swap his lock-up behind Fratton Road for some tumbledown ruin in Normandy. A third student, a woman this time, had a lifetime's ambition to read *Madame Bovary* in the original French. They were all friendly, all good fun, all down-to-earth, and their lives took place way outside that circle of wagons Faraday and his colleagues drew up around themselves. Within a month or so, Faraday had found himself looking forward to Wednesday evenings. By Christmas, these people all felt like good friends.

'*Encore du vin?*'

'*Bien sûr. Pourquoi pas?*'

There was something else, too, that had come as no less of a surprise. Far from being intimidated by the challenge of French, Faraday had positively revelled in it. He loved its subtlety and its strangeness in his mouth. He loved the precision with which the course tutor, herself French, insisted it be used. And most of all he loved the linguistic jigsaws he was slowly able to put together, not just shop-dialogue or the kind of French you used on a waiter, but oral descriptions of places he loved, of things that moved him and, of course, of birds. *Rossignol* was absolutely perfect for the nightingale. Just the sound of the word would send him to sleep with a smile on his face.

Month by month, his fascination for the language had grown. For Christmas, Ruth had bought him a serious dictionary. By February, he'd been turning out half-decent pieces of written work. He still wasn't quite ready to tackle Valerie, but the gradual discovery of the pleasures that awaited him at the end of the hard grammatical slog was a constant incentive to learn more. He was used to piecing together jigsaws. That was what detection was about. But the difference with French was the places it took you, the destinations that beckoned. A decent bit of detective work would often leave you in the heart of darkness. French, on the other hand, seemed flooded with light.

In the restaurant, Faraday was seated opposite a Spanish woman, Marta. She'd confessed from the start that her interest in French was purely social, a way of getting to meet new people in a city that could be tough going for outsiders, and she'd made no secret that she fancied Faraday.

She was a vivid, good-looking woman in her late thirties with a wonderfully stylish dress sense, and the social arabesques she wove had become the talk of the class. She was always the one to suggest a drink in the pub after Wednesday classes, just to unwind, and when one or two of the married men mistook her flashing eyes for a come-on, Faraday had been fascinated by the ease with which she played them. To his near certain knowledge, no one had laid a finger on her. Yet at least three members of the class, none of them stupid, were convinced she was besotted by them. It was a game at which she excelled, and part of her charm was the fact that it remained so totally innocent. Faraday knew this because she'd told him. Married men, she said, just weren't her style. Faraday, whom she'd ringed as single, most definitely was.

The meal broke up around eleven. There'd been the usual swapping of addresses and talk of a class reunion as soon as the summer was over, but now the crowd had melted away, leaving Faraday at the kerbside, looking vaguely for a cab. One sped past on the other side of the road, ignoring his outstretched hand, and he was on the point of using his mobile when a car drew up beside him. He recognised the low shape of the Alfa Romeo. It was Marta's.

She lowered the window on the passenger side and leaned across.

'Get in.'

Faraday did what he was told. The inside of the car smelled exotic. Leather and a perfume so subtle it had to cost the earth.

'How much have you had to drink, then?' he asked her.

'Very little. I don't need drink.'

It was true. Faraday had watched her in the pub. Most nights she limited herself to a single glass of wine, a sip at a time.

'I'm pissed,' he announced. 'My apologies in advance.'

He looked across at her for a moment, realising what he'd said, then started laughing. The laughter lasted the length of Copnor Road.

'Did I really say that?' he kept asking her. 'Was that really me?'

She just grinned back. She wanted to know where he lived. She needed directions.

'By the water,' he said, 'I live by the water. With the birds.'

'Comment?'

'Les oiseaux. Partout.'

'C'est vrai?'

'Oui. Absolument.'

She glanced across at him. She'd glimpsed the blackness of the harbour beyond the end of the road. They were nearly there.

'I like you drunk,' she said. 'Even more.'

She parked outside the house, looking up at the stars

and taking deep lungfuls of the warm night air. Faraday was having difficulty with the front-door key. After a while, he felt a hand on his.

'Here,' she said.

The door opened. By the time his hand found the light switch, she'd shut the door. Hearing the sound of the bolt sliding across, he looked at her with some surprise.

'Fine,' he mumbled. 'Why not?'

She led the way upstairs, pausing to look at each of Janna's photos in the spill of light from the hall.

'Who took these?'

'My wife. A long time ago.'

'You're divorced?'

Faraday shook his head. 'She died.'

They were on the top landing now. Marta found another light. The door was open to Faraday's bedroom, but she moistened a finger and held it to his lips.

'A moment,' she said.

Faraday got undressed, holding onto the corner of the wardrobe for support. Down to his pants, he felt the light press of her body behind him. He turned round. She was naked. She kissed him softly, then sank to her knees, slipping his pants off, smiling up at him.

'In France they do this first.'

Much later, waking up again, Faraday remembered the videos he'd watched, the stuff that Addison put together, and he bent over Marta, trying to rouse her with a whisper. She'd wanted to know what pleased him, what turned him on, which way he fancied next, and she'd brought a frankness and a sense of wild abandon to his bed that he'd never once managed with Ruth. There was nothing this woman wouldn't do, literally nothing, and what made it all the more enticing was the fact that she so obviously enjoyed the role she'd cast for herself.

She awoke with a tiny start, her big brown eyes staring up at him. When he explained a second time, she nodded, her teeth white in the darkness.

'Why not?' she murmured.

Dawn Ellis was asleep when her mobile began to ring. She rolled over, fumbling among the debris on the carpet beside the bed. According to the big alarm clock, it was 0248. Shit, she thought. Night call-out.

'Yes?'

It was a voice she dimly recognised, a male voice, very Pompey. He spoke slowly, spelling it out. He had a proposition to put to her. It was a proposition that she'd find incredibly attractive, a proposition that might put a lot of money her way.

Dawn was up on one elbow now. Jimmy's, she thought. The guy with the dangly little number nine.

'What is it? This proposition?'

'We need to talk.'

'We are talking.'

'Face to face, I mean. Ring me tomorrow.'

He gave her a number. She was to call him in the morning, any time, and they'd fix to meet. His place or hers, he didn't care. He had nothing to hide. All he was offering was a chance to better herself.

'Know what I mean?'

Dawn was still looking for a pen. Bastard things were never there when you needed them. Finally, she found the stub of a pencil.

'Just give me that number again,' she murmured. 'I missed it.'

Thirteen

Thursday, 22 June, 0800

Marta had gone by the time Faraday awoke. He felt for her body the way a blind man might, his hands reaching out in the expectation of warm flesh, but the bed was empty and the only evidence he could find of her presence was his own clothes, neatly folded on the chair by the bedroom door. He got up, knowing at once that it was going to hurt. The sun was already high and the dazzle of light from the harbour spiked the inside of his skull.

Downstairs in the kitchen, swallowing his second glass of water, he caught sight of the note. She'd retrieved an old envelope from somewhere and scrawled a mobile number on the back. 'Call me', she'd added. 'Before lunch'.

Call me? Faraday, still naked, gazed out of the window at the spot where her car had been. He'd built an entire working life on the painstaking assembly of evidence and he found himself doing it now, amazed at how little he really knew about her. She lived somewhere out beyond Fareham, in the sprawl of suburbs that stretched west towards Southampton. She had a dog called Gaudi, a spaniel of some kind. She had a job at IBM at the big headquarters up at North Harbour, something moderately high-powered. She drove a sexy car with immense panache. And she was great in bed. About everything else – her private life, her friends, whether or not she had any kids – Faraday was literally clueless.

He filled the washing-up bowl and plunged his face in. The shock of the cold water made him gasp, but the thunder in his head began to quieten and he managed a couple of slices of toast without throwing up. The pleasures of nights like that were distinctly double-edged. The sex was brilliant because it had been so long coming, but the hangover was brutal because you just weren't used to it. Reasonable trade-off, though. And long overdue.

Back upstairs, he checked his watch, then began to dress. This morning there was another session with Hartigan and the senior management team, the second of the week's visits to Planet Make-Believe, and the last thing he needed was one of those reproving silences that followed a late entrance. On his way out of the house, back in the kitchen looking for his car keys, he spotted the photocopy of the accident report that had come down from Accident Investigation in Winchester. Marta must have been taking a look at it because it lay open at one of the location photographs that showed the whole scene. Goodbye Fairyland, Faraday thought. Welcome to real life.

Prentice's Vectra had come to rest at a slight angle across the road, leaving a trail of broken glass from the shattered front headlights and indicators. The bonnet of the estate car had folded upwards, distorting the frame around the windscreen, and the windscreen itself had become dislodged. The Fiesta lay some ten metres down the street, spun backwards by the impact. The front of the car had virtually ceased to exist and there were gouge-marks in the tarmac where the gearbox and engine outriggers had scored the road surface.

Faraday gazed at the image, aware of the blood

pulsing to his head again. He'd been through the report a number of times now, trying to follow the calculations Accident Investigation had made. They had started with the available evidence and worked backwards. They had used computer software and measurements of distortion in the body shells to calculate relative impact speeds. They had done complex sums around something called momentum exchange to reconstruct exactly what had happened. Taking into account a margin of error of three per cent, they'd sworn by the accuracy of their figures. Which was just as well, because that was exactly what the court would require them to do. And their conclusion?

Faraday closed the report and slipped it into his briefcase. Matthew Prentice had been travelling at fifty-three miles an hour when he'd killed Vanessa Parry. There'd been no skid marks on the road, and to Faraday this was the conclusive evidence. The guy had been on the phone, checking some figure or other in the file the young traffic cop had retrieved from the car. Prentice had had the mobile in one hand and a biro in the other and he was probably steering with his knees. Whether or not he'd looked up before smashing into the Fiesta was immaterial. Average response time in a situation like this was a second and a half. At 23.6 metres a second, he could have been thirty-five metres away and been able to do absolutely bugger all about it.

Faraday closed his eyes a moment, fighting the hot gust of nausea bubbling up from his stomach. Life, in the shape of Marta, had suddenly been kind to him, but those last few seconds, from where Vanessa sat, didn't bear thinking about.

Dawn Ellis was a couple of minutes away from

Southsea nick when she remembered that Rick Stapleton had a couple of days off. Somehow, among all the grief about abstractions and lack of cover, he'd managed to persuade Faraday to honour a long-ago promise. His partner's fortieth birthday was tomorrow. Rick had lots of time off stacked up and he wanted to make the occasion special.

The house that Rick shared with his partner was in one of the leafy Thomas Owen crescents in the heart of Southsea. They'd only been there since Christmas, but Dawn already felt she knew the place inside out. Sharing a car on one of the more tedious surveillance jobs, Rick would agonise for hours about the choice of wallpaper for the upstairs lounge, or the aesthetic consequences of favouring whisper grey over string beige when it came to offsetting the pastel shades in the larger of the two bathrooms. To Dawn, whose interest in decorating began and ended with the B&Q catalogue, this kind of talk was a joke, but it was altogether typical of Rick that he should have plunged in with such gusto. The day he bought himself a year's subscription to *Traditional Homes* was the day she knew he was hooked.

The house lay in a terrace of five, with big pillared entrances, tall sash windows and ornate wrought-iron verandas on the first floor. When Rick came to the door, he was wearing an apron flaked with prawn shells and looked harassed.

Dawn was grinning.

'Aren't you going to invite me in?'

Rick stepped back without a word. After the heat of the street, the house felt almost sepulchral: cool greens in the spacious reaches of the hall, beautifully framed pictures on the wall, extravagant stands of flowers in tall Chinese vases and a glimpse of a carpeted staircase winding grandly upwards. The contrast with the suburban chaos Dawn normally associated with the domestic side of CID life couldn't have been more marked. No wonder so few of Rick's colleagues had ever made it past the door.

Rick led the way downstairs. The basement seemed to extend for ever, as carefully thought-out as the hall, and Dawn found herself in a huge kitchen at the back of the property. The terracotta tiles on the floor looked new and the room was flooded with light from a pair of big glass doors that opened into an exquisitely landscaped garden.

Rick was obviously in the middle of preparing something elaborate. A long pine table was covered in baking trays, and there was a big heap of discarded prawn shells on yesterday's copy of the *News*. Rick's partner, Callum, ran a legendary French restaurant down in Old Portsmouth, but the fact that the man had been cooking most of his life wouldn't have put Rick off for a second. Competitive as ever, he'd have bought himself a handful of books and set to.

Dawn was looking at the cafetière bubbling softly on the Rayburn. Under pressure, Rick could get incredibly crabby, but she asked for coffee just the same.

'Help yourself,' he grunted, mashing several cloves of garlic and scraping the results into a blender.

'Expecting company?'

'Coupla friends.'

'How many?'

'Forty-five, give or take.' He frowned with concentration, adding yoghurt and a spoonful of spices to the blender.

'Tonight?'

'Tomorrow.' Rick waved a hand at a line of casserole

dishes, carefully sealed with clingfilm. 'This lot goes in the chiller. Along with everything else.'

'What's that, then? The Baden Powell school of cookery?'

'Very funny.'

Dawn poured herself a mug of coffee. She wanted to talk about Shelley Beavis.

'That's work.' Rick was chopping spring onions now. 'How fucking dull.'

'Not to me.'

She told him about the encounter at Jimmy's and the late-night phone call that had followed, repeating the dialogue word for word. The rhythm of Rick's chopping began to slow.

'What's all that about, then?'

'I don't know. But I'm going to find out.'

She explained her need to build a better case against Addison. He was looking across at her, one hand still on the blender, impatience written all over his face. As far as he was concerned, the Donald Duck thing was history. They'd nicked Addison, dredged up loads of evidence, and the rest was down to the lawyers. The mask alone should put him away.

'What if he didn't do it?'

'He did,' Rick said shortly. 'You obviously weren't listening.'

'I thought I heard him say he didn't do it.'

'You did, love. How rude of me not to believe him.' Rick was washing watercress now, shaking each sprig out over the sink. When he'd finished, he turned to face her again. 'Look, where is this getting us? Only, I'm really busy.'

'It's getting me a date with my new friend.'

'Are you serious? You're really going to meet this guy?'

'That's right. That's why I'm here.'

Rick gazed at her a moment longer, trying to work out whether she meant it or not, then began to shake his head.

'No way,' he said. 'There's absolutely no fucking way I'm getting involved.'

'I just need back-up, that's all.'

'You're right.'

'You needn't actually meet him. Outside will be cool. Nearby. Whatever. It's your call. You choose the time.'

'You're talking *today*?' He flapped a hand at the dishes around the kitchen. 'What am I supposed to do here? Just abandon it? Just walk out? This is supposed to be a *surprise*, love. Callum's back this afternoon. Three. Just after. I've got all this to do, plus two other courses, all before three. Tonight we're going over to Bosham. Friends.'

'Just after three, then. Perfect.'

'But *why*? What makes you so sure we've got it wrong?'

'Shelley. The girl.'

'What about her?'

'There's shitloads of stuff she's not telling us. And most of it has to do with Addison.'

'Yeah? And just how can you be sure about that?'

Dawn looked at him a moment, then dipped a finger in the yoghurt mix and licked it dry.

'Womanly intuition.' She gave him an extra-big smile and then nodded at the apron. 'Half-three be OK? Give you time to change?'

Ronald McIntyre, Nikki's father, lived in a handsomely converted barn on the edge of the village of Meonstoke, tucked away in the Meon Valley north of Fareham. Winter parked his car on the curve of gravel in front of the barn and took a moment to admire the view. A newly mown lawn stretched down to the river where a couple of ducks, in convoy with their young, were paddling slowly upstream. On the other side of the house, a sizeable kitchen garden featured a stand of runner beans and several lines of tomato plants. In the little window beside the front door, someone had stuck up a poster for the forthcoming village fête.

Winter got out of the car, smelling the sweetness of the air. Joannie would have loved this, he thought, realising that his choice of tense had already consigned her to the grave.

Ronald McIntyre was a thin, erect, troubled-looking man in his late sixties. His hair, combed straight back, was beginning to curl over the collar of his shirt and his blotched face suggested a serious interest in alcohol. Despite the weather, he was wearing a heavyish blazer, badged with some kind of naval insignia.

Sherry in a cut-glass decanter was already waiting on a silver tray in the lounge. Winter stood in the window while McIntyre poured two glasses. The view stretched down to the river and up to the soft green folds of chalk downland beyond. The ducks, Winter noted, had gone.

'What's your interest in Hennessey, Inspector?'

Winter accepted the promotion with the faintest of smiles and explained about the scene in the Marriott hotel room. McIntyre listened attentively, taking tiny sips of sherry in between nods. Winter, who preferred sitting to standing, wondered why this man was treating the encounter like a cocktail party. He'd rarely met anyone so insistently formal.

'A lot of blood, you say? In the bathroom?'

'Fair amount.'

'Good.' He offered Winter a small, chill smile. 'Couldn't happen to a nicer chap. Here.'

He led Winter across the lounge. Among the collection of framed photographs on top of the grand piano were half a dozen of a striking-looking girl with a lovely almond-shaped face, a near-perfect mouth and a cap of very black hair. Looking harder, Winter could see McIntyre in the tilt of her chin. The same determination not to be bested, the same sense of an answer readied for a question yet to come.

'Nikki,' he announced bleakly.

The photographs charted Nikki's progress from childhood to her mid-twenties. She'd shed weight early on. She liked horses. And, in what seemed to be the most recent of the shots, she'd acquired an admirer in the shape of a thickset young man in a polo-neck sweater with glasses and an uneasy smile.

'Married?'

'Boyfriend. Local chap. Young farmers club. Never really liked him, to tell you the truth.'

Winter was peering at the other photographs, most of which featured McIntyre himself in a variety of foreign-looking locations. He was wearing naval uniform in all of them, and as the face aged, the gold braid became heavier.

'Captain by the finish.' McIntyre reached for one of the bigger frames. 'Not a bad life.'

'You ever miss it?'

'To tell you the truth, Inspector, yes. It hasn't been a picnic lately, believe me.'

Over a second sherry, still standing, McIntyre told Winter the story of his last few years. The account was strangely clipped, as if he'd been reading it, each succeeding crisis carefully tagged with a date. It sounded more like a briefing than a chunk of someone's life, and it slowly dawned on Winter that this formality of McIntyre's was nothing more than an attempt to reimpose control on something that had obviously gone so catastrophically wrong. Join the club, Winter thought grimly, accepting a third glass of Tio Pepe.

Nikki had been just nineteen when she was first referred to Hennessey. She'd gone to her GP with severe period pains. The GP could find nothing obvious and had referred her to the gynaecological specialist at the local hospital. Hennessy was the best, he'd assured Nikki. And so she'd bought herself a consultation.

'We were on BUPA,' McIntyre explained. 'Had been for years.'

Over the next seven years, Nikki had undergone eleven operations at Hennessey's hands. All the operations had been private, the bulk conducted at the Advent Hospital up in London where the man appeared to have some sort of deal. Each operation had come with the promise that it would be the last, that it would rid Nikki of pain, and after each operation the pain had got worse. By the time her twenty-sixth birthday had come round, Hennessey had robbed her of her uterus and one ovary. On two occasions, through gross negligence, she'd nearly died. In the opinion of another surgeon, only last year, none of Hennessey's operations had been either effective or even necessary. They had, of course, been back to him, demanding an explanation, but he'd refused even to meet them. From the man who'd wrecked his daughter's life, not one word of apology, not a single hint of regret.

McIntyre nodded, his eyes swimming with alcohol. His wife had walked out several months ago, unable to bear it any longer, another casualty.

'He's wrecked our lives,' he said bitterly. 'He's wrecked our lives, and I see absolutely no evidence that he's ever given it a second thought. Can you believe callousness like that? Can you?'

'They can be bastards,' Winter said at once, 'I agree.'

McIntyre appeared not to have heard. He was staring out of the window, his knuckles white around the empty glass, and Winter had a sudden vision of just how purposeless this man's existence had become. He'd bang around all day in this house, furiously trying to distract himself with the garden, or arrangements for the village fête, knowing all the time that nothing could supplant what had gone, what had been taken from him.

'Where's Nikki now?' Winter asked.

'Jersey,' he said stonily. 'And that's another thing.'

'What's another thing?'

'She never comes back. Never writes. Rarely even phones. She might be in touch with her mother. I've no idea. It's true what they say about grief, you know. It doesn't bond people at all. It isolates them.' His voice trailed off, then he pulled himself together, fixing Winter with one glassy eye. 'Terrible thing, grief. Drives you mad in a way. Turns you into someone else.'

Nikki, as far as he knew, was trying to make it as a singer in some big hotel on the seafront in St Helier. She'd always been good at music. She'd thumped around on various instruments since she was a kid, and it was her mother who'd first realised that she might have talent. Her teacher in those early days had brought her along in leaps and bounds, and McIntyre had been only too pleased to invest a chunk of his Navy gratuity on a grand piano. To be honest, he'd rather hoped she might make something of a mark in the classical repertoire, but kids are kids and she'd chosen another route. She wrote her own stuff, her own lyrics, her own music, and the last few years, thank God, she'd started to earn a bit of money for herself on the club circuit.

'People say she has talent. In fact, people say she's very good.'

'You haven't heard her yourself?'

'Never.' He was looking at one of the photos. 'But then she's never asked me.'

Winter made his excuses and left soon afterwards. The sherries had gone to his head and he wanted to get back to the bungalow, sort himself out, make a few phone calls. On the doorstep, in the bright sunshine, he shook the outstretched hand. McIntyre evidently popped down to Pompey a good deal in the evenings. There was a pub he liked by the Camber Dock. Maybe they could meet again, have a drink or two.

Winter nodded, aware again of how lonely this man was, and how broken.

'I'm really sorry about your daughter,' he said. 'You wouldn't wish that on anyone.'

McIntyre gazed sightlessly down towards the river.

'Apparently she's as beautiful as ever,' he muttered, 'on the outside.'

Hartigan asked Faraday to stay on after the senior management meeting. Faraday watched the uniforms filing out of the office, his heart sinking. He owed Hartigan a paper on crime prevention initiatives they might be able to launch in the Portsea area, and so far he'd done absolutely nothing about it.

To his relief, Hartigan appeared to have forgotten about the Portsea proposals.

'Gunwharf,' he said briskly. 'Tonight.'

'Sir?'

'There's a get-together I want you to attend. Tour of the site first, followed by' – he frowned, reaching for a letter on his desk – 'a light buffet supper and a chance to meet the team. Harry was coming with me but had to pull out. Sorry about the short notice.'

Harry Barnes was Hartigan's Chief Inspector. Still struggling with the aftermath of last night, Faraday could think of no good reason for refusing. Not that he intended to let Hartigan off without a fight.

'Is this straight PR, sir? Or do I have a choice?'

'Straight PR, Joe. And no, you don't.' His finger was already on the intercom button that summoned his management assistant from the outer office. 'Well done for the Donald Duck business, by the way. A result, I understand.'

Dawn Ellis phoned the number Lee Kennedy had given her from the car. The mobile at the other end appeared to be switched off because all she got was the roar of a large crowd. '*Pompey Play Up!*' went the recorded message, '*Play Up Pompey!*' She hesitated a moment, realising she didn't have an address, then began to leave a message, but the moment she began to speak a voice she recognised interrupted. The same gruff Pompey mumble.

'Knew you'd be on. When do you fancy a meet?'

'Half-past three. Not into small talk, are we?'

'No point, love. We know what we're about, don't we?'

It was a statement, rather than a question, and as she confirmed the North End address Dawn began to wonder about Shelley again. Was this the way he'd talked her into bed? With the number of a house and a promise that she wouldn't regret it? Or was there something a little less blunt, a little less brutal, going on here?

'OK, love? Three thirty?'

'Sure.' She might have been making a dental appointment. 'And it's Dawn, by the way. Not love.'

Winter was back at the bungalow in Bedhampton by lunchtime. He'd bought a Big Mac and fries from the drive-in at Cosham and he ate them at the kitchen table, Hennessey's files spread around him. The conviction that he was driving an inquiry, exploring avenues, putting various leads together, was deeply comforting. For one thing, it gave him a purchase on the anger that had come with the news of Joannie's cancer. He wasn't helpless any more, he wasn't a pawn in the hands of the bastard medics; on the contrary, he was doing something about them. Plus – a real bonus – the spread of the paperwork across the kitchen table kept the emptiness of the bungalow at bay.

Reaching for his mobile, Winter keyed in the 1471 number he'd retrieved from Hennessey's New Forest cottage. When the number answered, it proved to be a nursing agency in central London. Winter announced he was phoning on behalf of Pieter Hennessey. The name prompted an immediate transfer to the accounts department. Hennessey, it appeared, was way behind on the settlement of invoices for the hire of theatre staff. Might there be some early prospect of payment?

Winter heard himself apologising profusely for the delay. He was a friend of Hennessey's. There'd been an unfortunate burglary. The thieves had got away with all kinds of stuff including, alas, the briefcase containing the invoices. Might the agency send down duplicates? He gave his own address for despatch, adding that Hennessey had abandoned the New Forest cottage for somewhere a little less remote.

'Burglary,' he explained. 'Amazing how many people it affects like that.'

The conversation over, Winter turned his attention to the other number. The last place Hennessey had phoned from the cottage was the marina at St Helier. St Helier was in Jersey, and so was Nikki McIntyre, a fact that Winter's CID years refused to ascribe to coincidence. He'd operated on this girl no fewer than eleven times. He'd never once got to the bottom of what was wrong with her, but he'd clearly never tired of trying to find out. Just what that might suggest in terms of motivation was anyone's guess, but a very good place to start might be Nikki herself. Here was someone infinitely younger than the bulk of Hennessey's victims and her loss, for that very reason, was all the more profound.

Winter gathered up the debris of his lunch and reached for his mobile again. Directory Enquiries took him to the information desk at Southampton airport. There were five flights a day to Jersey. Winter checked his watch.

'Book me on late afternoon,' he said. 'I'll pay when I pick up the ticket.'

Fourteen

Thursday, 22 June, mid-afternoon

Dawn Ellis and Rick Stapleton took separate cars to the North End address. Salamanca Road, like the rest of the city, had been built for an age when car ownership was the exception rather than the rule, and the unbroken lines of parked vehicles on both sides did nothing for Rick's temper. His prawn vol-au-vents had been a disaster. Now he'd have to dream up something else to tickle forty-five discerning palates.

'So where do we park?'

He was talking to Dawn on the mobile. Dawn was fifty metres ahead of him, cruising for a space. Eventually she found a couple. Four streets away.

'You'll have to come back on foot,' she told him, bending to his lowered window. 'Here's too far to stay in the car.'

'So what am I supposed to do? Blend?'

'Whatever it takes.' She peered down at him. 'Just as long as you keep listening.'

The arrangement, much practised, was simple. Dawn had wired herself with a mike and a radio transmitter. The transmitter would stay in her jeans pocket, with the mike already built into a specially adapted mobile which she'd link-clip to the waistband of her jeans. The mike would be transmitting from the moment she walked up to Lee Kennedy's front door. Rick would be half a minute away, monitoring the conversation through an earpiece. As long as she kept her jeans on, as he rather acidly pointed out, the loop was foolproof.

Rick shrugged, parked his car and joined Dawn on the pavement. Once they'd tested the transmitter, he accompanied her as far as the corner of Salamanca Road.

'Number forty-five,' she pointed out, 'yellow door.'

She left him buried in the bits of yesterday's *News* that had survived the prawns, and crossed the road towards Kennedy's house. The curtains were drawn in the big bay window upstairs. Bad sign.

She rang the bell, wondering why she didn't feel nervous. She heard feet clattering down a flight of stairs, then Kennedy was holding the door open, inviting her in. He was wearing tennis shorts and a Lacoste top. His feet and legs were bare and lightly tanned. He had the legs of an athlete, leanly muscled, little whorls of blond hair, and the slow smile spoke volumes about how much he enjoyed her eyeing them.

'Come in,' he said. 'I won't bite.'

To her surprise, the house felt comfortable and lived in. There was a newish sports bike propped in the hall, drop handlebars and thin wheels, with a rolled towel bungeed to the rack at the back. Through a half-open door at the end of the hall, she glimpsed a kitchen. It looked clean, well equipped.

'Something to drink?'

'Please.'

'Cappuccino again?'

Despite herself, she was impressed. This man remembered what she'd been drinking in Jimmy's. Not a complete fuckwit, then.

She followed him into the kitchen. A big fridge with a clear-glass door was stocked with every kind of booze: lager, beer, wines, plus three kinds of vodka.

'Thirsty man.'

'Not me, love. I don't.'

'Not at all?'

'Never. Fruit juice, mainly orange. Boring, innit?'

'Thirsty friends then?'

He didn't answer, busying himself instead with a huge, chrome Gaggia coffee machine that dominated one corner of the kitchen's beechwood surfaces. She watched him at work. His hands, like his feet, were big. Long fingers. Clear, unflecked, well-shaped nails.

Dawn looked round, wondering who else was in residence.

'None of you work, then?'

'None of who?'

'You. And whoever else lives here.'

'What gave you that idea?'

'About working?' She nodded at a couple of tennis racquets, propped by the door. 'This time of day? Just in from the courts?'

'I teach the game,' he said simply. 'It's one of the things I do.'

On his own, without Shelley, Lee Kennedy might have been a different man. The banter, like a radio, was turned down. He was subtler, altogether more human.

'That call last night,' she began. 'Do you often phone complete strangers in the middle of the night?'

'Yeah, since you ask.'

'Why?'

'Because I felt like it. And because I knew you'd be exactly right.'

'Right for what?'

He smiled at her, and for a moment she thought he was going to make a move, but he was simply readjusting himself slightly, fitting his long body into the angle between the fridge and the wall.

There was a pinboard on the wall, covered with newspaper cuttings. Photos of a footballer featured in a couple of them, action photos from some game or other. The shots were too small for her to be sure about the face, but the number on the shirt was clear enough.

'Is that you?' She gestured at the board, 'Number nine?'

'Yeah.'

'Football too, is it?'

'Yeah. June's my month off. The rest of the year I'm a pro-footballer.' He opened the fridge with his foot and reached in for a carton of juice. 'Do you know anything about football?' His eyes didn't leave hers.

'Nothing, I'm afraid. Does that make me very stupid?'

'Not stupid, no. Not when we can't even get a result against bloody *Romania*.'

He shook his head, more pity than anger, enquiring whether she'd watched England dumped from Euro 2000 a couple of weeks back, then shrugged when she said no.

'I don't blame you. Pathetic, it was. Worse than pathetic. They played like wankers, all of them. Fifty grand a week? You have to be joking.'

He smiled his secret smile again, and Dawn suddenly remembered the intro on his recorded message tape, the roar of a huge crowd . . .

'The Pompey Chimes,' he explained when she asked. 'You're telling me you've never heard of the Pompey Chimes?'

'Should I have?'

'Yeah, you should, living here. It's a city thing. The football doesn't matter. It's the Fratton End. Anyone'll tell you that. Even Shel.'

'Is that who you play for? Pompey?'

'No.' He shook his head as he handed her a steaming cappuccino. 'I went close once, a while back, then I got scouted. Gillingham. Half a season at Brighton. Then back to the Gills again. I was only a kid, but I thought I was Pele.' He paused. 'Pele?'

Dawn's laughter was genuine. Try as she might to reinterpret them, the vibes were anything but menacing. The guy was happy to chat.

'Brazilian,' she said. 'Even I know that.'

'OK, then. Gillingham isn't Santos. And I wasn't Pele. That's the point I was making. Not that it mattered then. I was in dreamland.'

'And now?'

'Doc Martens League. Number five last year. Old Trafford it ain't, but I still get paid.' He nodded, refusing to take the conversation any further.

Dawn lifted the cup to her lips, realising she'd forgotten all about Rick. The cappuccino was delicious.

'Do you mind if I ask you something?'

'Go for it.'

'Shelley's face. Was that your doing?'

'She told you I lumped her?'

'No. She didn't tell me anything. I was just wondering, that's all.'

Kennedy thought about it for a moment or two, then nodded.

'Yeah,' he said simply. 'That was me.'

'Can I ask why?'

'Because she pissed me off.'

'How?'

'Don't ask.'

'Do you lump every woman who pisses you off?'

'No, not normally. It was just' – he shrugged – 'a spur of the moment thing.'

'Not your fault?'

'Oh, no, definitely my fault, definitely. It's just . . .' He frowned, as if genuinely puzzled. 'I dunno really. She was there one minute. The next, I'd smacked her.'

'Wouldn't be booze, would it?' Dawn nodded at the fridge.

'Definitely not. Coffee OK?'

'Nice, yeah.' She looked around at the neatly folded tea towels and the rack of spotlessly clean washing up. A woman's touch. Definitely. 'What's the deal here?' she asked at last.

'Deal? There isn't a deal.'

'Yes, there is. You phone me in the middle of the night and you tell me you've got a proposition to make.'

Kennedy looked briefly pained.

'You're telling me you don't want it?'

'Want what?'

'A fuck.'

'Is that the proposition?'

'It's part of it, yeah.'

'So what's the other part?'

'That depends on you.'

'On how good I am, you mean?'

'Yeah.'

Dawn couldn't help smiling. She'd been propositioned dozens of times in her life, but never like this. Filling in a form would have been more romantic.

'What about Shelley?' she enquired. 'Doesn't she count in all this?'

'No.' He shook his head. 'She's cool about it. Every time.'

'OK, then.' Dawn gestured towards the draining board. 'What about your wife? Your partner? Whoever lives here with you?'

Kennedy looked at her for a moment, then burst out laughing.

'You think there's someone else lives here? You think I can't run a plate under a tap?'

'All this is yours?'

'Yeah, and mine alone. That's the beauty of it. Listen' – he took a tiny step towards her, easing a stiffness in his lower back – 'I've got a proposal. This afternoon happens to be shit. Not a good idea at all. You've got my number. You know the address. When you've worked out whether you fancy it or not, just give me another ring. I meant it about the money, by the way. You'd be a right little earner, you would, and if you want to bring someone else with you next time, a mate, feel free. Bloke or bird, makes no odds.' He grinned at her again, 'Fair play?'

Not long afterwards, back at his car four streets away, Rick was incandescent.

'I gave up half my afternoon for that drivel?'

Dawn put a finger to his lips. She was genuinely grateful he'd minded her back. She wanted him to know that.

'And you're telling me it was worth it?' he insisted.

She was still thinking, still letting the pieces swirl around in her head.

'He's running a business there,' she said at last. 'The bad news is we'll have to go back.'

Rick was staring at her.

'*We?*'

Paul Winter was in Jersey by that evening. From the airport, he phoned a DC in the St Helier CID office he'd done business with before, keeping an eye on luxury cars stolen to order on the island and shipped into the Portsmouth freight terminal aboard sealed containers. The guy's name was Steve Brehaut, but the girl in the office said he was away on a job in France and wouldn't be back until the weekend. Winter thought for a moment about going through the proper channels but decided against it. Talking to the management might mean a referral back to Faraday. Quicker, safer, to play private eye for the evening.

He took a taxi into St Helier. The driver dropped him at Tourist Information where he waited impatiently behind a small queue of Germans before explaining his problem to the girl behind the counter. A friend's daughter was singing at one of the local hotels, big place, somewhere on the seafront. Her name was Nikki, Nikki McIntyre. Might she appear on a poster or in publicity for the hotel? Might there be a quick way of running her to earth?

There wasn't. The girl had never heard of her, but was happy to help in whatever way she could. Minutes later, Winter left with a handful of hotel brochures and a map. The seafront stretched away before him, around the long curve of the bay. The first six enquiries were useless. Most hotels assumed their clientele would be sixty-plus and supplied entertainment to match. Then, as the office blocks and seafood restaurants began to give way to winding drives and shuttered houses, Winter found her.

The hotel was called L'Abbaye. Tucked away behind thick stone walls and a frieze of silver birches, it had an intimacy and a sense of quiet good taste that suggested serious money. The woman behind the reception desk studied Winter over a pair of pince-nez glasses before confirming that Nikki McIntyre did indeed entertain guests there three nights a week.

'Tonight?'

'Indeed.'

'What kind of time?'

'About nine o'clock.' She raised an enquiring eyebrow. 'Will you be requiring a room, Mr . . .?'

Winter had been studying the tariff. A couple of nights at L'Abbaye cost more than a season ticket at Fratton Park.

'I'm staying with friends,' he said. 'Would you happen to have a number for Nikki?'

'I'm afraid not, sir. We're not permitted to give out information like that. As I say, nine o'clock. I'd advise you to get here earlier than that, though. High season, we tend to be pretty busy.'

'She attracts a big crowd?'

'Thursdays are certainly popular.' She offered Winter a quiet smile. 'Especially with the menfolk.'

Minutes before Faraday's tour of the Gunwharf Quays site was due to begin, he took a call on his mobile. He was stuck in traffic at roadworks outside the main dockyard gate, a Strauss waltz on the radio, trying to get in the mood. The voice on the phone took him straight back to bed.

'Marta,' he said, 'I've been meaning to phone.'

'But you couldn't?'

'I left the number at home.'

'Really?'

She sounded slightly reproachful, as if they'd been lovers for months, and Faraday found himself wondering about the question of etiquette. What kinds of obligation lay at the end of a night like that? What on earth happened next?

Marta was talking about some concert or other at the city's Guildhall. She had a couple of complimentary tickets and no one to keep her company. The concert was on Saturday night. How did Faraday feel about coming along?

'I'll take a rain check,' Faraday said quickly. 'Saturday might be difficult.'

'You'll ring me? Tomorrow?'

'Definitely.'

The traffic began to move at last, and Faraday eased his way through the cones. He was curious to know how Marta had got hold of his number.

'You gave it to me, Joe.'

'Did I?'

'*Oui.* I thought detectives had fantastic memories.'

She rang off without bothering to say goodbye, and Faraday was left shaking his head. Just the sound of her laughter was enough to stir him.

At the Gunwharf site, he left the car beside a muddy encampment of portacabins and joined Hartigan in the headquarters building for a pre-tour brief. A young project manager bounced through a Powerpoint presentation and fielded questions from the couple of dozen invited guests, each of them carefully badged.

There were envoys here from companies Faraday recognised from the Gunwharf brochures: business development managers from Levi Strauss, Gap and Adidas, an events co-ordinator from the Crew Clothing Company, a pretty executive from Bar 38, as well as a smattering of the more go-ahead councillors and local government officers with whom Hartigan was clearly on first-name terms. These were business-orientated people only too familiar with the bigger numbers, and as the graph lines climbed ever higher on the screen, Faraday began to understand why Hartigan had been so keen to have him along.

A one-hundred-million-pound investment. A catchment area of 2.72 million people within an hour's drive. Underground parking for thousands of cars. World-class shopping. Dozens of pubs and restaurants. Malaysian cuisine. Pacific-rim cuisine. A fourteen-screen multiplex. An open-air amphitheatre. A twenty-six-lane bowling alley. Two hotels. In a city addicted to smoky pubs, snatched take aways and a helping or two of recreational on-street violence, this was a radical makeover.

Back outside, Faraday joined Hartigan to tramp around the site itself, listening to the project manager map out the vision that lay before them. The gigantic hole in the ground that would anchor the shopping and leisure complex. The muddy swamp that would become Millennium Boulevard. The dumper park where Vulcan Square would be. The plans, just finalised, that would transform a dry dock puddled with oily water into City Quay. And, over on the other half of the site, the stubby little forest of deeply sunk piles that would soon support the harbourside apartment blocks.

Hartigan was standing by the new seawall, gazing out across the water. The sun was beginning to dip towards the rooflines of Gosport. Yachts from one of the up-harbour marinas were slipping past on the ebbing tide. A warship, grey and sleek, was ghosting in through the harbourmouth, the whine of her turbines barely audible above the laughter that had greeted a joke about the nearby car ferry terminal. The top floors of Arethusa House, on the southern flank, would be barely a stone's throw from the top deck of the Isle of Wight ferries. Imagine those long Sunday mornings in bed with your mistress, one guest remarked, with a couple of hundred ferry passengers cheering you on.

Hartigan hadn't heard the joke. He took Faraday by the arm, conjuring up in his mind's eye the apartment blocks from the muddle of cranes, pumps and bright yellow dumper trucks.

'If I had a spare half a million,' he said, 'I'd be down here like a shot.'

Only yesterday, Faraday had caught a rumour that Hartigan was preparing the ground for some kind of private policing deal with Gunwharf, and now he realised that it was probably true. Over in Kent, the Bluewater Centre was paying serious money for the exclusive attentions of a sergeant and half a dozen uniforms. On-site crime was largely plastic – credit-card fraud – but the Kent posse were invaluable as a training resource for the security staff and kept a high profile for the benefit of shoppers. Faraday's vision of police work had never extended to flogging his services to commercial bidders, but Hartigan was a different kind of animal. He could sense the way the commercial winds were blowing. And he knew that offering headquarters a modest profit on a six-figure policing deal would do him no harm when it came to the next promotions board. Partnership was an elastic concept. As Hartigan kept pointing out.

Minutes later, the party made its way to the show flats already completed on one corner of the site. The penthouse apartment at the top had its own lift, and Faraday emerged onto waxed parquet flooring to be greeted with champagne and canapés. Now came the softer sell. No more figures, no more graph lines, simply the chance to admire the developers' taste in soft furnishings and ovenproof tableware, and to fantasise that all this, one day, might just belong to you.

Faraday was still gazing out at the view when he felt a hand on his arm. It was the deputy editor of the *News*, a thin, intense thirty-something who never tired of daring life to take him by surprise. He'd been meaning to give Faraday a ring since yesterday. Nicking the Donald

Duck flasher sounded like a definite result. Faraday nodded, giving nothing away.

'We'll see how it goes,' he said.

'But a bloody academic, eh? Who'd have thought?'

Faraday hesitated a moment, knowing only too well where this conversation might lead. The last thing he was going to provide was the filling for one of the *News*'s feature supplements, and the arrival of the woman who headed the developers' residential sales team gave him the perfect opportunity to beat a retreat. He allowed her to take him by the arm. She wanted to show him a state-of-the-art kitchen.

'It's Liz, by the way,' she added, 'Liz Tooley.'

They talked for a while about the way sales were going. The apartments were released in batches. The first release had prompted queues round the block, would-be buyers prepared to camp out all night for the chance to put down their thousand pounds and secure a foothold in this wholly transformed, new-look Portsmouth. Already, she said, the options had become negotiable assets, changing hands at a sizeable premium, proof-positive that communities like these were the shape of things to come.

'Communities?' Faraday couldn't keep the smile off his face. '*Communities?*'

'Of course. Why on earth not?'

Liz Tooley swept on. Demand for the top-end properties, she said, was overwhelming. At half a million a pop, she was beginning to wonder whether they might even have underpriced them. And why? Because people were buying more than the view, more than the latest in designer chic. They wanted gated entry systems, exclusive access, electronically controlled gates on the undercroft parking areas. They wanted security locks and smoke alarms and centrally monitored intruder detection. Their investment was in peace of mind. They wanted, above all, to feel *safe*.

'You mean protected.'

'Exactly.'

'And you think that's realistic? Or even possible?'

'Of course it is. That's why you're here, Mr Faraday.'

The challenge was blunt, a reminder that nothing came for free, and Faraday turned away, swamped by a sudden anger, staring out at the lights mirrored on the blackness of the harbour. The city, with all its rough imperfections, lapped at the walls of this new development. So far, Gunwharf's security headaches had been limited to the theft of materials from the building site, but there'd soon come a point when they'd have to sort out exactly who this gleaming lifestyle vision was for. Would closed-circuit TV and smart doorlocks really keep the inner city where it belonged? Or were they prepared to face the social consequences of building paradise next door to one of the most deprived urban areas in the country?

'Call for me and it's probably too late,' he murmured. 'We're the guys who clear up afterwards.'

'Not true.'

'I beg your pardon?'

Liz shook her head, as vehement as ever. Faraday's guys had already been more than helpful. In fact, they were priceless.

'Like who, exactly?'

'Like Pete. Pete Lamb.'

Pete, she said, had been helping them out on the sales side, running checks on potential buyers, tidying up one or two of the dodgier applications, making sure that the punters could deliver what they'd promised. She'd passed his name on to her colleagues in the commercial operation. Access to someone with Pete's experience was a big, big bonus.

'Nice guy, too.' She spotted someone else, and began to move away, flashing the last of her smile at Faraday. 'Don't you agree?'

Nikki McIntyre was already at the piano by the time Winter got back to the hotel. A solitary meal at a Chinese restaurant in the maze of streets behind the seafront had gone on much longer than he'd anticipated, chiefly because the bloody waiters couldn't tear themselves away from serving the bigger tables. He'd have walked out had he not been so hungry, though in the end the food had been as crap as the service.

Now, in the hotel's cavernous basement-bar, he leaned against a pillar studded with tiny mirror tiles, transfixed by the figure at the keyboard. She was smaller and slighter than Winter had imagined. She wore black jeans, beautifully cut, and a simple black T-shirt. The cap of black hair had grown to shoulder length and the whiteness of her face was offset by a slash of crimson lipstick. Everything about her spoke of harshness, and hurt. If you'd spent seven years in the hands of a man like Hennessey, Winter thought, this is exactly what you'd look like.

He ordered a double Scotch from the tiny bar and took up another vantage point on the other side of the room. From here, she was in profile, her upper body moving slowly in time with the chords of the song, back and forth, utterly mesmeric. She sang wistful, bluesy ballads, perfectly scored for a slightly breathy voice that occasionally surged for a particular lyric or chord, and the longer she played, the warmer grew the ripples of applause that greeted each new song. Oddly enough, she appeared not to care about the audience. On the contrary, she seemed totally apart, totally oblivious, occupying a small private space she'd made her own, and as each song developed she seemed physically to grow, raising her eyes from time to time with a look so distant, so unnerving, that Winter could sense the stirrings around him. This is what you do when life lets you down, he thought. This is the bid you make for sanity.

None of the songs was announced, but towards the end of her one-hour set, she bent forward, her lips brushing the microphone.

'This is for a friend of mine,' she murmured, 'who died.'

Winter watched, following every movement of her hands, every dip of her head, remembering the little march of photos across her father's grand piano. The plump baby in the apple orchard. The shy ten-year-old aboard her pony. And now this, the chalk-faced survivor with a lifelong debt to call in.

The song came to an end, to more applause. Nikki got to her feet and closed the lid on the keyboard. Winter managed to intercept her as she hurried towards the stairs.

'That was incredible,' he said.

'Who are you?'

'The name's Winter.'

She seemed unsurprised.

'You're a policeman.'

'CID.'

'Whatever. My father rang. Have you got a pen?'

She gave Winter a mobile number and suggested he ring if he wanted to talk. Not tonight. Tomorrow maybe.

'Lunch?' Winter suggested.

She shrugged, ignoring the sea of watching faces.

'Ring me,' she repeated. 'And we'll see.'

Kids from the neighbouring estate, out late on the patch of wilderness by the beachside fort, were the first on the scene. They circled the burning car in the darkness, shrieking with excitement at each new yellow spurt of flame, fascinated by the way the fire seemed to strip the thing of flesh, licking at the seats inside, reducing the body to nothing but a shell, black against the dancing reds and yellows. Excitement smelled of spilled petrol and melting rubber. One of them legged it back to the flats to dial 999. All they needed now was the fire engine and ambulance and a couple of police cars. Then it would be just like the telly.

Fifteen

Pete Lamb was still at home in his new flat in Whitwell Road when the doorbell went. Looking down from the bay window, he recognised the car at the kerbside and the greying cap of tightly curled hair at the door. Faraday. How did he find me? he thought. How did he know where to come looking?

'You get this address from Cathy?'

'Your mum. Her number's on file. I said I was a friend. She was nice enough to believe me.'

They were upstairs now, standing uncomfortably in the big sunny lounge. Faraday didn't want coffee. Didn't want anything. He knew about the moonlighting job and the cosy little channel Lamb had opened up for himself on the Gunwharf job. He knew where it led and who else it involved. And he knew, above all, that his first call should have gone to headquarters.

A breach of regulations this wide was meat and drink to the Professional Standards Department, but formal notification would mean curtains for more than Pete Lamb. Cathy, too, would lose her job. Not only that, but if she'd been silly enough to run a name or a vehicle registration through PNC on Pete's behalf, she could land herself a prison sentence.

'Cath's doing a great job,' he grunted, 'in case you were wondering.'

Pete was still trying to work out what Faraday was doing here. Social calls just weren't his style.

'Glad to hear it,' he said.

'It isn't easy, believe me, especially when you haven't done it before.'

'I bet.'

'Stressful.'

'Yeah?'

'And sometimes tricky to get the balance right. Conflicting interests. All the time.'

Faraday was inspecting a row of paperbacks in a bookcase by the window. Most of them were nautical, a mix of well-thumbed yachting thrillers and colourful accounts of round-the-world voyages.

'Keeping yourself busy?' he enquired lightly.

'So so.'

'Never bored?'

Faraday turned to face him. One glance confirmed that Pete Lamb had begun to catch the drift of what he was really saying, but he knew he had to be careful here. The moment Pete realised for certain that he'd sussed the jobs he was picking up from Gunwharf, then Faraday himself would be implicated. DI on division might be the job from hell, but there were days when Faraday rather liked it, and the last person he intended to hazard his own career for was Pete bloody Lamb.

Pete was explaining the way he spent his time. Bimbling around mostly, plus the odd excursion afloat. Faraday stepped very close. He wasn't interested in this thin tissue of lies. Neither had he very much time for a man who'd put his wife's future on the line. What concerned him more was hauling Pete back from the brink, before he lost his balance and took Cathy with him.

'Policing's changed,' Faraday said softly. 'Do you

know that? It's just PR now, a lot of it, PR and all kinds of other bullshit. The right paperwork, the right connections, the right outcomes. You know how I spent last night? Banged up in some poxy penthouse being nice to a bunch of developers. And you know why? Because some ambitious prat wants to fast-track himself upstairs. I can eat a plateful of oysters with the best of them, my friend, but you know what really sticks in my throat? Finding out from other people, estate agents for fuck's sake, what's really going on.' He paused, his face inches from Pete's. 'We kiss these people's arses because they smell of money. And just look where it gets us.' He turned away for a moment, a touch on the brakes, then he was facing Pete again. 'Cath tells me you're training for Cowes Week. Is that right?'

'Well, training sounds a bit formal.'

'Then maybe it should. Maybe training's what you need. Lots of it. Every fucking day. Are we speaking the same language here?'

There was a long silence. Finally, Pete cleared his throat. He looked shaken.

'Do you want to know about Hennessey? Only—'

'Bollocks to Hennessey.'

'Only it's Cath's job, isn't it? Her patch? Up at the Marriott?'

Faraday fought the hot gusts of anger welling up inside him. Pete, as reckless as ever, was offering a trade. Information in return for Faraday's silence. Pathetic. He was in close again, close enough to smell the bacon on Pete's breath.

'Uniform was called to a torched Mercedes last night,' he said. 'I won't bore you with the details because I expect Cath'll tell you anyway.'

'Tell me what?'

'About the chassis number. It's badly deformed, but

my money's on Hennessey. It's right what people say, you know. You want a result, you leave it to the professionals. OK?'

Without waiting for an answer, Faraday turned on his heel and left the room. At the door on the top landing, he glanced back. Pete was right behind him.

'Shame,' Faraday said softly. 'You might have made a decent copper.'

Winter spent the latter half of the morning at the St Helier marina, several acres of wooden pontoons and gleaming yachts. The marina offices were under siege from a small army of visiting skippers, all of them with one problem or another, and when Winter finally managed to corner the guy who seemed to run the place he got nowhere with Hennessey's name. The guy might or might not have phoned. A walk up and down the pontoons would tell Winter whether he was here at the moment, and while he might have booked ahead, or stayed recently, late June was no time to be combing through the records. If the guy had a mobile, why not phone him?

None the wiser, Winter made a last precautionary check on the pontoons. Pete Lamb had given him a mobile number for Hennessey, but the bloody man never answered it. Without the name of a yacht, or even a description, he knew he was reduced to relying on a chance sighting, and with only a video surveillance still and a couple of photocopied mug shots from the newspapers to go on, even then he was riding his luck. Towards noon, with time pressing, he jacked it in. On the phone, Nikki had stipulated half-twelve for lunch and he still hadn't a clue where the restaurant was.

It was a Thai place, wedged into the ground floor of a tall, narrow, sturdy-looking building that must once have been a warehouse of some kind. Winter managed to get a table at the back, set slightly apart, and he stood up the moment Nikki stepped in from the street. She was wearing a lightweight leather jacket, black again, over a grey T-shirt, and she didn't appear to have changed the jeans. With any luck, thought Winter, she might give him another song.

The Chardonnay he'd ordered was already a third down. She nodded when he pulled it from the cooler, and then cupped the full glass in her hands the way a child might if she was very, very cold. In daylight, she was even more striking: wide blue eyes in that same almond-shaped face, eyes that never seemed to blink, eyes that looked right through you. When Winter introduced his interest in Hennessey, she simply nodded. Her father had been through all this already and she'd help him any way she could.

Winter, keen for her to see him making notes, took her back to the beginning: her referral from the GP, her first dealings with Hennessey, the endless trips to London, the interminable examinations, the way he was so sure he could rid her of pain.

'But he didn't,' Winter pointed out.

'No, but I didn't know that then. This thing was a learning curve and I was at the bottom.'

'Did you like him? Get on with him?'

She shook her head. Her glass was already empty.

'Liking him wasn't in it. You don't go to church because you like God, do you?'

'He thought he was God?'

'No, I did. I was nineteen, twenty. He was the big man up in Harley Street, the man everyone said was the best. Sometimes I used to think he had a little package, like a present, in a drawer in that big desk of his.

There'd be a cure in it, for me, and as long as I was good it would all turn out OK.'

'*Good?*'

'Polite, you know. Respectful. Know my place. Lie back. Open my legs. Do what I was told. The last thing that crossed my mind was whether I liked him or not.'

Winter's pen slowed and then stopped. There was a question here, an important question.

'Do you think he liked you?'

Nikki was looking at the bottle. Winter didn't move. At length, her face creased into a smile and she nodded.

'Yes,' she said. 'I think he liked me very much.'

Cathy Lamb intercepted Faraday in the car park at Southsea nick before he had had a chance to make it to the entrance door at the back of the building. Faraday could tell she'd been waiting for him by the expression on her face. Pete Lamb's been on to her already, he thought, and she's driven down here to sort it out.

'Get in the car,' he told her.

He returned to the Mondeo and unlocked it. Parked in the sun, the temperature was already beginning to climb inside.

Cathy was about to unpack all the baggage she'd brought down from Fratton, get it all off her chest, but Faraday beat her to it. She'd lied to him about her one-time husband. And lying was the last thing he expected from someone with her kind of ambition.

'You're an acting DI, for God's sake, Cath. This force relies on people like us. Not just all the service performance targets crap, but stuff that matters. Pete's a lunatic. First he gets pissed and nearly blows someone away. Then he gets suspended on full pay and promptly sorts himself a job. What's he got? Some kind of death wish?'

'He's bored,' she said stonily. 'Needed something to do.'

'Yeah, and you told me he was sailing, getting ready for Cowes Week. Do you know what really hurts? Not him busting the regulations. Not even him touting for a bunch of estate agents. No, what really hurts is the fact that you lied. To me.'

'I had to.'

'*Had* to?' He stared at her.

'Yeah.' Cathy turned her head away and began to wind down the window. 'If I'd been straight about it you wouldn't have known what to do.'

'How come?'

'It would have been awkward, split loyalties. So I thought it best, you know, to gloss it a bit.'

'To lie.'

'Yeah.' She nodded, looking at him at last. 'To lie.'

There was a long silence. Faraday thought of all the things he wanted to say. That she'd taken him for a prat. That she'd laid herself wide open to compromise. That she'd started a sequence of events she couldn't control. That the clatter of falling dominos would haunt her service record for years to come. That she could have ended up selling shampoo in Boots. That she could have ended up inside. Instead, he dealt with it in the only way he knew would really hurt her.

'Willard wants me to take over the Hennessey inquiry,' he said coldly. 'The SOCO's still sorting out the Mercedes and I'll have a squad put together after lunch. It's just as well you're here because one of the things I'll need to do is debrief Winter. As long as he's up for it.'

Cathy stared at him. Her mouth had compressed into a very thin line and she was fighting to contain her temper. Finally, she snapped.

'Shall I tell you why I really did it?'

'Did what?'

'Pulled Pete in? Took advantage? Because this job's not just hard, it's fucking near impossible. You might have forgotten about legwork, about getting out there, about putting whispers about, but I haven't, thank God, and neither have people like Winter. If sitting in an office put villains away, we wouldn't have any criminals left. If paperwork took care of it, we'd all be in the fucking West Indies by now, lying on some beach and getting pissed all day. But it doesn't, does it? It's the paperwork and the regulations you have to box off. Otherwise we'd be dead in the water. You know it and I know it. Only difference is that I've done something about it.'

'Is that some kind of explanation?' Faraday reached for the door handle. 'Only I'm really busy.'

Cathy ignored the sarcasm.

'Another thing,' she said hotly. 'Hennessey's the first bit of decent crime to come my way. And now you've stolen it. Just the way I knew you always would.'

Faraday glanced across at her. She was practically shaking with rage.

'You don't lie to friends, Cath,' he said quietly, 'not if they mean anything to you.' He began to get out of the car, then paused. 'And it's not theft, by the way. Just a reassignment.'

Nikki McIntyre was drunk. The second bottle of Chardonnay, which Winter had barely touched, had filmed her eyes and brought a strange animation to her manner. Her upper body dipped and swayed over the bowls of *haw mok* and *pla chien*, in much the same way as she'd addressed the piano, and when Winter pressed her for details, she became almost voluble.

'He never wore gloves,' she murmured, 'not once.'

'Didn't you wonder why?'

'Of course I did. But it's horrible asking questions like that. I thought there must be some good medical reason. I could hardly insist, could I?'

'Why not? You were paying, weren't you, or at least BUPA were? That makes you the client, doesn't it?'

'Yes, but client is the last thing you feel. That's not the way it works with Hennessey. You're his patient. You've been referred. You're his property, his chattel. He's the top man. He's in sole charge. And he makes bloody sure you know it.' She lifted a chopstick and poked at a glistening hillock of mangetout. 'It sounds medieval, and in many ways it is. You're forever on the receiving end, and if it hurts, then too bad. Your duty is to shut up. You never make a fuss.'

Winter nodded, scribbling down another note, struck by her use of tenses. This experience of hers was so vivid, so real, it might have happened only hours ago.

Nikki was talking about Hennessey's little jokes. Winter reached for the Chardonnay and refilled her glass.

'Jokes?'

'He used to make me these promises. One was about babies. He said I'd always be able to have babies. The other promise was about my play pen.'

'Play pen?' Winter was pursuing a sliver of fish.

'Here.' Nikki gestured below the table cloth at her lap. 'How he'd always treat it with the respect it deserved. How lucky I was to have one so beautiful.'

Winter looked up.

'He *said* that?'

'Every time.'

'Did it go any further?'

'Of course. He examined me.'

'Without gloves?'

'Yes, and every time – *every* time – he insisted on an operation.'

'Then and there?'

'Absolutely. He used to get me up to the hospital, the Advent, for consultations, but every time it would end in the operating theatre. I think he must have had the theatre pre-booked. It got so I'd automatically pack my overnight case every time. He made a joke about that, too. Me and my little case. Like I was his girlfriend on some sordid date.'

'And these were serious operations?'

'Serious enough to need anaesthetic.'

'Did he explain them? Justify them?'

'Not really. Information wasn't something he was ever really into. He probably thought I was too thick to understand. No, he just went ahead and did whatever he did.'

'And this went on for . . .?'

'Seven years.' She offered Winter a small, bitter-sweet laugh. 'You're talking to the world's expert on ankle stirrups and those dilator things. Ever wondered how vulnerable that might make you feel? Someone like Hennessey poking around inside you?'

'But you stayed with him,' Winter pointed out. 'You put up with it.'

'Of course.' Nikki shrugged. 'But then he was a doctor. And doctors are people you can trust.'

Winter looked away for a moment. He'd phoned Joannie in Hove first thing this morning, just to check how she was getting on. Her mum had taken the call, explaining that Joan wasn't too good. Rough night. Little sleep. And a constant, nagging pain in her tummy. She hadn't gone as far as spelling it out, but the inference was plain enough. Her daughter should be tucked up at home under proper medical supervision. Not abandoned by a husband too busy to care.

'Doctors can be bastards,' he said softly. 'Take it from me.'

Nikki gazed at him, seeming not to understand. The nod was automatic. He might have said any bloody thing.

'This Hennessey,' he continued, leaning forward, trying to get her to concentrate, 'have you seen him at all recently? Heard from him?'

She gave the question some thought. Then she shook her head.

'No.'

'Are you sure?'

'Positive. I'd remember that, wouldn't I?'

Winter imagined she would, but wasn't happy with the answer. There was something in there, something opaque he couldn't penetrate. He tried again, mentioning Hennessey's interest in the marina. Had he ever talked about having a yacht?

'Never. He went to the races. He talked about that all the time. But not boats, no.'

'And he hasn't tried to get in touch with you? The last couple of weeks?'

Nikki threw back her head and laughed.

'Socially, you mean? For a chat about old times?' The laughter died. She leaned forward, suddenly intense. 'There's a guy you ought to talk to, Mr Detective. My poor old dad might have mentioned him, I don't know, but I'm going to write down his name for you. You'll find him in the big hospital in Portsmouth, the QA. He saved my life after the last time Hennessey had a go at me. I'd come back home from London. I had a pain like you wouldn't believe. I was screaming half the night. I was climbing the walls it was so bad. The GP put me in an ambulance and got me down to the hospital and this guy sorted me out. Go and see him. Ask him what he found. And then ask him what it adds up to.'

Winter watched her reach for his pen and pad and scribble down a name. Alan Ashworth.

'And you're still telling me you haven't seen Hennessey since? You're absolutely sure about that?'

'I'm telling you, I'd see him in hell first. That man is evil. He's been inside me. He's robbed me. He's pillaged me. Bits of me have gone for ever, Mr Detective. I can't tell you what that feels like.'

Winter, slightly chastened, reached for the bottle again, but it was empty. Then he turned back to Nikki, struck by another thought.

'That song you did last night. Who was the friend who died?'

Nikki stared into her glass.

'Me,' she said softly.

Sixteen

Friday, 23 June, afternoon

Faraday finally got to see Willard shortly after lunch.
The Detective Superintendent's office lay in the Major
Crimes Suite, a heavily secured first-floor complex at the
rear of Fratton police station. Five-digit locks barred
entry to the suite, home to a sizeable task force of
specially selected detectives who devoted themselves
exclusively to long-running major crime investigations.
To warrant the attentions of these men, you had to have
murdered, raped or got yourself involved in a serious
drugs or robbery scam.

A posting to a Major Incident Team was regarded as
a top career move by many detectives, a chance to
escape the treadmill of volume crime, but Faraday had
never fancied it. All detection boiled down to teamwork
and co-ordination, but blokes on the MITs of Faraday's
rank, DIs, rarely had the kind of freedom that came
with the job at divisional level. Instead, wrestling with a
stranger rape or a complex drugs case, they would
inevitably be reporting to a senior investigating officer
like Willard himself. Not that Faraday had anything
against Willard as an SIO. He simply preferred running
his own squad, drawing up his own battle plan, and if
that meant missing out on quality crime, then so be it.

Willard had just come back from a civil unrest
exercise over at the big force training HQ at Netley. In
an earlier phone conversation about Hennessey, he'd

agreed that they were now looking at a missing-person inquiry and asked Faraday to take formal charge. While the surgeon's disappearance didn't yet justify investigation by an MIT, it did need someone of Faraday's experience at the helm. Cathy Lamb was doing a terrific job in the northern part of the city, but dumping this on her would be a lousy use of resources.

'Agreed?'

Faraday nodded, thinking of Cathy in the car park. At full throttle she could be very impulsive, and Faraday had half-expected her to get to Willard first. For the fact that she obviously hadn't, he was deeply grateful.

'I talked to the SOCO about the Mercedes,' Faraday said. 'He's got the arson investigator down from Chepstow and they had a good poke through the residues. He's pretty confident about accelerants, but there's nothing in there to suggest a body. The thing was gutted come the finish.'

'House to house?'

'I've had blokes on the estate all morning. So far it's a blank. First most of them knew, the car was on fire.'

'And the kids?'

'Still at school. We've got names and addresses. We saw some of them last night.'

Willard, who made a speciality of doing at least two things at once, was looking at next week's duty rosters.

'How many bodies do you need, then?'

'Half a dozen for now, and we can blitz it. Hennessey has a house in Beaconsfield and another rented place in the New Forest. Then there'll be the consulting rooms in Harley Street and wherever else he worked.'

'I thought you said he was struck off?'

'He is, but it's pretty recent. In my view, we need to start at the beginning again, the Marriott, and work outwards. Winter's ahead of the game already, and I've told Cathy we'll need to debrief him.'

'She must love losing Winter.' Willard's eyes returned to the roster. 'She's down to the bone already.'

'I know. I thought Dawn Ellis might help her out. She used to work from Cosham, so she knows the turf. Mates with Cathy, too.'

Willard took off his jacket and hung it carefully on the back of the chair at the head of the long conference table. Down the corridor, Faraday could hear a burble of conversation as the troops massed for the next big meeting.

Willard was asking about Winter. Why the compassionate leave?

'Problem at home, sir.'

'The wife?'

'Afraid so.'

'The usual?'

'No.' Faraday shook his head. 'She's dying.'

Willard, in the act of stooping to retrieve a file from a drawer, paused. Dealing with sudden death was food and drink to a man like him, part of his job description, but Faraday had often noticed how different it was when death crept closer to home.

'Dying?'

Faraday nodded.

'Cancer,' he confirmed. 'We've given him seven days' compassionate and, under the circumstances, I think he's coping rather well.'

Winter was back at Jersey airport, waiting for his return flight to Southampton, by the time he put another call through to Joannie. Once again, it was her mother who answered, and this time she left Winter in no doubt about her real feelings.

'You should have been here, Paul,' she said at once. 'It's horrible leaving her alone like that.'

'But she's with you.' Winter was outraged. 'And anyway, it was her idea in the first place. Put her on. Let me have a word.'

'I can't.'

'Why not?'

'She's gone.'

'*Gone*? Where?'

'She went home this afternoon, around half-two. She didn't want any lunch or anything. She just decided and that was that. There was nothing I could say, Paul. She just called a taxi and off she went. Imagine how that made me feel.'

'And you're sure it's home she's gone to?'

'Positive. Where else would she go? In the state she is? Honestly, Paul, I don't know what's got into you. One minute you're—'

Winter cut the conversation off and checked his watch: 1639. The fast trains to Havant left Brighton on the hour. If she'd made the 1500, she might just be home by now. He dialled the number, letting it ring and ring, then did the calculation again. Maybe she'd missed the 1500. The state of Connex South, maybe they'd cancelled the bloody train. Either way, he'd put another call through as soon as he got to Southampton.

He glanced up at the departure board. The Southampton flight had yet to show a boarding gate. He pulled out the phone again, checking the number in his notebook. Nikki had told him that it was a direct line to the consultant's desk at the QA. This guy was obviously important to her, a tiny ray of sunshine after seven years on the butcher's slab.

Finally, the call was answered. It was the secretary again.

'DC Winter,' he announced briskly. 'Is Mr Ashworth back yet?'

Dawn Ellis was in the CID office talking to Joyce when Faraday returned from seeing Willard. Faraday signalled that he wanted a word, and she followed him down the corridor to the office at the end. Joyce had already been at the big wall board with the dry-wipes and had listed the four DCs and the DS who'd comprise the Hennessey squad.

The skipper would be DS Grant Ferguson, an ex-Met detective who'd recently joined the force after running out of patience with the hassle of living in London. Quite what he was making of leafy North End, as busy and traffic-choked as Walthamstow, was still a mystery, but Faraday liked his working style. Ferguson had originally come from Aberdeen and managed to combine a combative punchiness with a gritty acceptance that things were always in the process of getting worse.

On the wall board, Joyce had also added a schedule for regular update meetings and, in red, the code to be used on overtime forms. Earlier, Faraday had noticed the difference a whiff of grapeshot had made to her. An enormous tin of chocolate digestives and several cartons of Red Bull had appeared in a cardboard box beside the electric kettle. Here was a woman, he thought, who just loved the prospect of battle.

Dawn was eyeing the names listed on the board. When she was fed up, she had a habit of biting her lower lip. Just now, she'd practically drawn blood.

'Was Hennessey the bloke at the Marriott?'

'Yes.'

'I thought that was down to Cathy?'

'It was. There's been a change of plan. We found his car last night, burned out near the Hayling ferry.'

'So why has Cathy been bumped?'

'Don't ask. Winter's on compassionate at the moment. That's why I'm putting you up with Cath for a bit. It's not permanent. Just to help out for a week or two.'

Dawn affected indifference.

'Makes no odds to me, boss.' She shrugged. 'Shoplifting's shoplifting, wherever it happens. Why should I complain about missing out on something tasty when I've got all those scrotes in Paulsgrove to look forward to?'

Faraday wondered briefly whether she was joking, but one look at her face told him she wasn't. Not that he could do much about it.

'What about the current stuff?' he enquired. 'Anything major to clear up?'

But Dawn still wanted to know about Cathy. Had she resisted the boarding party? Was she happy to have Hennessey nicked from under her nose? Faraday ignored the questions.

'I was asking about loose ends,' he insisted. 'Anything I need to be aware of? Or is everything boxed off?'

Dawn finally abandoned the wall board. She had a small, private smile on her face that made Faraday feel briefly uncomfortable.

'Nothing worth worrying about,' she said.

The incoming flight from Jersey was late landing at Southampton, the result of an air traffic snarl-up, and it was nearly half-past five before Winter was able to try Joannie again on his mobile. The number rang and rang but there was no answer, and he was on the point of asking the neighbours to pop next door when his mobile began to trill. He checked the incoming number. It was Faraday.

'How's Joan?'

'OK. Not too bad.'

'Taking it easy?'

'Pretty much.' Winter was making for one of the exits. A Tannoy announcement on the concourse was the last thing he wanted Faraday to hear. 'Hang on, boss. I'm in the kitchen. Reception's terrible. I'll just go out in the garden.' Winter pocketed the phone. Outside, he hurried across the departures lane and into the car park, resuming the conversation once he'd caught his breath. 'That should be better. Can you hear me?'

Faraday told him about the burned-out Mercedes. The recovered chassis number had finally confirmed it was definitely Hennessey's. The call from the manager at the Marriott had turned into a misper inquiry. As divisional DI he was now in the process of putting a squad together.

'I've mustered five blokes,' Faraday said, 'but I'd appreciate a debrief.'

Winter's heart sank. The last twenty-four hours had enabled him to draw a bead on the missing surgeon and everything he'd learned about the man had confirmed his instinctive belief that something had happened to the guy. The fact that no one else was remotely interested had been a bonus. It kept the hunt private, just himself and Hennessey. He liked that. He liked the thought that this had become a purely personal vendetta, a form of intimate hand-to-hand combat untainted by paperwork. It permitted him a very special kind of freedom. And one day, maybe sooner than anyone expected, it might lead to a settling of accounts. Dierdre Walsh's account. Nikki McIntyre's account. And even, in some deeply important way, Joannie's account. But here, all of a sudden, was Faraday, the boss dog, about to piss all over his private lamp-post.

'It's difficult, guvnor,' he said.

'I know. This must be the last thing you need.'

Winter frowned, turning his back to shield the phone from the whine of nearby turbo-props. On the one hand, he needed to keep closing on Hennessey. On the other it was very evident that Faraday might get there first. Might there be some way he could dip in and out of the investigation? Strictly when it suited him?

'It's not just Joannie,' he said at last, 'it's her mum as well. She's staying with us now. You know how territorial they get.'

'And?'

'It's OK so far, no big deal, but there's going to be a problem when I start getting under her feet.'

'Meaning?'

'Meaning I might be more use to you. On the Hennessey job.'

Faraday didn't sound convinced. Three days' compassionate wasn't very much when your wife was dying.

'I know, boss, I know. All I'm saying is I'm up for it.'

'Up for what?'

'Hennessey. D'you mind if I discuss it with Joannie and bell you back?'

Faraday asked Joyce to sort out the briefing. Ferguson was already en route to Hennessey's New Forest Cottage, armed with a warrant to search the premises. If there was any sign of a struggle, Ferguson and his accompanying DC would be sending for a SOCO and digging in for the full forensic trawl, including the running of any prints through automated fingerprint recognition, the computerised system which included the stored prints of all police officers.

The other two DCs, meanwhile, were next door in the CID office, working the phones in a bid to get the

Beaconsfield uniforms organised. If the local guys up there could take a look at Hennessey's house, maybe even ask a question or two locally, it might go a long way towards eliminating the possibility that he'd gone to ground at home.

Joyce stood by Faraday's desk, translating his orders into busy little flurries of shorthand. Chances were that Ferguson wouldn't be back from Newbridge until late evening – even later if he had to call in a SOCO. The guys next door had a stack of other phone calls to make. Faraday himself was still awaiting a fuller report from the Mercedes search. Might not the briefing wait until tomorrow?

'Tomorrow's Saturday,' Faraday grunted.

'Sure. But the sheriff never sleeps.' She tapped her notepad. 'Or are you telling me we're headed for a Monday start?'

Faraday was looking at his wall board. At moments like this he felt like the high-wire act in some circus troupe, balancing available resources and overtime budgets against a particular set of demands. Misper inquiries were always tricky. A single phone call, and they could turn into a murder investigation. A chance sighting, and the subject might turn out to be alive and well, wondering what on earth all the fuss was about.

'Well, sheriff?'

Joyce was eager for a decision. Faraday couldn't make one. Apart from everything else, he'd rather been wanting to fence off the weekend for personal reasons.

'Anything nice?'

Faraday gazed up at her. There was a fine line between presumptuousness and friendship, but the distinction seemed altogether lost on Joyce. Maybe it's the fact that she's American, thought Faraday. Maybe, where she comes from, it's perfectly natural to turn your boss into your buddy.

'It's my birthday,' he said with some reluctance. 'I was thinking of popping over to France.'

'Hey, neat idea.'

'But that obviously depends . . .' Faraday nodded at the pad clutched in her hand, not bothering to finish the sentence.

She beamed down at him for a moment longer, evidently thrilled by the news that he was about to turn a page in his life, then backed out of the office. Minutes later, with Faraday busy on the phone, she was back with a large white envelope. She sealed it with a lick and left it balanced on the keyboard of his PC.

Faraday studied it while he finished his conversation. The Mercedes had been lifted onto a recovery vehicle and trucked to secure storage by a firm on Hayling Island. Among the items recovered from the residues in the footwell on the passenger side was seventy-five pence in coins and a tempered steel blade that just might have belonged to a surgical scalpel.

The conversation over, Faraday opened the envelope. Inside was a Larsen Far Side card featuring a field full of cows. 'I bought this for my nephew's birthday', Joyce had written, 'but I guess you beat him to it. I talked to Vodafone, by the way, and the number you need is 07772 456372.'

Vodafone?

Faraday looked up. Joyce was back in the doorway with her third coffee since lunch. She nodded at the card, scolding him for opening it a day early.

'Vodafone?'

'They rang this morning and tried to give me the run-around. They've got Prentice's account details but there's some kind of waiting list for print-outs. You have to sit tight and take your turn.'

Faraday was up to speed now. Vodafone had supplied Matthew Prentice's mobile. One look at his account would tell them whether he'd been on the phone when he killed Vanessa Parry.

'And this is the number he was phoning?'

'Yep.'

'So how come you got hold of it?'

Joyce, anticipating the question, was already grinning.

'The girl was American.' She handed him the coffee. 'We Yanks stick together.'

Winter was home by just gone six. He left the car in the street and tried the side door that led into the kitchen. If Joannie hadn't made it back, he'd drive to the station and wait for her there.

The side door was unlocked. Winter looked round the kitchen, calling her name, wondering whether she might be asleep again. The kettle was cold and the cat, winding itself around his ankles, appeared not to have been fed. He went next door, into the lounge, finding the television on but the sound turned down. His wife's slippers were on the carpet beside the sofa.

Winter turned towards the open door, raising his voice.

'Joannie? You here, love?'

Again, no reply. The front door was secured on the deadlock. Retreating back down the hall, he pushed softly at the bedroom door. The curtains were drawn against the early-evening sun but the little window at the top must have been open because he could hear the put-put-put of next door's sprinkler. He peered into the shadowed room, relieved to see the shape of Joannie's body under the light summer duvet. He whispered her name again but got no response. Asleep, he thought, stepping back into the hall.

For a moment, he thought about getting some food ready for when she awoke, then decided against it. What Joannie's mother had failed to suss was the state of her daughter's insides. She no longer took regular meals. Instead, at the oddest hours, she snacked on mush.

Back in the bedroom, he tiptoed across to the bed. Joannie lay on her side, her greying hair splayed across the pillow, her knees drawn up the way she always slept. Her breathing was very slow, the way you might breathe if you were in some sealed chamber way underground. Her lips were a strange shade of blue and there was a flecked white chalky deposit caked in the corners of her mouth. Winter, looking at her, felt the first faint stirrings of panic. He'd been in situations like this before. He recognised the symptoms, knew where clues like these might lead.

They kept all the tablets in a cabinet in the bathroom. Joannie had the middle shelf, a carefully sorted collection of painkillers, sinus tablets and sleeping potions, lately supplemented by heavier prescription drugs. Winter stared at them now, not knowing quite what he was looking for. Anadin? Ibuprofen? He could see neither.

Beside the bed, he bent down to Joannie and began to shake her, gently at first, then with more force. Her body felt floppy and sack-like. No matter what he did, he couldn't rouse her.

'Joannie? Shit...'

On his hands and knees, he began to search under the bed, looking for a discarded bottle of pills, a note, anything. The other side, his side, was also empty. He fumbled for his mobile, dialling 999, asking for an ambulance, still hunting for whatever it was she'd taken. Only when the operator was checking his address did he find what he was looking for.

He'd pulled back the duvet and the sheet. His wife's thin body was curled protectively around a small white plastic container. The label read PARACETAMOL: 40 tablets. The container was empty.

At the hospital, hours later, Winter was still sitting beside Joannie's bed. The ICU staff kept appearing to check the drips and the monitor read-outs, but Winter barely registered their presence. Outside, he thought it was getting dark. Inside, in the very middle of him, it was pitch black, an inky nothingness that seemed to have put the future beyond rational calculation.

Instinctively, he knew why she'd done it. In her place, had he been brave or desperate enough, he might well have tried something similar. But that wasn't the point. The point was that by giving life a nudge, by accelerating the inevitable, she'd forced Winter to acknowledge what awaited him. Now, or later, he'd be totally alone. There was no way round it, no escape. It was Joannie slowly dying by his side, but it was more than that. It was the whole of his adult life, the whole of that long sequence of minor and major betrayals he'd turned into a twenty-four-year marriage. He didn't feel remorse. He didn't regret that he'd never apologised for not making life sweeter for her. It wasn't about that at all. It was about him. And about what came next.

Past midnight, with the doctors worrying about the possibility of brain damage, he phoned Faraday. He'd never felt so cold in his life.

'Me,' he said, when Faraday answered. 'Winter.'

'What's the matter?'

'Nothing. That squad of yours. Count me in.'

He was still looking at Joannie. Her face was grey against the whiteness of the pillow. She gave a little sigh – regret, perhaps, or maybe even amusement – and then her breathing resumed the same slow rhythm, the trace lines barely spiking against the black of the overhead monitor screens.

Seventeen

Saturday, 24 June, morning

Half-awake, Faraday was still dreaming about the lamp-posts. They were brand new, a boldly modern design, street furniture to garnish the city's huge harbourside restoration scheme. Already they'd appeared in Old Portsmouth, eyecatching lines of them. The lamps themselves were hung from crescent-shaped supports, bolted to the upward slash of the post, and each lamp was topped with a glass filter, the deepest blue, so that every night the harbour was necklaced with tiny jewels. In the paper, they'd said that the filtered light was visible from the moon, something to do with the colour frequency, and Faraday half-believed it because the effect after dark was so magical.

Colour was the key. The blue of the jewels and the white of the lamps stole into this dream of his, a squad of lamp-posts on the march, implacable, terrifying, locked together in perfect formation. On Hot Walls, the fortifications overlooking the approaches to the harbourmouth, they paused beside Tower House for a conference. Dawn was approaching. The clouds were pinked with the rising sun but it was still chilly. Faraday hid behind the thick stone battlements, desperate to catch what they were saying, desperate to find out whether he'd been seen. Haunted by a lifelong terror of rats, he felt a scuff against his shoe and peered down in the half-darkness. Nothing. Then he heard a sigh, and the beginnings of laughter, and when he looked up again he found himself staring at a lamp-post, the white light in his eyes, barely feet away.

He awoke at last, fumbling for the alarm clock. Six o'clock exactly. Late. He lay motionless for a minute or two, ridding himself of the nightmare, then padded through to the bathroom and doused his face in cold water. Joyce had managed to organise a briefing of sorts last night and he knew there was little he could add to the Hennessey inquiry until the crop of current actions yielded some kind of harvest. Ferguson, his DS, had searched the New Forest cottage. He'd called out the security firm to disable the alarm before forcing an entry, but found nothing to warrant a Scenes of Crime operation. Sour milk in the fridge and a pile of post on the door mat suggested that the place hadn't been lived in for a while. The neighbours next door were out, but the folk across the road hadn't seen Hennessey for nearly a week.

Only at the village pub did inquiries turn up a positive lead. Hennessey had booked himself one of his regular rides at a local stables for Thursday morning, but had failed to turn up. The owner of the stables had been concerned enough to try his mobile, but several calls failed to get through. Armed with the mobile number, Ferguson had commissioned urgent inquiries but was still awaiting a response from Cellnet.

Faraday's other DCs, meanwhile, were pursuing inquiries in Old Portsmouth. Already, at the Sally Port, they'd drawn a blank. Staff at the hotel confirmed that he often stayed, but no one seemed to have seen him for at least a week. Pete Lamb, to Faraday's disgust, had been right. Once he'd left the Marriott, up in the north of the city, Hennessey had simply disappeared.

The postman came at a quarter to seven. Faraday, still wrapped in a towel, sat in the kitchen sorting through the half-dozen envelopes. The fact that there was nothing from Ruth wasn't really a surprise – she seemed to regard birthdays, including her own, with total indifference – but more hurtful was the total absence of anything with a French stamp on it. Maybe J-J had muddled up the date, he thought. Maybe there's been a strike or something over in Caen. Maybe the card's with the rest of the mail on the midday ferry and won't be delivered until Monday.

He didn't know, and wished he didn't care, consoling himself with a double-rasher bacon sandwich and a retreat upstairs to his study, where his second-hand coastguard binos, mounted on a refurbished stand, awaited him in the big picture window. For a while, he did his best to bury his disappointment among the turnstones and oyster catchers feeding on the foreshore below, but the thought of his absent son wouldn't go away. What was he up to? How was he coping? Had Hennessey not gone missing, Faraday would be on the ferry now, en route for Caen and a surprise weekend visit, but as it was he was trapped by the ongoing inquiries, obliged to wait at the end of a telephone in case anything important turned up.

A cormorant settled on a distant piling, spreading its wings to dry, and Faraday reached for the focus ring, wishing it hadn't been one of J-J's favourite birds. As a kid, he'd gone through a phase of drawing cormorants on the big flip-charts that Faraday occasionally liberated from the CID stationery cupboard. The best of them, a wild confection in mauve and green Pentel that made the birds look positively prehistoric, still hung on his study wall.

Nearly an hour later, motionless at his scope, Faraday

heard a car pull up outside. Moments later, someone was ringing at the front door. It was Marta. She stood in the sunshine in a pair of denim shorts and a Prada T-shirt. Her hair was tied up in a twist of scarlet and she was carrying a large present, flamboyantly wrapped in lime-green paper.

'*Bonne anniversaire*,' she said, kissing him. 'Happy forty-second.'

Faraday, astonished, invited her in.

'How did you know?'

'I asked your age the other night. You told me. To the day.' She kissed him again. 'You don't remember anything, do you?'

It took Winter most of the morning to get a home number for Alan Ashworth. He was still at the hospital, still haunting the long corridor outside the intensive care unit, but from time to time he'd take little excursions down in the lift and out into the sunshine, making calls on his mobile, grateful for the chance to think of something else beside Joannie. This morning the ICU staff were more optimistic about her chances. Her vital signs were better, they said. She was still unconscious, but there was definitely an agreement that she'd pull through. Be nice to have her back again, they seemed to be saying. If only for a couple of months.

It was the woman who ran the press office for the hospital trust who finally came through with Ashworth's number. Winter knew her from way back, an inquiry about a serious Saturday-night assault in the A&E department, and this morning he'd played the CID card again in his determination to trace the consultant who'd saved Nikki McIntyre's life. Normally, decisions to release home numbers could only come from way up the management tree, but on this occasion, at Winter's suggestion, the press officer rang Ashworth herself and secured his consent. He lived out in Denmead. He was off sailing after lunch but could spare Winter a couple of minutes if he got up there smartish.

Ashworth was in his back garden when Winter arrived, a tall, fit-looking man who pushed the mower up and down the quarter acre of lawn with a stern sense of purpose. His cropped hair was greying at the edges and his eyes, deep set, gave little away. When Winter apologised for intruding, he simply nodded. Normally, he'd never dream of discussing a patient's case history. Only the fact that Nikki had rung him personally had made him break this iron rule.

'She's been on?'

'Yesterday afternoon.'

'And what did she say?'

Ashworth didn't answer. His wife came out of the house with a couple of glasses of something cold.

'Apple juice,' Ashworth explained shortly. 'What is it you want to know?'

They talked on the long flagstoned terrace at the back of the house. Winter explained his interest in the operation that Ashworth had performed after Nikki had been rushed in by ambulance. She said she'd been in pain. Pain so terrible she couldn't find the words to describe it.

'I can believe that,' he said.

The pain had been in the abdominal area. An external examination had revealed a gross swelling and he'd operated within the hour, finding her single remaining ovary ballooned to the size of a honeydew melon. Another twelve hours, he said, and septicaemia would have killed her.

'Whose fault was that?'

Ashworth was toying with his empty glass.

'It's difficult to say.'

'But she'd just had another operation, hadn't she?'

'Yes.'

'Done by Hennessey.'

'Yes.'

'So was there a connection? Cause and effect?'

Ashworth frowned, unhappy with the crudeness of the linkage.

'Every operation carries a modicum of risk. You have to be careful about attribution of blame.'

'But Hennessey was the only one who'd operated before, no?'

'That's true. And I must say his work wasn't pretty.'

'Does that make him incompetent?'

'Possibly.'

'What else could he have been?'

There was a a long silence. Ashworth was gazing out at his half-mown lawn, deep in thought. At length, he asked whether this was a criminal investigation. Winter told him it wasn't. Not yet.

'Then I want you to understand that this is off the record. I have no intention of giving you a statement or of appearing in court. If you ever quote me back, I shall deny it. Is that understood?'

'Perfectly.'

'Good.'

Another silence. Still Ashworth seemed undecided. Winter mentioned Nikki again. They'd talked at length. She'd gone into great detail. The suggestion that Winter should bother Ashworth was hers, not his.

'I know,' he said. 'She told me. That's why I agreed to this.'

His wife appeared with another carton of apple juice.

Again, Ashworth didn't introduce her. When she'd gone, he sat forward on the wrought-iron chair, his elbows on his knees, his decision made.

After that first afternoon in theatre, he'd operated on Nikki twice more, repairing the worst of Hennessey's work. An investigation of her internal scars, coupled with an exhaustive patient history, had led him to conclude that most of the operations performed by Hennessey had been unnecessary. Her original problem was gastro-enteric, nothing to do with her reproductive system. There was absolutely no clinical reason to have removed her womb and one of her ovaries.

'So why did Hennessey operate at all?'

'That's a very pertinent question. First time round, he might have done it blind, strictly as an exploratory option. Surgeons do that all the time. It's standard procedure. But after that, you'd be looking for another explanation.'

'And?'

Ashworth glanced up at him. He wasn't enjoying this.

'In my opinion,' he said slowly, 'I think he wanted her back.'

'But how could he do that?'

'By making deliberate mistakes. Every time he operated, he left a little calling card, an unstitched incision, a deliberately loose suture. Once you knew what you were looking for, his signature was all over her. In time, the wound would break down. And then she'd be on the phone again, wanting – needing – to come back.'

Winter was staring at him, mesmerised.

'But why? Why would he want to do that?'

Ashworth tipped back his head, staring up at the blueness of the sky. Then he glanced at his watch and extended a hand.

'I can't say it's been a pleasure, Mr Winter.' His grip was firm. 'But good luck, all the same.'

Cathy Lamb sat on the pebbles at Hayling Island, watching Pete racing out towards the distant curve of the sandbar, his body hanging way off the windsurfer in the stiffening breeze. The invitation to join him for the day had come first thing. With another empty weekend yawning before her, Cathy had been happy to say yes. Half-close your eyes, she thought, and the events of the last year or so need never have happened.

She'd thrown a picnic together in the time it had taken for him to drive up to the neat little Portchester semi he'd once called home. She'd made sandwiches with thick wedges of Cheddar and coated them with Marmite, the way she knew he liked. She'd run down to the corner store and bought crisps and a four-pack of Guinness. By the time he arrived, she'd even managed to change into something that proved she'd shed the stone she'd put on over the winter. A big woman, sturdily built, she'd managed to absorb the extra weight without too many dramas, but now, with the help of a gym subscription and twice-weekly aerobics, she was back in shape again. She knew exactly what turned Pete on when she'd first met him and she believed Dawn Ellis when she said that men never change their ways. Lately, somewhat to her own surprise, she'd begun to ache for him.

Pete was coming back now, tramping the board over the waves, hauling in the boom and skidding sideways to avoid a gaggle of swimmers trying to coax a ride from the modest surf. He sailed the board the way he seemed to organise this new life of his, with minimum effort and maximum pleasure, and watching him Cathy was glad that all the angst, the endless letters and midnight phone calls, was over. He was recognisably the guy she'd first dragged off to bed during Nationals week at Weymouth. She'd been crewing for a friend of her brother. Pete had been helming on a borrowed 470. They'd got pissed together in a pub down near the harbour and they'd gone back to her B&B after closing time. She'd fancied him then, like she fancied him now. Dawn again. And the way life just went round and round.

Pete wanted to know whether she wanted the board. The wind was great, picking up nicely. She shook her head, throwing him a towel and spreading the blanket. If the sun stayed this hot, she might have to go topless. The last thing she wanted to talk about was Joe bloody Faraday.

'He's totally out of order.' Pete was inspecting the inside of his sandwich. 'I've been thinking about what you said.'

'It doesn't matter. Forget it. It's what blokes like him do. I thought he was better than that, but I got him wrong. He's greedy, that's all.'

She dismissed him with a shrug, but Pete wouldn't let it go. She should do something about it. Put up a fight.

'Like how?'

'Like go and see Willard. There are two sides to every story. He's only heard one.'

'And what do I say?'

'You say that the Hennessey thing happened in your patch, that there are procedures here, a kind of protocol thing, and that people like Faraday don't have the right to just' – he shrugged – 'take it away from you. You're a DI, Cath. You have rights here. He's treating you like a bloody infant.'

'Yeah, or a woman.'

'Whatever. But you have to do something about it. Otherwise it'll happen again and again. Believe me. That's what men do. Let him get away with it once and you're stuffed.'

Cathy nodded, gazing out at the crescent of broken surf. She knew Pete was right, but somehow, just at this point in time, she couldn't summon the interest or the energy to imagine going through with it all.

'He'd stuff me anyway,' she said softly, 'if I kick up a fuss.'

'How?'

'By threatening to blow the whistle on you. So far he's just made me feel this big about it.' She closed a gap between her forefinger and thumb. 'And I don't think he's going to take it any further. But the moment I threaten to go gobbing off to Willard, he'll say it's a disciplinary thing. I know he will. He's just a ruthless bastard, like they all are.'

'Listen.' Pete was lying on one arm now, reaching for another sandwich. 'If it's me you're worried about, forget it. If he makes it official, if he puts it in writing, tells the suits what I've been up to, then too bad.'

'They'll hammer you,' Cathy pointed out. 'They'll probably sling you out completely. No full pay. No gratuity. Nothing.'

'Tough.'

'You mean that?'

'Yes. If you want to fight him on Hennessey, then do it. You should, Cath. In fact, you must.'

Cathy looked at him for a long moment. She was touched. It was a big thing to sign away £30,000 a year plus a big fat pension, but she could tell by the expression on Pete's face that he meant it. She leaned across and kissed him on the lips.

'That's a nice offer,' she said, 'but it's not just you.'

'No?'

'No.' She shook her head. 'He'd get me busted too, I know he would.'

Pete finished the last of the sandwiches and then lay back on the blanket, his eyes closed, his blond hair stiff with salt. There was a smear of Marmite at the corner of his mouth and Cathy moistened a finger, rubbing it off. He smiled at her touch. His eyes were still closed.

'There's some other stuff about Hennessey I never told Winter,' he murmured. 'Maybe I'll tell you instead.'

It was early afternoon when J-J and Valerie arrived. Faraday was upstairs in the bathroom, taking a shower. Marta was still in bed, sprawled full-length across the rumpled sheet, her eyes closed, sound asleep.

Faraday, hanging out of the bathroom window, couldn't believe his eyes. Six foot two. Jeans and a rucksack. Hair down to his shoulders. As gangly and loose-limbed as ever. He answered his father's yelp with a wild burst of sign: first his flattened hands sliding over each other, then his hands cupped in the shape of a hull, and finally an expression of astonishment that animated his whole face. *Took the early ferry. Thought we'd surprise you.*

You did, Faraday signed back. *You bloody did.*

He shook Marta awake. My boy's here, he told her. *Mon fils et sa petite amie.* Absolutely bloody wonderful. She looked up at him, still naked, rubbing the sleep from her eyes, and wished him a happy birthday again.

Faraday made a huge brunch, everything he could find in the fridge, while J-J hung over him, his hands and face a blur, describing the way things had been over in Caen. Valerie had found him a job with a travel company. They paid money, real money, good money, nearly seventy francs an hour, and he and Valerie had been to Paris a couple of times, staying with friends of hers, rich friends with big houses. Did he know the 16th *arrondissement*? Had he tasted Moroccan food? Was there ever a scarier journey in the world than the lift to the top of the Eiffel Tower? J-J made wings, the old gesture, his long skinny arms outstretched in the kitchen. Men dressed as birds had leapt off the top of the tower. They really had.

The meal over, Faraday insisted on a walk. They took the footpath up round the harbour as far as the RSPB reserve at Farlington Marshes and they lay in the warm grass with the wine that Marta had bought Faraday for his birthday. There were three bottles of Rioja, a 1994 reserve from a vineyard she knew personally, and they drank it in the hot sun while J-J scanned the sky above them with Faraday's binoculars. Marta and Valerie had been talking for hours now, a spontaneous friendship, and Faraday was amazed at the fluency of Marta's French. How come she'd ever bothered with Monday nights at the sixth-form college when she could speak the language like this? And how come she'd kept it such a secret?

He didn't care, putting it down to modesty, glad only that a day which had begun so grimly had turned out like this. His son beside him, very obviously sorted. And a woman who had taken his own life and given it such a thorough shake. This morning, in bed, she'd told him that he'd already begun to turn into someone else, and one clue that she was probably right was the fact that he'd so readily agreed with her. Do this, then this, then this. Now relax. So easy, my love, *n'est-ce pas?*

J-J had spotted a bird. He didn't know what it was. He pointed upwards, handing Faraday the binoculars. At first, Faraday found nothing but sky. Then he caught a sudden blur, brown and tan, and he followed it, racking the focus, following the bird as it plunged down.

'The saker,' he murmured. 'Back again.'

The saker was a falcon, a favourite with rich Arabs but foreign to UK shores. It must have escaped from a private collection, but it had learned survival over Langstone Harbour, feeding from kills among a colony of little terns recently established on an island near the Hayling bridge. Faraday had watched it on a number of previous occasions, revolted by its table manners.

Unlike the occasional visiting peregrine, which devoured its kill at a discreet distance, the saker tore its prey apart at once, in the midst of the colony on the shingle beach, with frantic terns circling and screaming overhead. The falcon was a killing machine solely preoccupied with its own needs, and as such there was something infinitely menacing about this alien intruder. To satisfy itself, it broke every natural rule, and Faraday was still trying to explain to Marta about the bird's sadistic pleasure in taking its prey when it suddenly folded its wings tight into its body and plunged after a pair of black-headed gulls.

The gulls, at first, didn't see it. By now, the saker was barely a couple of feet above the water, arrowing in for the take. Then, abruptly, one of the gulls sensed the imminence of danger and tried to veer away. A tiny change of course brought the saker within a couple of metres. Both gulls, in blind panic, plunged into the water, totally submerging themselves, desperate to escape, and the saker swooped upwards, no longer remotely interested.

J-J was beside Valerie, waiting for the gulls to appear again. Marta couldn't take her eyes off the saker.

'What happens now?' she asked.

Faraday had the falcon in perfect focus.

'He's playing with them,' he murmured. 'He's not even hungry.'

Eighteen

Sunday, for Faraday, was a delight. Marta stayed over on Saturday night and all four of them went to a fish restaurant in Old Portsmouth where J-J ignored the blackboard offers of turbot and monkfish, settling instead for the biggest plate of cod and chips Faraday had ever seen. Early next morning he was up before anyone else, and Faraday watched him from his study window as he rambled aimlessly along the foreshore, kicking at tangles of seaweed and skimming the flatter stones across the mirrored flatness of the harbour. This was a scene from countless summers gone, a perfect cameo Faraday was determined to tuck away and treasure. Wind back the clock, he thought, and this son of his might never have left.

After breakfast, Faraday put a call through to Ferguson, who was driving the Hennessey inquiry over the weekend. A decade with Met CID hadn't softened the dour Aberdeen accent and he seemed to take a positive pleasure in reporting a lack of progress. There had been no sightings of Hennessey in Beaconsfield. The redial on the telephone at his New Forest cottage had led to a marina in Jersey but inquiries there had drawn a blank. Staff at the Advent Hospital hadn't seen him since April. Apart from confirming the use of accelerants – petrol, in this case – forensic had nothing solid on the burned-out Mercedes. And preliminary word from

Hennessey's bankers had now established absolutely no movement in any of his accounts since 18 June. In Ferguson's view, the man had either had an accident, done a runner, or been killed, but there was absolutely no evidence to indicate which.

'Boils down to fuck all,' he concluded grimly. 'Is Winter still coming on board?'

Cathy Lamb contacted Winter mid-morning. She stood at the back of her knocked-through lounge, waiting for the phone to pick up at the other end. Pete's shortie wet suit was still hanging on the line in the garden, sluiced with fresh water from last night.

When Winter finally answered, Cathy at first assumed he was drunk. She could hear music in the background, the Walker Brothers, and Winter's voice was slurred and indistinct against the driving lyrics. *The sun ain't gonna shine any more*, they sang, *the moon ain't gonna rise in the sky*.

'Paul? What's the matter?'

Winter was mumbling about his wife, Joannie. Something had happened. Something he didn't want to talk about.

'Is she there? Paul, tell me.'

'What?'

'Joannie . . . your wife . . . what's happened?'

The phone went dead. Cathy rang the number again, but it was engaged. Winter lived in Bedhampton, a pretty little bungalow on the slopes of Portsdown Hill. She could picture it now. Roses in the front garden. Ruched curtains in the windows. Not like Winter at all. She turned off the toaster in the kitchen, scribbled a message to Pete, and ran to her car.

On a Sunday, Bedhampton was less than ten minutes away. Winter's Subaru was parked on the hardstanding beside the bungalow. Cathy could hear the music as she hurried across the pavement and down the side. Still the Walker Brothers. She knocked on the door, then tried the handle. The door was locked. Another knock produced no response. Running back to the big rectangle of grass at the front, she leaned across the neatly planted border, shading her eyes against the glare of the sun, trying to see inside. Winter was sitting in the armchair in front of the television. His head was back against the squab and his eyes were open, staring at the ceiling. At first she thought something truly terrible had happened, then she saw the movement on the arm of the chair. Winter's fingers, tap-tapping along with the music.

She knocked on the window.

'Paul!' she yelled. 'It's me, Cathy. Open the bloody door.'

Winter's head slowly came up. He looked round, the expression of a man aroused from deep slumber. He seemed surprised to see her. She wasn't sure, but she thought he managed to raise a smile. He got up, very slowly, and tottered towards the open door. He looked, Cathy thought, like an old man: bent, uncertain, somehow defeated. That wasn't the Winter she knew. No way.

She made him tea and settled him in the armchair again, listening to what had happened to Joannie. She'd tried to top herself. Not because she was in great pain. Not because she wanted to get it over with. But because she'd come back to an empty house.

'Empty because of me.' He nodded. 'Because of me not being here.'

Cathy was kneeling beside him. She'd had her moments with Winter, everybody had. Put an artist like that on your squad and you know it's only a question of time before the relationship hits a brick wall.

Winter and paperwork had never been made for each other. He had no patience for mission statements and the squeaky-clean bureaucrats who'd taken over the upper echelons of the force. He saw no point in signing up to performance indicators and total abstinence. He was a relic, a dinosaur. He did his business in car parks and deserted trading estates and ran his informants like goldfish, tossing them the odd scrap, treating them with the matey contempt he thought they deserved.

From time to time, when she was DS under Faraday, Winter had driven Cathy nuts, partly because he hadn't got an ounce of honesty in his body, and partly because he still turned in such consistent results. Show Winter a villain and he'd make a friend of him. Show him two, and he'd form a little gang, lying his socks off when the likes of Cathy tried to nail down how many rules he'd just broken. He was, she'd always thought, the cross every DS had to bear, at once bent and brilliant.

But this was different. Winter was in deep, deep trouble. And that mattered more than anything.

He was telling her about the tablets, about the hospital, about the tangle of drips and monitor leads with which the ICU staff had hauled Joannie back from the edge. He'd sat there and watched her. All night. And the truth was that he just couldn't cope.

'That's why I'm doing it, Cath.' She was stroking his hand. 'That's why I'm what I am.'

Slowly, the story began to trickle out. How he was going after Hennessey. How he'd flown to Jersey to meet the girl, Nikki. How he'd checked out exactly what this so-called surgeon had done to her. And how there were umpteen other people just itching to knock the bastard off.

'I just need to know, Cath.'

'Know what?'

'That someone's done it, that he's paid the price. That's all I need. Just to be sure.'

'And what if he isn't dead?'

'Then I'll find him.'

'And then what?'

Winter stared at her. His eyes were swimming with tears.

'I need to hurt somebody, Cath,' he whispered. 'I really do.'

Cathy gazed at him for a long moment. His hand was warm in hers and he clung to her like a child.

'But what about your wife?' she said at last. 'What about Joannie?'

'She was with her mum. She shouldn't have come back.'

'But she did.'

'I know she did. I know. And I should have been here, shouldn't I? But I wasn't.'

'Why not? Why weren't you here?'

'Because I can't fucking handle it, love. End of story.'

'*You* can't handle it?'

'Yeah, I know, I know, don't lay it on. Pathetic bastard, me. Totally fucking useless.'

He gestured round the lounge at twenty-four years of mementos and, watching him, Cathy sensed he'd got to the heart of it. It wasn't about Hennessey at all, or Nikki, or whatever the surgeon was supposed to have done. It was about him, Winter, and about this marriage of his that had suddenly run its course. He'd taken it all for granted, somehow assuming it would always be there for ever. Joannie in the recliner doing her lottery numbers. Joannie combing the *News* for the best car-boot sales. Joannie giving the roses a seeing-to.

With his wife gone, what would be left? Fuck all. That's why his world had fallen apart. That's why he wanted – needed – to hurt somebody.

'You have,' Cathy said softly. 'And it's Joannie.'

'I know.' He sniffed. 'But she's in good hands now, isn't she? They'll take care of her. They'll know what to do.'

Cathy nodded and got to her feet. She'd check at the hospital, but she thought that Winter was probably right. Joannie would be in there a while. They'd insist on some kind of psychiatric assessment. And in the meantime, Winter would be at a loose end, banged up in this trim little bungalow, going slowly round the bend.

She looked down at him, wrestling with a private decision.

'I've been talking to Pete,' she said at last. 'There's some more stuff about Hennessey he's found out.'

'Does Faraday know?'

'Nobody knows except Pete and me.' She smiled down at him. 'And now you.'

The transformation was remarkable. Winter gazed up at her, a sparkle in his eyes. The angst, the self-pity, had suddenly gone. He wanted to know more, needed to know more, because one way or another, dead or alive, he was going to sort that fucker Hennessey out.

'Legally, though,' Cathy reminded him. 'There are procedures here. You've got enough problems without an assault charge.'

Winter hadn't heard a word. He was smiling now, sunshine after the rain.

'So how come your ex-hubbie's so generous all of a sudden? Are you bunging him or what?'

Cathy shook her head, then began to laugh.

'"What",' she said, 'would be closer.'

*

Dawn Ellis was at the Tesco hypermarket at North Harbour when she got the call from Shelley Beavis. She paused at the head of the aisle, stocking pre-cooked convenience foods, making space in her trolley for half a dozen of their own-brand vegetarian specials. Back with Cathy on the volume-crime treadmill next week, she'd have neither the time nor the inclination to knock something up herself.

Shelley wanted to meet, preferably that afternoon.

'Why?'

'Just to talk . . . you know . . . as friends.'

'What does that mean?'

'I just want it private. You and me.'

'I don't do private, Shelley. Not in my job.'

'Yeah, but—'

'But nothing, love. Of course we can talk, but it has to be for real.' Dawn reached for a frozen cauliflower cheese. 'Is it Lee again? Has he been on to you about me?'

'Yeah, but it's not him. It's my dad. I just . . . look, it'll take five minutes. I'm really sorry, but . . .'

Dawn had paused in the aisle, remembering the state of Kevin Beavis's place. Rick had described it later as a film set, the kind of squalor you really have to work at, and he'd been right.

'Why your dad?'

'It's just something I need to tell you.'

'On the record?'

'If you like, yes.'

Dawn glanced at her watch. Tonight, for once, she had a date with a guy who'd never dream of joining the police force.

'Half-three.' She named a café five minutes from Rawlinson Road. 'I'll see you there.'

*

The afternoon ferry for Caen left at three o'clock. Faraday and J-J said their goodbyes in the ferry terminal, a hug all the more unusual for being so spontaneous. J-J disentangled himself and beamed down at his father. Marta stood to one side, telling Valerie how much she'd love to come over and visit.

Nice lady. J-J's big, bony hands described eloquent shapes in the air. *And good for you.*

Cheeky bugger, Faraday signed back.

No, I'm serious. He held his thumb and index finger in a smiley U-shape under his chin. *Fun to be with.*

Marta had turned to watch the exchange, deeply amused, and Faraday knew at once that she had understood every gesture.

'The boy's drunk,' he explained. 'Gets over-emotional.'

'Just like his dad?'

'Maybe.'

He took J-J to one side, walking him slowly towards the mouth of the tunnel that led down to the quayside. The towering bulk of the white Brittany ferry lay beyond the line of embarking cars. Mid-summer, the terminal was packed.

J-J was repeating Valerie's invitation to stay. The flat was tiny, but there were *chambres d'hôte* everywhere, really cheap, and he could find somewhere nice.

Double room? He extended his index and third finger, then prayered his hands together against his sleeping head.

Faraday shrugged. *Maybe.*

For sure. You must.

You really think so?

This time, J-J just nodded, looking glassily through the mill of passengers at Valerie and Marta saying their goodbyes. At the pub, earlier, he'd already told Faraday

how much he'd enjoyed the visit. J-J had never understood the dividing line between candour and hurtful-
ness, and after the third pint he'd confessed how days
alone with his dad could sometimes be just a bit tense.
Lately, before he'd embarked on his new life with
Valerie, he'd got the feeling that Faraday was frightened
of him growing up. His dad, he said, had always wanted
the relationship to stay the way it had been when he
was a kid, with excursions out in the car and wet
afternoons on the marshes: adventures scored for wellie
boots and tripods and, if they were lucky, a bird or two
they hadn't seen for a while. But for him, J-J, the world
had moved on. Birds bored him now, and so did being a
kid, and the wonderful thing about Marta was the fact
that she wasn't afraid.

The sign for 'afraid' is a claw hand against the heart,
coupled with a fearful expression, and in the pub,
gazing at the remains of his steak and kidney pie,
Faraday had at first thought the boy had made some
kind of mistake.

Afraid?

J-J had nodded. Marta wasn't afraid to have a bit of a
laugh, to let herself go. She wasn't afraid to get drunk
and put her arms around Faraday and pinch his cheeks
like a baby. She didn't hold herself back. She wasn't
afraid of laughter.

At the time, barely an hour ago, Faraday had slightly
resented J-J's frankness. As driver, he'd been on the
orange sodas all day and hadn't quite kept pace with a
riotous lunch. But now, watching the two women
picking their way towards them through the crowd, he
realised that J-J was absolutely right. Laughter had
bonded the weekend together like glue. And laughter
would take them, just as soon as he could organise it, to
Caen.

J-J was struggling to heft up his enormous rucksack. Faraday gave him a hand.

Love you, he signed, as the boy grabbed Valerie's hand and turned to go.

The Country Kitchen was nearly empty by the time Dawn made it down to Southsea. Shelley Beavis sat at a table in a corner of the window, nursing a glass of camomile tea. To Dawn's relief, she seemed to have incurred no further damage since they'd last met.

'Your dad . . .' Dawn was determined to be business-like.

Shelley looked startled, as if she'd never suggested this conversation.

'What about him?'

Dawn gave her a look. It was Sunday. She hadn't had time off for over a week. This was a kind of favour. The least Shelley could do was stop pretending.

'I don't pretend.'

'Yes you do, love. Addison said so, and he's right. You pretend all the time. That's what acting's about. You pull all these numbers on me and you expect me not to notice. Shelley, that's not what we're about. We're in the noticing game. That's what they pay us for. OK?'

She leaned back. She could have been this girl's mother, scolding her for staying out late. Shelley had ducked her head. She looked genuinely chastened, but that, too, might well have been part of the repertoire.

'Your dad,' Dawn repeated. 'You wanted to get something off your chest.'

'Yeah.' Shelley nodded, her face briefly curtained by her hair. 'But it's going to sound . . . you know . . . a bit odd.'

'Tell me why.'

'It just is.' She stared at her glass for a moment, frowning with concentration. Then she looked up. 'You'll just have to make allowances. That's all I want to say.'

'Allowances for what? Come on, Shelley, just tell me.'

'For the kind of bloke he is.'

'What does that mean?'

'It means that . . . well . . . he's not all there. Actually, he's never been all there. You don't suss it at first, not as a kid, because you think all dads are like that. But when you get older and you've got friends and so on you realise that most dads aren't like that at all.'

'Like what?' Dawn was staring at her.

'Like . . . different. He's not bad or anything. He's just missing a bit, in the head. It's like he had an accident or something once. Maybe he did. He's been riding those bikes all his life. I just dunno. All I can say is that he's not a bad man. Not when it comes to the things that really matter. He's been a good dad. He really has.'

'You mean it's not his fault?'

'Exactly.'

'What's not his fault?' Dawn leaned forward, moving the glass out of the way, repeating the question. This was it. This was what the girl had phoned to get off her chest. Something terrible in her past. Something Dawn had to know. 'Are we talking abuse here? Is that what you're trying to say?'

Shelley sat back, her hands picking at a loose thread in her cardigan. She wanted no further part in this conversation and no amount of pressure from Dawn would prise any more out of her. Her father needed a bit of sympathy, a bit of understanding, and that was all she was prepared to say. Dawn, close to losing her temper, pushed and pushed, trying to wheedle out what was really on her mind, but the girl simply shook her head.

Finally, Dawn changed tack.

'Tell me more about Lee Kennedy,' she said.

Shelley stared at her. This time, the bewilderment was for real.

'But I thought you'd been round to see him?'

'I have.'

'Then you'd know, wouldn't you?'

'Know what?'

'Know—' Dawn saw the first flicker of alarm. 'He hasn't asked you to . . .?'

Dawn, at last understanding, got to her feet. She was right about Lee Kennedy running some kind of business. This was about money, as well as sex. She stood beside Shelley's chair for a moment, but the girl wouldn't look up at her.

'He's pimping, isn't he?' she said at last. 'I should have sussed that days ago.'

Nineteen

The Weather Gage was a pub in Old Portsmouth, tucked into a corner of the Camber Dock, the tiny, centuries-old anchorage protected by the curl of shingle known as Spice Island. The first medieval settlement had grown up here, a huddle of roofs around the harbourmouth, just visible from the distant chalk ridge of Portsdown Hill. Fishermen and traders had settled along the lanes and alleys snaking back from the water. In search of Channel access for his infant navy, Henry VII had despatched surveyors and craftsmen to dig a dry dock, establishing the town's dependence on the tides of war and peace.

Five hundred years later, the Royal Naval Dockyard now sprawled to the north, hundreds of acres of handsome Georgian boathouses, Victorian repairing basins and state-of-the-art workshops, but the Camber Dock still survived: a muddle of fishing boats, tugs, moored yachts and the sleek, deep-throated launches which ran pilots out to the huge container ships inbound to neighbouring Southampton. If you were going to have a pub anywhere, Winter thought, then this would be the place.

The Weather Gage, though, had seen better days. The timber cladding on the upper floor was badly in need of paint, and in rough weather the guttering leaked torrents of water onto the flagstones below. Worse still, the current owner's bid to grace the area with a brand-new restaurant featuring dishes from the Nelsonian navy had come unstuck after a much-publicised run-in with the environmental health inspectors. Accused of buying dodgy beef, the would-be restaurateur had been fined a total of £4,500.

The guy's name was Rob Parrish. Winter didn't know him personally, and neither did Cathy, but that wasn't the point. The point was that Parrish, according to Pete Lamb, was a great mate of Hennessey's. And Hennessey, until last week, had been a lunchtime regular at the Weather Gage.

By early evening, the weekend crowds had largely gone. Winter left his Subaru in the safety of the nearby Wightlink car park. Local Portsea kids were screwing everything that moved these days and the car park surveillance cameras might just keep them off. The Subaru locked, Winter sauntered back towards the pub. The quayside was cluttered with empty lobster pots and hanks of fraying rope. A big container lorry belonging to one of the fish wholesalers dripped water onto the oil-stained tarmac. Beyond the nearby Wightlink car ferry terminal, huge construction cranes towered upwards over the harbourside Gunwharf Quays site. The area smelled of fish and tar, of seaweed and diesel, and the only note that faintly jarred was a frieze of expensive new maisonettes, *faux*-Georgian in red brick, for incomers with a taste for instant history.

The pub, as Winter had half-expected, was empty. The wood-panelled walls were hung with sepia pictures, wild-eyed trawlermen with pipes and flat caps, and Winter was still trying to work out what had happened to the grubby-looking shacks in the background when a door banged shut in the depths of the building and footsteps came clattering into the bar.

Pete's description had been more or less right: medium height, mid-thirties, well turned out, blond hair pinned up at the back, nice legs, lots of make-up. She looked, Winter thought, like someone who'd auditioned for a certain role and got it, only to find herself badly let down.

Winter ordered a pint of HSB. It tasted foul. The woman took it back without a word, substituting it with a pint of lager.

'How come?' Winter enquired, nodding at the beer as she poured it down the sink.

The woman's name was Tara Gough. She had little taste for conversation, beyond a series of rather bland comments about the weather and the passing trade, but Winter persevered. The beauty of the next hour or so was the fact that he knew exactly where it had to lead.

'You want to *eat* here?' The hint couldn't have been plainer.

'Thought I might give it a go. Is there a problem?'

'Not at all.' She gave him a suit-yourself look. 'Are you insured?'

This was fighting talk, but Winter was too canny to succumb. There were other things he wanted to find out first, little things, things that would flesh out the bigger picture.

The restaurant was called Aubrey's.

'Why Aubrey's?'

'That was my idea, actually. You've never heard of him?'

Winter shook his head. Jack Aubrey, it transpired, was the lead character in a series of immensely successful novels set in the Revolutionary and Napoleonic Wars. At the time, like the sea-going Nelsonian cuisine, it had seemed a good idea. In fact, a great idea.

'This area attracts those kinds of people, you know, people who read books, people who like history. We thought we couldn't go wrong.'

'We?'

'The guy that owns it, and me. I ran the restaurant. Still do, for my sins.'

Winter was looking across at the eating area, a dozen or so tables carefully set with prime views across the Camber. Even at this time of night, they should have been filling up with diners for the early sitting, people settling in, a warm hum of conversation.

Winter turned back, one eyebrow cocked, his question unvoiced.

'Dead in the water,' she said. 'And a great lesson in how not to do it.'

Winter bought her a drink. She settled for a hefty slug of Pernod with ice rather than water and, watching her drink it, Winter realised she'd taken more from this pub than the disappointments of running an empty restaurant. Not that she was thinking of sticking around.

'Ten days and counting,' she confided. 'And to tell you the truth, I can't bloody wait.'

'Why hang on? It's a free world.'

'I can't.' She gestured towards the door. 'You won't believe the MOT bill I got for that bloody car out there. Plus it's kids, isn't it? Once it used to be a ticket to the multiplex. Now it's the top-up card for the mobile.'

Winter offered his sympathies. She drove a clapped-out old Peugeot 205. She never got paid until the first Monday in every month so bailing out before then would be suicidal.

'He'd love it if I did that. I'd never see the money again.'

'Who's he?'

For the first time, she hesitated. Winter sat back on

his barstool, his hands held up in a gesture of apology. Sorry to intrude. None of my business.

'No, it's OK.' She shook her head, annoyed with herself. 'His name's Rob, Rob Parrish. He owns the place.'

'And you were with him? From the start?'

'More or less. I knew his sister. Rob was a diver, out in the Gulf. He earned pots of money on the oil rigs and came home to spend it all.' She gestured towards the window. 'He learned his diving over in Vernon, when he was in the Navy. This place was next door. He said he'd always fancied it.'

Winter nodded. HMS *Vernon* had once stood on the Gunwharf site before the developers moved in.

'He bought the freehold?'

'For a song. The place was practically derelict. He spent loads doing it up, adding the restaurant, all that. Then he asked me to sort it out.'

'For wages or a share?'

'A *share*? Rob Parrish, cut anyone in?' She shot Winter a look. 'This man will screw anyone for money. This is a guy who'd sell his mother for another half per cent. A *share*? You have to be joking.'

An elderly couple arrived, both Americans, and Winter wandered around, looking at the pictures again while Tara served them. From the window beside the door, he could see her rusting Peugeot 205. Blue. N365 FRT.

With the lone Americans shedding their anoraks at a table in the corner, Winter returned to the bar. Had trade always been this dire?

Tara was polishing the counter where she'd spilled beer from an overfilled pint. She had the kind of hands that appear in adverts for the more expensive Swiss watches: long, elegant fingers, perfectly lacquered nails.

'It was OK for a while,' she said. 'We had a good first summer with the tourists and a decent regular lunchtime crowd from Gunwharf. It got busier once they started building, of course, but the management lot used to come in before that, and they'd eat, too. I think they were just glad to get out of the office, to tell you the truth.'

Winter was thinking of Hennessey. It all stacked up. He'd nose around the site, study the plans, choose the apartments he wanted, and when it came to lunchtime the sales girls would point him at the Weather Gage. Simplest thing in the world.

'They still come in? The Gunwharf lot?'

'Not after the business we had with the health inspectors. One mention of beef these days, everyone thinks it's BSE. They never come in now, and who can blame them?'

'So what happened about the beef?'

Tara was drying her hands on a cloth.

'I thought you said you were local? It was in the *News*. Front page. Rob did a deal with a guy up in Hilsea. Turned out the meat had been condemned. Somewhere up in the Midlands. How to kill a business for a couple of quid off your butcher's bill.' She shook her head. 'Madness.'

The American, the husband, had returned to the bar. He wanted to know about the steak and ale pie. Was it home-made? Tasty? Tara reached for her order pad and glanced at her watch. The pies were made daily, she said. Chef's speciality.

'Even on a Sunday? Hey . . .' The American relayed the news to his wife. They both settled for new potatoes and a salad alongside. Plus lots of that nice French mustard.

Tara was still scribbling the order when Winter

enquired about the chef. How could they justify the wages with trade this thin? Tara glanced up.

'Rob does the cooking,' she said, 'if he ever makes it back.'

Winter had retired to a corner with his *Sunday Telegraph* and a second pint by the time Parrish turned up. He was a lanky, sunburned man in his early forties. He was wearing patched jeans, a pair of scuffed deck shoes and a white T-shirt. His Rod Stewart crop of blond hair looked dyed, and he sported a thin gold ring in one ear.

He paused inside the door, looking round at the empty bar. He had an elaborate dragon tattoo on the inside of one arm and a tense smile that failed to warm his face. The logo on the T-shirt advertised a Virgin Islands windsurfing school.

Tara was already tapping her watch and nodding at the American couple. Parrish rolled his eyes and disappeared through a door marked PRIVATE. The meal must have been microwaved because it appeared within minutes. As did Parrish.

Winter returned to the bar. He'd barely touched his second pint.

'A word?' Winter beckoned Parrish over.

Tara was standing by the till. When she saw Winter show Parrish his warrant card, she turned away.

'Police?' Parrish said blankly. Flat, south London voice.

'CID.'

Winter had produced one of the video stills of Hennessey. He laid it carefully on the counter where Tara would be able to see it. The surgeon was standing at the reception in the Marriott, his smile wide, his little eyes fixed on the receptionist's blouse.

'Do you recognise this guy?'

Tara was looking too, and Parrish knew it. He picked up the photo, stared at it for a moment, then nodded.

'Sure,' he said. 'He comes in here sometimes. Lunchtimes.'

'Do you know his name?'

Parrish glanced at Tara.

'Peter someone?'

'Hennessey.' Her voice was cold. 'Used to drink with the Gunwharf lot.'

'When was the last time you saw him?'

Once again, Parrish looked to Tara for help, but this time she spared him the effort of repeating the question.

'Last week some time,' she said. 'Maybe longer.'

'Mr Parrish?'

The fact that Winter knew his name tightened Parrish's smile even more.

'Dunno,' he said.

'You can't remember?'

'No, I can't. It might have been longer, like Tara says. Faces are a blur in this trade. New people all the time.'

'Business OK, is it?'

'Never better, mate. You eating as well, are you?'

He fetched a menu and spread it on the bar. Winter ignored it. He wanted to establish how often Hennessey had used the pub, how well Parrish had got to know him, whether or not he'd been showing any signs of stress lately, whether or not he'd talked about going away at all. He wanted to know about the three apartments he'd reserved for himself over at Gunwharf, whether he was serious about exercising the options, and quite who the other two might have been intended for.

To all these questions, Parrish offered little more than a grunt and a shrug. He didn't know the guy at all well.

260

Short-handed as always, there was precious little time for social chit-chat.

'Was he always alone?'

'Always.' It was Tara this time.

'He was a surgeon, by the way. Did he tell you that?'

'Yes.' She nodded. 'He did.'

Parrish interrupted. He was looking at the video still again.

'Why all this?' he said. 'What's happened to the guy?'

Winter stared him out, curious to know why the question had been so long coming.

'We don't know,' he said. 'That's what we're trying to find out. Shame you can't help, really.'

'Yeah.' Parrish suddenly checked his watch. 'Sorry about that.'

He glanced across at Tara and muttered something about catching up with a mate. She shrugged, long past caring, and Parrish disappeared again. Winter reached for the video still.

'Why didn't you tell me?' Tara blurted out.

'Tell you what?'

'That you were police.'

'You never asked.' Winter folded the still into his pocket. 'And anyway, it's Sunday.'

'Does that make a difference?'

'Not really, but I'd hate you to carry a grudge.'

She looked at him for a moment or two, her face stony, then she began to rearrange the beer mats on the bar top.

'Actually, I thought he was lonely,' she said quietly. 'Lonely and a bit pathetic.'

'Hennessey?'

'Yes. And I'll tell you something else.' She glanced over her shoulder. 'Rob's lying. He used to talk to the guy a lot.'

'What about?'

'I haven't a clue. They were really thick, head to head. You know, boy's talk.'

'Friends?'

'Looked like it.'

'So why' – Winter gestured at the space where Parrish had been – 'not admit it?'

'I've no idea.'

Parrish returned from upstairs, running a hand through his hair. He was wearing a thin suede jacket over the T-shirt. Pausing briefly beside the bar, he threw a sideways glance at Tara. He'd be gone a couple of hours. There was stuff for the microwave in the smaller fridge. Not that they were expecting a coach party. He laughed at his own joke, a dry, mirthless bark of laughter, and Winter turned on his barstool to watch him leave. Something struck him about the shape of Parrish's shoulders, the cut of the jacket, and as he disappeared into the last of the sunshine Winter suddenly realised that he'd seen this man before. On the Marriott surveillance video. Leaving the hotel. With Hennessey.

Faraday was trying to fix the coffee percolator when he heard the front-door bell. He put the plug to one side and was halfway to the door when he recognised Marta's footsteps up the hall. Her feet were bare on the polished wooden boards and she was still wearing Faraday's dressing gown.

The door opened and there was a moment of silence before he heard a woman's voice, surprise hardening into something much terser.

'I'm intruding,' she said. 'I'm sorry.'

It was Ruth. She was carrying a present of some kind. She looked tight-lipped.

'Marta,' Faraday muttered, 'meet Ruth.'

The two women eyed each other. Then Marta stepped aside with a flourish and invited Ruth in. Ruth hesitated, then shook her head. Her eyes didn't leave Faraday's face.

'Wrong house,' she murmured. 'My mistake.'

She turned on her heel and disappeared into the gathering dusk. Then Faraday heard the sound of a car door closing and the cough of an engine.

'Friend of yours?' Marta was looking amused.

'I'm not sure.' Faraday closed the door. 'I think so.'

Later, when Marta had showered and gone, Faraday sat alone in his upstairs study, staring at the pictures on the wall. Some were etchings and lithographs, trophies from long afternoons in Winchester antique shops. Others were colour photographs plundered from birding magazines. One or two he'd taken himself, using Janna's camera in the hope that some of her magic might just rub off. All the pictures were of birds, and collectively they bridged the years that stretched backwards to his marriage.

In a solitary life, under siege from the demands of an impossible job, these images never failed to offer Faraday a certain kind of consolation. In these frozen moments – a turnstone rooting for lugworm, a skua caught against the sun – he'd always found warmth and solace. Until now.

The weekend with Marta, Valerie and J-J had opened his eyes, and Ruth's abrupt appearance, so typically unexpected, had simply confirmed a deep-down suspicion that the time had come for a change. There was, after all, a place for laughter in this life of his. It was, to his faint surprise, perfectly safe to let whole days unfold without plans or preparations, holding nothing but the promise of gossip and good company. There was, in J-J's phrase, no need to be afraid.

The image of Ruth's face at the door came back to him. She was disappointed because he hadn't fitted in with whatever expectations she had of him. She'd walked away because he'd dared to wriggle off this hook of hers and head for warmer waters. He sat back, eyeing a favourite shot of J-J's, a gannet plunging into the boiling waves off Bempton Cliffs. Ruth belonged in this museum of moments. She'd been important to him, but her reclusiveness, her self-regard, her carefully preserved sense of mystery had, in the end, been no more than a taunt. He could chase her all his life, but that would be as far as he'd ever get because the take, if it ever happened, would satisfy nothing more than a momentary hunger.

Ruth knew this. That's why she rationed herself so carefully. That's why she stayed so eternally beyond reach. She'd found a lifetime's perch in a certain kind of detachment, and the games she played were, in the end, strictly for her own amusement. In return for her company, Ruth exacted certain dues, and in his heart Faraday knew that he was no longer prepared to pay them. She really was beyond his grasp, and after this weekend he wasn't going to chase her any more.

The thought of Marta enveloped him again, close, intimate, overwhelming. Here was a woman without fear, without scruple, without shame. A woman who spoke the direct physical language of appetite and pleasure. Who knew how to loosen his knots and sort through his baggage. She was direct. She was stylish. She was funny. And the games she played were games for two.

He got up and left the room, turning off the light as he did so.

Later that night, back at his bungalow in Bedhampton, Winter got a call on his mobile. It was Faraday, wanting to know about tomorrow. What was the situation with Joannie? Was he joining the Hennessey squad or not?

Winter wondered whether he'd been talking to Cathy, but decided that he hadn't. No way would Cathy be helping Faraday out just now. Not in her current mood.

'One way or another, we have to stitch this job up,' Faraday was saying. 'The last thing we want is an upgrade to Major Crimes. Willard's onside at the moment, but it may not last.'

Winter, barely two fingers into a bottle of Bell's, smiled to himself. It was the same old story: Faraday desperate to square off a bit of decent crime in between all the other crap they had to deal with. CID work, increasingly, was like panning for gold. Upstream, the guys on the Major Crimes Suite had first dip. Downstream, the blokes on division were left with the tailings. Just what kind of hero spent his life hunting down serial cycle thieves?

'Well?' Faraday sounded unusually impatient.

Winter was contemplating the bottle.

'Difficult,' he said. 'I'm back at the hospital first thing, but maybe later.'

'Hospital?'

He definitely hadn't been talking to Cathy.

'Joannie's had a bit of a ...' Winter frowned. 'Relapse.'

'She's OK?'

'More or less.'

'Shit, I'm sorry.'

'That's OK, boss.' Winter reached for his glass. 'Phone you in the morning?'

Twenty

Winter hadn't slept so well for what felt like weeks. He awoke to the alarm, washed and shaved, and remembered to collect the scribbled address from the pad by the phone before he headed for the door. Last night's vehicle check through the PNC had yielded all the information he needed. By seven o'clock, with the city barely awake, he'd even found himself a parking spot with a perfect line of sight to her front door.

Playfair Road was on the borders of Southsea and Somerstown, one of a series of streets that fed into a warren of council housing, gaunt high-rise blocks shadowing the graffiti and litter beneath. There were still survivors from the blitz years in these terraces of little bay-fronted houses, bent old couples you might catch tottering down to the community centre around the corner, but recent years had seen tides of students, together with huge, colourful Bangladeshi families, turning the houses into multi-occupation. To Winter, who drew many of his informers from hereabouts, the area had a slightly post-war feel, as if armies of displaced persons were forever moving through, leaving nothing but chaos in their wake.

Tara Gough, according to the records at DVLC, lived at number 4. Her blue Peugeot was parked outside and the curtains in the upstairs window were still closed. Behind the Peugeot stood a silver BMW Z series sports car, a fashion statement wholly out of place in a street like this. Just parking for the night was a reckless act of faith, and the fact that it seemed intact was truly remarkable. In this area, Winter had come across Transit vans, L reg. for God's sake, chocked up on bricks after a hard night's recreational theft.

He put a call through to the PNC operator in Fratton control room, and read him the number plate on the Beamer. Within a minute, he had a name and a London address. Richard Savage, Aubrey Rise, London N5. Winter scribbled it down, then gazed up at the windows. Odds on, Savage was tucked up with Tara Gough. He'd put money on it.

He settled down again, tuning the ancient Blaupunkt to Radio Two. Whatever anyone else told you about forensics and multi-disciplinary teamwork, the key to nicking people was motivation. You had to understand what it would take for a man or a woman to kill or rape or thieve, or embark on a thousand other misdemeanours that might end in serious grief. Normally, to his surprise, it was pretty straightforward: they were either jealous, greedy, desperate or simply pissed off to the point where there seemed no other sensible option but to bury an axe in someone's head. They were the easy cases. Other times, though, you'd come across something so devious, so maniacally clever, that it took a real understanding of the darker side of the human psyche to get any kind of result. That's where Hennessey belonged. He'd felt it from the start, and now, after last night, he was all the more certain.

At one minute to eight, just after the weather forecast, a man in a suit appeared at the door of number 4, pulled it shut behind him, and climbed into the little silver sports car. He had an executive haircut and nice shoes. Winter judged him to be in his early thirties.

Five minutes later, Winter was at the door of number 4. Tara Gough opened it within seconds of his first knock. Judging by the milk carton in her hand, she must have been in the kitchen. She was wearing a long blue T-shirt and not a lot else. When she saw it wasn't the postman, she tried to close the door.

'The name's Winter. You've seen the warrant card already.'

With enormous reluctance, she let him in. Despite the weather, the house smelled of damp, and Winter could hear someone else moving about in the kitchen at the back.

'My son,' Tara explained. 'He's late for school already.'

A tall youth had appeared in the hall. He was eating a slice of toast in one hand and trying to tuck a white shirt into dark trousers with the other. Winter nodded at him.

'I thought you had a daughter?'

'I do. She's still upstairs.'

'Cosy.'

'We think so. I suppose it's all right to get dressed, is it?'

Winter watched her climbing the stairs. Nice legs. No knickers. The youth had beaten a retreat to the kitchen, drowning the silence in a blast of music from Ocean FM.

The two downstairs rooms had been knocked into one, but the separate carpets were still in place and bits of plasterwork remained to be finished. An ironing board had been set up with a good view of the big widescreen TV, and the pile of shirts was topped with a black basque and a collection of thongs. Beside the back window, a cheap DIY bookcase was brimming with copies of *Vanity Fair* and *Cosmopolitan*, and there was a cardboard box on the floor full of rubber work gloves.

The front half of the room was empty except for the long curve of a four-seat sofa, and Winter sank into the dimpled leather, waiting for Tara to return. She was dressed for work when she appeared again, a smart-looking blouse over a full cotton skirt.

'Been here long?' Winter didn't bother to get up.

'What's it to you?'

'Just asking.'

She didn't answer for a moment. She was trying to ready herself for work, gripping half a dozen hairclips between her teeth while those busy, elegant fingers combed through the long blonde hair. Finally, she checked her efforts in the mirror on the chimney breast.

'Since Christmas,' she muttered, 'give or take.'

'And before that?'

'Before that, we were somewhere else.'

'Where?'

She was losing patience fast. Winter sensed she wanted to shout, to have a real go, but couldn't because of the kids.

'Why don't you just tell me what this is about?'

'It's about Hennessey,' he said peaceably. 'I thought I'd explained all that.'

'But what's that got to do with me?'

Winter didn't answer. Footsteps down the hall were followed by the crash of the front door being pulled shut. Through the net curtains at the front, Winter watched the youth in the kitchen set off down the road. He was still eating.

'I asked you a question.'

'I know.' Winter frowned, plucking at the crease in his trousers. 'Who's Richard Savage?'

The name brought the blood flooding to Tara's face. Winter watched it rise and spread.

'You've been watching us.' A statement, not a question.

'Since seven o'clock,' Winter confirmed. 'Who is he?'

'You've no right to ask that. It's none of your business.'

'Is it Parrish's business?'

'He knows already.'

'And you leaving? Does he know about that too?'

Tara stared at him, trying to work out how seriously to take this new threat, then, abruptly, she shut the door and sank onto the other end of the sofa.

'Richard's one of the site engineers at Gunwharf. We're' – she shrugged – 'together.'

'Does he live here full time?'

'No. He's got a place in London.'

'And your husband? Partner?' Winter's gesture took in most of the house.

'He's long gone. We divorced years ago.'

Winter nodded, arranging the pieces in his mind. The sleek young engineer with the BMW. The recent move to Playfair Road. The fact that the Gunwharf people used to decamp to the Weather Gage at lunchtimes.

'You met him in the pub,' Winter suggested. 'When you were still serving half-decent food.' Tara didn't say a word. 'You met him in the pub and you began some kind of affair, and that led to this.' He bent forward, his hands on his knees. 'You could help me on this but it doesn't matter if you don't.'

'Why not?'

'Because there's nothing illegal in screwing around.'

'So why are you here?'

'Because I think your friend Hennessey's been murdered.' Winter smiled. 'And that's not legal at all.'

For the first time, he had her full attention. The antagonism, the anger, had gone. She wanted to know what he meant. Winter paid her the courtesy of being frank. He explained about the damage to the room at the Marriott, about the bloodshed in the bathroom, and then he offered her a date.

'Sunday the eighteenth of June,' he said. 'Do you keep a diary?'

She did. She used it to keep a tally of the hours she worked. She went upstairs to fetch it.

'I was on that night,' she said when she returned. 'Alone?'

'Not to begin with. Rob was there until ten, maybe even closing time.'

'And then?'

'He went out somewhere.'

'Do you happen to know where?'

She hesitated a moment, the diary still open on her lap. Then she shook her head.

'There's something you ought to know,' she said. 'Rob and I used to live together. There are rooms over the pub. The kids were up there with us too, of course, but that wasn't the reason we split up. He would have been just as impossible without the kids. I know he would.'

Winter still wanted to know about Sunday the eighteenth. Had she been there when Parrish returned?

'No, I don't hang around after closing time. But that's exactly it, you see. What he does, where he goes, that's down to him. He makes a point of not telling me. It's a game he plays. He must see it as revenge or something. It's nothing of the kind, of course, but that's the kind of animal he is. He has to win. He has to be in the driving seat. Losing's not an option.'

Winter gazed at her, struck by something else.

'You're telling me he lost you to Savage?'

'No, though that's what he'd think. He lost me because he was a miserable self-centred bastard who thought he was God's gift. Men are strange that way. Buy them a bottle of blond rinse and one of those bracelets and they think the battle's over. The guy's nearly fifty, for Chrissakes. Thank God I got out.'

Winter wanted to get back to Hennessey. He and Parrish had been buddies. Yes?

'Yes, definitely, though I don't think Rob knows what the word "buddy" means. He's not into friendship or any of that drivel. As far as he's concerned, people are there to be used. Once you've sussed the way he does it, it's quite blatant. Believe me. I'm an expert.'

'You're telling me that's the way it's been with Hennessey?'

'I'm telling you he uses everybody. He and Hennessey seemed to be close, really close. You'd watch them talking, and you'd swear they'd been mates for ever, but I know they hadn't. He only met the bloke when I did, a couple of months back. He just smothered him. Puppy love. He does it with everybody. He did it with me.'

'Until he got what he wanted?'

'Yes. And then you realise what a bastard the man really is. My kids saw it, they saw it straight off. They couldn't get over what a mistake I was making. They hated him.'

The door opened and a girl of about fourteen appeared. She was wearing a a school uniform, blue top, grey skirt.

'In the fridge, Becca.' Tara barely spared her a glance. 'Pull the door to when you leave.'

Winter heard the girl returning to the kitchen. He wanted to know about Hennessey again.

'He was a nice bloke actually. Old school, you know.

Bit of a bullshitter, but at least you could have a laugh. I think he wanted company more than anything else. Like I said last night, I almost felt sorry for him.'

'Bullshitter?'

'He's South African, still got the accent. He used to tell me all these stories about the girls he'd had when he was at medical school over there. They were all incredibly rich and incredibly beautiful and, you know, just queuing up for him, and he was forever trying to work it out so they never bumped into each other.'

'You believed him?'

For the first time, she laughed. It warmed her whole face.

'Of course not,' she said. 'Total fantasy.'

'How can you tell?'

'Just by looking at him. You meet men like that all the time. What they're really trying to do is ask you out but they haven't got the bottle. So they make it all up instead.'

'You think he fancied you?'

'I think he'd fancy any woman. Not that he'd ever do anything about it.'

Winter sat back a moment, staring up at the ceiling. Nikki McIntyre, he thought, every encounter wrapped in heavy doses of anaesthetic. Maybe this woman was right. Maybe Hennessey was just a pathetic old bluffer who couldn't get it up.

'You say he told you he was a surgeon?'

'Yes.' Tara frowned. 'Heart transplants or something, wasn't it? No wonder he had so much money.'

Dawn Ellis attended the 0900 squad briefing in the CID office at Cosham nick in the north of the city. The overhang of jobs from the weekend included a B&E at a cattery in Drayton, an episode which had resulted in the theft of an Abyssinian moggie called Jason along with nine dozen tins of salmon Whiskas. Dawn was still trying to work out whether the pet food was worth more than the cat when Cathy took her aside. She wanted to know whether Dawn was happy to work single-crewed. Squad numbers were now so depleted that the normal practice of working in pairs would effectively halve the hit rate.

'No problem,' Dawn told her. 'I'll do whatever.'

'Any unfinished business?'

'Only Donald Duck. The rest I left with Faraday.'

Cathy frowned. The arrest and charging last week of Paul Addison, the lecturer, had been the subject of several crowing e-mails from Southsea CID room.

'I thought you lot had put that to bed?'

'So did I.'

Dawn quickly outlined the case against Addison. The guy made porno movies in his spare time. The dad of one of the students was alleging harassment of his daughter. The guy had no real alibi for any of the Donald Duck dates. And they'd found a mask in his garden.

Cathy was lost.

'So what's the problem?'

'I don't think he did it.'

'And Faraday?'

'I'm not sure he's bothered.'

Cathy gazed at her for a moment, then smiled.

'How much longer would you need?'

'Not long.'

'Do you want to spend a little more time on it then?'

'But we're snowed under, skip. You just told me. You just told us all. We've got volume crime coming out of our ears and no bloody time to sort any of it out.'

Cathy touched her lightly on the shoulder, a gesture of reassurance.

'It's all about priorities, my love.' Dawn thought she was going to get a kiss. 'Keep me briefed?'

Faraday tried Winter's mobile five times before ten o'clock but for some reason it was switched off. Only the thought that he was probably at the hospital prevented him from sending someone to physically deliver the simplest of questions: yes or no? With us or not?

Finally, against his better judgement, he gave in to Joyce's offer of yet another coffee, hoping to God she didn't go mad on the sugar again. American obesity wasn't down to anything as remotely complicated as greed. They simply couldn't count.

'You had a great birthday. I'm really glad.'

'How can you tell?'

'The mood you're in. Folks with faces that black have always had a great time. They just didn't want it to end, is all. Take it from me. I know about disappointment.'

'You might be right. What's this?'

Joyce had left a brown envelope beside the brimming cup of coffee. There were a couple of pictures inside. She'd been clearing out the cupboard behind her desk and she'd found them tucked away behind some printer ribbons.

'That was Vanessa's cupboard,' Faraday pointed out.

'I know. That's why I rescued them.' She nodded at the envelope. 'You might want to keep them. Your decision.'

Faraday opened the envelope and shook three photographs onto the desk. They'd been taken last Christmas, souvenirs from the CID party. In one, Vanessa was

276

posing beneath a pair of reindeer antlers, the green-tinged darkness behind her swimming with faces. In another, her glass was raised to the camera. The third showed Vanessa and Faraday together on the dance floor, umpteen glasses down, enjoying the slowest of smooches.

Looking at the shot, Faraday could hear the music again, a Celtic folk band, the creation of a wild DC from the Drugs Squad up at Havant. They seemed to have played for most of the night, an unending mix of tempos, keening ballads one moment, frenzied foot-stamping rebel songs the next. Vanessa had loved it, surprising Faraday with her knowledge of the words, and afterwards, walking her to the taxi rank, he'd learned that an aunt of hers had once had a holiday home out in County Kerry.

Sleepy-drunk, she'd hung on his arm at the kerbside, describing the taste of the wind in the early mornings and the rags of cloud that blew in from the ocean, wrapping themselves around the mountains behind the cottage. She'd spend hours alone on the beach, she'd said, just watching the waves. They'd come three thousand miles to die at her feet, and she'd dance barefoot in the shallows, celebrating their final moments, because a little death like that was a gladness.

A gladness?

Faraday looked up, a knuckle in his mouth, to find Joyce still there.

'I did give you that number, didn't I?' she asked.

'What number?'

'The number I got from Vodafone? The one you were gonna try for yourself?'

Faraday stared up at her, totally lost, then he was back in the world of twenty-five-year-old commercial salesmen and Vanessa's broken body, painstakingly extracted from the wreckage of the crushed Fiesta. Not a gladness at all, he thought, letting Joyce scribble the number afresh on a corner of the envelope.

Twenty-One

Monday, 26 June, mid-morning

At the Southsea CID office, Rick Stapleton was waiting to check out a couple of details with Ferguson on the Hennessey inquiry when the call came in from Dawn Ellis. She needed a word with him, strictly private, preferably face to face.

'When?'

'Now.'

Rick looked around at the empty desks. The rest of Ferguson's squad were out and about, knocking on doors, but the truth was the inquiry was dead in the water. He himself had talked to the sales people over at Gunwharf, and they'd certainly confirmed that Hennessey had bought three twenty-eight-day options, but he'd got the impression they thought him a bit flaky, and it was therefore no surprise that he hadn't turned up with the full ten per cent. The fact that anyone could kiss goodbye to three grand was inconceivable to Rick, but the girl in the sales office had told him it was no big deal. Out there, she'd said, people have money you wouldn't believe. Three grand, to someone like Hennessey, would be small change.

Rick bent to the phone again.

'Where?' he said.

They met on the seafront half a mile from Southsea nick. Rick settled himself in the passenger seat of Dawn's diesel Escort and wound down the window, eyeing a couple of barechested roller-bladers as they cruised past.

'Missing me already?'

'Like you wouldn't believe.'

Something in Dawn's tone brought his head round. 'What's the matter?'

Dawn had been rehearsing this conversation in her mind since the morning's conversation with Cathy. The last thing Rick wanted to hear about was the Donald Duck job. Never pick old scabs. Always move on.

'There's something I have to do,' she said. 'I'd handle it on my own, but frankly that isn't an option. You need to be there too.'

'Where?'

'Forty-five Salamanca Road.'

Rick frowned for a moment, trying to place the address, then began to laugh.

'Kennedy's drum?'

'Yep.'

'*Again?* What's the matter with you? The guy's off the planet, all that gobbing on about what he can do for you. You'd be better off down Guildhall Walk.'

'I'm serious, Rick.'

'Yeah, but why? Why go back?'

'Because Addison didn't do it.'

'That's what you said last time.'

'I know. And I'm certain now.'

'How can you be?'

'I went back over the statements. You remember that last woman? The woman with the dog? The one who got hurt?'

'The duty DC talked to her. Up at the hospital.'

'Yeah, and one of the points she made was the smell on the bloke. Remember?'

Rick looked down for a moment, picking at a cuticle on one of his nails.

'No,' he muttered, 'remind me.'

'She said he stank of tobacco, cheap tobacco, roll-ups. She made a big point of it. That's partly why she felt so yukky about the clothes she was wearing. That's why she threw them in the washing machine.'

'So?'

'So the guy's a smoker. A heavy smoker. Probably rolls his own.'

'And?'

'Addison doesn't smoke.'

'We don't know that,' Rick said at once. 'That's supposition.'

'*Supposition?*' Dawn couldn't believe it. 'Is it my imagination, or did we turn his house over?'

'We had a look round.'

'Yeah, exactly, *we*, me and you. You were there, Rick. No ashtrays. No fag packets. No matches. No lighters. No fag ends in the fireplace. No smell. Nothing. That guy hasn't touched a cigarette for years. He's probably never smoked. And we're trying to kid ourselves he climbed all over the woman with the dog? Reeking of fags? Are you kidding?'

'It's borrowed gear. He's laying a false trail.'

'Yeah? So where is it?'

'He burned the stuff. Dumped it. Binned it. God knows. Happens all the time.'

'That's bollocks. And if *I* think it's bollocks, what's a half-decent QC going to say?'

Rick frowned again and returned to his nails, avoiding her gaze, and Dawn suddenly realised that he'd known all along.

'You owe me,' she said quietly. 'This thing about Kennedy, I shouldn't even have to ask.'

The Weather Gage, for the second day running, was empty. Winter gave Tara Gough a little wave as he came in. The place smelled of stale beer laced with disinfectant, and it crossed Winter's mind that the non-existent profits probably wouldn't stretch to a cleaner in the mornings. Maybe Tara did it. Maybe that's why she bought rubber gloves by the boxful.

'Long time,' he said, 'no see. Where's our Mr Parrish?'

'Out at the cash and carry,' she replied, 'and he's your Mr Parrish, not mine.'

There was a single glass on the bar top, just under half-full. Winter studied it a moment, wondering who'd be starting this early. Tara nodded towards the toilets.

'One of our regulars,' she said. 'I count them in and I count them out.'

'Both hands?'

'Very funny.'

Winter glanced at his watch.

'When's he back, then? Parrish.'

'Midday at the earliest. He's got a session with his accountant, too. He was talking about putting the place on the market this morning.'

'You think he will?'

'He thinks he may have to. He nearly did it back in the spring, but that was different.'

'Yeah?'

They were friends now, allies in a common cause. Winter could see it in her eyes. She just loved gossiping, especially when it included an element of revenge.

'Yes. Don't ask me the details, but I know he was trying to raise money for the Gunwharf bid. He had his eye on one of the pub franchises in the leisure complex. He's convinced he could do huge business if he got the formula right, but the commercial people blew him away.' She smiled. 'That was just after me and the kids moved out. Really made his week.'

'How do you know all this?'

'About the franchise?' Winter nodded. 'Richard told me. He tells me everything. That's another reason he's such a sweetie. Drink?'

Winter shook his head. He'd be off now. This afternoon, once Parrish was back, he'd maybe have a word or two.

He folded his copy of the *Daily Telegraph* and turned to go. Behind him, he heard the sigh of the door that led through to the lavatories. He glanced over his shoulder, briefly registering the tall, erect figure making its way back towards the barstool. Tara was in conversation with him already, producing a saucer full of peanuts, and as the lone drinker made himself comfortable Winter realised where he'd seen the man before. The converted barn beside the river with the ducks paddling past. The long sweep of the grand piano, laden with photographs. The mottled, liver-spotted hand that had poured him sherry after sherry. Ronald McIntyre. Nikki's father.

Winter walked the length of the quay before finding a public phone box. Directory Enquiries gave him the phone number of the pub. He dialled it on his mobile. There'd been an extension at the back of the bar. He'd seen it.

'Tara? Paul Winter.'

He asked her to take the phone out of earshot.

'Who are you worried about?'

'The guy at the bar.'

Winter heard the rustle of movement as she decamped. Then she was back on the phone.

'He's fine. He's no problem. He's a nice old boy. What's going on?'

283

'You say he's a regular?'

'Couple of times a week. Sometimes more. Why?'

'Always this time of day?'

'Normally evenings. He tells me he can't stand the traffic during the day, though how he makes it home at all some nights defeats me.'

'And Hennessey? Has he ever bumped into Hennessey?'

There was a longish silence. Winter was watching a pair of swans preening themselves on one of the pontoons. No, he thought. The answer is no.

'No,' she said at last. 'Hennessey only comes in at lunchtimes. When he's down, that is.'

'So they've never met?'

'No.'

'OK.' Winter walked on. He felt the sun on his face. He felt warmth flooding his whole body. Just one more question, he thought. Just one. 'Tara?'

'Yes?'

'Tell me about Parrish and the guy at the bar. Do they chat like old mates? Old buddies? Is Parrish all over him? The way you described with Hennessey?'

'Like a rash.' He could hear Tara laughing. 'That's why the old boy keeps coming in.'

It took Faraday less than five minutes to find the Half Moon Café. He'd driven up from Southsea and parked at the back of Cosham nick. The Half Moon was midway down the high street, wedged between a charity shop and Woolworth's. Today's special offer, according to a handwritten square of cardboard in the window, was a choice of roasts at £3.99. Including tea and a slice.

The café was busy, mums with babies mainly, and the air was blue with cigarette smoke. Meals and prices were chalked on a blackboard and a weary-looking woman perched beside the till at the end of the counter took the orders. Faraday asked for a cup of tea and found himself a table at the back. Perfect, he thought. Grandstand seat.

The café got even busier. After a while, Faraday produced his mobile and dialled the number again. He heard an answering trill from the steamy, neon-lit space behind the counter, and then came the same voice, a kid's voice, thick Pompey accent, a voice barely out of adolescence.

'Yeah?'

'Just checking.'

'Yer what?'

'Come next door. There's someone needs you.'

'Yer *what*?'

'You heard me, son. Just step next door.'

Faraday was watching the counter, his phone back in his pocket. After a moment or two, a pale, pock-marked youth appeared, looking carefully around. He wasn't spoiled for choice. Among a couple of dozen women, Faraday's was the only male face.

As soon as they made eye contact, Faraday waved him across. The boy promptly disappeared. On his feet, Faraday squeezed past the woman at the till, ignoring her protests. The cooking area was at the back. Oil bubbled in a blackened chipper while a fat woman in her sixties did her best to wrestle pre-cut chips from a big plastic bag.

'Where's the lad?'

The woman turned to look at him, an expression of mild curiosity on her face. Then she jerked a fat thumb towards a tiny office area round the corner. Over the desk was a Pompey football poster. The door to the alley at the back was open. Faraday stepped through, avoiding a dustbin full of discarded slops, following the alley round to the side. The lad was at the end, his back to a big iron gate that was plainly locked. He was thin and of medium height, wore baggy, grease-stained jeans, a Pompey football top and trashed runners. His hair, black and lank, fell sideways from a centre parting. His head lowered, he peered through the hair at Faraday. He looked terrified.

'I'm gonna call the police!' he shouted. 'You can't do this!'

Faraday had his warrant card out.

'I am the police,' he said, 'and I'm afraid I can.'

Faraday offered him the choice of the nick round the corner or the table he'd just abandoned in the café. The youth, whose name was Brent, settled for the café. Faraday sat him down with his back to the street. He wanted to talk about a man called Matthew Prentice. Did Brent know him?

'What if I do?'

'Just answer the question.'

'Yeah.' He tipped up his chin, defiant now. 'I knows him.'

'You know him well?'

'Yeah.'

'Mates?'

'Sort of, yeah. He's older than me, like, but . . . yeah.'

Faraday produced a notebook and scribbled down a line to himself, aware of Brent watching him. This was a youth off one of the estates, Paulsgrove maybe, or Wymering. Faraday had done business with hundreds of them over the years. Without a qualification to their names, most of them had a sharp, streetwise intelligence it would be foolish to underestimate.

'He does business here,' Faraday suggested, 'your mate.'

'He comes round with the crisps and stuff, yeah.'

'How often?'

'Dunno.' The youth shrugged.

'Every week?'

'No. More like two.'

'OK.' Faraday nodded. 'You remember that last time he came?'

For the first time it dawned on Brent where this conversation was going. Faraday could see the curtains coming down. It was like being in the theatre. End of act one. He made another note, then looked up.

'He had an accident, didn't he?'

'Did he?' Brent picked at the formica around the edge of the table. 'I dunno nothing about no accident.'

'You're mates with this guy, and you don't know he nearly got himself killed?'

'It weren't that bad,' he said hotly.

'What wasn't?'

There was a long silence. One or two of the women, curious, were exchanging glances. Brent announced he'd had enough of talking. Said he had to get back to the kitchen. Faraday reached across as he tried to get to his feet.

'Sit down,' he said, 'while I tell you something.'

He described the accident the way Accident Investigation had pieced it together, the Vectra racing down Larkrise Avenue, the Fiesta slowing in its path. The impact, a couple of degrees off head on, had spun both vehicles. The Vectra had been doing fifty-three miles an hour. The Fiesta was practically stopped.

'Do you know Larkrise Avenue?'

The youth, with great reluctance, nodded a yes.

'Good. Because that's where I lost a very close friend. She was driving the Fiesta. And your mate Matthew killed her. And you know why he killed her? Because he was on his mobile. Talking to you.'

Faraday meant it to sound like a hanging offence, taking a phone call, and he knew he'd succeeded. Brent was shaking his head.

'I don't remember no phone call.'

'Yes, you do. He was on his way here. We've checked, Brent. You were his next stop. He was late. That's why he phoned.'

'I didn't have the phone then.'

'Where was it?'

'At home, I'd left it at home.'

'Then how come you made another call right afterwards? Five minutes afterwards?'

'How d'you know that, then?'

'We've got the print-out, son. It's all there, black and white, timed to the second.'

'It was someone else. I lent it to someone else.'

'Really? You want me to go and talk to the person you phoned right afterwards? You want me to find him, like I've found you, and put these questions to him?' He paused. 'There's an offence here. It's called perverting the course of justice. I can put you away for this, Brent. And the next guy you talked to. And the guy after that. OK by you? Or shall we get back to your mate Matthew?'

Brent was weighing it up. Mateship meant a great deal to kids like these. The last people you did favours for were the filth.

'I don't remember,' he said finally. 'It might have happened but I don't remember.'

'You don't remember what he said?'

'I don't remember nothing.'

'You don't remember a conversation that ended with a huge fucking bang?'

The word 'fucking' had the impact of the accident itself. It shook Brent but made him, if anything, even more determined not to remember. He was busy. The phone was always going. There were people in and out all the time, just like today. How the fuck was he supposed to remember a conversation that old?

'Because someone got killed.'

'Yeah?' He looked down again, bit his fingernails. 'Well, he never told me that.'

'You don't believe me?'

Brent wouldn't look up, wouldn't look Faraday in the eye. Instead, he just shrugged.

'Fuck knows,' he muttered.

Something snapped in Faraday. He got to his feet and stepped round the table. He'd had enough of trying to coax out the truth. He'd had enough of trying to funnel all his neat, textbook questions through the proper channels. There were moments that called for something a little more direct, and this, in front of a largish audience, was one of them.

'Get up,' he hissed.

One look at Faraday's face brought Brent to his feet. He looked about ten years old.

'Get back in the kitchen.'

Faraday followed him through to the area behind the counter. One or two of the women were shouting out now, telling Faraday to leave him alone, but Faraday ignored them. When the youth made a bid to escape, Faraday pinned him in a wristlock. The old woman in the kitchen was standing at the range, giving the chip pan a good shake. Faraday explained to her that he was police.

'Brent here took a phone call a couple of weeks back. You'd have remembered it because it ended with a car crash. Literally. A big bang. He'd have told you that. I know he would. He'd either have told you then, or maybe later. Either way, it was news.'

The woman was still shaking the pan.

'Yeah?' she said.

'Yeah. But Brent can't remember that phone call any more, which is a shame.'

'Why's that?'

'Because someone was killed.'

The woman put the hot chips to one side and adjusted the temperature on the oil. Only when she'd wiped her hands did she finally turn round. She wasn't looking at Faraday. She was looking at Brent.

'I read about that woman in the paper,' she said. 'Why don't you tell him about the season ticket, you little tyke?'

Twenty-Two

Monday, 26 June, early afternoon

Ever patient, Paul Winter waited until McIntyre had drunk his fill at the Weather Gage before intercepting him en route to his car. He must have had at least three pints in that time because the old man was having difficulty working out which of the two keys on his Rover ring fitted the driver's door.

Winter made his way towards him and touched him lightly on the sleeve.

'Ronnie,' he said with a smile, 'a word.'

McIntyre was taking a while to put a name to the face. Winter spared him the trouble, adding that it might be wise to let the last pint settle before getting behind the wheel.

'You're police, of course.' McIntyre frowned. 'That's right, isn't it?'

Winter walked him to a bench on Point at the tip of Spice Island. From here, they had a grandstand view of the Gunwharf construction site. Tourists milled around the explanatory display boards, trying to superimpose the stylish computer-generated images of shopping malls and waterside apartments onto the muddy chaos across the tiny stretch of water. McIntyre watched them from the bench, as awkward and as stiff as ever.

'Used to sail from there.' He nodded in the direction of an area further upharbour. 'HMS *Invincible*. He glanced sideways at Winter. 'Falklands War.'

Winter let him ramble on for a while, making himself comfortable, setting down this unexpected conversation in a warm bath of reminiscence. How the bloody acquisition radars never worked properly. How the MoD consistently underestimated the Argie pilots. What a shock it was to see the first pictures of HMS *Sheffield*, adrift and abandoned, the victim of a single bloody Exocet.

'French missile, of course,' he added bitterly. 'Never miss a trick, do they?'

Finally, he ran out of stories. There was a companionable silence. Then Winter began to talk about his wife. How she'd had grumbling little pains in her tummy. How she was never the complaining sort. How her GP had given her a couple of aspirin and a pat on the head. And how the bad news had come crashing into their lives, a direct hit from their very own little Exocet, the consultant consigning Joannie to the early grave she didn't, for one second, deserve.

'Bastards,' Winter said softly. 'Absolute bastards.'

'Medics?'

'This one, certainly.'

McIntyre blew his nose. He couldn't agree more. He was desperately sorry to hear about Winter's wife. His own dealings with Hennessey had opened his eyes. If you couldn't trust a doctor, where would it all bloody end?

Winter nodded. Under the circumstances, he thought Nikki had coped incredibly well. Real strength, real character.

'Of course, you've met her, haven't you? So you'd know.'

'Know what, Ronnie?'

'Know what a man like that could do to her.'

'Too right. And not just her.'

'Excuse me?'

'You, Ronnie. You and your whole family. There must be times when' – Winter hunted for the exact phrase – 'you could do with a little compensation.'

'Compensation?'

'Revenge.'

McIntyre didn't say anything. Instead, he was staring up the harbour, towards the jetty where his wife and daughter had waved goodbye the morning he'd sailed for the Falklands. He'd never had a moment's doubt about the Task Force. The Argies had taken without asking. The islands were British. And British they would stay.

Winter wanted to know about the Weather Gage. Did Ronnie pop in there a lot?

'Often enough. It's difficult in the village now. People know about Penny going. You can imagine, can't you? The gossips had a real field day.'

'Whereas down here . . .'

'Exactly.' McIntyre offered an emphatic nod. 'Nothing like a fresh start.'

'And Parrish?' Winter smiled. 'Rob?'

'You know him?' McIntyre sounded surprised.

'Of course.'

'A good man. Enterprising. And a bloody good landlord too.' McIntyre fumbled for his handkerchief again. 'Makes it a pleasure to pop down of an evening.'

Winter let him wipe his nose. One of the Isle of Wight car ferries churned past, executed a deft three-point turn, and began to inch backwards into the terminal berth.

'Do you have any financial relationship with Rob Parrish?'

Winter was still watching the ferry. He might have been asking about the weather.

'I beg your pardon?'

'Have you given him any money recently?'

'Good Lord, no. Why should I?'

Winter left the question unanswered. Side by side on the bench, he could sense the sudden tension in McIntyre's body. He glanced across, offered a reassuring smile.

'Would you have any objection to showing me your bank statements?'

'My what?'

'Bank statements.'

'That's what I thought you said.' He blinked. 'What an extraordinary thing to ask.'

The response was wholly ambiguous. Winter put the question another way, patting him on the arm, ever friendly, ever supportive, a fellow victim at the hands of the bastard medics.

'How much did you give him, Ronnie?'

'What?'

'How much is she worth? Nikki? How much did you give Parrish to sort out Hennessey?' He paused. 'I could get a court order on your bank statements. 'It's not a hard thing to do.'

McIntyre was staring at him. Three pints and this sudden change of tack had left him hopelessly confused. Was this man friend or foe? A harmless blip on the radar screen, or something infinitely more menacing?

Winter bent towards him.

'Tell me, Ronnie. You're not under caution.'

'I'm not?'

'No. We're friends here. Trust me.'

He nodded, heartened by this small reassurance. Then he slumped again, completely defenceless.

'You know, don't you?' He wouldn't look at Winter. 'You know already. I can tell.'

Winter didn't say a word. McIntyre moistened his lower lip.

'It was a loan,' he said at last, 'strictly a loan.'

'How much?'

'Twenty thousand.'

'When?'

'A couple of weeks ago.'

'And you've still got the paperwork?'

'I'm still drawing it up.'

'You gave this man twenty thousand pounds and he didn't sign anything?'

'He will. It's a formality.'

Winter shook his head. He couldn't even begin to believe him.

'So how do you know?' he asked. 'What's the deal here?'

'I don't understand.'

'How do you know Hennessey's dead? Where's the proof? You spend twenty grand on the man. You want him good and dead. But how can you be sure?'

McIntyre stared at him for a long time. Behind the affronted expression, Winter could see all the misery, anger and emptiness of the last few years. Things had piled up. He'd been to hell and back through no fault of his own. And now, to cap it all, comes a conversation like this.

'Put yourself in my place for a moment,' he said. 'Don't you think that man *deserves* to die?'

'Yes.' Winter placed a hand on his arm. 'But very slowly.'

For all his misgivings, Rick had agreed to accompany Dawn Ellis back to Kennedy's place. It was half-past two in the afternoon. Dawn had made the call privately, standing alone on the pavement while Rick pretended not to watch from the car. She'd told Kennedy she was up for it, but she wanted to bring a friend. When Kennedy said no problem, she pointed out it was a male friend.

'So what?' he'd drawled. 'Share and share alike.'

'Share what?'

'You.'

He'd laughed. Half an hour's time would be fine. He'd get everything ready. Two guys, and they'd make it last the rest of the afternoon.

'Any preferences?' he'd enquired, still laughing.

She'd rung off without answering. Now, she and Rick stood on the pavement outside the house. Rick, under his weekend tan, was less than eager. A year of working with Dawn had made it obvious that she had designs on him and he wasn't convinced that she hadn't stitched him up. Women could be so devious that way. Men were an infinitely simpler proposition.

'Who draws the line?' he asked for the second time.

'I do,' Dawn muttered. 'I told you just now. I'm the one with most to lose.'

She rang the doorbell, wondering where the next few minutes would take them. She was more convinced than ever that Kennedy was running a brothel, a knocking shop with a difference, offering students for sex. Girls like Shelley, skint most of the time, had a brain as well as a body and there'd be plenty of middle-class, middle-aged punters more than happy to pay Kennedy for the pleasure of screwing someone their daughter's age. What she needed now was evidence, and a lead on exactly how Shelley Beavis fitted into Kennedy's little enterprise.

Footsteps came crashing down the stairs. Kennedy must have been in the shower. His shaved head glistened with tiny drops of water and he smelled of something from one of the more expensive bottles of *après-douche*.

'Hi.' He extended a hand towards Rick. 'Awright?'

'Fine, thanks. You?'

Rick walked straight past, ignoring the hand. Kennedy and Dawn exchanged looks.

'Where d'you find him, then? Crufts?'

Kennedy was already leading the way upstairs, Rick and Dawn in pursuit.

'Sorry about the short notice,' she called. 'My friend's got a train at six.'

'And you?'

She laughed. 'I hate trains.'

Upstairs, four doors led off a carpeted landing. The walls were hung with Japanese-looking erotic prints, strangely tasteful. Rick paused to look.

'Where did you get these, then?'

'Paris. Friend of mine runs a market stall. *Loads* of oriental stuff. Like it?'

'Yeah.'

'I'll bring you some back. Next time I'm over.'

Kennedy pushed his way in through a door at the end. The room at the front, thought Dawn, with the permanently pulled curtains. She hesitated outside for a second, checking with Rick. To her surprise, he was beginning to look interested.

The room was bigger than she'd expected. In the middle was a huge bed, king-size at least, with an assortment of pillows at both ends. There were no blankets, just a sheet. The ceiling was painted black, and from it hung a number of lights, all of them directional and all of them pointed at the bed. In a shallow semi-circle on the far side of the bed stood three tripods. There were cameras on each of them. Dawn was no expert, but you didn't buy cameras like these at

Boots. Maybe not simply a pimp, she thought. Maybe something else as well.

Kennedy had seen the surprise on her face.

'Shel never mentioned it?'

'Never.'

'I'm amazed.' He nodded towards the bed. 'This is what turned her on to acting in the first place. Proper little drama queen.' He pointed at the rug by the deep bay window. 'Dump your gear there. Thank Christ it's summer, eh?'

He loosened the knot on his dressing gown. Rick was watching his every move.

'You mentioned money,' Dawn began. 'For what, exactly?'

Kennedy didn't answer. Instead, he went to the only piece of furniture in the room, a chest of drawers that must have come from a half-decent antique shop. Dawn found herself looking at a selection of vibrators.

'Help yourself.' Kennedy winked at Rick. 'First course is on us.'

Dawn didn't move.

'I'm serious,' she said 'I want to know whether we get paid.'

'The answer's no.'

'Why not?'

'Because you're first-timers. It's like football. This is a try-out. If you're any good, then we might talk business. Either way you still get to have a good time.'

'And you video us?' Dawn was examining one of the cameras.

'Not this time, no. Next time, maybe.'

The dressing gown was off now. Naked, Kennedy was bent over a small fridge in the corner. Rick eyed him for a moment, then glanced across at Dawn.

'Say we're good,' he began. 'Say we pass the screen test. What happens then?'

Kennedy turned round. He had a couple of Becks in one hand and a high-energy drink in the other.

'On the house.' He grinned.

'I asked you a question.'

'I know you did.'

'Well?'

Kennedy passed Rick a Becks.

'If you shag OK, there's money in it,' he said.

'How much?'

'Depends on sales. I pay a flat rate up front, plus a percentage of sales.'

'Sales of what?'

'Videos.'

'You make videos? Up here?'

'Of course. That's the deal. That's why I asked you over. If it's cool, you get to be a movie star.'

'How do we know how many you sell?'

'You don't. You take it on trust.'

'Are you kidding? What kind of sales are we talking about?'

'Depends how far you want to go.' Dawn shook her head when Kennedy offered her the other Becks. 'Something really tasty, we could shift thousands.'

'Shelley?'

He grinned, and then nodded. 'Thousands.'

'So who cuts it all?' Dawn gestured at the cameras. 'Who does all the technical bits afterwards?'

Kennedy just looked at her, the Lucozade tipped to his lips. Then he glanced across at Rick.

'Tell she's a student, can't you? Real turn-on, all these questions.'

Rick told him to ignore her. She was the only student he'd ever met who got all her essays in on time.

'Good point about the editing, though,' he went on, picking up Dawn's thread. 'Who does put these things together?'

Kennedy looked from one to the other, weighing them up.

'You *are* up for this, aren't you?'

'Definitely.' Rick nodded. 'I'm just curious, that's all. I've got a mate who does video. He's got all the gear, everything, he's really good. I was just wondering . . .' He shrugged. 'If you ever wanted a hand . . .'

'That's cool.' Kennedy was watching Dawn. 'Actually I have got a problem. Bloke let me down big time. I'd been relying on him and he just won't come through.'

'And this bloke puts it all together? Whoever you're talking about?'

'Yeah, and he's good. In fact, he's cracking. Does it for a living, know what I mean? That's what you need in this game. Good post-production.' He nodded at the cameras again. 'I can get the pictures OK but it's what you do with them afterwards that really counts. This guy's a genius. If only the bastard would come across.'

'What's his name? Matter of interest . . .'

At last it dawned on Kennedy that there was more going on here than he'd anticipated. He studied them both for a long moment, then reached for his dressing gown.

'You're the Old Bill, aren't you?' he said quietly. 'I'll murder that fucking Shel.'

Back in the car, an hour later, Rick couldn't contain himself. Justice, for once, had been done. He'd gone in there feeling a right prat and now here they were, back in one piece with a story that would keep the CID office going for months. Not only that, but he'd had one of his great all-time assumptions confirmed.

'And what's that?'

'Footballers really are fucking apes. See the body on that guy? What a waste.'

They'd arrested Kennedy on suspicion of aiding and abetting unlawful sexual intercourse. They'd organised a proper search of the premises and stayed long enough to find a stack of videos. One of them, labelled 'Shel', had contained uncut footage of the girl in action with Kennedy. It carried a date and time on the top right-hand corner of the picture, when according to Dawn's calculations Shelley would have been barely fifteen – ample evidence to justify Kennedy's arrest. The issue now was Shelley's safety. Kennedy would be in custody for at least twenty-four hours, but after that it was anyone's guess what would happen next.

'I'll get her out of Rawlinson Road,' Dawn said. 'I'll park her in the Travelodge until we sort something out.'

Twenty-Three

Monday, 26 June, late afternoon

At Winter's insistence, Tara Gough gave him a proper tour of the Weather Gage. Parrish, like Hennessey, seemed to have disappeared. He always took over in the late afternoon, giving Tara the chance to get home for the kids, but it was nearly twenty-four hours since she'd last seen him and she couldn't hang on for ever.

'It'll take fifteen minutes,' Winter told her. 'I just need to take a look.'

With some reluctance, she agreed. Upstairs was the living accommodation, a dozen rooms on two storeys. Parrish had been here for nearly three years now, yet some of the rooms still hadn't been touched – bare boards, cobwebbed windows – and Winter began to sense the kind of life this man was leading.

With Tara and her kids here, it would certainly have been cosier, but now she'd gone, he'd reverted to a cramped, chaotic existence in a bedroom, a lounge and a filthy L-shaped kitchen. Old newspapers and magazines were strewn everywhere, as were sundry items of food: biscuits still spread with Kraft cheese, open packets of crisps, the remains of a takeaway korma, green with mould. This was graphic enough, evidence of a life spooling out of control, but when Winter examined just a handful of the invoices piled high on the faded baize card table Parrish obviously used as a desk, it became clear that this same chaos had spilled into his business life. Bills for hundreds of pounds' worth of frozen pizzas. Four-figure demands for electricity arrears. Tara was right. The pub was on its knees.

Downstairs again, Winter wanted to know what was out the back. Tara checked her watch. She was late. The kids would be worrying.

'Phone them,' Winter told her briskly, pushing at a door that was obviously locked.

Tara fetched the key. This was the outhouse, the place where Parrish kept the big fridge freezers he used to store food for the restaurant. There were cases of wine here too, and, along the inner wall, specially built cradles for the wooden barrels of real ale that had once given the Weather Gage a reputation for decently kept beer.

The door creaked open and Tara reached for the switch inside. Spookily lit with a single flickering neon tube, the outhouse was enormous, much bigger than Winter had imagined. Double doors at the far end were bolted and padlocked on the inside, and Winter could see a thin strip of sunshine at the bottom where the wood didn't quite reach the flagstones.

'Does he ever keep cars in here?'

'Sometimes. When he's got one.'

'What's this?'

There was a sturdy wooden table in the middle of the outhouse, big but still dwarfed by the space around it. Winter bent to examine its top. The table looked old, the surface stained and scored from years of use.

'Rob's pride and joy,' Tara told him. 'He bought it from a butcher in Southsea. When we first started the restaurant, we'd get whole sides of beef from a farm up near Petersfield and Rob would pay the bloke we'd got the table from to come and chop the carcass up.'

'Has he used it recently?'

'Not as far as I know.'

'What's it doing here then? Centre stage?'

'Haven't a clue.'

Winter took a tiny step backwards, his head cocked. The overhead light had a definite problem. As well as the flicker, there was a loud hum, almost a buzzing. Control unit, he thought. Ten quid from B&Q.

He reached out to touch the table, then had second thoughts. Scenes of Crime, he thought. The guys with the white paper suits and the face masks. The guys who just love crawling over items like this.

'That Sunday I asked you about? Just over a week ago?'

'Yes?'

'You say Parrish came back?'

'No, I told you I locked up without him. I've no idea whether he came back or not.'

'But he could have done, no?'

'Of course.' The neon light danced on her face. 'He lives here.'

Outside in the sunshine, Winter walked Tara to her car. He wanted to know about Parrish and the old boy, Ronald McIntyre. Had they really been close?

'"Close" isn't the right word,' Tara muttered, dying to get away. 'Like I said, Rob isn't close to anyone. But if you're asking whether they chatted, then yes, all the time.'

'What did they talk about?'

'I don't know. All sorts. There's some problem about Ronnie's daughter. She's had a bad time. Some gynae mess-up. Sounds horrific.'

'Does he ever talk to you about that?'

'Never. He's very old-fashioned. That's one of the things I like about him. To women you talk about flowers and horseriding. The nasty stuff might upset me.'

'But he discusses it with Parrish?'

'Definitely.'

'Anything else?'

'Look. I—' The watch again, and the key poised to open the car door.

'Anything else?' Winter repeated.

'No, not really. Boats, of course. But all the men I know bang on about boats.'

Cathy Lamb was so pleased by the news of Kennedy's arrest she fetched the coffees herself. The machine along the corridor was playing up, so she couldn't guarantee the sugar.

'Doesn't matter.' Dawn's smile was equally bright. 'I shouldn't take it in the first place.'

'OK.' Cathy passed the brimming plastic cup across. 'Just go through it again for me.'

Dawn consulted her notes. What she knew for sure was that Kennedy was making porn movies in his upstairs bedroom and that Shelley had been one of his first volunteers.

'She admits that?'

'Yes.'

'How old?'

'Fifteen. Which means we can have him.'

'You've got evidence? A statement?'

'I've got better than that. We've seized a video featuring him and Shelley at it. It's got date and time on it. April 1997.'

'And she's been working for him ever since?'

'Big time. But recently it's been getting tricky.'

'Why?'

'He's started beating her up.'

'Any particular reason? Or just for kicks?'

'She says it's because of Addison, the guy we nicked for the Donald Duck jobs. Kennedy heard about the porno movies he does for the Kosovan girl and wanted him to work on his own stuff. The guy's really good with the editing. Really, really good. Kennedy needed some of that, which is why he steered Shelley towards him in the first place.'

'She didn't want to be an actress?'

'No, she did, and she still does, but it took Kennedy to point her at Addison. All his students have to do a little video of their own, a kind of intro thing. It's all part of the selection process. Vamping it up the way Shelley did was Kennedy's idea too. He thought Addison wouldn't be able to resist it, and it turns out he was right.'

'So she's at it with Addison?'

'She still says not.'

'You believe her?'

'Yes, I do.'

'Does Kennedy?'

'No. He thinks she's screwing him. That's bad enough, but the fact that she won't lean on him to do the editing drives him up the wall.'

Cathy sipped at her coffee and then pulled a face, swapping the cup with Dawn's.

'So who's Donald Duck?' she asked at last. 'Does Shelley know?'

'She says not.'

'What about you?'

Dawn didn't answer for a moment or two. A name, at this stage, would be dangerous. She didn't have the evidence, and another mistake would simply cancel out the pleasure she had in store for Cathy. Finally, she reached for her notebook and slipped it into her jeans pocket.

'Give me one more day?'

'Gladly.'

At Southsea nick, Faraday convened a squad meet on the Hennessey job for five o'clock. He'd heard about the Kennedy arrest, but Cathy was dealing with it up at Fratton and he'd yet to make the connection with Addison. Ferguson rustled up the bodies for the Hennessey squad and launched the brief with an update on current progress. He was about to reach the usual gloomy conclusion after another wasted day when Winter finally appeared. Heads turned. Faraday was the first to speak.

'How's Joannie?'

'A bit better, boss.'

'Still at the QA?'

'Afraid so.'

'Are you with us now or' – Faraday frowned –' not?'

'Yeah.' Winter perched himself on the edge of a desk at the back. 'Definitely.'

Ferguson took up the running again, with what little remained to be said. There'd been no sighting of Hennessey at the ferry port. Photos from the Marriott surveillance had been circulated on an inter-force digest. No evidence had turned up of an ex-wife, or a close relative, or even a friend. On that big, busy drawing that was life, the man had simply rubbed himself out.

'Not quite, skip.' It was Winter.

'You've got something for us? Thank fuck for that. Draw up a seat. Make yourself comfortable.'

There was a ripple of laughter around the CID room. Some of the support staff were here too, clerks who'd spent long, fruitless hours trawling through records of one kind or another, looking for Hennessey's tracks. An inquiry this complex at divisional level was unusual, to say the least. Only the fact that a body hadn't turned up had so far prevented an upgrade to the Major Crimes Suite.

Winter, with a slightly apologetic look in Faraday's direction, explained that he'd had an hour or two off from the hospital, time he'd been more than happy to devote to Hennessey.

'Lucky us.' It was Ferguson again.

No one else laughed this time. Winter had a certain reputation among these men: bent, for sure, but exactly the kind of guy to find gold when everyone else was running their arses off trying to make the system work.

'OK?' Winter was looking at Faraday, who nodded.

'Go on.'

Winter said he'd picked up word about the Weather Gage. He'd no idea whether it had already figured in some action or other, but he'd thought it was worth a visit.

'I went down there first thing this morning,' Ferguson growled. 'And it was shut.'

'Sure,' Winter countered. 'I went down there mid-morning, and it wasn't.'

'And what did you find, Mr Winter?'

'This guy.'

Winter produced the car park video still from the Marriott and tapped the figure helping Hennessey towards the Mercedes. Later, in the bar up at Fratton, there was talk of the rabbit and the hat. From somewhere, God knows how, Winter had conjured a definite lead. Not just a definite lead, but potentially a case-cracking lead.

'And who the fuck is he?' Ferguson looked positively baleful. Even Faraday was enjoying it.

'His name's Rob Parrish. He owns the pub.'

'You've talked to him about it?'

'I can't. He's disappeared.'

'So how do you know it's him?'

'The woman who runs the pub restaurant ID'd him.'

'She's certain?'

'One hundred per cent.'

'Fuck me.' Ferguson was looking at Faraday. 'TIE him, boss? All hands?'

TIE was shorthand for trace, interview and eliminate. Ferguson had a lot of ground to make up.

Faraday was still looking at Winter.

'So what are you saying?'

Winter took his time. You didn't get to play scenes like this very often and he wanted to squeeze it for every last drop of advantage. Faraday's curt dismissal still burned in his memory. *'Tends to lack strategic perspective'*. Strategic perspective, fuck. Who else in the room had anything to match this?

'We know this guy was at the Marriott that Sunday night. Video puts him and Hennessey in the car park at two in the morning. They get in the Mercedes. They drive away.'

'Where do they go?'

'My bet's on Old Portsmouth. They drive back down, back to Parrish's place, the Weather Gage. They go inside. Fuck knows what happens next, but Parrish has a big storehouse place at the back, properly secured. There's an old butcher's table inside.'

Ferguson couldn't contain himself.

'Don't tell me.' He was looking wonderingly at Winter. 'He chopped Hennessey up.'

'Yeah.' Winter nodded. 'Something like that.'

'Why?'

'Some kind of contract. Hennessey's got a list of

enemies as long as my arm. I've said so from the start. Ex-patients of his who are seriously pissed off.'

'Pissed off enough to kill him?'

'Pissed off enough to have him killed, yes.'

Faraday was making notes. He looked up.

'When?' he asked. 'When did this happen?'

'I'd say early Monday morning, after the Marriott. Parrish drives him back to the pub and then kills him.'

'So where's the body?'

'Pass.'

'And where's this man Parrish?'

'Fuck knows.'

There was a long silence. After three days of blank leads, an eternity of doorsteps and phone calls, no one except Ferguson was in the mood to second-guess Winter. It was the old story. He'd been out on his own. He'd backed a hunch or two. And here he was, back in the delivery business.

Faraday stirred. Decision time.

'Number one, we need some shots of Parrish.'

'He was in the *News* recently.' It was Winter again. 'Big fuss about condemned meat, I think it went to court. They're bound to have photos.'

'OK?' Faraday was looking at Ferguson. 'Number two, we need to check every bloody inch of traffic video for Monday morning, two onwards. Cameras on the roads in, and not just the obvious route, plus cameras around Old Portsmouth.'

'There aren't any.' Ferguson, for once, looked almost happy. 'Old Portsmouth's not on the council's priority list.'

'Begging your pardon, skip, but there's always the Wightlink terminal.' Winter sweetened the news with a smile. 'It's bang next door to the pub and they've got twenty-four-hour video coverage. It's where you leave your motor if you want to keep it in one piece.'

'Wightlink.' An order, Faraday to Ferguson again.

Faraday ran quickly through the other actions, covering the obvious bases. PNC checks on Parrish. The guy might have a criminal record. DVLC checks on any vehicle he might own.

'The woman at the pub says not.'

'Check all the same.'

'OK.'

'Then the pub. We need to box it off. Get a SOCO in, full treatment, especially the place you mentioned with the table. Go through the place with a toothcomb. I want floorboards up, the lot.' He glanced at his watch. 'It's a quarter past five. Willard will want an upgrade to Major Crimes, but it would be nice to spare him the bother before he gets the chance. Let's get it bottomed out, nice and tidy.' He looked round, then nodded at Winter. 'Agreed?'

Faraday was back home by eight. Forensic had gone into the Weather Gage and the building was now in the hands of the Scenes of Crime team. Until they'd completed their fingertip search of the premises, there was very little he could do. A bleak, handwritten notice on the main door announced that the pub was shut until further notice.

In the kitchen, Faraday poured himself a large Scotch, added a finger of water, and retired to the big lounge. With the doors open to the garden, he could smell the falling tide. Winter's sleight-of-hand, as ever, perplexed him. Not how he managed to pull off coups like this, but why. What was it about his colleagues that made it so difficult for him to be part of a team? Why, in God's name, was he so determined to step outside the rulebook and run little private investigations of his own?

Last year, after the business with Charlie Oomes, they'd almost been friends for a while, and one night, over too many whiskies, he'd tried to find an acceptable way of asking questions like these. Winter had listened, as matey as ever, and when Faraday had tired of tiptoeing around the point he'd just sat back and put the question himself.

'You want to know why I go my own way? *You*, of all people?'

Faraday hadn't understood, and had said so. At this, Winter, not unkindly, had laughed.

'It's because we're out of the same egg, boss. Difficult bastards. And devious, too.'

At the time, Faraday had been slightly shocked. Now, his chair half-angled towards the warm evening breeze off the harbour, he wasn't so sure. Another Scotch might pin it down, he thought. Another Scotch might fix it.

He awoke to the sound of the doorbell and glanced at his watch. Ten to ten. Nearly dark. He put the empty tumbler on the table and padded down the hall. It was Ruth. She stood in the throw of light through the open door and held out the present she'd brought the evening before.

'I'm not stopping,' she said at once, 'in case you're worried.'

'Not at all. Come in. Great to see you.'

She shot him a look as she walked past. The present felt pleasantly heavy. They met again in the kitchen, Ruth in her jeans and denim jacket, her face glowing from a day in the sun. She was running her eyes over the dishes in the sink.

'Just me,' Faraday told her. 'Promise.'

'Open it.' She nodded at the present. 'Please.'

Faraday did what he was told, looking for a knife to ease back the Sellotape.

'Just tear it. Did I ever tell you how much that pisses me off?'

He looked across at her, wondering whether she was joking or not. The paper came off in a single pull, and he found himself looking at a leatherbound album.

'Go on, open it.'

The album was full of photographs. They were exquisite, full colour, beautifully captured. Lapwing and grey heron. Dunlin and redshank. Curlew and mistle thrush. As Faraday turned the pages, recognising the backgrounds, he began to realise what she'd done.

'You took these?'

'Every one.'

'When?'

'Over the course of the year. It was meant as a special present.'

'It *is* a special present.' He was looking at a turnstone, the bird perfectly caught on the shimmering mud, the beak engaging with some mollusc or other. 'You shouldn't get the wrong idea.'

'About what?'

It was a direct challenge. He looked up at her again, recognising the cold glint of anger in her eyes. She's been rehearsing this scene for a while, he thought. Ever since last night.

He didn't know what to say. He felt completely stupid, completely outflanked.

'You're sure this is for me?' he managed at last.

'Of course it's for you. Who else?'

She gazed at him for a long moment, then something softened in her face and she stepped closer, and kissed him on the lips.

'My poor lamb,' she said softly. 'You really haven't a clue who you are, have you?'

Faraday stared at her, still nursing the album. Then, quite suddenly, she was gone.

Winter made it to the hospital far too late to see Joannie. He stood outside the ICU, trying to work out a line that would get him to Joannie's bedside. It had been a good evening, an epic evening, and he'd very much enjoyed taking drinks off the rest of the squad. Not that they weren't working their arses off. No, they'd simply sent out for a bulk order. And Winter had consumed most of it.

Now, at last, a nurse appeared. He knew her vaguely, recognised her face.

'My wife . . .' he began.

'She's conscious, Mr Winter. She's back with us.'

He gazed down at her. She was pretty: brown hair, big chest, neat legs. He was about to ask her name, enquire further, when she beat him to it.

'I'd come back tomorrow, if I were you. Your wife'll be with us for a while yet.'

Twenty-Four

The forensic team were about to pack it in when Faraday arrived at the Weather Gage next morning. The hot spell had finally come to an end and the oily green water in the Camber Dock was dimpled with raindrops.

Faraday hurried across the slippery cobbles, spotting the looming figure of DS Jerry Proctor at the front door of the pub. Proctor was in charge of the local SOCO teams, working from a cramped little office at Fareham nick, and he'd been up all night, supervising the room-by-room trawl for the tiniest scrap of evidence that might link Parrish to the missing surgeon. Exhausted now, he was arranging for the premises to be sealed for six hours, doors locked, uniforms front and back, permitting him and his team to get their heads down before resuming the search.

'What do you think?' Faraday was watching the rain cascading down from a broken gutter.

Proctor was still in the one-piece paper suit the SOCO guys were obliged to wear. He looked wrecked, and smelled worse.

'The outhouse round the back. Put money on it.'

'What did you find?'

'There's been blood on the table in there, lots of it. Goes back years according to Winter, but we'll take the thing away and give it a thorough going-over. If there's any that's recent and human, we'll find it.'

'Anything else?'

'Yeah. Someone's had a vehicle in there recently. There's fresh oil on the flagstones. Fibres? Rubber?' He shrugged. 'We might get a match with the Mercedes, what's left of it. Then there's this, through here.'

Faraday followed Proctor round the pub. At the back, beside the outhouse, was one of the plain white vans the SOCOs used. Proctor unlocked the rear doors and propped them open. Sealed and tagged in separate plastic bags were two items. One of them was a solid meat cleaver of the kind the Chinese use, the other a saw.

'Feel the weight of that.'

Proctor picked up the cleaver and passed it across. Even through the plastic, the steel handle felt cold in Faraday's palm. Was Winter right? Had Parrish gone to work on the surgeon – dead or alive – in an abrupt reversal of roles? He gave it a practice swing, tried to imagine it chopping down through flesh and bone, then he peered at it more closely. There were tiny dark incrustations on the blade.

'Blood,' Proctor grunted, 'for sure.'

The saw carried the same trademark stains. Under the microscope, there would be tiny nests of precious DNA among the rusting teeth.

Faraday glanced across at the doors of the outhouse. He wanted to have a look inside, put these items in their proper context, try and picture how Parrish might have done it, but he knew that Proctor wouldn't let him anywhere near. Until the search was complete and the premises were released from his control, the SOCO was boss here. Any suggestion of contamination – a nosy DC, an impatient DI, even a stray cat – could wreck a prosecution case before it even got to court.

The older of Proctor's two colleagues ambled round

the corner of the building. His paper suit was blotched with raindrops and he was in the process of removing the mask that protected his nose and mouth. Faraday had met him a number of times before. His name was Dave.

'All right?'

Dave nodded. There was someone round the front, he said. Might pay to have a gander.

Faraday checked his watch. The *News* had already been in contact. The reporter had taken down some details over the phone and wanted to send a photographer. A story like this would be front page for sure, especially if they could dress a shot of the pub exterior with the guys in the white suits. The punters, as Faraday had agreed, just loved to see the telly intruding into real life.

Faraday took Proctor and Dave by the arm. Their moment of fame. Dave stared at him.

'It's not the *News*,' he said.

'Who is it then?'

'Bloke called Parrish. Says he owns the place.'

Dawn Ellis, parked across from the eyesore that was Kevin Beavis's house, wondered yet again whether she had really got it right. His daughter, Shelley, was safely parked in the Travelodge. She hated the isolation, and daytime telly bored her witless, but she was as reluctant as ever to get everything off her chest. Last night, after Dawn had turned up with a couple of bottles of decent Rioja and poured a great deal of it down her young throat, she'd finally admitted that she knew who'd done the Donald Duck jobs, but, pressed for a name, she'd still shaken her head. 'I know, but I can't tell,' she'd said.

In strict procedural terms, Dawn had already broken

every rule in the book. The last thing you did in any inquiry was buddy up with a key witness. But there was something about Shelley – a vulnerability, a sense that deep down she was struggling to do her best – that Dawn frankly admired. Add her now absolute conviction that they'd charged the wrong guy, and Dawn felt almost justified in pushing so deep into forbidden territory.

I know, but I can't tell.

Dawn got out of the car and crossed the road. There were bits of motorcycle engine in the tiny scrap of front garden; she'd last seen them in Beavis's kitchen sink. The hood of her anorak turned up against the rain, she knocked at the door again, gazing down at the rusting piles of junk.

I know, but I can't tell.

Was Shelley being protective? Was that the reason she'd phoned yesterday? Asked for the meet in Southsea? Told Dawn that her dad was blameless? Handicapped? Couldn't really help it? And was simple loyalty – father, daughter – the reason she wouldn't venture as far as a name?

The door opened. Kevin Beavis was in a grubby pair of tracksuit bottoms and not much else. He could do with losing a bit of weight about his middle. And he could use a shave as well.

At first, he didn't recognise Dawn. Then she pushed the hood back and his face lit up.

'C'mon in, love. How you doing?'

Dawn followed him through to the kitchen. If anything, the house smelled even worse than before. Chip fat and dodgy drains, Dawn thought, watching Beavis fill the kettle after she'd said no to tea.

Beavis wanted to know if she'd seen young Shel at all. He'd been trying to get hold of her the last couple of days but there was no answer at that flat of hers. Probably up London with her mates. Does that sometimes, if she's got the dosh.

The mention of money took Dawn back to last night. According to Shelley, Kennedy had been paying her for her video performances for nearly a year. The money was pretty irregular and he held most of it back for reasons he never explained, but she'd taken nearly four hundred quid off him and that definitely helped with the bills. She'd got through her student loan in a couple of months and her dad, with the best will in the world, hadn't got a penny to his name.

Looking at Beavis now, Dawn could believe it. He'd had the decency to wrap an old cardigan round his upper half, but for someone who couldn't have been more than forty-five, he already had the stoop and pallor of an old man. Dawn was ferociously aware of diet. What you ate was what you were. Kevin Beavis was the walking evidence of what the frying pan and too much sugar could do to you.

He was tipping hot water into a chipped old tea pot. Dawn had a list of dates. She read them out one by one: 19 February; 12 April; and finally, that warm June night just nine days ago when the figure in the Donald Duck mask had struck for the third time.

'Shit.' Beavis backed away hastily from the sink. 'S'cuse me, love.'

He'd splashed boiling water over his bare feet. Dawn threw him a tea towel.

'I need to know where you were on those three dates, Mr Beavis. We're talking evenings here.'

'Haven't a clue, love.'

He levered one huge foot into the sink and ran cold water over it. He seemed genuinely untroubled by her questions.

'What about that last date? It was the Sunday before last. What do you normally do Sunday nights?'

'Pub, when I can afford it.'

'And the Sunday before last?'

'No chance. Skint.' He looked across at her with a slightly wolfish grin. 'The telly's free, and Sunday nights they sometimes show good movies.'

'Can you remember watching anything on the night of the eighteenth?'

'No chance. Memory's shot, love.'

'What about if I get hold of a copy of the listings? Might you remember then?'

'Yeah, might do. Give it a go. Why not?'

He'd done the other foot now and he gave them both a wipe with the cloth. He seemed pleased by all the attention she was showing him, pleased she was so interested, and Dawn realised that Shelley had been right. He was simple, like a child. He had simple needs, and friendship – attention – was probably one of them.

Dawn decided to change tack.

'There's a bloke called Lee. Lee Kennedy. He's a footballer. Do you know him at all?'

'Lee?' The face had come alive again. 'Of course I knows him. Known him all my life.'

'Really?'

'Yeah. He's my cousin, ain't he?'

'*Cousin?*'

Dawn stared at him. Not just under-age sex. Incest, too.

'Well, not a real cousin like. Step-cousin? I dunno. Anyway, like I said, me and Lee . . .' He crossed two fingers, grinning at her. 'Do anything for me, Lee would. Tell you something, love, he was the one that told me about that lecturer bloke, Addison, what he was up to with Shel.'

'*He* told you that? Lee Kennedy?'

'Yeah, comes round here, tips me off about it, says I gotta do something. That's when I come and told you lot. Can't have that, can we? Shel and some tosser twice her age? Ain't right.'

The memories had taken the smile off his face. He clumped around the kitchen, looking for the bread he had left over from last night, grumbling about the evils of the academic world. No wonder he has no sense of time, Dawn thought. As far as Beavis was concerned, the visit to Fratton nick might have happened years ago.

He left the kitchen for a minute or two and returned with two slices of Mighty White. Next on the list was the toaster.

'I was mending it.' He was looking under the table. 'I had it somewhere.'

Dawn waited until he was upright again. She felt like an old-style copper, come to break bad news.

'It wasn't Addison, the lecturer,' she said quietly. 'It was Lee Kennedy.'

'What, love?' Vague now, still looking for the toaster.

'Lee. Lee Kennedy. He's the one who's been ... who's been having sex with Shelley.'

The word 'sex' stopped Beavis in his tracks. He stared at her. He obviously didn't believe a word of it.

'That's crap,' he said. 'Not Lee.'

'I'm afraid so.'

'Knocking off my Shel?'

'Yes.'

'Who says?'

'Shel, for a start.'

Beavis sank into the other chair. Tobacco and a packet of Rizlas were in the drawer on the table. He began to roll himself a cigarette with thick, oil-stained fingers, a tongue the colour of fresh liver. Dawn half-expected him to offer her the roll-up, but he didn't. Lost in a world of his own, he fumbled around for a match but finally settled for the gas stove.

Cheap shag tobacco, Dawn thought. The kind of smell you wouldn't forget.

Beavis was back in the chair, looking blankly at the wall.

'Not Lee,' he muttered. 'Girl must've got it wrong.'

Back at his desk at Southsea nick, Faraday was rehearsing the moment when Parrish's name would appear on a charge sheet. It would be the sweetest pleasure to leave a message with Willard's secretary, and another with the management assistant who worked for Hartigan. Parrish was in a cell over at the Bridewell. Winter and Rick were readying themselves for the first interview. By the end of play, with luck, they'd have the whole shebang squared away. It would be a brilliant result. A brilliant, brilliant result.

He reached for the phone and dialled Marta's mobile. It was still barely nine, and he wondered whether she'd be at work yet.

The moment she recognised his voice, she told him to hang on. He could hear a radio in the background and something else he couldn't quite place. Then came footsteps, and the radio began to fade. She's on the move, he thought, trying to imagine the house she lived in. A newish place, she'd said, over towards Locks Heath. A door slammed shut, then she was back again, her voice low, almost a whisper. Faraday was curious. Was this some new game? Yet another twist?

He began to tell her about Parrish, the way the case had suddenly cracked open, leads spilling everywhere. He was still describing this morning's scene at the Weather Gage when she interrupted.

'Listen,' she said, 'I have to go. Ring me later. After lunch.'

'Why?'

'My husband's still here, bloody man.' The voice lower still. 'Promise you'll ring?'

She hung up, leaving Faraday staring at the phone. *Husband?*

The first of the interviews with Rob Parrish began at 1104. Winter and Rick Stapleton sat on one side of the table in the interview room at the Bridewell, Parrish on the other. He was still wearing the suede jacket Winter had recognised from the Marriott video, though the Virgin Islands T-shirt had now given way to a light denim shirt that badly needed an iron. Offered a lawyer by the Custody Sergeant, Parrish had said no. They could ask him whatever they liked. He had nothing to hide.

While establishing those present for the benefit of the three audio tapes, Winter described Parrish as a publican.

'Fair?'

'And restaurateur,' Parrish drawled.

Winter nodded. He hadn't had much time to plot this first interview, but he'd agreed with Rick that he would lead, and he saw no point in not going in hard. This interview formed part of an ongoing investigation into the disappearance of Pieter Hennessey. Winter had reason to believe that Parrish could help them in their inquiries. He should be aware that anything he said might be used in evidence against him.

'OK?'

'Sure.'

Winter wanted to know about Hennessey, and about Parrish's movements on the evening of Sunday, 18 June.

Parrish's account, as detailed as possible, would become the source material for subsequent and more detailed interviews. Whatever he said now was the rope that might hang him later.

'You know Hennessey well, then?'

'I know him. Let's put it that way. He comes into the pub lunchtimes when he's down in Pompey. We talk, you know, like you do.'

'You know he was a surgeon?'

'Yes.'

'You know he's been struck off?'

'I know he's had his problems.' He was beginning to sound guarded. 'He's not the happiest bloke you'll ever meet.'

Winter waited for him to offer more, but he didn't. Rick asked him again about that Sunday night.

'Where were you that evening?'

'At the pub. Working.'

'You didn't go out at all?'

Parrish eyed them both, then offered a slow smile. Traps like these were easy.

'I went out around ten.'

'Where to?'

'The Marriott.'

'Why?'

'I got a call from Hennessey.'

'On the hotel phone?'

'No.' He shook his head. 'On his mobile. I've got his number stored. I remember the name coming up.'

'Do you call him a lot?' Winter this time. 'Pals, are you?'

'I'm supposed to call him if there's anything happening on some Gunwharf flats he wants. He's put money down. He lives out in the New Forest somewhere and he wants me to keep an eye open for him, just locally, you know. Kind of agent, if you like.'

'Has he left your name with the Gunwharf people?'

'I've no idea. If he has, they've never been in touch.'

Winter paused. Parrish was impressive. He'd no idea how much they knew, yet so far he hadn't put a foot wrong. Present tense, too. Clever.

'Hennessey phoned you that night.' Rick again. 'What did he say?'

'He was pissed out of his head. He had a bottle of Scotch with him and by the time I arrived, most of it had gone.'

'Why did you go up there?'

'Because he was threatening to do himself in.'

'Why didn't you call the management? On the phone?'

'Because he wanted to talk. To me. He was one fucked-up bunny, that man. OK, I didn't know him well, but, hey, you do what you can.'

He shrugged and spread his hands wide, a gesture of comradeship, and Winter remembered Tara Gough's words. 'He uses people,' she'd said. 'He uses them all the time.'

'Fucked-up how?' Winter enquired.

'Guilt. You probably know about all those women he screwed up on, all those operations he got wrong. Guy doesn't sleep too good these days and that can do anyone's head in.'

'So what happened when you got there?'

'He was sitting on the bed, crying his eyes out. I didn't see it at first, but he had a scalpel tucked under the pillow. I tried to get it off him and there was a bit of a scuffle.'

Winter remembered the state of the room: armchair upturned, shards of china on the carpet.

'How much of a scuffle?'

'Nothing too serious. We rolled around. I managed to see off the scalpel. I think the tea tray got the worst of it. After that I tried to calm him down and we talked for quite a while before he went for a piss. At least, that's what he said he was doing.'

'And?'

'He tried to open a vein. He had another blade in the bathroom. Lucky I got there in time. He'd slashed his wrist, just here' – he touched the wristband of his watch – 'and I think it dawned on him then that he was being a bit of a cunt. There wasn't a lot of blood but, you know, enough to make him think.'

Rick leaned forward.

'You stopped the bleeding?'

'I put a towel around it. He did the rest.'

'What do you mean?'

'Applied pressure. Stopped the bleeding. The guy's a surgeon. He knew what he was doing.'

'Then what?'

'He wanted me to take him out to his car. He had some suture needles and twine in the first-aid box he carries.'

'Why didn't you take him to the QA?'

'He wouldn't hear of it, and actually I don't blame him. Can you imagine it? A surgeon turns up, pissed out of his head, with a wound like that? They'd section him if they had any sense.'

Rick was beginning to look glum. By his elbow were the video stills from the Marriott. Normally, in an interview like this, he'd use them for leverage, letting the suspect talk the usual bollocks then suddenly producing them as evidence of the way things had really been. It was an obvious tactic, having one hundred per cent undisclosed evidence like that up your sleeve, but it was amazing how often it worked. On this occasion, though, all the stills offered was corroboration. There they were, Parrish and Hennessey, pushing out through the Marriott's main entrance at two in the morning, just the way Parrish had described. Look hard, and you could even see a tiny curl of white where Hennessey still had the towel pressed against his dripping wrist.

Winter didn't spare the stills a second glance.

'So where did you go?'

'I took him back to my place, back to the pub. He was going to tell me what to do, and I'd ...' He shrugged. 'Just sort him out.'

'By sewing up his wrist?'

'That's right.'

'Where?'

Winter saw the answer coming a mile off. Parrish was enjoying this.

'On an old table of mine,' he said, 'in the outhouse.'

'Why there?'

'I've got running water, a sink, everything I needed. Plus it wouldn't make a mess inside.'

'Neat.'

Winter offered a tiny, private nod of applause. Proctor had already found a couple of human hairs on the flagstones beneath the table. Human blood would doubtless be next. There was a sluice in the outhouse, and gunk from the drains would also yield all kinds of forensic treasure. Yet here was Parrish, plausible to the last, methodically sealing off each of Winter's precious leads. An explanation for everything, he thought. Far too fucking perfect.

Rick pushed the story forward.

'So what happened next?'

'I gave him a bed. He got his head down. Then he left.'

'Did he bleed at all? In bed?'

'Yeah. I wasn't the greatest with the needle.'

'What happened to the sheets?'

'I threw them out.'

'The mattress?'

'That went too. I'd been meaning to bin it for months.'

Winter stirred again. This guy was becoming a serious irritation.

'Where did he go?'

'He didn't say, and I didn't ask. It was broad daylight and he was still pissed out of his head, but to tell you the truth I didn't fucking care. All this shit about guilt and suicide and not being able to cope. I'm a publican, not a fucking shrink, know what I mean? Next time, I'm taking him straight to casualty.'

'You haven't seen him since?'

'No way.'

'He hasn't been back at all? Hasn't rung you?'

'No.'

'Not even to say thank you?'

'No. And no flowers in the post, either. I'm telling you, the guy's out of his tree. That's the problem in my business. You do your best with your customers and half of them turn out to be nutters.' He made a big show of looking at his watch, then yawned. 'Time is money, guys. Can I go now?'

It was Ferguson who passed word to Faraday about the surveillance tape from the Wightlink car park. Faraday joined him in front of the video monitor in the CID office, staring down at the screen. The floodlights around the car park revealed a yawning expanse of empty tarmac, white-lined queueing lanes leading down towards the ferry ramp. In the distance, small at first, a figure appeared. It was a man carrying something bulky in a black plastic sack. He was tall, in jeans and a hooded top. The hood was pulled low, obscuring his face, but it could easily have been Parrish. Easily. Foreshortened by the height of the camera, the figure and his baggage disappeared off the bottom of the screen.

Faraday, checking the clock read-out on the top right-hand corner of the picture, did the sums. 0332. A hint of dawn over the rooftops of Old Portsmouth. Just about right.

Ferguson had a great deal of ground to make up. Now, he spooled the tape forward. Another camera picked up the figure with the bag as he made his way past the booking hall and the first-floor café. Seconds later, at the end of the jetty that hung over the ramp, he disappeared.

'Where does that go?' Faraday asked.

Ferguson had frozen the video on the last frame.

'Gunwharf,' he said. 'There's a ladder gives you access to the site.'

The first interview with Parrish ended at 1244. Winter and Rick Stapleton broke for lunch. They were still in the canteen at the Bridewell when Faraday appeared, and he knew without asking that cracking Parrish was proving to be a great deal tougher than they'd ever anticipated.

'He's worked it all out,' Winter said. 'It's like chess. He counters before we even fucking move.'

Faraday collected a pie from the hot shelf and spiralled brown sauce over it. Then he described the contents of the Wightlink tape. Winter confirmed that the time seemed to fit.

'Did it look like Parrish?'

'Yes. Not enough for court, but yes.'

'Any sign of the Mercedes?'

'No.'

Winter gazed into the middle distance while Faraday asked Rick about a further complication. Even if Parrish coughed, and they managed to turn up a body, that was only half the story. If Winter was right about a contract, who put Parrish up to it? The long list of Hennessey's surgical victims was an obvious place to start, but Faraday could see the inquiry disappearing to the Major Crimes Suite if that much legwork was involved. He turned to Winter.

'Any ideas about who might have hired Parrish? Assuming it's a hit.'

Winter blinked. He seemed not to have been listening.

'Pass,' he said. 'But I tell you something. He hates those bastards. Absolutely loathes them.'

'What bastards?'

'The Gunwharf lot. They wouldn't let him near a pub franchise. They nicked the bird he was shagging. They don't come to his pub any more. He doesn't like them at all.'

Faraday was looking blank.

'So what?'

'So what?' Winter suddenly seemed a great deal more cheerful. 'Say you had a body, or bits of a body. And say you were looking for somewhere to dump it.'

Rick exchanged looks with Faraday. Faraday had abandoned his pie.

'Go on.'

'You'd be looking for a hidey-hole, wouldn't you? You'd be looking for a place where no one would ever dream of digging.'

'Gunwharf?'

'Spot on. And say you had something against all

those bastard suits who'd screwed you over. What you'd do, you'd bury it under one of those bloody great apartments before they went up, and then, if you were really nasty, you'd fuck off somewhere hot and sunny, give it a couple of years, then ring the *News* and tell them all those rich punters were sitting on a corpse. Parrish would love that. He'd count that as evens.'

Faraday's instincts told him that Winter was talking bollocks. It was too complicated, too contrived. But the more he thought about it, and the more Winter told him about how accomplished Parrish had been in the interview room, the more he warmed to the theory. Not one target, but two. Not simply the price on Hennessey's head but a big fat whack at the guys across the way who'd treated him so badly. Winter, after all, had a point. Rarely was revenge more elegant.

'Think about it,' Winter was saying. 'They'd have to dig the whole place up. Years afterwards.'

Twenty-Five

Tuesday, 27 June, 1330

The interview with Parrish resumed within the hour, and Faraday sat in the tiny monitoring room next door, listening through speakers.

Winter and Rick walked Parrish through the chronology again, testing every link, every tiny episode that bridged the four hours between the initial phone call and the moment when Hennessey had walked through the doors of the Marriott and disappeared. Once again, despite challenge after challenge, Parrish was word perfect on every detail, not once backtracking, not once changing his story. Even without seeing him face to face, Faraday had to admit that Winter was right. This man had worked out every last detail. And it would take more than Winter's silky changes of tack to shake him.

Finally, after getting nowhere with the burned-out Mercedes, Winter brought up the Wightlink video.

'We've got some other shots,' he said. 'That ferry car park place across the way from the pub. A bloke like you, your size, your build, everything. Half-past three in the morning, with a bloody great sack. Heading for Gunwharf.'

Next door, Faraday was trying to interpret the possibilities that might account for the ensuing silence. Was Parrish flustered? Had they shaken him? Had they at last found a way in?

332

Alas, no. He heard a tiny cough and the scrape of a chair. Then came Parrish's voice. He sounded, if anything, amused.

'Is that right?' he said softly.

Faraday's first meeting that day was with Willard. As he'd thought, the Detective Superintendent was beginning to feel uncomfortable with the potential scale of the Hennessey job. A straightforward misper inquiry was one thing. A full bells-and-whistles murder inquiry, with no corpse and a suspect list as long as your arm, was quite another. Just now, as it happened, Major Crimes were swamped with work, but it was Willard's job to pull in extra bodies from elsewhere, and if necessary he'd do just that. Divisional resources weren't supposed to cover crimes like these. That's why they put Major Incident Teams together.

In the end, Faraday managed to negotiate a stay of execution. He had another forty-eight hours to sort the job out. Otherwise it was a surefire upgrade.

After Willard, Hartigan. Once again, face to face was the only way to resolve it. Faraday accepted the offered seat in front of Hartigan's desk. As ever, the divisional superintendent had absolutely no time for small talk.

'Bring me up to speed, Joe. I'm hearing all kinds of rumours.'

Faraday explained about developments over the last twenty-four hours. They'd achieved a major breakthrough. They'd established a chronology and a sequence of events, and speaking personally, Faraday had absolutely no doubt where they led.

'Where's that, then?'

'Gunwharf.'

Hartigan was horrified. The way Faraday described

it, the possibility of a body having been buried beneath the apartments site was truly bizarre.

'This is crank stuff, Joe. You can't possibly be serious.'

Faraday went through it again, endlessly patient. Motivation, opportunity, outcome – classic textbook stuff. For once, it was a pleasure to quote it all back to Hartigan. Not that it made the slightest difference.

'Think of the practicalities, Joe. Do you have any idea how big the place is?'

'Thirty-three acres, sir. You showed me.'

'Exactly. And where do you propose to start?'

'I haven't a clue, not at this point in time. My betting's on the apartment block.'

'Blocks, Joe. There are two of them, three of them, four of them. And they're all behind schedule.'

'Is that a factor?'

'Strictly speaking, no.' He frowned, conjuring fresh nightmares from this terrifying scenario. 'And what about the publicity? Can you imagine the *News* getting hold of this?'

'Begging your pardon, sir, but that isn't our problem.'

'Of course it isn't, but have you thought it through resources-wise? It'll cost a fortune. Have you seen the overtime audit for the last quarter? Dear God . . .'

For a moment, Faraday thought Hartigan was on the verge of a coronary. This was what happened if your interpretation of police work went no further than public relations. Hartigan was pale with foreboding.

'This is ridiculous, Joe. I'll talk to the Detective Superintendent. It's his responsibility, not ours.'

'I have already. He's given me until Thursday.'

'Then stick with what we know. Keep hammering at

the man Parrish. If you need an extension, I'll be only too happy to oblige.'

Faraday stared at him for a long moment. Every officer in charge of an investigation keeps a Policy Book, a minute-by-minute account of exactly where an investigation is going. On a complex inquiry, it becomes an invaluable reference tool: every action recorded, every decision justified. Faraday, too, was keeping a Policy Book.

'I'll bring it up, sir,' he said quietly, 'and perhaps you'd like to note your objections to the search. In writing, if you don't mind.'

Hartigan watched him leave. Ten minutes later, Faraday took a phone call from his management assistant. The Gunwharf search could go ahead.

When Winter finally made it to Meonstoke, Ronald McIntyre was on the point of leaving. Suitcases lay beside his little Toyota and Winter could see him through the open front door. He was standing in the hall, erect in his blazer and cravat, the phone pressed to his ear.

When the conversation came to an end, Winter stepped inside and took him by the elbow. Gentle pressure, friendly pressure. McIntyre, to his alarm, found himself in the big lounge. The curtains were already half-drawn in anticipation of his exit.

'I need to know about the deal with Parrish,' Winter explained.

McIntyre didn't want to think about Parrish any more. That was over, done. He was off to the West Country, he told Winter, a fortnight's day-sailing with a chum down in Salcombe. He'd finished with evenings in the Weather Gage.

'Do I make myself clear?'

Winter ignored the challenge. He nodded towards the sofa and told McIntyre to sit down.

'You have a choice,' he explained softly. 'Either you start telling me about Parrish or this relationship of ours becomes a bit more official.'

'Meaning?'

'I arrest you.'

McIntyre looked startled.

'What for?'

'Conspiracy to murder. You've virtually admitted it.'

'I've done no such thing. I agreed I lent the wretched man some money. Is that a crime?'

'It depends why you did it. Parrish is under arrest. We've talked to him twice already and I must say there's every prospect of him telling us exactly what happened. You're part of that story, Ronnie. You know it, and so do I.' He paused. 'Pleas in mitigation can count for a lot.'

'What's that supposed to mean?'

'It means that I can have a word with the judge. In these circumstances, it helps to understand what you and Nikki have been through.'

'*Judge?*'

'I'm afraid so. Unless . . .' Winter frowned, as if struck by a sudden idea. 'Unless we can sort something out about Parrish.' He gestured at the space between them. 'Here and now.'

McIntyre, at first, wasn't having it. OK, he'd lent Parrish the money, as he'd already admitted, but in time he'd get it back. There'd never been any question of services rendered. He'd be crazy to hire a hit man. If he really wanted to see Hennessey dead, he'd do it himself. With the greatest pleasure.

Winter let him come to a full stop. Then he patted him on the shoulder.

'Crazy is a good word,' he agreed. 'No one's blaming you here, Ronnie, least of all me.' He nodded towards the piano and the gallery of framed photos. Nikki as a kid, sprawled on a blanket on the lawn. Nikki on the beach at Seaview, guarding a circle of perfect sandpies. Nikki on Graduation Day, champagne and smiles. 'Are you really telling me you'd let him get away with it? Is that what fathers do?'

McIntyre was less certain now. Winter suggested a drink. There were two decent glasses of sherry left in the decanter. McIntyre emptied his without a word.

'I can help you here,' Winter told him.

'How?'

'By keeping this . . . between us.'

'Private, you mean?'

'Yes.'

'I have your word on that?'

'Yes.' Winter sipped at the sherry. 'I just need to know about proof.'

'What kind of proof?'

'Proof that the man's dead. You don't part with twenty grand without proof.' He tipped the glass in a mock-toast. 'Do you, Ronnie?'

McIntyre was gazing out of the window, his eyes filmed with alcohol. He sat there bolt upright for perhaps a minute, then carefully replaced his empty glass on the presentation silver tray and left the room. CAPTAIN RONALD ARTHUR MCINTYRE, went the inscription, FROM THE WARDROOM OF HMS NOTTINGHAM. WITH RESPECT AND GRATITUDE. He was back moments later. Winter watched him slip an audio cassette into the hi-fi and press the play button. Then he sank into the nearby armchair, his eyes returning to the lawn and the river beyond the window.

At first, Winter couldn't make any sense of the tape,

it was just a series of scraping noises. Then he heard a grunt, followed by a man's voice. It was Parrish. He sounded out of breath. He was telling someone to hold still. This shouldn't take long, he was saying, just relax. Then another voice with a distinctive South African accent. Do this, then this, now pull, now carry the needle through, not like that, the other way, yes, and again, yes, much better. The dialogue went on for a while, a master class in suturing, then came a moment of complete silence followed by the sound of a heavy thud, cold steel splintering through bone. A man screamed. Another thud, the screaming fainter this time. Then, finally, a return to silence.

McIntyre nodded. His eyes were bright with excitement.

'Hennessey,' he confirmed. 'Definitely Hennessey.'

'You know that for sure?'

'I talked to him on the phone a number of times, when Nikki was seeing him. You don't forget a voice like that.'

Winter was still gazing at the hi-fi.

'Where did Parrish do it? Did he tell you?'

'He's got a garage, or workshop or something, round the back of the pub. He's got fridges in there for the meat and what have you.'

'And that's where it happened?'

'Yes.'

'And what did he do with the body?'

'He cut it up, there and then.'

'And?'

'I didn't ask. It's somewhere very safe. That's all he told me.'

Winter drained his glass and stood up. McIntyre stared at his outstretched hand.

'That's it? We've finished?'

'Of course. You're off on holiday aren't you?' He smiled. 'Have a great time. You've earned it.'

Winter was on the long sweep of motorway that cuts through Portsdown Hill when he finally managed to raise Tara Gough on her mobile. She'd been engaged for the last twenty minutes while he raced down the Meon Valley.

'It's Winter. Where are you?'

'At home. The pub's still sealed off.'

'OK, listen. That light.'

'What light?'

At ninety-five miles an hour, Winter hit the brakes. Why did people still bother with seventy in the outside lane?

'The neon tube in the outhouse,' he explained tersely. 'The one with the fucking great hum.'

'The flicker, you mean?'

'Yeah, and the noise. How long's it been like that?'

'Weeks, months. I keep telling Rob but he never gets round to fixing it. It's worse than not having a light at all.' She paused. 'Why do you want to know?'

The van had finally moved over. To the right, beyond the roofs of Paulsgrove, the city was laid out like a map, sunlight winking off a distant tower block.

'You mentioned boats,' he said.

'Like . . . how?'

'Parrish and McIntyre. You said they talked about boats.'

'That's right. They did.'

'Has Parrish got a boat?'

'Yes, love of his life, big motor cruiser thing.'

'Name?'

'*Crazy Lady*.'

'Where is it?'

'In the Camber. Last time I looked.'

The last person Faraday expected to see was Dawn Ellis. She appeared at the door of his office, asking for a brief chat, and it was several seconds before he realised she had company.

'Cath,' he said, fetching a couple of chairs. 'Some kind of deputation?'

Cathy Lamb allowed herself the faintest smile. Dawn was obviously the one who was going to do the talking.

'Well, girls?' Faraday was awaiting word from the Bridewell. Winter wanted another crack at Parrish.

'It's about Addison,' Dawn began.

Faraday gazed at her. She sounded strangely formal, almost strained. Was this what half a day with Cathy Lamb did to you?

'What about him?' he asked.

'I think he's innocent. I think we've nicked the wrong guy.'

She went through the evidence. Shelley's career as an apprentice porn star. Lee Kennedy's ambitions as a movie producer. The fact that the girl herself was sure that Addison had nothing to do with the Donald Duck incidents. The fact that Kennedy had a major grudge against him. Finally, she brought herself full circle.

'Addison didn't do it, boss. Believe me.'

Faraday was looking at Cathy Lamb. She hadn't taken her eyes off Faraday for a second.

'Just thought you ought to know,' she said quietly, 'before the CPS get their hands on the file.'

Faraday acknowledged the favour with a nod. He knew exactly what was going on here. Cathy was enjoying a moment or two of the sweetest revenge. And, God knows, she probably deserved it.

He turned back to Dawn.

'So who are we looking for now?' he enquired drily. 'Who *is* Donald Duck?'

Dawn exchanged glances with Cathy.

'I think it's Beavis,' she said.

'Have you put it to him?'

'No. But everything else adds up. He's got no alibi. He smokes like a chimney. And he's thick as a brick.'

'But why would he want to do it?'

'Because Kennedy told him to. He worships Kennedy. He worships the ground he walks on. If the man said jump, he'd jump.'

'But *exposing* himself? You're telling me he'd go that far?'

'Yes. Definitely. Kennedy was the one who told him that Addison was shagging his daughter. Kennedy wanted to screw Addison himself. Putting him in the frame for the Donald Duck job was perfect. Except he needed some guy actually to put the mask on and do it.'

'And you're saying Beavis?'

'Yes.'

'Not Addison at all?'

'No.'

There was a long moment of silence. From away down Highland Road, the distant blare of a two-tone. Faraday's gaze never left Dawn's face.

'Shit,' he said quietly.

The third session with Parrish bogged down almost immediately. For one thing, he'd decided to accept the offer of a lawyer. For another, he was as ready with answers as ever.

Winter wanted to know about the boat, *Crazy Lady*. How long had he had it?

'I bought it when I came back from Dubai. I made a whack of money out there and I fancied something, you know, really flash. It was a Boat Show offer, San Remo thirty-five, good discount for cash.'

'When was that?'

Parrish frowned. 'Ninety-three,' he said at last.

'You used it a lot?'

'To begin with, yeah. Women loved it. We used to bomb over to France or the Channel Islands. Boat like that, you could be there as quick as the ferries. It was like driving a sports car. You just put your foot down and *boom*.'

'So where is it now?'

'I sold it.'

'When?'

'A couple of weeks back. French bloke, businessman of some kind, comes over here a lot. Turned out he'd been eyeing it for months.'

'How did he pay for it?'

'Cash.' Parrish was enjoying himself, anticipating Winter's next question. 'Hundred and fifteen grand, can you believe that?'

Winter sat back for a moment, only too aware that the figure Parrish had just mentioned was exactly the sum Hennessey himself had withdrawn from his bank account before he disappeared. Coincidence, bollocks. Parrish was starting to take the piss. The cassette he'd given to McIntyre was supposedly recorded in the outhouse behind the pub. Yet where was the evidence of the dodgy neon tube? The hum you couldn't miss if you were in there for more than a second or two?

'This French guy,' Winter said slowly. 'You wouldn't have an address by any chance?'

The lawyer began to protest at the question, but

342

Parrish told him he wasn't bothered. Then he turned back to Winter.

'Afraid not,' he said sweetly. 'Real nomads, these business types.'

An hour later, Winter phoned the hospital. The sister in charge of the ICU confirmed that his wife had been transferred to another ward and was awaiting a full psychiatric assessment.

'How is she?'

'Awake. Cogent. Remarkably well, considering.'

Winter nodded, glancing at his watch. Rick was already down in the Camber, checking out the story on Parrish's boat. Depending on the outcome, Winter might just make the evening Jersey flight out of Southampton. Either way, he needed to get home for a shower and a change of clothes.

The ICU sister was telling him the name of Joannie's ward. He didn't bother writing it down.

'Give her my best,' he said. 'Pecker up, eh?'

En route home, Winter phoned Rick. So far he'd talked to half a dozen locals, most of whom remembered Parrish's boat. The landlord of the Weather Gage had never quite mastered the art of berthing and the hull of *Crazy Lady* was scarred from countless small collisions. The fact that the cruiser had now gone for good was, said Rick, the cause for some rejoicing.

'Anyone see it go?'

'Not so far, but there's a guy runs the tugs. He lives on top of Parrish's old mooring. If anyone can help us, he can. Bloke's back in an hour or so.' He paused. 'I also phoned a magazine called *Motor Boat*. Ran the price past some guy who seemed to know about the second-hand market.'

'What price?'

'The hundred and fifteen grand Parrish got for his boat.'

'And?'

'Way over the top. At least twenty thousand over the top. Whoever paid him that was off his head.'

Winter sealed the conversation with a grunt. Twenty grand was the price Hennessey had paid for making good his escape. He wasn't interested in appearing in front of the GMC. He didn't want to be dragged through the courts. And he certainly didn't need his face plastered all over the papers yet again. And so Parrish, with Ronald McIntyre none the wiser, had ghosted him away. Clever.

Back home in Bedhampton, Winter found a small pile of post on the mat. Most of it was cards for Joannie. Only a typed envelope with a London postmark was of any real interest.

Inside, he found a sheaf of unpaid duplicate invoices from the nursing agency Hennessey had used for the supply of theatre staff for the operations he conducted. Most of the nurses were obviously paid through the agency, but in one case they'd included photocopied invoices that had come direct from the nurse herself. Her name was Helen O'Dwyer, and there was a telephone number with her Guildford address.

She took a while to answer. Winter explained that he was CID. Hennessey had gone missing and various lines of inquiry were being pursued. She had absolutely no obligation to help him out, but he'd be really grateful for a steer or two.

There was a long silence. She wanted to know how she could be sure he was police. Winter gave her the control room number at Fratton and asked her to check him out before phoning back.

'No, that's OK.' She'd made up her mind. 'What do you want to know?'

Winter established that she'd done lots of operations with Hennessey. Indeed, she was the nurse he normally called on first.

'You're aware of the trouble he's in?'

'Of course.'

'Have you seen him recently?'

'Not for a while, no.'

Winter mentioned Nikki McIntyre. Was she familiar with the name?

'Yeah. She was one of the regulars. Pretty girl.'

'Was there anything in particular you remember? Anything' – Winter paused – 'special he did for her?'

'Not really, he was slower, that's all.'

'What do you mean, slower?'

'With most patients, he raced through the operation. He was famous for it.' She offered a sour laugh. 'Some days he even used to bring in an alarm clock. He'd set it for, say, thirty minutes' time, then off we'd go. We'd have to be out and sutured by the time the bell went.'

'He could do things like that?'

'Of course he could. He was the client. He'd hired the theatre, hired the anaesthetist, hired us. He could do damn well what he liked.'

Anger had given her voice a sharper edge. She didn't like Hennessey, Winter thought. No wonder she's got so much to get off her chest.

'And Nikki McIntyre?'

'He never brought the alarm clock in. He'd take his time.'

'Yeah?' Winter could almost see her face now. 'And anything else?'

There was a long silence. Then Winter heard a sigh.

'He'd take photos,' she muttered. 'Lots and lots of them.'

An hour later, Winter lay full length in the bath, making his plans for Hennessey. He'd find him in Jersey, he knew he would. He'd be tucked up aboard Parrish's motor cruiser, moored in the marina. Between them, the two men must have been plotting this for weeks. Probably longer.

Strictly speaking, Winter should now level with Faraday – telling him about McIntyre, the audio tape and the scam that Parrish had undoubtedly worked – but it was far too early for this kind of disclosure. Better, by far, to tie up the loose ends first. And if that meant a settling of personal scores, then so be it.

But what next?

For more than a week now, Winter had been doing his best to cast himself as some kind of crusader, righting wrongs on behalf of the poor bloody women Hennessey had maimed. Dierdre Walsh was one of them, Nikki McIntyre another. Conversations with both had taken the inquiry to the brink of success, but in his heart Winter knew that his pursuit of Hennessey had fuck all to do with philanthropy. He just wasn't like that. He'd never fought other people's battles and he wasn't about to start. No, this was for him. Hennessey was his. When he'd told Cathy Lamb that he needed to hurt someone it was as close as he could get to the truth, and in the shape of a fat old pervy gynaecologist, he now had the chance. Squaring it with Hennessey wouldn't be a duty but a pleasure, and afterwards he knew he'd feel a whole lot better about things.

So what next?

He gave Joannie's plastic duck a little poke with his

big toe, watching it bob around among the bubbles, then closed his eyes, considering afresh the possibilities. Hennessey, he thought. Mine, and mine alone.

Twenty-Six

Rain had begun to fall by the time Faraday and Ferguson met up with the Gunwharf site engineer. He was young and fresh-faced with a mop of curly black hair, and he occupied one end of a stuffy, neon-lit office in a Lego city of portacabins at the top of the site. The uniformed Inspector in charge of the POLSA team had been here since nine and he wanted to know why Faraday and Ferguson were late. He had a million things to do this morning. A site survey ahead of a full-scale search was just another cross he had to bear.

'Traffic,' Ferguson grunted. 'Sir.'

The engineer gave them each a hard hat. Faraday's was too small so he wore it tipped down over his eyes, letting the rain drip onto the front of his anorak. The weather was horrible, not just rain but a cold, hard wind that blew across the harbour from the Gosport side and played havoc with the huge sheets of polythene stretched across lattices of scaffolding. For late June, it felt arctic.

The Gunwharf's thirty-three acres were broadly divided by the cavernous dry dock which would soon become City Quay. To the north, the leisure and retail complexes were already taking shape: huge grey boxes, metal clad, which would house the shopping malls, pubs and restaurants. Carrying anything heavy this far would be a pain, and logic told Faraday that they should be much more interested in the south-west corner of the site, the couple of acres that abutted directly onto the harbour and the Wightlink ferry terminal. This muddy chaos, criss-crossed by dumper trucks and gangs of sodden navvies, had yet to support the gleaming elevations of Arethusa House, though foundation work had been going on all winter, the steady thump-thump of the huge pile-drivers audible all over the city.

The uniformed Inspector caught Faraday by the arm. The weather had done nothing for his temper.

'When was all this supposed to have happened?'

Faraday had already had this conversation with someone else in his office. Clearly messages didn't get passed on.

'We're interested in the night of the eighteenth.'

'That's ten days ago.' The Inspector gestured at the churned-up mud and pools of standing water. 'And you're telling me we're looking for *footprints*?'

'I'm telling you we're looking for human remains.'

'Like where?'

Faraday glanced at the site engineer. As yet he hadn't fully grasped quite what Faraday and Ferguson were trying to investigate. Were they really saying that someone had turned up with a dead body?

Faraday took him by the arm. Only yards away, there was access to the site from the jetty of the Wightlink terminal. A metal ladder climbed the newly piled seawall, and at the top it was child's play to squeeze around a poorly secured stretch of fence.

'Our suspect came in here,' he explained. 'That's the way we see it.'

'With a corpse?'

'Probably with parts of a corpse. Maybe a couple of journeys. We don't know.' He stepped across a tangle of pipes, aware of the boom of the enormous construction crane revolving slowly above their heads. 'So how do you build these flats? How do you put them together?'

The site engineer looked relieved. Here was a question he understood. He walked Faraday around the boundaries of the apartment block. Dozens of sunken piles poked up through the yellow mud. These piles, he explained, would be linked laterally, creating a raft of reinforced concrete on which the structure itself would rise. Faraday, trying to picture it, asked about the space beneath the concrete raft. To the naked eye, there would appear to be a gap between the base of the building and the soil beneath.

'That's right.' The engineer nodded. 'You'll get voids. Bound to.'

'But the building is obviously walled on all four sides.'

'Of course.'

Faraday glanced at the Inspector, but the uniformed man was deep in conversation with Ferguson. He was asking about site security. His POLSA search team included specially trained sniffer dogs, and a look at the on-site video tapes might short-circuit all this guess-work bollocks.

'Any intruder would be caught on camera, right?'

'Afraid not, sir.'

'Why's that?'

'There are no cameras.'

The Inspector didn't believe it.

'What about patrols?'

'One guy, on all night.'

'One guy? For this lot?' He gazed round. 'There must be a fortune in gear here. Doesn't anyone keep an eye on it?'

350

The site engineer admitted that stuff went missing. Break-ins at night were frequent. Hence the management's interest in a close working partnership with the police.

'That's above my head,' the Inspector grunted. 'But I'd suggest more bodies and a decent camera set-up. Still, that's your decision.' He turned back to Faraday. 'What's the story then, Joe? Bloke climbs up your ladder. Bag full of bits. Then what?'

Faraday scrambled down the earth bank and into the wide trench that surrounded the base of the apartment block. The mud was glutinous underfoot and there were big puddles of standing water, pitted with rain. Everyone else followed.

'Say he came down here.' Faraday was looking at the site engineer. 'And say he dug sideways into this lot.' He nodded at the banked earth on the inner side of the trench. 'Or went much deeper into the site, in among the pilings there. What would we be looking at in, say, a year's time?'

'An apartment block. Arethusa House.'

'Starting where?'

'Starting where we're standing now.'

'So everything inside this line would be' he was still looking at the site engineer – 'under what?'

'Under two feet of reinforced concrete.'

'So if you wanted to dig it up? Get at it?'

The site engineer at last understood. He plunged his hands into the pockets of his anorak and shook his head.

'Don't even think about it,' he said bleakly.

Winter had been waiting for nearly two hours in the drenching rain before the golf umbrella finally appeared. It was striped blue and white and the bulky figure beneath held it low, angled into the howling wind.

Crazy Lady was berthed towards the end of the outer pontoon, riding uneasily on the swell. According to the marina authorities, she'd been there for a couple of days, though Hennessey had booked in under a false name. Winter wasn't good with boats, but he judged the motor cruiser to be about forty feet, moulded in sleek white plastic, with a high exposed bridge at the rear of the superstructure and a wide sitting-out area at the stern where you'd pose with your evening drinks. In a different setting, with better weather and a couple of semi-naked women, it might have come straight from the pages of *Hello!* magazine. How fitting, thought Winter, watching the umbrella approach.

The early morning flight out of Southampton had brought him to Jersey. He'd taken a cab to the marina, walking the pontoons until he found Parrish's motor cruiser. When he'd tried the big glass access doors at the back they were locked, but he could see the glow of a television in the saloon and there were clothes strewn everywhere. Over at the marina office, the girl behind the counter thought that *Crazy Lady* had been on the pontoon for a couple of days, but she couldn't be sure. When asked for the name of the skipper, she'd just looked blank.

Not that it mattered. Tucked into the meagre shelter of the big seawall, Winter was certain he knew. The same slight roll to the walk. The same impression of size and bulk. And, as he collapsed the umbrella, retrieved his shopping and stepped carefully aboard, the same long, jowly face that had stayed with Winter ever since he saw the Marriott video tape. Hennessey wasn't dead at all. He'd just been to the supermarket, and now he was due a little surprise.

Winter gave him a minute or two to settle in. Then he picked up a bag of his own, a black hold-all, double-zipped, and began to walk. The portable electric drill and lengths of rope were heavier than he'd thought and he was out of breath by the time he got to the seaward end of the pontoon. *Crazy Lady* was moored stern-on. Winter paused to pull on a pair of leather gloves, then stepped aboard, feeling the deck stir beneath him. The tall smoked-glass doors still barred the way to the saloon. Winter wiped the rain from his face, then tried one of the doors. This time it wasn't locked.

Hennessey was sitting at a kidney-shaped table, his thinning hair still tousled where he'd just towelled it dry. A copy of the *Daily Telegraph* was open in front of him and he was nursing a large glass of red wine. He looked up, confused by this sudden intrusion, this black silhouette against the grey light outside.

'What's going on?'

Winter didn't reply. The tall glass door locked on the inside. Hennessey was struggling to his feet now, penned in by the table. He was trying to reach his mobile. Winter got there first.

'Pieter Hennessey?'

'Who the hell are you?'

'I asked you a question.'

Hennessey paused. Something in Winter's voice prompted a nod.

'That's me,' he confirmed. 'I'm sorry, but I can't recall the name.'

For the first time, Winter saw the bandaged wrist.

'Sit down,' he said.

'You have absolutely no right—'

'I said sit down. You have a choice. Either you do what I say or I'll hurt you.'

Hennessey, with some reluctance, sank back onto the

buttoned velour. Despite his bluster, and his evident unfitness, Winter could sense him measuring up the distance between them. Winter stepped closer, then paused before extending a gloved hand in greeting. Hennessey gazed up, relief flooding his big face.

'Christ,' he said. 'For a moment there, you had me worried.'

It was Dawn's idea to confront Beavis with the video, and it was Faraday who insisted on coming along. With Winter's unexplained absence, and with an hour to snatch between conferences, he was determined to get at least one job properly sorted.

Beavis, this time, was dressed to go out. He was wearing jeans and an old leather jacket with a faded transfer of James Dean on the back, and just as soon as the rain eased up, he was off to Lidl's for a spot of shopping. Shel had just rung. Girl never really knew her mind, but it looked like she might be coming for tea. He beamed at Dawn and told her to come in. Bloody weather. Never stopped.

Faraday followed them down the hall. Beavis led the way through to the kitchen, but Dawn called him back. Did he have a video player?

'Yeah.' Beavis looked blank. 'Old thing. Got it off a skip then had a bloke mend it. Works OK though.'

The player was upstairs. There were motorcycle magazines stacked beside Beavis's bed and the tiny square of carpet was crusted with something yellow and sticky. Over by the window, water dripped steadily through the ceiling into a carefully positioned cake tin. Faraday looked round, wondering about the smell. Dawn had been right. Beavis needed a good scrub.

He was still talking about his daughter. He'd been on at her about Kennedy and, just like he'd thought, she'd told him it was all crap. Lee was like an uncle to her, or maybe a brother. No way would she get involved. He'd also phoned Lee.

'What did he say?' Dawn was on her hands and knees, trying to sort out the video player.

'He said it was crap too. Must be Addison, he said. Just the kind of thing that little bastard would do.'

Beavis looked round for Faraday and nodded, making the point twice. Dawn had introduced him as her boss, but Faraday wasn't certain he'd made the CID connection. I might be Dawn's dad, Faraday thought grimly, or some passing stranger she'd pulled in off the street.

Dawn had finally got the video player to start. She hit the pause button and looked up at Beavis.

'We came across this the other day,' she held up the video cassette. 'Thought you ought to see it.'

'Lovely.' He settled down on the end of the bed. 'Why not?'

Dawn exchanged glances with Faraday. He hadn't seen it either, though a brief conversation in the car coming over had prepared him for most of what followed.

Dawn bent to the video again. The picture wobbled on the screen, then a bed swam into view. It was the big double bed in Kennedy's upstairs room. Shelley was sprawled across it on her back. She was naked and she was mugging a big stagey orgasm for the camera, her back arched, her head thrown back. Then she collapsed in giggles, earning a reproof from an unseen voice.

'Shel, for fuck's sake . . .'

It was Kennedy. Even Beavis knew it. He was gazing at the screen, fondness spiked with disbelief.

'Silly bitch,' he muttered to himself. 'Stupid cow.'

Kennedy stepped into shot. He was wearing a tennis

shirt and a pair of briefs. He took the shirt off first, disappeared for a moment, then returned with a bunch of grapes.

'Go on,' he said.

Shelley caught the grapes one by one, positioning them across her body, starting with the hollows at the base of her neck. Then, very slowly, she spread her arms wide, the perfect take-me cameo.

Kennedy was on his hands and knees. He had a grape in his mouth and he crushed it very slowly, letting the juice drip onto her face. Then he began to work downwards from grape to grape, biting into the purple flesh and licking at her glistening skin. The last of the grapes lay in a little cluster between her thighs, and soon it was clear even to Beavis that this daughter of his was enjoying herself. Kennedy's face was buried between the spread of her thighs and she kept reaching down, both hands on the gleaming baldness of his scalp, making tiny adjustments, fitting herself to him. No one could pretend a pleasure this intense, and when it was over, and Kennedy took her place on the mattress, she had a skill and a theatricality that could only have come with practice. She was eager, too, and by the time Beavis finally stumbled from the room, Kennedy was doing conjuring tricks with an empty bottle of Becks. First you see it. Then you don't.

Minutes later Beavis was still washing his mouth out in the tiny bathroom. Dawn stood in the open doorway, Faraday behind her.

'We're here about the Donald Duck business,' Dawn said. 'We need to know who did it.'

Beavis tried to throw up again. Finally, he sat back against the side of the bath. Faraday could hear the steady drip-drip of water into the cake tin next door.

'Can you believe any of that?' He shook his head. 'Bastard.'

'Who?'

'Fucking Lee Kennedy. Do you know how old that man is? Twenty-eight, and he does that kind of stuff with my Shel.' He reached for a flannel and wiped his mouth. 'Bastard.'

'Donald Duck?' Dawn queried.

Beavis hadn't heard her. His voice was almost a whisper.

'I wouldn't have believed it,' he said. 'I wouldn't. I'll be honest with you. She's never been an angel. But that . . .' He shook his head. 'Fucking outrageous.'

Dawn squatted beside him. She wanted to know about the mask. About the three little excursions, out into the night. About the three times Beavis had dropped his drawers and given the women a good look. He stared at her, blinking, trying to follow the logic. At last, he got there.

'Me, love? You think I did that?'

'I do.'

'Them Donald Duck jobs?'

'Yes.'

'No.' He wiped his mouth again, this time with the back of his hand. 'Not me. Wrong bloke.'

'Who, then? Who was Donald Duck?'

Faraday would remember the silence for years to come. The drumming of the rain on the roof overhead. The drip-drip-drip from next door. And the moment when Beavis finally arrived at some kind of decision, the floorboard creaking beneath him as he staggered to his feet. When he came back, he was carrying a battered old sports bag.

'Inside, love,' he said.

Like a retriever, he dropped the bag at Dawn's feet. Dawn looked at Faraday, who shook his head.

'You.' Dawn glanced across at Beavis. 'You do it.'

Beavis pulled the bag open. The mask was on top, Donald Duck, the manic cartoon smile leering up at them. Underneath, the rumpled black of a tracksuit.

'There's trainers and gloves in there as well,' he said. 'You want to see them?'

Faraday shook his head, reaching out to stop him as he prepared to rummage through the hold-all.

'Leave it,' Faraday said. 'We'll need to bag this for forensic.'

Dawn's eyes hadn't left Beavis's face.

'So who does it all belong to?' she said.

Faraday braced himself for another silence, more rain, but Beavis hesitated for less than a second.

'Lee's,' he said stonily. 'This is his gear. He asked me to look after it for him. He wanted me to do it first off, but I wouldn't so he did it himself.'

'Did what?'

'Wore that.' He nodded at the mask.

'*Lee* did the Donald Duck jobs?'

'Yeah. To screw Addison.'

'And he wore that stuff?'

'Yeah.'

Dawn was staring down at the contents of the sports bag. Faraday was right, she thought. The smell of roll-ups would have come from here, this house, but the DNA would be Kennedy's. On the tracksuit. In the trainers. Everywhere. She looked up at Beavis again, just to make sure she had it right, but he was miles away.

'Should have worked it out for myself, shouldn't I?' he muttered. 'He'd wave it at any fucking woman. Even Shel.'

*

In Jersey, the weather had got worse.

'Where do you sleep?'

'Through there.'

Hennessey's head jerked towards the bow. Twice already he'd complained about the tightness of the handcuffs, but Winter had ignored him.

'Go on, then.' Winter gave him a push.

Hennessey shot him one last despairing glance. He'd offered money, a lot of money, for Winter to leave him alone. He'd got out his cheque book and promised a handsome dip into offshore funds, here in Jersey, and when Winter had shaken his head he'd even owned up to five thousand in cash on the boat, his for the taking, but Winter had just laughed. There were some things that money couldn't buy, he'd said. And this, the sweetest settling of accounts, was one of them.

Hennessey was manoeuvring himself sideways down a flight of four steps. Beyond the bulk of his body, Winter glimpsed a heart-shaped bed draped in a shiny mauve coverlet. Yuk.

Winter told Hennessey to strip.

'I can't.' He gestured helplessly at his cuffed hands.

'Do it,' Winter said, 'or I'll do it for you.'

With infinite slowness, Hennessey managed to rid himself of his brogues. The corduroy trousers came off next.

'That's it,' he said. 'The top's impossible.'

'It doesn't matter about the top.'

'What?' Hennessey's face was the colour of putty. He held out his cuffed hands. 'There. See that?'

Fresh blood had appeared through the crêpe of the bandage on his wrist. The fact that Winter plainly didn't care deepened the alarm on Hennessey's face.

'What are you going to do?'

'Take your pants off.'

'I beg your pardon?'

'I said, take your pants off. Then lie down on the bed.'

Winter had already looped the ends of two lengths of rope he'd picked up from Joannie's potting shed.

Hennessey hadn't moved.

'I meant it about the money,' he tried again.

'Fuck the money. I know where that money came from. I know how you earned that money. That's the last thing I'd want, believe me.'

'Are you a relative?'

'Yes, in a way.'

'Should I know your name?'

'No.' Winter nodded at his belly. 'Get them off.'

Hennessey pulled down his underpants and stepped out of them. His eyes never once left Winter's face.

'You meant it about the bed?'

'Yes. Just do it. Before I get fucking annoyed with you.'

Hennessey crawled onto the bed and lay face down.

'Turn over.' Nothing happened. 'I said, turn over.'

Winter lashed out with the rope, scoring an angry scarlet weal across Hennessey's buttocks. He did it again, and then a third time, until it occurred to him that Hennessey was crying, his huge white fleshy torso shaken by uncontrollable sobs.

Finally, Hennessey rolled over. His glasses had become dislodged, giving his face a strange, skewed look. Never had Winter seen anyone so vulnerable, so pathetic. Quickly, he unlocked the handcuffs and pulled Hennessey's arms back over his head. With the cuffs on again, Hennessey's wrists were now anchored to the brass rail that ran along the top of the bedhead. Back at the foot of the bed, Winter was about to remove the surgeon's socks when he had second thoughts. He knew exactly the tableau he wanted to create, the effect he wanted it to have, and he realised that socks, especially red socks like these, would help. Immeasurably.

The loops at the end of the lengths of rope he slipped over each of Hennessey's ankles. Winter pulled them tight, then looked for anchor points in the master bedroom to tie them off. Grab handles on both walls were perfect. Winter tightened each of the ropes until Hennessey's legs were scissored open. In the en suite closet, he found a big roll of Elastoplast which he used to tape Hennessey's mouth. On the shelf above, from a largish bag marked SURGICAL, he took a scalpel, a pair of metal dilators, a pair of forceps and – a late thought – a pair of rubber gloves. Back in the master bedroom, he laid them carefully on the pillow beside Hennessey's head.

The surgeon watched his every movement, plainly terrified. Winter looked down at him, and winked.

Back up in the saloon, still gloved, Winter began his search. He was as methodical as he'd ever been – every drawer, every cupboard, every crevice, every last inch of space Hennessey might have used as a hidey-hole – and when, after an hour, he'd turned up nothing, he went through exactly the same procedure in the guest bedroom and the little galley.

Around lunchtime, still with no result, he at last found them under an astrakhan rug, back in the master bedroom. They were in a thick, battered envelope with the address of the Advent Hospital on the front. He shook them out onto the bed, looking down on a shot of Nikki McIntyre, her legs up in stirrups, her genitalia exposed. The other photos were variations on the same theme, different angles, different framings, insistently explicit. These were shots Hennessey had looked at time and time again, pulling them out of the envelope and spreading them over the bed. These were the shots he pawed over, drooled over. This was the way he went to sleep every night.

'Clinical aids?'

Hennessey had his eyes closed. Winter gave him a shake, forcing him to look at a couple of the photos.

'For the file or the album?'

Hennessey just stared up at him. Finally, he closed his eyes again and turned away. He'd had enough of this, more than enough, but Winter was far from finished.

He bent down low, his lips to Hennessey's ear.

'You knew she was here, didn't you? You knew where to find her and you came looking.' He paused. He was word perfect. He'd been rehearsing this conversation for days. 'Do you go there every night? The Abbey? That nice hotel along the way? Do you slip into the club downstairs? Have you got a table at the back? Do you listen to her singing? Do you remember all those times when she was yours? Your patient? Your slave? Do you come back here afterwards? Fetch out this lot? Have another look? Remember what she felt like? No gloves on? Is that what you do? Eh?'

Winter's hold-all was over by the steps. He'd got a fresh roll of film in the camera. He circled the bed, taking shot after shot, Hennessey's favourite angle, total exposure. He'd give some of these to Parrish, little souvenir, little reminder of a scam that very nearly came off. Two guys with money to burn. Two guys after services to hire. Twenty grand each. One wanting revenge. The other, an escape to invisibility. Play both ends against the middle and you ended with a murder so perfect that there wasn't even a body. A murder so perfect that people like Faraday would go digging up whole apartment blocks on a fool's hunt for a non-existent corpse. A murder so perfect it would buy you a whole new life.

The film rewound, Winter circled the bed and settled briefly in a chair by a porthole. Hennessey was watching his every move.

'Were you going to fuck off, then? After here? Just nod or shake your head. Go on. Just do it.'

Hennessey didn't react. His eyes were filled with tears again.

'What about your name? Were you going to change it? New passport? New ID? New life?'

Again, no reaction. Winter pursed his lips for a moment, regretful, then fetched the hold-all. Hennessey stared at the drill as Winter went slowly through the choice of bits, weighing each in his hand, eyeing Hennessey's lower body. 2mm? 5mm? 10mm? Something big enough to make a serious hole? Finally he settled on a 7mm, tungsten-tipped for longer life.

'Brand new.' He showed Hennessey. 'That's supposed to be hygienic, isn't it? Less chance of infection?'

This time he didn't wait for a reaction but laid the drill beside Hennessey's head and busied himself with the photos, returning them to the envelope.

'These I get to keep,' he explained, 'just in case there's enough of you left to think about going to the police. OK?'

Winter glanced up at Hennessey. He thought he detected the faintest nod, but he couldn't be sure. He told him again about the photos, before tucking the envelope into his hold-all. Any kind of investigation, and the photos would go to all kinds of interested parties. OK? This time, for sure, Hennessey understood.

'Good.'

Winter crossed the cabin and knelt beside the opposite porthole. The shag pile carpet was secured with anodised battens where the floor met the outward curve of the hull. With a screwdriver, he loosened a batten, then levered it free. He'd rolled the carpet back less than a metre when he found the inspection hatch.

'This would go into the bilges, wouldn't it?'

He glanced over his shoulder. Hennessey's eyes were shut again. He might have been dead already.

'Shame,' Winter murmured, 'making a mess like this.'

He pulled the carpet back, exposing the entire hatch, then retrieved the drill from the pillow. Hennessey didn't move a muscle. When Winter pulled the hatch open, there was darkness beneath and the hollow slurp of water against the hull. At full stretch, Winter could reach the roughly textured interior of the hull. He pressed the trigger and the screech of the drill echoed back at him, amplified by the empty bilges; then, to his infinite satisfaction, the tungsten tip began to bite into the GRP. Revenge smells of hot glass fibre, he thought, pushing down even harder.

Forty minutes later, Winter stepped off the boat and made his way back along the pontoon. There was a public call box outside the marina office. When he got through to the newsdesk on the *Jersey Evening Post*, he gave them the name of Hennessey's motor cruiser and the number of the marina berth. The owner was having a rather special party. They'd be crazy if they didn't get down there sharpish, and crazier still if they didn't take a photographer.

'Big story,' Winter promised. 'Exclusively yours.'

When the reporter pressed him for details, he repeated the name of the boat and told him it belonged to a national figure.

'Like who?'

'Bloke called Hennessey. He's a gynaecologist. Been in all the papers.'

The brief silence told Winter he'd rung a bell or two. Asked for his own name, he laughed and hung up.

Stepping out of the call box, Winter ducked his head against the driving rain. He'd already chosen the restaurant, a first-floor bistro across the road. Two o'clock, he thought. Perfect for a late lunch.

With the restaurant emptying, he settled at a window seat with an uninterrupted view across the marina. He ordered skate with chips and a light salad, and sent the first bottle of Chablis back because it wasn't cold enough. Three glasses down, with the food yet to appear, he offered a private toast to Hennessey, still bound and gagged aboard his £115,000 hideaway. He'd drilled two holes. He was no expert in hydraulics, but already *Crazy Lady* was visibly nose-down beside the pontoon.

The reporter arrived while Winter was busy with the skate. There was a photographer as well, with an aluminium camera case, and Winter watched while they hurried along the pontoon, bodies bent against the weather. They both clambered aboard Hennessey's boat, and it was several minutes before the journalist reappeared, running back towards the marina office. Winter returned to the last of his skate, imagining the photographer making the most of the tableau he'd so carefully prepared. Humiliation, he'd decided, deserved the widest possible audience. He smiled to himself mopping up the caper sauce with the remains of his bread roll, then reaching for the menu again.

By the time Winter had finished his lemon sorbet and paid the bill, *Crazy Lady* was attracting a great deal of attention. Among the figures clambering aboard were two paramedics in hi-vis jackets. He was curious to know what they might find in the master bedroom, but a glance at his watch told him there was no point hanging round to find out. With luck, he thought, Hennessey might just have succumbed to a heart attack.

The restaurant obliged Winter by phoning for a cab. It took five minutes or so to arrive, a sleek Peugeot with a guy young enough to be his son at the wheel. Winter threw his hold-all onto the back seat and settled cheerfully beside it.

'Airport, please,' he said. 'Flight's at half-four.'

Epilogue

Friday, 7 July, 1400

Just over a week later, Dawn Ellis ran into Rick Stapleton at Fratton nick.

'I just wanted to say thank you,' she said, waiting for the plastic cup to drop in the hot-drinks dispenser.

'Thank you for what?'

'Keeping Kennedy out of my knickers.'

Rick smiled. On the basis of statements from Kevin and Shelley Beavis, Kennedy had been charged with GBH in relation to the Donald Duck incidents. In view of his previous convictions, he'd been refused bail and was now on remand in Winchester prison.

Rick waited for Dawn to finish with the machine, then inserted a coin of his own. There was something bothering him about Addison. He was OK now about the guy being innocent, but why hadn't he fingered Kennedy? The bloke had put on all kinds of pressure to enlist his editing skills. According to Shelley, he'd even made verbal threats. Wasn't it obvious that the mask was Kennedy's plant?

'Of course it was.'

'So why didn't he tell us?'

'Because he was certain he'd get the verdict in court. Plus he wanted to protect Shelley. He thought she'd be genuinely at risk if Kennedy thought she'd been talking.'

'Really? Was she that great a shag?'

'It's nothing to do with shagging. He believes in her. He's convinced she'll go the whole way.'

'Yeah, and some . . .'

The best part of a year with Rick should have prepared Dawn for this. There was no way he wouldn't interpret every human relationship in terms of body fluids. Motives like generosity or belief just didn't figure.

'Listen.' Dawn was watching Rick over the brim of her milkless tea. 'There's something else you ought to know about Addison.'

'What's that?'

'He's gay.'

'*Gay?* Who says?'

'Shelley.'

'And you believe her?'

'I do. It takes time with Shelley, but you get there in the end.'

Rick was staring at her. Disbelief gave way to bewilderment, then irritation, and finally an expression dangerously close to embarrassment. He should have known. He should have picked up the clues: the obsessive tidiness, the way the guy dressed, his enjoyment of the subtler touches, the icy self-control. It was all there. And he, of all people, had missed it.

'You wanted a result,' Dawn pointed out. 'And you thought you'd got one. Why bother with the rest of the story?'

Rick was still staring at her.

'Have you told anyone else?' he asked at last. 'About him being gay?'

'No.'

'Thank fuck for that.' He checked both ways down the empty corridor. 'Our little secret, eh?'

Faraday escaped early from an informal sandwich lunch

with Hartigan and drove north through the city, out towards Petersfield.

His divisional boss, somewhat to his surprise, had been almost effusive. The Hennessey investigation, by confirming that the surgeon was alive, had been a masterly demonstration of exactly what lengths Hartigan's CID squad would go to in a bid to establish the real truth in a misper inquiry. The bag of bones and pig offal recovered by the POLSA team on the Gunwharf site wasn't, alas, enough evidence to warrant any kind of charge against Parrish, but the developers, nonetheless, had been generous in their thanks. It was, wrote the company's MD, a perfect example of the police and big business working in partnership for the greater good of the city as a whole. The consequences of disinterring that same bag a couple of years down the line just didn't bear thinking about.

Willard, in an earlier meeting, had been somewhat blunter. As far as Hennessey was concerned, the whole job had been down to Winter. He'd set the hare running and he'd led most of the pursuit. Not because he'd been especially conscientious or dutiful, but because the guy's MO was starting to verge on professional suicide. Pursuing hunches was one thing. Doing what Winter had done – declaring total UDI and running his very own investigation – was quite another. Only the fact that his missus was dying had kept his name off the internal charge sheet.

And Addison?

Both Willard and Hartigan had ignored it. Never underestimate the persuasiveness of circumstantial evidence. Never penalise guys hungry for a quick result. Mistakes happen. Gold star to young Dawn for sticking with it. Damages, alas, for Mr Addison. But here's hoping Lee Kennedy goes down.

Faraday's route took him past Bedhampton. Winter's bungalow was up there somewhere, and as far as Faraday knew, his wife was back in residence, buoyed by a care package from social services. One of her daily visitors was evidently a psychiatric nurse, and Faraday hoped that he or she had the time to spare for Winter as well. It was still far from clear exactly what had happened in Jersey, but the front-page splash in the *Jersey Evening Post*, gleefully pinned to noticeboards in police stations throughout Portsmouth, had been explicit about Hennessey's luck in escaping with his life. Another hour or so and the guy would have been history. As it was, the journos had got there in time. Thanks to an anonymous phone call.

Had Winter somehow been implicated in this little stunt? Faraday didn't know, and the fact that Hennessey had set his face against any kind of formal investigation made it unlikely that he'd ever find out. Pumped dry and repaired, *Crazy Lady* had already slipped away, bound for God knows where. Winter, meanwhile, was now on extended compassionate, trying to do his best for Joannie. Forty paracctamol had done nothing for her prognosis, but, fingers crossed, she might just see the summer out. Unlike Vanessa Parry.

Matthew Prentice lived in an estate on the southern edges of Petersfield. The houses, judging by the rash of extensions, had once been council but were now privately owned. Prentice lived in the one with a purple door near the end of the street. Faraday knew he'd be in because the young lad he'd talked to at the café had phoned him and said so.

'He wants a word,' he'd mumbled. 'Said it would be cool if you called round.'

A middle-aged woman in jeans and a nice-looking

blouse opened the door. To Faraday's surprise, she turned out to be Prentice's mother.

'It's my house,' she explained briefly. 'He's in the front room.'

Faraday remembered the face from the car park after the funeral: the gelled hair, the diamond ear-stud, the tilt of the chin shadowed by a couple of days' growth of beard. Prentice got up from the sofa and extended a hand. Another surprise.

'Well?'

Faraday wasn't in the mood for small talk. Prentice was looking confused.

'Is this, like, official? Only—'

'Of course it is, Mr Prentice. You got a message to me. You've got something to say. So just say it.'

Prentice was looking at the carpet. Faraday was aware of the open door behind him. Was the mother still outside in the hall? Was this her idea?

'It's about that woman,' Prentice began.

'Vanessa Parry?'

'The woman who died. I was gonna leave some flowers.'

'Yeah, without your name on. I saw them in the car park. In the back of that motor of yours. Brave man. Say you're sorry. Leave a blank for your name. Then piss off.'

Despite his every best intention, despite telling himself that he had to stay calm, be grown up about it, Faraday knew it would come to this. A moment's recollection of the photographs, a single remembered glimpse of the interior of the crushed Fiesta, and he'd thrown the rulebook out of the window. Maybe Winter had a point. Maybe, in the end, it came down to this. Red, the colour of anger. Red, the colour of blood.

'So what happened?' Faraday was trying to rein himself in.

'I was on the phone. I remember now.'

'Oh, yeah? And why's that?'

Prentice didn't answer. Faraday had established that the lad in the café had just been given a season ticket for Fratton Park, £320 worth of spontaneous present. The name on the credit-card slip had been Prentice's. Beyond any reasonable doubt, he'd bought the lad's silence.

Faraday could hear Prentice's mother in the kitchen now, noisily putting the kettle on. All she'd wanted was her boy to tell the truth. And at last, for whatever reason, he'd done it.

The door was still open. Faraday closed it.

'OK, son, this is what you're going to do. You're going down to Kingston Crescent police station. You're going to ask for PC Barrington. You're going to tell him the truth about the crash. You're going to tell him you were on the phone when you hit the Fiesta, and that afterwards you bribed the lad to cover for you. PC Smith will sit you in an interview room with your solicitor and a tape recorder and you'll go over the whole story again.' Faraday nodded towards the door. 'You want your mother to go with you?'

Prentice shook his head.

'What happens afterwards?' he muttered.

'You'll be charged.'

'What with?'

'Perverting the course of justice. You've interfered with a witness. Courts take a dim view of that. You'll be lucky to avoid a jail sentence.'

'*Jail?*' Prentice sank onto the sofa. For a while, he did nothing but study his hands. When he finally looked up, his eyes were glistening. 'I just wanted to say I was sorry,' he said hopelessly. 'I don't need any of this.'

Faraday gave him time to compose himself. If he felt anything, he felt weary. The longer he did the job, he thought, the less certain his take on what really made people tick. We've all got in a muddle. We've all lost the plot. Actions and reactions, causes and effects. One tiny moment, and a life blown away.

'The whole story,' he repeated stonily. 'OK?'

If you have enjoyed

The Take

don't miss

ONE UNDER

Graham Hurley's latest novel featuring
DI Joe Faraday

coming soon in Orion hardback

Price £9.99
ISBN 978-0-7528-6883-7

Monday, 11th July 2005, 04.30

Every driver's nightmare.

Assigned to the first train out of Portsmouth, he'd checked in at the Fratton depot before dawn, double-locking his Suzuki 900, stowing his helmet in the crew room, and then making his way upstairs to glance through the emergency speed restrictions and confirm his station stops. This time in the morning, the five-car set would be virtually empty. A handful of staff hitching a ride to stations up the line, maybe a dozen or so City-bound commuters, occasionally a drunk or two, slumped in the corner of the carriage, unconscious after a night in the Southsea clubs.

He was two minutes late off Portsmouth Harbour, waiting for a lone punter off the Isle of Wight Fast Cat, but made up the time before the miles of trackside terraces began to thin and the train clattered over Portsbridge Creek, leaving the city silhouetted against the fierce spill of light to the east.

The station at Havant looked deserted. Coasting to a halt, he waited barely fifteen seconds before the guard closed the doors again. Picking up speed, heading north now, he wondered whether the promised thunder storms would really happen, and whether his partner would remember to close the greenhouse door in case the wind got up.

Beyond the long curve of Rowlands Castle station,

the gradient began to steepen. Ahead lay the dark swelll of the South Downs. He added more power, watching the speedo needle creep round towards seventy. These new Desiros knocked spots off the old stock. German kit, he thought. Never fails.

Minutes later, deep in a cutting, came the sudden gape of the Buriton Tunnel. He slowed to 40 mph and sounded the horn, raising a flurry of wood pigeons from the surrounding trees. Then the world suddenly went black, the clatter of the train pulled tight around him, and he peered into the darkness, waiting for his eyes to adjust. Moments later, still enfolded by the tunnel, he had a sudden glimpse of something ahead on the line. In the dim throw of light from the front of the train, the oncoming shape resolved itself into a body spread-eagled on the nearside rail, then – for a split second – he was looking at a pair of legs, scissored open, and the unmistakable whiteness of naked flesh.

Instinctively, in a single reflex movement, he took the speed off and pushed the brake handle fully forward, feeling his body tensing for the impact, the way he might on the bike, some dickhead stepping out onto the road. Thenn came a jolt, nothing major, and he knew with a terrible certainty that his eyes hadn't betrayed him, that what he'd seen, what he'd felt, was even now being shredded to pieces in the roaring darkness beneath the train.

The cab began to shudder under the bite of the brakes. The tunnel exit in sight, he pulled the train to a halt and reached for the cab secure radio that would take him to the signalman back at Havant. When the signalman answered, he gave him the train code and location, asked for power isolation, declared an emergency.

What's up then?' the man wanted to know.

The driver blinked, still staring ahead, aware of the guard trying to contact him on the internal coms. 'One under,' he managed, reaching for the door.

One

Monday, 11th July 2005, 07.53

This time, Faraday knew there'd be no escape.

He'd taken to the water an hour or so earlier, finning slowly out of the bay, scanning the reefs below, enjoying the lazy rise and fall of the incoming swell. An evening with a reference book he'd picked up in Bangkok let him put a name to the shapes that swam below.

Beneath him, he could see yellow-ringed parrot fish, nosing for food amid the coral; half a dozen milky-white bat fish, stately, taking their time, slowly unfurling like banners; even, for a glorious minute or two, the sight of a solitary clownfish drifting over the underwater meadows of softly waving fronds. The head of the clownfish was daubed with a startling shade of scarlet but it was the huge eyes, doleful, disconsolate, that had Faraday blasting water from his snorkel tube. The little fish reminded him of an inspector he'd once served under in his uniformed days. The same sense of tribulation. The same air of unathomable regret. Laughing underwater, Faraday discovered, wasn't a great idea.

Further out, the colours changed and with the blues and greens shading even deeper, Faraday became aware of the schools of fish beginning to thin. He'd never been out this far, not by a long way, and a lift of his head told him that he must have covered nearly a mile since he'd slipped into the water. He could see the tiny wooden bungalow clinging to the rocks above the tideline. A line of washing on the veranda told him that Eadie must have finally surfaced. Shame.

Adjusting the mask and clearing the snorkel again, Faraday ducked his head. It was hard to judge distance underwater but twenty metres down, maybe more, he could just make a tumble of boulders on the seabed. This, he imagined, would be the point where the coral shallows suddenly plunged away into something infinitely deeper. In the beachside bar, only yesterday, he'd heard a couple of French lads describing a dive they'd just made. Faraday was no linguist but his French was adequate enough to understand *profondeur* and *requin*. The latter word came with a repertoire of gestures and had raised an appreciative shiver in one of the listening women. *Requin* meant shark.

Floating on the surface, barely moving, Faraday was overwhelmed by a sense of sudden chill. A mile was a long way out. There were no lifeguards, no rescue boats. Trying to slow his pulse rate, he scanned the depths below him. A thin drizzle of tiny particles was drifting down through the dapple of surface sunlight, down towards the inky-blue nothingness. Then, way off to the right, he caught a flicker of movement, the briefest glimpse of something much, much bigger than the carnival of cartoon fish he'd left in the shallows.

Faraday shut his eyes a moment, squeezed them very hard, fought the temptation to turn in the water, to kick hard, to strike for home. This is exactly what you shouldn't do, he told himself. In situations like these, panic was the shortest cut to disaster.

He opened his eyes again, watched his own pale hand wipe the toughened glass in the facemask. He'd been wrong. Not one of them. Not two. But half a dozen. At least. They were circling now, much closer, sleek, curious, terrifying.

All too aware of the quickening rasp of his own breath, Faraday watched the sharks. Every nerve end told him that something unimaginable was about to happen. He hung in the water, his mouth suddenly dry, feeling utterly helpless. He'd never seen creatures like this, so perfectly evolved for the task in hand, so ready, so close. The water rippled over the gills behind their gaping mouths as they slipped through the shafts of dying sunlight, and as they circled closer and closer he became mesmerised by their eyes. The eyes told him everything. They were cold, unblinking, devoid of anything but the expectation of what would happen next. This was their territory. Their world. Trespass was a capital offence.

Faraday had a sudden vision of blood in the water, his own blood, of pinked strips of torn flesh, of jaws closing on his flailing limbs, of line after line of those savage teeth tearing at the rest of his body until nothing was left but a cloud of chemicals and splinters of white bone sinking slowly out of sight.

One of the biggest sharks made a sudden turn and then came at him, the pale body twisting as it lunged, and Faraday felt himself brace as the huge jaws filled his vision. This is death, he thought. This is what happens when you get it so badly wrong.

Another noise, piercing, insistent, familiar. The shark, he thought numbly. The shark.

His heart pounding, Faraday turned over and groped in the half-darkness. The mobile was on the chair beside the bed. For a second or two, listening to the voice on the other end, he hadn't a clue where he was. Then, immeasurably relieved, he managed a response.

Buriton is a picturesque Hampshire village tucked beneath the wooden swell of the South Downs. A street of timbered cottages and a couple of pubs led to a twelfth-century church. There were 4x4s everywhere, most of them new, and Faraday slowed to let a harassed-looking mother load her kids into the back of a Toyota Land Cruiser. Buriton, he thought wearily, is where you'd settle if you still believed in a certain vision of England – peaceful, safe, white – and had the money to buy it.

He parked beside the pond at the heart of the village. Already, there was a scatter of other cars, most of them badged with the familiar chequerboard of the British Transport Police. Faraday was still eyeing a cople of BTP officers pulling on their Wellington boots, wondering quite why a suicide had attracted so much police attention, when there came a tap at his passenger window.

'Jerry . . .'

Surprised, Faraday got out of the Mondeo and shook the extended hand. DS Jerry Proctor was a Crime Scene Manager, a looming, heavyset individual with a reputation for teasing meticulously presented evidence out of the most chaotic situations. The last couple of years, he'd been seconded to the British effort in Iraq, teaching local police recruits how to become forensic investigators.

'How was the posting?'

'Bloody.'

'Glad to be back?'

'No.' Proctor nodded towards the parked Transport Police cars. 'These guys have been here a couple of hours now. They've got a DI with them and it needs someone to sort him out.'

Faraday looked away for a moment. Proctor had never seen the point of small talk.

'You're telling me the DI's a problem?'

'Not at all, sir. But they haven't got the bodies, not for something like this. You want to come up to the tunnel?'

Proctor was already wearing one of the grey one-piece discardable suits that came with the job. While Faraday pulled on the pair of hiking boots he kept in the back of the car, Proctor brought him up to date.

The driver of the first train out of Pompey had reported hitting a body in the nearby tunnel. The power had been switched off, and control rooms in London alerted. Calls from Transport Police HQ in St James's Park had roused the duty Rail Incident Officer who'd driven over from his home in Eastleigh. By then, the batteries on the train were running out of juice and the twenty or so passengers aboard would soon be sitting in the dark.

'No one got them off?'

'No, sir.'

'Why not?'

'The driver didn't think it was appropriate. Young guy. Cluey.'

'Cluey how?'

'He'd taken a good look underneath the train, gone back with a torch, brave lad.'

'And?'

They were walking round the pond by now, following the narrow lane that wound up towards the railway line. Proctor glanced across at Faraday.

'He found the impact spot, or what he assumed was the impact spot. Bits of our man were all over the bottom of the train but the torso and legs were still in one piece.' Proctor touched his own belly. 'Chained to the line.'

'*Chained?*'

'Yeah.' Proctor nodded. 'We're talking serious chain, padlock, the works. Our driver friend thought that was a bit over the top, made another call.' He shot Faraday a bleak smile. 'So here we all are.'

'And the train's still in the tunnel?'

'Yes, sir.'

'Impact point?'

'About fifty metres in. That's from the southern end.'

'How long's the tunnel?'

'Five hundred metres. Transport Police are organising a generator and a lighting unit. Plus they've laid hands on half a dozen or so blokes to check out the tunnel. Don't get me wrong, sir. The DI knows what he's doing. It's just resources. Not his fault.'

Faraday was doing the sums, trying to imagine the size of the challenge that awaited them all. At worst, he'd assumed they were looking at some kind of complicated suicide. The fact that this body had been physically tied to the line changed everything.

'The DI's established a common path?'

'Yes, sir. Down this lane, under the railway bridge, along a little track, then up the embankment and into the tunnel. The train's maybe forty metres in.'

'And that's the way we get the passengers off?'

'Has to be. The Incident Officer tells me the rest of it's fenced miles back in both directions. We've got no option.'

Faraday pulled a face. In these situations, absolute priority lay in isolating the crime scene. If Proctor was right about access to the track, then whatever evidence awaited them was about to be trampled.

'We need Mr Barrie in on this.' Faraday fumbled for his mobile. Martin Barrie was the new Detective Superintendent in charge of the Major Crimes Team. If it came to any kind of turf war, then Barrie was the man with the ammunition.

Proctor watched while Faraday keyed in a number, then touched him lightly on the arm.

'That's another problem, sir.' He nodded towards the nearby embankment. 'This is a mobile black spot. Either end of the tunnel, there's no signal.'

The train was visible from the mouth of the tunnel. Faraday stood on the track, peering into the darkness, trying to imagine what five carriages would do to flesh, bone and blood. Like every policeman, he'd attended his share of traffic accidents, successful suicide bids, and other incidents when misjudgement or desperation had taken a life, but thankfully he'd never witnessed the cooling remains of a human body torn apart by a train.

Other men, less lucky, spoke of unrecognisable parcels of flesh, of entrails scattered beside the track, of the way that the impact – like the suck of high explosive – could rip the clothes from a man and toss them aside before dismembering him.

The image made Faraday pause. Only days ago, three Tube trains had been ripped apart by terrorist bombs in London and some of the media coverage of the consequences had been unusually candid. Was his incident, in some strange way, a twist on that theme? He let the thought settle for a moment, then he was struck by another image, altogether more personal, and he found himself fighting a hot gust of nausea, remembering the oncoming shark of his nightmare and that moment before consciousness when he knew for certain that he, too, was a dead man.

'Sir?'